/12

Don't Mess with Travis

Also by Bob Smiley

Follow the Roar: Tailing Tiger for All 604 Holes of
His Most Spectacular Season

Don't Mess with Travis

Bob Smiley

Thomas Dunne Books
St. Martin's Press
New York

THOMAS DUNNE BOOKS.
An imprint of St. Martin's Press.

DON'T MESS WITH TRAVIS. Copyright © 2012 by Bob Smiley. All rights reserved. Printed in the United States of America. For information, address St. Martin's Press, 175 Fifth Avenue, New York, N.Y. 10010.

www.thomasdunnebooks.com
www.stmartins.com

Library of Congress Cataloging-in-Publication Data

Smiley, Bob.
    Don't mess with Travis : a novel / Bob Smiley.—1st ed.
        p. cm.
    ISBN 978-1-250-00119-1 (hardcover)
    ISBN 978-1-250-01518-1 (e-book)
    1. Political satire, American.   2. Texas—Politics and government—
Fiction.   I. Title.
    PS3619.M47D66 2012
    813'.6—dc23

                                                            2012004613

First Edition: May 2012

10 9 8 7 6 5 4 3 2 1

For Jim Hays. The real Ben Travis.

Prologue

The cows were the first to know. At least the ones that were awake. It was four thirty in the morning and most of the herd was fast asleep, dreaming of, well, whatever cows dream about. India, probably . . . that magical land of vegetarians where cattle can do no wrong.

It wasn't a loud sound. That would have spooked them and sent them scampering through the dark in a dozen different directions. It was soft and low, like a distant vacuum sucking on commercial-grade carpet. The cows searched the long valley around them for clues and saw nothing. The noise grew louder, only for a moment, and then disappeared altogether. After a few more seconds of scanning the blackness, some went back to grazing. The rest went back to sleep.

The limousine exploded on impact. The fireball blew out and then up, instantly destroying every living thing within fifty feet. Grass was reduced to ash. Barbed wire melted into nothing. A hubcap escaped the blast and sliced through the air like a Frisbee. The body of the reinforced Cadillac buckled under the nine-hundred-degree heat, then disappeared into its own grave.

The fire raged long after the sun came up, feasting on tires, gasoline, and beef. Two fields away, resting by itself, detached but otherwise unscathed, was the driver's door. On the outside was a silver five-pointed star. Beneath it, in simple block letters, were three words: STATE OF TEXAS.

1

The president of the United States eyed the downhill four-footer from three different angles. "It's not every day you shoot eighty-nine," he said, still panting a bit from the walk between the cart and the eighteenth green at Congressional Country Club. The caddies in his group shared a look, knowing there was no way President Leary had broken a hundred, even if you ignored the water ball on hole number six, the "gimme" he putted anyway—and missed—on eleven, and the fact he'd played the entire round with sixteen clubs in his bag, two over the limit. His regular Sunday morning playing partners had given up years ago on the prospect of ever winning a bet against the Leader of the Free World, seeing the six-hour saga as yet another tax on the rich.

The president had, in turn, given up years ago on the idea of spending his Sunday morning in the front pew of St. John's Church in Lafayette Square. For one thing, it was boring as hell. For another, the pastor wouldn't let him smoke during the sermon.

Confident of his read, he tossed his cigarette to the ground and settled over the knee-knocker. The sun bounced off his hair, vibrant and flawless, the color of a freshly minted penny. Sweat beaded off his freckled Irish skin. *Left edge and firm,* he reminded himself. His putter was halfway back to the ball when the BlackBerry in his pocket buzzed, sending his Titleist wobbling wide right, never scaring the cup. "Damn it!" he barked. "That didn't count!" The sprawling red-roofed clubhouse was a hundred yards away, but the outburst easily carried, loud enough to cause an elderly member to spill her hollandaise sauce as she lunched on the patio with her Jamaican nurse. Leary raked the ball back and tried again, this time missing left.

The president's short game wasn't the only thing in the crapper. It had been two years since he declared America's Great Recession over and the Great *Recovery* in full swing, a speech that culminated with a balloon drop (eco-friendly, of course), a blast of confetti (biodegradable), and a rousing rendition of Neil Diamond's "America" sung by the cast of the hit TV show *Glee*. There was just one problem—it wasn't true.

It wasn't for lack of effort. In the three and a half years Leary had been in office, he'd funneled over four trillion federal dollars to troubled banks, upside-down homeowners, and mismanaged corporations. In cases where free money couldn't rescue a company or a mortgage, the government went ahead and bought it outright. The thinking was that the backing of Washington, D.C., would free up credit and ease everyone's fears, like a rich parent's signature on an apartment lease. Leary's intentions appeared good, his commitment unwavering, but the president's Keynesian approach had not delivered.

Instead, the sick economy he thought he was reviving had been suffocated by wasteful spending, increased regulations, and a general demonization of free market capitalism. Wary investors dumped stock and ran to gold. Small business owners ignored Washington pleas to hire new workers and sat on what capital they still had. Entire housing developments stood empty. Others were bulldozed and returned back to nature. Inflation was on the rise, the dollar was dying, and the unions, the president's most loyal voting bloc, had taken to the streets with increasing violence to make it known that if anyone was going to take a cut in pay or in benefits, it would not be any of them.

The world was losing faith in America. On more than one occasion, the first lady found her husband staring out the window of their

White House bedroom, shaking his head and wondering aloud, *I thought people loved* Glee . . .

His wife wasn't making things any easier. Where most first ladies choose one cause célèbre, she had a dozen, each of which appeared purposefully targeted at fixing the flaws she saw in her own husband. Cigarettes, sugar, swearing—she had taken public shame and made it her most powerful weapon.

At least he had his golf—but apparently now even that wasn't sacred. It was a standing rule that he was not to be contacted on the links unless there was a national emergency, and even then, it had to be *really* bad. Like missile-heading-toward-a-DNC-Hollywood-fund-raiser bad. He read the waiting text message and wasn't sure this qualified. TX GOV FEARED DEAD AFTER CAR CRASH. He walked through his partner's line as he dialed. Mark "Ruffles" Ruflowski, his flabby forty-five-year-old chief of staff and omnipresent adviser since his days as a Massachusetts state senator, was trained to answer on the first ring and always let Leary talk first.

"Feared dead or actually dead? Because if he's not *really* dead you just cost me a par."

Ruffles blew his nose into his handkerchief. He was still a hanky guy; one of a shrinking handful of men under fifty who saw nothing off-putting about blowing mucus into a rag and then stuffing it back into one's pocket. "Yes, he's dead," Ruffles said. "So is Lieutenant Governor Rice."

"Yowzers. A twofer."

"Apparently Rice's limo had a flat, and rather than wait, he broke protocol by driving back with the governor. That's what Fox News is saying at least."

"Fox News?" Leary could hear Ruffles's TV click back to the comforting voices of MSNBC. "Any clue how it happened?"

"NTSB's working on it," Ruffles said. "There were no survivors, no witnesses. They drove right off a cliff."

"I thought you said this happened in Texas."

"It did. A hundred miles outside Austin."

Leary dropped his putter back into his bag. "I didn't think Texas had any cliffs."

"Well, they got at least one."

Leary peeled the plastic from a fresh pack of Benson & Hedges and let the wind carry it away, paying no heed to the Secret Service agent who shuffled off to retrieve it. "Alright, let's issue a statement. 'Tragic loss' . . . 'our hearts go out to the people of Texas' . . . mention the wives by name, boilerplate stuff."

"You got it."

Leary had always liked Governor Allen. Not in a friendly way, but more in the way you like someone who is putty in your hands. In public, he referred to Allen and similar Republicans as open-minded, reasoned, and, if he was feeling especially charitable that day, bipartisan. Guys like Allen ate that stuff up for some reason. In most cases, it was because their wives were secretly Democrat and the husbands could use compliments from the other side of the aisle as proof they weren't complete monsters. In private, the administration simply referred to people like Allen as ETs. Easy Targets. *Damn it all,* Leary thought. He'd miss the big idiot.

The president's golf-gloved thumb moved to hang up, but the reminiscing about Governor Allen triggered one last question. "Hey, Ruffles."

"Yes, Mr. President."

"Who the hell's in charge of Texas?"

Ben Travis was working without his gloves again. Kate used to say that his hands doubled as her calendar, and by the looks of things, the blisters of early April had finally given way to the calluses of late May.

He liked the heat. A lot of people in North Texas cursed it, but it made him sweat and become occasionally dizzy, which, in its own strange way, made him feel young. At age fifty, those moments were becoming fewer and farther between. When his new driver's license arrived a few weeks earlier, it was hard not to wince when he noticed that his hair was now listed as "gray" and not brown. He'd lobbied hard for "salt and pepper," but the surly pumpkin-shaped woman behind the counter at the DMV informed him that it wouldn't fit. At least Travis *had* some hair. And his looks. Probably for another six or seven years. After that, the chiseled chin would soften and the boyish dimples would slip into the cracks and valleys of an old man who'd had a good run.

No matter how old or ugly he became, he couldn't picture himself in gloves. Gloves were for gardening. His ranch hand, Gene, a thirty-year-old raisin in a cowboy hat, still didn't get it. "Remind me again what's wrong with that black pair in the shed?" Gene had been pushing those on Travis for months. They were a Christmas gift from a fellow senator, and Travis loathed everything about them: the color, the synthetic material, the extra rubber grip on the thumbs . . .

"They're like Darth Vader's gloves," Travis said.

"Exactly!" In Gene's eyes, this was yet another selling point.

"Yeah, well, I know I haven't seen those movies for a while, but I don't seem to remember him clearing a lot of brush with them. Now if you could get me one of those light swords . . ."

"Light*saber*," Gene corrected.

While Travis may have looked and acted the part, he didn't consider himself a rancher in any real sense of the word, and he certainly didn't think of himself as a politician. He'd had too many careers to be labeled anything other than occupationally schizophrenic.

He got rich drilling oil and gas wells in West Texas and went penniless owning a string of 1950s-themed diners across Oklahoma. He made half of it back in the oil and gas commodities market before a third of that disappeared on a "sure thing" racehorse that he'd later discover never actually existed. He took his family and what little was left of his fortune and returned home to the town of Prosper, his unassuming birthplace thirty-five minutes due north of Dallas. First he bought the ranch, and then he bought a struggling Prosper company that made heating and air-conditioning ducts for commercial buildings. There was nothing sexy about it. Five years later, it cracked the Fortune 500. *Forbes* summed up Ben Travis the best when it dubbed him "a business savant with the Midas touch . . . but only about half the time."

The original ranch was eighty acres, with a cheery, two-story, pale blue clapboard house in the middle. Over time, he befriended his neighbors, and as they moved—or moved on—he always bid first and bid highest. Then, somewhere near the five-hundred-acre mark, Travis's marriage fell apart. What had started off as a man building his empire had ended up bearing a closer resemblance to a middle-aged divorcé living in depressing isolation.

His pickax arced through the air and took aim at a line of mesquite bushes that were encroaching on his back porch. He hated mesquite. It was a total nuisance, the raccoon of the plant kingdom. It wasn't pretty, its sharp thorns could penetrate sneakers, and it never stayed away for long. It was all due to its taproot, the vertical root that stretches all the way down to the water table. The longest one ever recorded on a mesquite was close to two hundred feet, or twice the length of a blue whale. He was fighting a losing battle and knew it.

A half mile behind him, a line of black cars, lights on, drove single file, kicking up dust and scattering jackrabbits as they went. Gene noticed them first. Among the advantages of a five-hundred-acre ranch on the outskirts of Prosper is the sheer impossibility of anyone ever being able to sneak up on you. As the vans and Suburbans came into focus, Gene eyed Travis accusingly. "What did you do?"

Travis stopped and looked. "Me? What makes you think they're not coming for you?" Gene had a habit of spending a few nights a year behind bars.

The fact that Ben Travis was third in line to be governor was one of those things that briefly registered in his brain the year before and was promptly forgotten, like the fire extinguisher he'd bought and placed under the sink, which, even if the kitchen was engulfed in flames, would never be remembered when its moment came.

The president pro tempore of the Texas Senate was a ceremonial position more than anything else. In the United States Senate it's bestowed upon the longest-serving senator of the majority party. Robert Byrd, Ted Stevens, and Strom Thurmond played hot potato with it for the better part of two decades. When Travis's peers in Austin bequeathed it to him, however, it wasn't because of his seniority. He'd only been in the senate two years, and there were plenty of old coots ahead of him. Lee Snyder, the same senator who gave Travis the Darth Vader gloves, was one of them, and he said they chose Travis because he was so well liked and respected. Travis suspected it was the best way they could think of to show sympathy for the messy way his divorce unfolded inside the Austin statehouse.

The caravan pulled to a stop in front of the house as the dust cloud moved on without them. A familiar face stepped from the passenger seat of a Suburban and waved. Hunter Reese was the governor's everexhausted chief of staff. He was stronger and wiser than he looked, and make no mistake, he looked terrible. His birth certificate claimed he was thirty-nine, but seven years in the same job had sucked the remaining youth out of him. His shirt hung loose off his shoulders, as if there were a hanger in there and nothing else. Eating was a luxury his schedule didn't often allow, and today the thought of it hadn't even entered his mind.

"We've been calling all morning, Ben," Hunter said. "Where were you?"

"Church. Then here," said Travis.

"Alright, second order of business, we're giving you a cell phone."

"What's the first order of business?"

From the other Suburban appeared another face Travis recognized. Owen Pokey was eighty-five and the oldest Texas Supreme Court justice on the bench. The thin laces on his brown leather shoes were still untied from the long drive. He shuffled along, dragging his feet and leaving parallel tracks in the dirt. Under his arm was a tattered leather book that could only have been a Bible.

Travis's mouth turned to chalk as he pieced together the evidence. "*Both* of 'em?" he said. Hunter nodded.

Travis let the handle of the ax slip through his hands. He tossed it to the ground, removed his hat, and flattened his hair. As he raised his right arm, Gene finally caught on, memorializing his boss's swearing in with an entirely inappropriate and perfectly understandable summation: "Holy shit."

2

Hunter Reese leaned against the frame of the paint-chipped doorway as the new governor of Texas wandered back and forth across his bedroom, only occasionally dropping clothes in a small black suitcase he'd laid open on the bed. Hunter walked over and peeked inside. "I think you might need more pants than that."

Travis was still in a bit of a daze. He agreed to run for the state senate for a few reasons, not the least of which was the fact that the Texas Legislature only meets for the first hundred forty days of each term, after which it takes the next year and a half off. No other state had a system like it, and the rationale was that doing so limited the damage the legislative branch could inflict upon the citizens of Texas. Travis loved it because he could be a public servant without losing his business or his sanity. He hadn't thought about politics or set foot in Austin for a year, which was fine by him. Now, with one simple oath, he was a full-time government employee.

"Who's going to take care of my horses?" he asked.

"What about that ranch hand?" Hunter suggested. "He seems to know what he's doing."

"Gene?" Travis shook his head and flung another pair of jeans into his suitcase. "Gene's hippophobic."

Hunter was paid well to know a little bit about a lot of things, but that didn't include phobias. "What does that mean?"

"Fear of horses," Travis said.

"Seriously?"

"It's pretty common, actually."

"With ranch hands?" Travis didn't answer, and Hunter wasn't going to belabor the point. "We'll find someone, Governor. Not a problem. There are probably lots of locals who'd love to say they work for you." A little ego massaging couldn't hurt, Hunter thought, but Travis was already on to his next concern.

"What about my truck?"

"Don't tell me Gene's afraid of cars, too."

"I want to bring it with me." Travis cherished his truck. It was a silver 2008 F-150, the last year Ford made them with manual transmissions. Unlike his ex-wife, it didn't argue with him and rarely needed maintenance.

"You can't take your truck, Governor. Especially given this morning's accident."

"It's not like *Allen* was driving the limo. And anyway, I've been driving since I was ten. Not legally, obviously, but—"

"How about we just get to Austin and then we can deal with all these questions?"

Travis didn't appreciate the patronization and showed it by disappearing into the walk-in closet. Reese rubbed his temples, working on his third headache of the day. Every media outlet in Texas as well as a number of nationals were waiting in Austin for Travis to arrive. On the drive through Prosper, they'd passed a news van searching in vain for Travis's ranch. It was only a matter of time before they found it. Time to change tack and go personal.

"Look, Ben," he said, "if you don't want to do this, it's your call. I think everyone would understand. This is a big change for you. Just resign. Put something in writing and we'll move down the list."

Travis didn't answer. He had avoided his bedroom closet for months. He had tried to vanquish her scent from it but couldn't do it. He tried mothballs, baking soda, even spraying cologne, nothing helped. Lavender orange blossom was eternally part of that closet, taking up residence like an overly moisturized ghost. He couldn't help but picture her clothes, organized by color and style and divided by season. Shoes lined up and pointing out. He often called it the world's smallest J.Crew store, and half-expected some teenager to pop out from among her sweaters and ask if he needed help.

Hunter sensed Travis slipping away. He walked to the closet. Travis had his back to the door and his hand wrapped around an empty wooden hanger rod.

"Ben?" Travis turned around. "Do you want us to move down the list?"

"I don't know . . . maybe."

Hunter liked Travis. Most people did. He was engaging. He was smart without knowing it. And he hated the prospect of defeat. That was during his senate campaign. His first term in Austin was marked by an aloofness written off as the understandable product of a man blindsided by the one woman he ever loved. Most of his peers felt that Ben Travis could be great—but right now he was a question mark.

Hunter always weighed his words. This time he was even more careful. "I'd like you to take this job, Governor, I would. But you need to understand that when you drive out that gate with us, you're the face of this state. I think everyone would prefer if it weren't a depressing one."

Travis gave him a look but didn't say anything, a sign Hunter took to mean proceed . . . with caution. "What I'm saying is that the people of Texas deserve your best. You need to decide if that's something you can give them. If it's not, let's stop before we start."

Hunter turned and made for the door, leaving Travis with his thoughts. He hadn't reached the second stair step when Travis popped his head over the railing. "Hunter." His chief of staff stopped and looked up. "If I pass on this, who's in line after me?"

Hunter cleared his throat, then answered softly. "The, um, Speaker of the House."

"Gabe Coggins?!" Hunter nodded as Travis choked the dull teak at the top of the staircase. "I hate that guy." Returning to the land of lavender orange blossom, Travis held his breath and was back a minute later with his black bag and his only three suits. He passed Hunter on the stairs. The keys to his F-150 were jingling in his pocket.

3

It was what reporters called "a three-pancake day." Not in terms of food, in terms of makeup. Most of the talking heads were already up when news broke that neither the governor nor lieutenant governor had returned from a climate change conference near Horseshoe Bay. They rushed en masse from Dallas, Houston, and San Antonio to the governor's office and reported live—*on the scene—with all the latest updates!* Of which there were none. That was pancake one. When the wife of the spokesman for the National Transportation Safety Board mentioned the location of the crash site in a Facebook update, the convoy of Econolines sped northwest, arriving in time to capture the last of the plume of smoke, impede firefighters, and harass local ranchers who didn't appreciate news vans crisscrossing their property without permission. Pancake two. Finally it was back to Austin to hear from the new governor on the south steps of the capitol building. Pancake three.

Back in 1881, when contractors Charles and John Farwell, brothers from Chicago, looked at the ambitious plans for the Texas capitol building, they set the price to build it at $3 million. The state, wary of more debt, offered them three million *acres* on the Texas panhandle instead. The result was the creation of the single largest ranch in the world and the largest state capitol in the Union. Its red granite dome rose over three hundred and ten feet into the air, almost fifteen feet higher than the top of the U.S. Capitol. No matter who was in office, conservative Texans rested easier knowing that, at least architecturally speaking, Austin was looking down on Washington.

It was an imposing backdrop for Travis's first public appearance. The thinking was that the setting would give the new governor some much-needed gravitas. After all, 95 percent of Texas had never even heard of the guy, let alone voted for him. A few minutes into his address, however, it was clear that something was wrong. It wasn't the speaker, it was the speech.

The writer who spit out that afternoon's prepared statement had spent the last five and a half years on autopilot, writing for a career politician whose voice had long ago absorbed the warm and yet robotic cadence of a network news anchor. A few years earlier, a grad student in communication studies at the University of Texas analyzed fifty separate speeches given by Governor Allen and discovered that, with almost no exceptions, Allen's voice rose one octave four beats into every sentence, stayed there through the middle, and then dropped two octaves for the final two beats. It was both remarkable and terrifying.

Travis was a different beast, however, with a different rhythm and different vocabulary. So those same speechwriter's words, when put into his mouth, felt all wrong, like dropping Mercedes parts into a '65 Mustang.

"And while we grieve for our fallen leaders, beloved though they be, the tumult of today will soon pass . . ." *Dang it,* Travis thought. Was that *tumult*? Or *toomult*? It was one of those words he'd read a thousand times but never said out loud. Whatever it was supposed to be, he was certain he did it wrong.

Travis's problems weren't just confined to the words on the page. There was also the problem of the page itself. Hunter had already told him multiple times to use the teleprompter and *not* the hardcopy statement on the podium.

"Why is there a hard copy if I can't use it?" Travis asked. It was a legitimate point.

"That copy is just for emergencies," Hunter said.

"You mean if the teleprompter breaks."

"Right."

"Does that ever happen?"

"N—"

"Yes," a junior aide interrupted. Hunter glared at him.

"On occasion," Hunter said, trying to sound reasonable.

The aide wasn't through. "Once it fell over and knocked out a kid in the front row."

"We replaced it with a new model, *Jeffrey*," Hunter said, defensive, and turned his attention back to Travis. "The MT4500. It has a much wider base. Larger screen. It's the same one used by President Leary."

"Are you trying to talk me into it or out of it?" Travis asked.

"Look, Governor, we just want you to look natural and relaxed, that's all."

Now Travis was really confused. "If you really want me to look natural and relaxed, how about I just go out there and wing it?"

"No!" Hunter was repulsed. "Whatever you do, don't do *that*."

Before being thrown into the spotlight, nearly every politician goes through a grooming process, both figurative and literal. In one room, aides discuss the appropriate position on the Mideast. Next door, another team debates which hair color will woo the most female voters. Phone surveys are done, experts are consulted, and ten days later, out pops a candidate with chestnut locks and a tough stance on Iran.

Travis had bypassed this entire process, and Hunter just hoped to get through Day One and then fix all of Travis's flaws, the most glaring of which was a disconcerting reputation for saying exactly what he thought and doing whatever he wanted.

Thus it was that when Travis came to the next period on the screen, he stopped. The pool of reporters and cameramen waited patiently, believing Travis was going for—and failing at—some sort of dramatic pause. After another two seconds, Hunter leaned in behind him to see if the MT4500 had frozen. It hadn't, but Travis was done embarrassing himself. He'd mispronounced "tumult," "visage," and the name of the lieutenant governor's wife. No one in Texas wanted to hear him say another word. At least not like that. Instead, he broke another pre-statement directive, scanned the room, and asked, "So, you folks got any questions?"

One reporter outyelled the rest. "Governor Travis, when exactly did you know you were the new governor of Texas?"

"Right after I took the oath," Travis deadpanned. *Hey,* he thought, if they were going to tee them up like that, he was gonna swing. A series of laughs worked through the press corps as the remaining color drained from Hunter's face. Travis looked through the sea of hands.

"Yeah, you with the"—he didn't know anyone's name yet—"hair gel."

"Governor, I know the NTSB's official report will take months, but is there any hint of foul play in the car crash?"

"Not that I've heard, no." Another scan of the crowd. "Sweaty Forehead."

Calling the chief political reporter from the *Austin American-Statesman* "Sweaty Forehead" killed what little hope there was of being asked a softball question. "Governor, I think you would agree with the sentiment that you're coming into this job fairly green. What do you see as your three big weaknesses and how do you plan on addressing them?"

"Three big weaknesses . . ." *What a twit,* Travis thought. He pretended to give the question some serious consideration. "Well, I'm not a very good liar. That's a big one. Probably need to work on that. I don't appreciate being bribed. That's going to make things difficult . . . And I don't get too upset if people don't like me. So yeah, I guess it's gonna be interesting." More laughs. Even from Sweaty Forehead. Travis had been more entertaining in one postmortem press conference than Governor Allen had been in five years.

He spotted a female reporter—Cindi Patti, Channel 13 ABC Houston—squished between two burly men and pointed her way. This was all part of Cindi's MO: look defenseless, appeal to a man's innate desire to help a damsel in distress, and then, when called upon, ask the most ruthless question of the day. Hunter tried to wave her off, but it was too late.

"Governor Travis, Cindi Patti, Channel 13 ABC Houston." She was on pancake number four. "Some people have suggested that in such a unique situation as yours, the appropriate thing to do is simply to carry on the major policy positions of Governor Allen for the remainder of his term. To see his vision and the will of the voters prevail. Can we assume that's your intention?"

Damn you, Cindi, Hunter thought. Travis knew this was tricky. The politically savvy response was to say that he had a great deal of respect for Governor Allen (a lie), and that he had yet to give those heavy questions any real thought (also a lie). Travis spent much of the four-hour drive between Prosper and Austin thinking about his predecessor. The truth was that Allen's mushy-middle Republican-*light* positions increased the size of the state government, got him invited to the right D.C. parties, but did little for the people of Texas. The answer to whether or not he wanted to continue that could not have been clearer.

"God, I hope not," he answered.

Cindi held the tip of her pen to her notepad, waiting for Travis to finish, take back, or at least soften his response. No one would claim Governor Allen was the nation's greatest politician, but he was still a Texas legend; not to mention dead for less than six hours. However, Travis wasn't going to expound on it any more than that. With a cordial wave to the throng, he turned and headed up the steps, unbuttoning his jacket as he went.

Hunter grabbed Travis's sleeve before he could reach the door. "What was that?"

"What?"

"You didn't finish the speech."

"Yeah," said Travis, "it was terrible. What was that anyway, the King James Version?"

"And then you took questions."

"And then I answered them," said Travis. "You do realize I was there, right?"

"Your answers were cold, insensitive, and blunt. It was a disaster."

"It was?" Travis turned and saw reporters swapping quotes. "Look, they're going to find something to say about me either way. Might as well show them who I am versus making them guess." He patted Hunter on the shoulder and ducked inside.

It was Hunter's worst nightmare. The more provocative things his boss said, the more phone calls he had to field. The more phone calls he fielded, the less sleep he got. Based on the current buzz from the steps of the capitol, this night would be a sleepless one.

4

The president's team assembled at nine thirty in the Oval Office, divided evenly between the two beige couches, while Leary sat behind his desk, legs up, revealing a flash of his trademark green socks.

His specific policies may have been wildly unpopular, but there were enough appealing things about the man himself that kept Americans infatuated with Michael Leary. His Irish freckles were disarming, making him look like Richie Cunningham in *Happy Days*. His toothy grin was delightful, a perfect cover for a temper that had sent more than one classic American oil painting to the Smithsonian for emergency repairs. And his hair . . . well, his hair was flawless. Thick and red on top, fading to a wispy peppery gray on the sides. Horses with hair like that won awards at county fairs.

The president's Monday morning briefings were the most thorough of the week, and Ruffles—as chief of staff—had the thankless job of deciding what to discuss first.

"Let's start with baseball."

"Ugh." Leary groaned and spun around to face the South Lawn.

During his presidential campaign four years earlier, Leary, at the time the junior senator from Massachusetts, made the mistake of telling a crowd in St. Louis that he was "America's biggest Cardinals fan." He weathered the rebuke from angry Bostonians and for the next three months was inundated with Cardinals paraphernalia. Hats, jerseys, foam fingers, seat cushions, beer cozies. Some nut from Cape Girardeau sent him an actual cardinal in a cage with instructions on how to care for it. For the rest of the campaign, if he came within three hundred miles of the city, a reporter would ask for his latest thoughts on the team, their playoff chances, last night's game, etc., etc. After Leary won the election that November, the team's owner devoted the off-season to building a presidential box and invited the first family to Opening Day, where the first fifty thousand fans through the gate received a President Leary Bobblehead.

Unfortunately, Leary wasn't a Cardinals fan. He wasn't even a baseball fan. If Missouri weren't a swing state, he might have just come clean, but with his poll numbers sagging, he needed those eleven electoral votes even more now than he did four years ago.

Ruffles pressed on. "This weekend was interleague play, and the Cards lost two of three to the Royals. The third-base ump made a bad call on Sunday that cost them the game."

"Why didn't they reverse the call?" Leary asked.

"You can't do that."

"That's not fair."

"That's baseball."

"Hmm . . ." Leary scratched his ear.

The six suits and skirts on the couch exchanged a look. They knew that scratch. It meant this benign thirty-second baseball update suddenly had the potential to become a three-week political detour with Leary pushing for federal oversight on all disputed major-league baseball calls.

Ruffles took back the reins. "Let's talk about your Supreme Court nominee." Aides had been busy coming up with a short list ever since Justice Ferraro stepped down for health reasons a month earlier. Ferraro had been the most stalwart conservative on the Court since the early 1990s. The general belief was that at age sixty-eight, he had ten more good years of jurisprudence in him, maybe fifteen. All that changed in April when he began behaving erratically, displaying memory loss, and attempting to write the majority opinion in a gun control case that he had ruled against. His doctor diagnosed him with early onset dementia, and his retirement was formally announced the next day.

"We still liking the Asian chick?" Leary asked.

His team winced. "Yes," Ruffles said. "Justice Chan is still the front-runner. Liz and her team have been doing as much digging as possible, making sure we don't get stung with something after we announce. We'll be ready to move soon."

"Good. What else?"

Ruffles nodded toward Lee Kurtz, the president's press secretary. Kurtz had spent most of his career as a public relations wizard in Los Angeles and was offered the White House gig after successfully navigating a Dodger pitcher through a high-profile paternity scandal in which he was accused of fathering children with nine different women. When the test results came back positive for all nine of them, Kurtz paraded the happy father in front of the cameras and declared that his client had achieved the biological equivalent of throwing a perfect game.

Early in the term, Kurtz would bounce to the podium in the pressroom, fully embracing his reputation as a svelte and witty raconteur. He could fill an entire press conference with just one long, colorful anecdote about the president trying to explain American football to the king of Bhutan. From a news perspective, the story would be completely useless, but Kurtz told it so well that every reporter in the room would return to the news desk and repeat it to their colleagues, who would laugh and then pick up the phone to share it with someone else.

As the domestic and international mistakes of Leary's last three years piled up, the press was less and less interested in Kurtz's one-man show. He had become a man shackled by reality and didn't seem to be handling it well. With his inner showman repressed, those closest to him noticed the only things that still made him smile were things devoid of humor, like homeless children or Christiane Amanpour.

"Mr. President . . ." Kurtz spoke like a man delivering a eulogy.

"I've already received a number of calls this morning regarding Governor Ben Travis."

Leary had caught some of Travis's speech the night before and wasn't impressed with his teleprompter skills. "What about him?"

"Reporters just want to know if the administration sees him changing the dynamics of our relationship with Texas."

"The guy's a zero," Leary said. "Just tell them we're anxious to forge a good relationship just like we had with Governor Allen."

Kurtz scribbled the comment as Ruffles waded in. "You don't think we need to adjust our plan for next month's announcement?" Everyone in the room seemed to know what he was talking about.

"Why should we? We're doing it no matter who's governor down there."

"Yes," Ruffles agreed, "but many of us think it would behoove us to have a friend on the Texas side of things."

"Of course it would, but this guy isn't a game changer," Leary said. "He's the biggest lame duck in the history of Texas politics. A man without a mandate. Believe me, first chance he has, he'll be back on his farm, in his overalls, playing the washboard and blowing on an empty jug."

The door to the Oval Office swung open as Hank Crudders, the vice president, a walking liability, loped in. "You guys started without me?"

They had. After three years of high-profile gaffes, keeping the vice president out of the loop as much as possible was standard procedure. Among many problems, the man was incapable of keeping secrets, having accidentally revealed the location of one of the country's nuclear missile sites to Al Roker during the Macy's Thanksgiving Day Parade.

"We're almost done, actually," Leary said. "Sorry about that."

"We'll brief you later on what you missed," Ruffles promised. They wouldn't.

Crudders squeezed onto the couch and took a sip of someone else's coffee. "You guys catch that Texas governor last night? A real quack, huh?"

Lee Kurtz was glad to see someone else reraise the issue. "He is, which is why I don't think we should discount him."

Leary thought he had already finished this discussion. "What do you want me to do, Kurtz? Just spit it out," he said.

"Well . . . for safety's sake, I say we release the wolves on him," said Kurtz. "See if anyone in the press wants to tar and feather him a bit."

"Sounds good to me," the vice president chimed in, believing his opinion mattered.

"Leave it alone, fellas," Leary said. He stood up and made his way to the men's room. "After all," he said, "do we even have to ask them to do that anymore? Pretty sure tarring and feathering is their Pavlovian response at this point."

Paige Travis set her iPhone to vibrate. Between the bings from voice mails and the bongs from text messages, her purse sounded like the casino inside Circus Circus. The highlights of last night's presser in Austin were the burning topic on all the morning news shows, with Travis himself appearing on many of them to discuss his vision for Texas; and every last friend of Paige was waking up to discover that the father she rarely acknowledged was this week's media darling.

She could ignore the cell, but not the landline.

"Department of Justice, Office of the—"

The voice on the other end of the line didn't let her finish. "So is it out of character for your father to speak ill of the dead or is this just one of his many winning qualities?" Paige gazed down at the caller ID—*Washington Post*—and smiled. Her friend Aubrey was a fellow Yale grad and scrub reporter.

"Hey, Aubs." Paige popped open a pocket mirror. At least she was having a good hair day. Her gentle brown curls held up well in spite of the late-spring humidity, and when she turned her head, they bounced around her neck and collarbone like a marionette being walked from one side of the stage to the other. She looked just like her mom. Petite but athletic, pretty without trying. Her eyes were her father's, green with a golden rim that was only visible from a few inches away. It had been fourteen months since any guy had been close enough to notice, not that she was counting.

"Have you talked to him?"

"No, but that doesn't mean anything. I think the last real conversation we had was the day before I came home from Yale with a butterfly tattoo and a Che Guevara T-shirt."

Yale hadn't made Paige liberal; it merely set in stone the direction she was already headed. At age twelve, she flummoxed the salesperson at a Dallas Foot Locker when she tried to purchase one black Converse and one blue one. "I'm trying to raise awareness of the growing problem of domestic abuse," she explained. By thirteen, she was a vegetarian. At fourteen, she stole her father's American Express and used it to make a sizable donation to John Kerry's presidential campaign. In Travis's eyes, she might as well have joined al Qaeda.

Kate assured her husband that their daughter's liberalism was just a phase. After a few years, Ben decided it was a simple matter of misinformation, and so one Saturday afternoon he sat her down to logically explain the errors of her ways. He came with statistics and tax returns. He dug up pay stubs from old jobs to show how much money he lost each week. His approach was both calm and reasoned. When he was finished, he looked at Paige, who had been silent the entire time, and said, "So? What do you think?" She called him a "heartless, money-grubbing Anglo-Saxon monster" and bolted for her room.

Ben Travis could only conclude that he and his daughter were just wired differently. He dwelled in facts, she in emotion, two approaches to life that rarely crossed paths. Even when he tried to be empathetic, he would say the wrong thing. He let Kate take over as Paige cried over puberty and boys and a hundred other problems he couldn't possibly solve. He lumped them all together in one radioactive category he dubbed *Double T:* Teenage Trauma.

Paige's decision to go to Yale seemed like a natural fit. She wanted to pursue acting, and he couldn't deny she was . . . dramatic. She quickly landed some bit parts in campus plays, only to find herself drawn more and more to political activism. When presidential hopeful

Michael Leary came to speak at Yale in the spring of her freshman year, she was in awe. Even his enemies recognized he had a spirit that inspired people, especially college kids. He seemed to get her generation in a way that her own father didn't. When summer came, Ben hoped she would come home. Instead, Paige became a Leary volunteer and headed off to a campaign office in Ohio.

When she found out her parents were separating, she had no problem taking sides, and not because her brief career in politics had made her so good at it. There was no adultery, no dirty secrets; the relationship died the same way Hemingway said people go broke—very slowly and then all at once. Still, the blame as Paige saw it fell squarely on her father. Her dad was a man of unparalleled tunnel vision. When something or someone grabbed his attention, everything else fell away. As the years went on, that focus seemed to fall everywhere but on his wife.

Paige felt her father viewed his family like one of his successful businesses: It pretty much ran itself. His time and his thoughts were better spent on new ventures. On the few occasions when she or her mom dared to open up about needs that weren't being met, her father brushed them aside as ridiculous if he even considered them at all.

She still remembered their last family vacation. She and her mom pushed for Paris since none of them had ever been out of the country. Her dad turned up his nose at the idea and countered with the Grand Canyon, then used the road trip as an excuse to schedule meetings with clients all across New Mexico and Arizona. The low point came when she and her mom pleaded to stop at an Indian jewelry store near the South Rim. After using the restroom, Travis returned to the family SUV and drove away. He made it halfway to Flagstaff before realizing he was the only one in the car.

Paige stood at her window, phone pressed to her ear, and looked down Tenth Street. A busload of tourists was headed north toward Ford's Theatre. "So how often do you see him?" Aubrey asked.

"I don't know. More than I see my gynecologist but less than I see my dentist."

"How often is that?"

"My dentist or my dad?"

"Your dad."

"Oh. Three or four times a year, I guess."

"Geez, what's wrong with your teeth?"

"Nothing. I just like clean teeth."

All the teeth talk made her reach for the pocket mirror again and see how they were holding up. She rubbed some lipstick off an incisor. "I don't know what else to tell you, Aubs. My father's sort of an idiot." Aubrey laughed . . . and furiously scribbled notes. She had her exclusive—and Paige had one more person she wouldn't be talking to anytime soon.

5

Ben Travis stared into the distant black square of the television camera and listened. He'd been on the same stool for the better part of eight hours and couldn't for the life of him remember who was interviewing him. It was definitely a woman. Rachel? No, no, *Raquel.* Or maybe Rebecca. A green plastic sheet hung behind him, held in place at the corners by five-pound sandbags. Those watching at home were seeing Travis hovering in front of the glistening night skyline of Austin, but in reality he was sitting in a four-room TV studio in a business park five miles outside of town.

Cable networks paid the studio eight hundred dollars an hour for its services, which included an on-site producer, a cameraman, a sound tech, a lighting guy, and a makeup-girl-slash-receptionist who mistakenly thought she was on the first rung of a glorious career in show business. Almost all Travis's interviews had been focused on his press conference comment about Governor Allen, RIP. He was so tired of the topic that when a local sports radio host was a no-show for a scheduled ESPN interview on University of Texas football, Travis offered to step in and give his own take. The producer called ESPN, and two minutes later he was on *SportsCenter* dissecting the holes in the Longhorn defense. The media could call him a heartless bastard—and yes, the Huffington Post and Chris Matthews already had—but there was no denying that Travis was having fun for the first time in years.

He finished his day at the historic grill inside the Driskill Hotel. Opened in 1866, the Driskill once featured a ladies-only entrance so female guests could bypass rough-talking cattlemen in the lobby. A hundred and twenty-five years later, it was the governor who hoped to avoid unnecessary attention. A perky hostess led him to a corner table in the darkest part of the restaurant. "Will this work for you?" she asked.

"What time's the séance?" he inquired as he slid across the leather bench seat. Dark or not, there would still be the problem of simply reading the menu, a side effect of turning fifty, about which Travis was still in some denial.

K Polopono, the governor's hulking Hawaiian bodyguard, explained the location. "It's for your safety, Governor." K was two hundred eighty pounds and hadn't seen his own neck since his sophomore year of high school. The "K" was short for OK, the nickname he received the day he signed a letter of intent to play football for the University of Oklahoma. Travis couldn't believe he was putting his life in the hands of a Sooner, but K was no slouch. A three-time All-American defensive end, he was drafted by the Jacksonville Jaguars right out of college, only to blow out his ACL the first week of camp. After a solid year of recovery, and then rehab, he was back in uniform, but the new ligament never took. All the speed and power that made him one of the most feared men in Division I football were gone for good. He rode the bench all season and retired from the NFL without ever seeing a single play.

Protecting the governor was a respectable fallback and made good use of K's ability to scan the field and look for holes, but it had yet to provide the drama, excitement, or women that came with sacking a quarterback in front of seventy thousand fans.

"Tell you what," Travis had said. "I promise to tick off one person enough to kill me, but only if you promise to stop him before he does."

The hostess materialized out of the dark. "Excuse me, Governor."

Travis jumped. *Seriously, could it be any darker back here?* "You have a phone call."

"Are you sure?" No one even knew he was here.

Travis was fine with taking the call up front, but the Bird Dogs—a rocking country band out of Dallas—were performing at B. D. Riley's pub, and traffic on Brazos Street was at a standstill. K had it transferred to the tiny manager's office in the back of the restaurant. A stack of timecards sat on the desk.

"This is Ben Travis," he said.

"Governor, it's Walt Thompson. I apologize for interrupting your dinner."

There was no need for Walt to introduce himself. His was the most recognizable voice in America. Finely tuned from a lifetime of on-again/off-again chain-smoking, it sounded like an 18-wheeler idling outside a coffee shop. Walt's morning radio show netted fifteen million listeners a week, many of whom disagreed with everything he said but tuned in anyway to get their daily dose of outrage. The liberals branded him the unofficial chairman of the Republican Party and made him their favorite target. No matter what they tried, he was impervious to their attacks. In the last three years alone he'd been labeled racist, cruel to animals, insensitive to the earth, homophobic, xenophobic, anti-Semitic, anti-Arab, pro-life, pro-gun, and, above all else, a fat slob. Walt believed he was an "equal opportunity hater," disliking people of every race, color, and creed, but never for that reason.

"This is a pretty cheap way to land an interview, Walt," Travis said.

"This isn't an interview, Governor. I tried to catch you before you left the studio. The girl there said you were headed out for dinner. She sounded cute. Was she?"

"How'd you know I'd come here?"

"I'm that good, Governor." Yes, that and the fact he had his cadre of assistants call every restaurant in downtown Austin till they found him. "I wanted to talk to you somewhere where I knew the call would not be recorded. I don't want anyone listening in."

Walt loved conspiracy theories, offering them up on his show with great regularity. Over the course of twenty minutes, he would connect the dots, work his listeners into a lather, and then transition seamlessly into a pitch for Goldmine®, the official gold supplier of *The Walt Thompson Radio Show*.

"For what it's worth, Walt, so far I'm only *half*-listening." He was proving himself a harder sell than Walt's typical audience.

"Governor, as you could probably imagine, I have a number of operatives scattered around Washington, including the White House. Undercover patriots, if you will."

"Of course," Travis said, wondering how many pictures of himself Thompson kept scattered around the house.

"And I say that not to toot my own horn . . ."

No. Never, Travis thought.

". . . but to let you know that this is based on a conversation that I personally had with someone on the inside. *Deep* on the inside."

"I hate to interrupt, but I'm curious," Travis said. "You still eating leftover cans stored up from Y2K?" He leaned back in the cracked leather chair and waited. This, as Travis knew from catching his radio show a handful of times, was when Walt would lose it, laying into Travis as he did on a daily basis to his most petulant of callers. Travis wondered what moniker he'd receive. "Moron" was Walt's standard one, but occasionally he would go for something so colorful that his technician would have to bleep it out.

This time he didn't. Instead, Walt Thompson's voice grew soft, almost gentle. "Governor, I received this tip months ago. I sat on it, not knowing myself what to make of it. Because the truth is that there's nothing even I can do to stop this. Governor Allen could have done something, but I knew he wouldn't. Then I heard you, and I thought . . . maybe this guy might." All traces of his blustery radio persona were gone. "I could be wrong. I could have misread who you are. Maybe you're just riding the media wave like so many other politicians, hoping it leads to a fat book deal and a speaking tour. Yet I hope not."

He was good, there was no doubt about it. "Go ahead," Travis said. He tried to sound disinterested, but the truth was that if Walt Thompson tried to sell him a Sleep Number® bed right then and there, he'd probably buy one.

"Are you familiar with the construction along I-10, I-20, and I-40?"

Of course Travis knew the job. Everyone from Texas to Arizona knew that job. The resurfacing of those three interstates had been going on for years. No other topic had bred as many angry letters to the editor as that one. It seemed like too obvious a place to be starting a Walt Thompson conspiracy theory. "What about it?"

"Any idea what they're doing?"

"Yeah, pissing off truckers."

"I mean *officially*."

"Officially, they're widening shoulders and improving drainage. Part of Leary's stimulus program."

"Right, and so far they've been at it, what, three years?"

"About that."

"How long do you think it should take?"

"That's not my area of expertise. I can only tell you how long it would take if they wanted to air-condition it or drop some wells along the center divider."

"Governor, the bottom line is that it's taken a long time given the amount of workers they've hired for that job."

Travis peeked through the door and saw a waiter circling their table. "Walt, I really hope you didn't waste this opportunity just so you could make a point about the slow speed of government projects."

"Ben," he said, dropping the formalities, "I can only drop the bread crumbs for you. My mole didn't tell me everything, and I'm telling you even less. It's the only way to give us protection if you turn around and try to bury us. The way we see it, we're the last line of defense."

"So you're saying there's more going on there than just adding lanes," Travis said.

"Uh-huh."

"Something illegal?"

"I sure think so."

Travis was in a high-stakes game of Twenty Questions whether he wanted to be or not. "Will it affect the citizens of Texas?"

"Yep."

"People outside Texas?"

"Oh yes."

Travis waited, hoping that Walt wouldn't be able to contain himself. He stayed silent. "You're really not going to tell me, are you, Walt?"

"I told you plenty."

Travis shook his head. Walt had successfully provided all of the threat and few of the details. "Well, thanks for ruining my dinner, Walt."

"Anytime, Governor." Walt Thompson laughed, coughed, then laughed some more.

6

It was sort of embarrassing to admit, but Travis needed a map of Texas. He knew that Interstate 10 was south of Austin and ran through San Antonio, but there had to be a faster way than down I-35. He didn't want to give away his after-dinner plans to his staff, so he found one of the night shift housekeepers instead.

"Map? *Sí, sí.*" The Latina maid led him down the hall, past stacks of boxes and rolls of bubble wrap. The mansion was still in a state of upheaval, with Governor Allen's possessions being prepped for a midweek move. A small funeral was scheduled for the following week. In light of his comments about the dearly departed, Travis's invitation had yet to arrive. After a few more turns, the maid stopped in the hallway outside the master bedroom and proudly pointed to, yes, a map of Texas . . . circa 1760. It wasn't just older than the interstates, it was older than the states themselves.

The guy at the Chevron down on Congress Avenue proved to be more helpful. "Just take 183 past Luling," he said, not recognizing the man in the ball cap whose picture was on the front of every newspaper he'd sold that day.

Luling was in the midst of a recent drilling boom, centered around a new oil and gas play in the Eagle Ford shale, but was better known as the watermelon seed–spitting capital of Texas. If there was another Texas town hoping for that title, it was wasting its time. Luling didn't merely have a watermelon-painted water tower and an annual watermelon festival; it had a permanent "spitway," recently upgraded with a roof to protect contestants from the vagaries of the wind, putting the emphasis of the sport back where it belongs—on spitting.

It was only forty-five minutes to Luling, and another two minutes got him onto the interstate. Travis pulled his F-150 off the shoulder and killed his headlights. It was raining, and Texans tended to stop at the sight of any and all broken-down vehicles, especially during a storm. Such benevolence was a nice quality to have, except in horror movies, where Samaritan Texans are regularly gutted by serial killers masquerading as hitchhikers. He pulled his cap snug over his head and felt under the passenger seat for his Maglite.

The south side of the four-lane interstate was already finished, with a wider shoulder and a deeper drainage ditch to increase safety and improve runoff during bad weather. Based on how it was handling tonight's deluge, so far so good. The north side wasn't as close. Travis ducked under the orange construction tape. Beyond the tape and cones, eight feet of fresh dirt lay flat and packed, ready for the base coat and then asphalt. He walked onto the mud and clicked off his flashlight. Pretty standard stuff, he thought.

A semi barreled down the highway, and Travis took another step back, not aware of his precarious position. Three feet behind him was the edge of a sheer thirty-foot embankment, heavy and weak from two straight hours of Texas rain. The governor's hundred eighty pounds were all the extra weight it needed. The bank crumbled and took Travis with it. He turned as he fell and slid feet first, his back to the hill. As the semi passed, its lights briefly lit the foreground. The shovel of a backhoe materialized out of the darkness. Travis pressed his head flat against the mud and watched as the jagged iron teeth passed no more than an inch over his head, snagging the bill of his cap as he went. He continued sliding, again through the darkness, and stopped with a cold splash at the bottom of the hill.

He wiggled his arms and legs, fearing the pain of a sprained ankle or broken bone. Nothing. He sat up and shook his head. *Way to go, idiot,* he thought. He fished for his Maglite and switched it back on. Mud cascaded down the hill through the trench he'd made when he fell. He wondered if this was where he'd be spending his night. That was sure to inspire confidence with the public. He could see the headline from the *Dallas Morning News*: GOVERNOR FOUND DISORI-ENTED AND WET, MILES FROM HOME.

As he looked for a path up the slope, something white caught his eye halfway up the embankment. It was a stark white slash against the brown earth and gleamed in the light of his flashlight like the rubber on an unused pitcher's mound. He struggled up the hill, first recovering his hat from the jaws of the backhoe, then continuing up the slope, slipping as he went, eventually arriving at the spot. He moved the mud away with his free hand, holding himself against the embankment with the other, flashlight under his arm. He worked slowly at first. It was white plastic. High-pressure PVC. A big sprin-kler pipe? That didn't make sense. He'd seen sprinklers along the freeways in California, but never in Texas. He dug his nails into the clay and moved more dirt. The white slash grew into a flat surface, ten inches high, eighteen inches across. He worked faster, clearing the dirt in giant swaths. Two more feet of white were exposed, then five feet, then seven feet up and ten across.

He slipped back down the hill and looked up at what was now a white wall. It ran dead straight east and west and, at the top and bottom, curved back into the dirt and under Interstate 10. He stood in bewilderment, looking through the rain as it poured off the brim of his chewed-up cap.

One thing was for certain: This was no sprinkler pipe.

7

Damon Cole always saved this lecture for the end of May. He knew that if he led off with it in January, no one would appreciate the unique challenge it presented. By now, though, the three hundred fifteen undergrads enrolled in Constitutional Theory knew with whom they were dealing. In turn, they were willing to fight back. Cole loved a good fight—as long as that fight was ideological, nuanced, esoteric, and, above all else, fistless.

He delicately placed his TAG Heuer watch—realigned once a week to match Greenwich Mean Time—on the wooden podium exactly thirty seconds before 10:00 A.M. The seats in Cole's classes always filled up early. "Raise your standards and the students will rise with you," he often remarked to jealous associate professors who struggled with late arrivals.

That wasn't the only reason for Cole's popularity. It helped that he was an anomaly. As a handsome, conservative, African American politics professor at Princeton, he was the circus freak of modern liberal academia. *Step right up, folks, and see for yourself! He's conservative, teaching politics . . . and yes, a minority.*

When Cole's name came up for tenure five years earlier, the Princeton trustees were in a pickle. They already had one outspoken tenured conservative professor in Robert George, and that was more than enough. George was a total nuisance to university life. He was always speaking out in favor of some extreme, embarrassing position. A few years earlier he had vocalized his support for the Anscombe Society, a student-led group committed to abstinence and promoting the role of families in society. They weren't convinced that Princeton needed *two* unstable people like that on the dole.

On the other hand, Cole was the only black professor in an all-white department. It wouldn't look good if they lost him. Until that January, they had two, but then Lynne Oxley died. The dingbat went to see the Costa Rican rain forest over winter break and fell off a zip line. They say she fell through seven hundred species of plants and animals on the way down, so at least she got her money's worth.

They knew that Damon Cole would never do anything that risky. He wouldn't even jaywalk across Nassau Street. If they gave him tenure, they'd be stuck with him for twenty years, maybe thirty. At least he was good-looking. Nice, round head. A blinding smile. He'd photograph well in the university brochure. When the debate was over, Cole secured his tenure by one vote.

Fifteen seconds to go, and the last few students shuffled into the hall. Mixed in with the stragglers were Ben Travis and K, fresh off an early-morning flight out of Austin to Newark. They snagged two seats in the last row just as Cole's watch struck the hour.

"I'm wrong, and I'm sorry," Cole began. That grabbed their attention. "I'm wrong, and I'm sorry. That is the goal of today. To get me to say *that* to *you*. You see, all semester I've stood here and indoctrinated you with my thoughts on every subject even tangentially related to the Constitution. And as the sponges you are, you've believed it all." Cole spotted some smiles. "Or you've at least *pretended* to believe it for the sake of a good grade." The class laughed, knowing that was closer to the truth.

"But as I hinted at last week, today is your chance to prove me wrong. To show me the error of my ways. To educate *me*. Impossible? Maybe. Yet it's worth a shot, isn't it? And here's the prize: If you get me to admit that I'm wrong, you will not have to take the written final." Now that was some incentive, especially with the late-spring sun beckoning through the lead-framed windows.

"Who wants to be the first victim?"

Cole left the podium and began to move around the stage. Most professors took tenure as a license to give up on fitted pants and basic hygiene, but not Damon Cole. His tortoise-framed glasses came from Brooks Brothers. His pinstripe suit was handmade during his last trip to Italy. A white silk handkerchief peeked from his left breast pocket and, unlike the one carried by the president's chief of staff, was purely for looks. As for his shoes . . . well, his shoes ate up all his lucrative speaking engagement fees and were the most talked-about part of his wardrobe. He had dozens of pairs, each with a story. Today's selection was a pair of Tanino Crisci birch-colored loafers, made of two-hundred-year-old Russian reindeer leather, which had been cured in baths of steel-cut oatmeal. The soles were made from the bark of fallen California redwoods. There were only three hundred pairs like them in the world. Price tag: $2,900. He spotted a hand halfway up on the aisle. "Ah, Mr. Brandel. Nice to see you're still awake this far into class." The other students knew this wouldn't end well. Clad in a T-shirt and flip-flops, Spencer Brandel was a blue blood who proved that gaining acceptance into an Ivy League school wasn't always based on merit.

"Um, yeah, Professor Cole, I think you were wrong about the legalization of weed. I don't think anyone has any, ya know, right to tell me what I can or can't put in my body. I mean that's what freedom is all about, right?"

"Mr. Brandel, if I may, would you agree with me that marijuana can impair your judgment?"

"No, I wouldn't. It doesn't."

"I see." Cole twirled his pen in circles with his right hand. "Just out of curiosity, have you ever tried marijuana?" The class laughed at the obvious.

"Yeah."

"I see. And is it safe to assume that you've tried it recently?"

"Maybe."

"Maybe?" Cole looked around the room to see if anyone else was buying this. "Maybe . . . this morning?"

Spencer weighed his words. "Off the record, Professor?"

"Of course," Cole said.

"Then yes. This morning."

"Thank you, Mr. Brandel. Next question." Cole looked around the room for the next hand.

Spencer stood up. "Wait, but Professor. You never answered me."

"Oh, I'm sorry, Mr. Brandel. I assumed the fact that you would admit to three hundred future leaders of America that you came to class high proved *my* point, not yours."

The class laughed and cheered, appreciating the verbal jujitsu. Cole pointed to a preppy girl toward the back.

"Professor, you've talked about affirmative action being unconstitutional, but the Declaration of Independence says all men are created equal. I just don't see how a desire to give people a chance to succeed—who might not otherwise have it—is anything but a thoroughly American ideal."

"Okay, good." Cole was glad for something a little meatier. "First off, your question shows how the left wing wins a lot of arguments—by appealing to our emotions. What *feels* right. Based on experience, one would think I'd agree with you. I was a kid from the inner city. I got out. A lot of friends didn't. However, to answer this question, we have to put aside emotion and look at who's doing the giving. I've said this before, I'll say it again: Government doesn't operate in a vacuum . . . though most of the time it does suck."

Travis elbowed the kid next to him and asked to borrow a pen and some paper.

"So," Cole continued, "when Washington gives something to someone—whether it's a job or 'free' health care—it must in turn take something from someone else. And suddenly what seemed so loving and American to begin with is suddenly not American at all. Because to give Person A a job, Person B, who is more qualified, doesn't get a job. In trying to pursue equality, the government has managed only to destroy justice."

Cole saw a few scattered nods and silence, a sign that he was being heard.

"Now, don't take that answer to mean that we shouldn't care. Helping someone at the bottom rise to the top is the most American ideal of all. Of course, liberals would have you believe that they have the market cornered on compassion—even though in 2008, Arthur Brooks from Syracuse published a study that showed conservatives give more money and devote more of their personal time to the poor and needy than liberals, and by a wide margin. Conservatives even give more *blood* than liberals! Yet liberals have the gall to call themselves bleeding hearts! Next question."

No one raised a hand. Cole singled out an Asian girl in the front row. "What about you, Rose? I know you came armed with something." Rose Hsia was his top student and took notes with four different pens, color-coding the different elements of his lectures for easier absorption.

"Okay," she said, steeling herself. She wasn't used to confrontation, but the possibility of one less final was too tantalizing. "I know you've said that Woodrow Wilson was the worst president the United States has ever had, but I think you're wrong."

Cole's disdain for Woodrow Wilson was unwavering. He spent two weeks a semester on the guy, destroying Wilson's legacy and the Progressive movement he elevated from academia to the national stage in the early twentieth century. As Cole had laid out in detail, "Progressive" was merely a smoke screen, a pleasant-sounding name consciously chosen by philosopher John Dewey when it became apparent that calling it "socialism" was never going to fly with the American people.

The first time Cole gave the lecture he was asked not to do so again. The reason why didn't need to be stated: Woodrow Wilson was a Princeton icon. He joined the faculty in 1890, teaching political economy and jurisprudence. In 1902 he became the university president, a title he kept until 1910. Multiple places around campus were named in his honor, as was the Woodrow Wilson School of Public and International Affairs, the department from which Damon Cole drew his paycheck. Cole refused to stop talking, and the administration backed off, not wanting their spat to become a public relations nightmare. If liberal academia was going to go to the mat for some-one, it should be for someone who hadn't been dead for eighty-eight years.

"Someone was worse than Woody Woo?" Cole asked. "That's a scary thought. Who?"

"President Leary," she said, triggering a few catcalls. It was a cou-rageous stand for Hsia. Among her peers, Leary was still beloved. He used an iPod and he tweeted and he made references to MTV shows, all hallmarks of a true statesman.

Cole was intrigued. "Alright, make your case."

"Well, first I think we need to agree on what our definition of 'worst' is." Cole was glad that all his homilies on defining terms hadn't been in vain.

"Fair enough," Cole said. "What's your measuring stick?" One could point to economic indicators or polling data, but the ultimate success or failure of any president tended to be cemented long after he was gone. That wouldn't be possible when discussing Leary.

"I think since presidents take an oath to 'preserve, protect, and defend the Constitution,' the worst president would be the one who fails to uphold its most basic tenets."

She was off to a rational start. "Fine," he said, "and the Constitu-tion, as everyone should now know, or forever risk a failing grade in this course, was designed to establish a system of government which would . . ."

Voices rang out from all corners.

"Establish justice . . ."

"Insure domestic tranquillity . . ."

"Provide for the common defense . . ."

"Promote the general welfare . . ."

"And secure the blessings of liberty to ourselves and our posterity."

"Good," Cole said. He leaned against the side of his podium and directed his attention back to the five-foot-tall girl in sneakers. "Ready when you are."

Hsia looked down at her notes. Her hands were shaking.

"*Establish justice.* President Leary has empowered the most politically driven Justice Department in American history. Its employees have falsified documents, ignored subpoenas, and dropped cases when it was to their own political advantage to do so. In cases from California to Vermont, activist judges have overturned election results, casting aside the will of the people with little concern. President Leary has responded in each circumstance by looking the other way."

Wow, thought Travis. *This girl isn't messing around.*

"*Insure domestic tranquility.* President Leary has encouraged his followers to 'get in the face' of their opponents. He applauds the efforts of left-wing protesters, many of whom are outspoken anarchists and communists. Near the Mexican border, gangs commit killings in broad daylight, without fear of repercussion from hamstrung federal troops. Leary and his cohorts push earmark-laden legislation through Congress that the great majority of Americans oppose, which is not only a blatant disregard of the principles of a democratic republic but also incites public anger and breeds distrust toward our entire political system."

Good point, Cole thought. Woodrow Wilson might have created the federal income tax, but at least he had the decency to pass it as a constitutional amendment rather than wedge it into a three-thousand-page bill that no one had read.

"*Provide for the common defense.* As strong as President Leary is at pushing his own agenda, he's weak when it comes to the most basic responsibility of government—protecting its people. The border remains porous, with ninety percent of those attempting to illegally cross it succeeding. He started a war with a Middle East country that bore no threat, but sits on his hands while another develops nuclear power. He puts our soldiers at risk by bringing some of them home earlier than his generals recommend in order to score political points in an election year."

Hsia waited for Cole to respond. He wasn't about to step in front of this train.

"*Promote the general welfare.* Leary is far more interested in promoting *class* warfare, and so not surprisingly his economic policies have done undue harm to the prosperity of Americans. The uncertainty about future taxes and further government intervention in the private sector has scared both individuals and corporations, forcing them to hold on to their assets rather than invest, spend, and grow. Greater regulations and a bloated bureaucracy have strangled innovation. Corporations are treated like diseases when they are the best source of rapid job growth. The man was elected on the promise that he was the answer to all our problems, and yet it seems that the only thing he excels at is causing them.

"*Securing the blessings of liberty to ourselves and our posterity.*" Hsia paused. She looked at her notes, then back up at Cole. "Well, Professor, I could go on, but if the other things I said are true, or even *half* true, do I really need to prove that the blessings of liberty are less secure than they were three and a half years ago?"

Cole didn't answer. He walked in a slow line across the stage, paralleling the first row of the class. His head was down, hands in pockets. A few students snickered, not used to seeing Cole so silent for so long. His shoes clicked—*thuck-tick, thuck-tick*—redwood soles against pine floors. "Miss Hsia." He was choosing his words carefully. "As I'm sure you know, the final exam for this class is on Thursday." *Thuck-tick, thuck . . . tick.* He stopped and faced his challenger. "I suggest you make alternate plans."

8

The last of the students filed out of the hall and down the stairs. Damon Cole flipped off the podium's green reading lamp and grabbed his insulated coffee mug. He shook it, found it empty, and dropped it into his attaché case.

"Since when do you drink coffee?"

Cole turned to find Travis standing in the back with K.

"Don't worry," Cole said. "It's Dr Pepper."

They met halfway up the aisle and hugged.

"Hello, Ben." Their friendship and the contents of that mug were the only remaining evidence that Damon Cole was Texan. The two met at Texas Christian University in the late 1970s when someone in the campus housing office decided a straight-A black kid from Houston would meld perfectly with a C-average country bumpkin from Prosper.

Back then Cole's wardrobe was more of the knee-high socks and ugly turtleneck variety, but his conservative politics had already been established. For that he thanked the postal service, which mistakenly delivered a copy of *National Review* to his family's two-bedroom apartment when he was fourteen. His father, Reggie, a loyal union leader, was the first one to find it. He stared at it for a while without touching it, then picked it up and carried it to the trash, holding it between two fingers at the corner as though removing a rodent that had up and died in their living room.

Damon had waited until everyone was asleep before fishing it out. He couldn't understand a third of it, but what he could was electric. It was unabashedly patriotic, a virtue that rang true in his mind despite going against everything he'd heard at home. He checked out a dictionary from his school library the next day and decoded the rest of the magazine that night, hiding it inside his older brother's *Playboy* just in case someone walked in on him.

Reggie became aware of his son's "issues" the following summer when Damon landed a summer job at a Houston car wash. Rather than work for minimum wage, Damon insisted the manager pay him what he was worth, citing various studies that showed how bloated government-mandated wages increase employee malaise and stifle long-term business growth. The manager, convinced he was being set up by Reggie's union, offered Damon $4.30 an hour, two bucks over the minimum. He was the highest-paid scrubber on the line.

By the time Cole arrived at TCU, he had his entire life mapped out for himself. Travis proved to be just what Cole needed, someone to remind him that school was about more than grades. Travis dragged Cole to frat parties and on countless double dates, kicking him under the table every time he tried to "spice up" the dinner conversation by sharing the history of the gold standard or ranting about the Ayatollah Khomeini. Cole, in turn, helped Travis, too, promising him that employers would definitely notice whether his résumé said "attended TCU" or "graduated from TCU."

During the first year after graduation, they talked weekly. Then monthly. By the time they hit forty, their entire relationship consisted of hastily written-out thoughts on the back of Christmas cards. *Hope all's well! . . . It's been too long! . . . Must meet soon!*

After college, Cole added a Juris Doctor from Harvard, a master's from Yale, and a PhD from Princeton. He referred to it as "the Trinity," a collection of degrees that individually were impressive enough but together would have the power to bring all rival scholars to their knees.

Somewhere in that extra eight years of East Coast schooling, he lost his accent and gained a wife, a fellow grad student named Beth who shared his love of pinot noir and supply-side economics. They decided early on that they didn't want kids, but after seven years Beth changed her mind and had one—with one of Cole's colleagues from Princeton. That was that. Travis's divorce had given them something else in common, but they remained as unlikely a duo as they were in the dorms in Fort Worth.

Travis and Cole crossed Washington Road and headed across campus toward Prospect House for lunch. Cole explained that for nearly a hundred years, the sepia-colored mansion was the private home of the university president, before the school took it over for formal events and faculty fine dining. Cole's restaurant selection wasn't lost on Travis. "So you bash Wilson, then eat in his old dining room?"

"I am terrible, aren't I?" Cole replied, holding the heavy oak door for his guest.

Their table sat against a floor-to-ceiling window and looked down on Prospect Gardens, an oval piece of campus ringed by pine trees and filled with hundreds of the season's most luscious flowers. Right now that meant tulips and poppies. Next week, everything would be pulled and replaced with roses and petunias—flowers that could thrive in the beastly New Jersey summer. Most students couldn't care less about the flora and fauna and used the gardens as a cut-through to the student center, their shoes crunching as they passed on the pebbled path.

"F. Scott was right, wasn't he?" Cole said, taking in the scene and being reminded of his favorite American author. "Princeton truly is the pleasantest country club in America . . ."

Travis was busy with the sugar bowl, turning his iced tea into sweet tea. "F. who?"

Cole had forgotten the company he was keeping. "Never mind."

Travis had read plenty of books, but rarely cover to cover. The last thing he wanted to do was spend his life sitting in a chair flipping pages. When he was given a book he absolutely had to read, he found reading the first chapter and last chapter was a handy short-cut. The first chapter gave him the setting, the tone, the style . . . and then he could skip past all the conflict and tension to the end where the hero from chapter one either lives happily ever after or dies alone. If he was blown away by the ending, he'd go back a chapter and read into it. If he was still intrigued, he'd go back one more. The biggest compliment one could get from Ben Travis on a book would be to hear that he liked it so much he made it all the way back to the middle.

"So I got a call last week from Walt Thompson," Travis said, finally offering up the reason for his spur-of-the-moment visit. "He gave me a hot tip."

"Oh Lord," Cole said, wondering what sort of rabbit hole Walt had pulled his friend into. "I suppose it's too late to say don't listen to that guy." Even though Cole and Walt Thompson shared many of the same political views, the radio host's lack of civility was off-putting to his Ivy League sensibilities.

"What would you say if I told you that there's a giant water pipeline system running under Texas?"

Cole cleaned his glasses with the edge of the tablecloth. "I'd say there are a lot of pipelines running under Texas. Of course, I don't have to tell you that."

"You're right. There's seventy-seven thousand miles of utility pipelines, but none like this. Eight feet in diameter, high-pressure PVC, and all of it buried under the interstates."

"Under the interstates?" Cole was suddenly interested. "Huh."

"Huh what?"

"You realize the ground under the interstates is federal land, don't you?" Cole asked.

Travis nodded.

"Well . . ." Cole slipped his glasses back on. "I'd say if Washington wants to pump a lot of liquid across the Southwest without telling anyone, that's how they'd do it."

"What are you saying? They want to take our groundwater and send it somewhere else?"

"West, most likely. California never has enough water. They're also bankrupt and loyal to Leary. Makes sense."

"Yeah, except for the fact that Washington can't do that! Each state owns its own water."

"That's true," said Cole.

"Then what the heck are they up to?"

"I didn't say they *weren't* going to do it."

Travis reached for the sugar and dumped another spoonful into his tea. Cole was surprised to see Travis so taken aback. They'd chatted a few times in the wake of his separation, and he knew his friend had been in a fog. He just didn't realize how thick it was.

"Ben, weren't you listening back there? The country is broken. I'm not talking job growth or home sales, though all of that is terrible. I'm talking about the foundations of this country: separation of powers, states' rights, the sanctity of private property, the power of the individual, the fear of government tyranny. All those things that set us apart from the rest of the world are being pushed aside in the name of progress, which we're all learning is no progress at all."

"I know Leary has some fringe ideas, but—"

"Come on, Ben. This goes beyond the president." Cole recognized that now *he* was sounding like Walt Thompson. "It's been a slow creep, going on for over a hundred years, all the way back to my dear pal Woodrow Wilson. Most of that time, we didn't even notice it. It was just a nudge. A push here, a push there. Look at income tax. When reformers introduced the idea in 1913, they promised that the highest rate would never go beyond seven percent. You know what that percentage was just four years later, Ben? *Sixty-seven* percent. Or then there's the national debt. George Washington said there was no more dangerous government practice than that of borrowing money. Then time passed, and people started to suggest that just a little debt couldn't hurt. It would help us pay for wars, free up the flow of money. It seemed reasonable. Then John Maynard Keynes writes a book and says that the best way to climb out of debt is to create more debt, and people believed him; especially politicians looking for an excuse to spend more money. Now that debt is fifteen trillion dollars and paralyzing our economy. It always starts with—"

Travis's pocket broke into song. Loudly. *The stars at night are big and bright ... ... deep in the heart of Texas!* Faculty members stopped and stared, as did K, who was standing guard at the entrance of the dining room.

It was Hunter Reese, unhappy that the governor of Texas was not *in* Texas. It wasn't like there was a lack of activity back home. Nearly every state official whose term was up in six months had called to request a face-to-face meeting with their new boss. They all did their best to sound relaxed and cheery on the phone, but none could cover up their fear that Governor Allen's early exit might also hasten their own. Travis refused to cancel his trip but compromised by finally agreeing to carry a cell phone on him at all times. "If something comes up, just call," he had said.

"Are you going to answer that?" Cole asked.

The sage in bloom is like perfume ... ...

"Don't know how," Travis said. . . . *deep in the heart of Texas!* It stopped and flipped over to voice mail. "You've met the president, right?" said Travis.

"Once. A few years ago." Leary had called for one of his famous blue-ribbon commissions, this one to discuss the nagging problem of stagnant economic growth. Lee Kurtz, the president's press secretary, boasted to the media that the event was bringing together "some of the greatest minds of our time, from all across the political spectrum." "Across the spectrum" equated to fifteen liberals and Damon Cole. Each brainiac made the most of his opportunity to be on C-SPAN, lecturing for ten minutes without interruption. When the microphone came to Cole, he offered a concise and simple suggestion: Cancel the collection of all income taxes for one year. The unprecedented window of opportunity would spur investment, hiring, spending, employee production, you name it. Leary smiled thoughtfully at the suggestion but left it out of the final report.

"And you didn't like him?" Travis said.

"Personally, I like him a lot. He's warm, engaging. Really draws you in. He's the cool kid in junior high who you wish liked you. Something about him makes you want to agree with him even if you don't."

"But politically . . ."

"Well, politically he's a naive, self-absorbed socialist masquerading as a liberal whose most significant contribution to America has been getting people to cough into their sleeve instead of their hand."

"Oh, you mean a turd."

Lunch arrived. A grilled chicken breast with brown rice and steamed broccoli for Cole. Travis went off menu and asked for a BLT and fries. "I'm stopping in Washington on the way home to see Paige. Just breakfast. I think maybe I'll try to grab fifteen minutes with Leary while I'm there. See what he can tell me."

Cole was aghast at the thought. "You can't be serious."

"Sure. Why not?"

There were a dozen suitable answers to this question. "Let's start with the fact you have no real evidence of a secret pipeline."

"Sure I do. I saw it."

"You saw thousands of miles of pipe?"

"No, I saw three or four feet of it."

"Did you take a picture?"

"Yes, in fact, I did." Travis had taken a picture using an old disposable camera he found in his glove compartment. He hadn't developed the film yet—if there were places that even developed film anymore—and without a built-in flash, it was undoubtedly going to be too blurry and dark to be of any use whatsoever, except in the case of this argument.

"Look, even with a picture, this isn't the way to handle this. Go through your attorney general. Have him snoop around, then he can draft a letter and—"

"A letter? I don't have that much time in office, Damon. This is faster. Especially if you come with me."

"Me?!" It was one thing to give Travis his opinion and some historical context over lunch, some casual pro bono work. Sitting next to him in the Oval Office was a different matter. "Why would I go?"

"To give me some extra credibility. Leary loves nerds."

"Not going to happen," Cole said. "The president's calendar is booked months in advance, down to the minute. You really think he wakes up in the morning, gets dressed and says, 'Well, what should I do today?'"

"Fine," Travis said. "I'll make you a deal. If I can't get him, you can stay here and polish your panda-skin loafers. If I can, you have to fly down and join me."

Thirty years earlier, Cole would have turned down the deal. He'd been duped by his college roommate too many times to count. That, however, was always in sports or cards or women. Politics was his domain. In this realm, at least, he felt snooker-proof—and, yes, he had the expensive shoes to prove it.

9

Paige Travis slipped between the doors of the Red Line just as they were closing. Most mornings she was moving in a herd, squeezing her way from Dupont Circle down to Judiciary Square. On a good day she'd find herself nuzzled against a twenty-something Hill staffer who smelled like the inside of an Abercrombie & Fitch. In those brief ten minutes, she'd map out their future: their first date, first kiss, the look on his face when he proposes on the steps of the Lincoln Memorial, their villa on St. Maarten . . . It was a talent, really. At least twice she had skipped her stop in exchange for spending another half mile pressed against the future Mr. Paige Travis. Yes, she expected her husband to take her last name. This may have played a role in why she was still single.

Most mornings she left for work at seven forty-five; right now it was only six fifteen, far too early for any steamy suit-on-suit contact. Instead, the Metro was populated with a scattered collection of early risers, brownnosers, and German tourists who'd been up since 2:00 A.M., unable to adjust to the time change and figuring they might as well get in line to climb the eight hundred and ninety-seven steps to the top of the Washington Monument.

The cars lurched as Paige took a seat and pulled the day's *Post* from her bag. Above the fold was the usual collection of grim news.

CONSUMER CONFIDENCE AT THIRTY-YEAR LOW, EXPERTS SURPRISED
AS UNEMPLOYMENT SWELLS, IRAN THREATENS ISRAEL . . .

She flipped the paper over and saw her breakfast date staring right back at her. The black-and-white photo of Ben Travis was an old one, a file photo from a cook-off he had judged in the late 1990s. It was the least flattering one the editors could find. Travis wore a cowboy hat and was in midguffaw. A layer of barbecue sauce ringed his mouth. Barely visible on the edge of the frame was a bottle of Shiner Bock beer, empty. It was an effective image, planting the thought that this man was no real statesman but merely a drunk slob with an unhealthy passion for rib tips.

Paige read the headline: NEW TEXAS GOVERNOR TAKES AIM AND (MIS)FIRES. *Uh-oh,* she thought. The unbylined article detailed Travis's rise to prominence in the business world, highlighting his failures while making his success look like the result of luck and not skill. It spoke of his political experience, or lack thereof: "just one hundred forty unremarkable days in the Texas Legislature." It covered Travis's "callous response" to Governor Allen's death, supported by a quote from a former governor—of Rhode Island no less—who felt Travis acted "without sensitivity" and "tarnished the reputation of governors everywhere." It was a hit piece if ever there was one.

The concluding paragraph was Paige's least favorite:

> Divorced at age 48, Travis has been described as a loner, prone to holing himself up for weeks at a time on his 500-acre ranch north of Dallas. His only child, Paige, 22, an assistant with the Department of Justice in Washington, calls the place "Dad's dungeon," and says she goes there as little as possible. "It has A/C but he won't run it. He has a TV but no cable. It's like taking a time machine back to a place no one wants to go." Their relationship is "dysfunctional at best," she tells the *Post.* As for that comment during his first press conference as governor? "What can I say? He's nuts."

A German tourist in sandals with socks saw Paige shaking. "Are you alright, miss?"

"Yes, I'm . . . fine," she said. "I'll be—I'm fine." Paige fumbled through her purse for her phone. She searched in her contacts, found AUBREY CELL, and dialed. No service. She'd forgotten she was twenty feet underground.

She popped up at the Farragut North station, only a few blocks from the Hay-Adams Hotel, where her father had spent the night. This time her call went through but went straight to voice mail. *Hi, you've reached Aubrey Garza at the* Washington Post. *I'm either away from my desk or on another call—*

"—or ruining friendships for the sake of my journalism career," Paige muttered before hanging up.

The sun was almost up, but the lights were still on in front of the Hay-Adams. The place was named for the two famous men who lived on the spot where the hotel now stands. John Hay was an assistant to Abraham Lincoln and secretary of state under Presidents McKinley and Teddy Roosevelt. He negotiated the end to the Spanish-American War and was instrumental in clearing a diplomatic path for the construction of the Panama Canal. Henry Adams was the grandson of John Quincy Adams (and great-grandson of John Adams) and won the Pulitzer Prize in 1919. He was also a rabid anti-Semite who once wrote that he lived solely to see the demise of the Jews. Not surprisingly, that was left off the gilded historical marker mounted near the entrance.

The white-gloved doorman wished Paige a chipper "good morning" as she climbed the marble steps. She was too shell-shocked to look up. Her father had to have seen the article already, she figured. Although it was still early.

A stack of papers was splayed out on a table in the lobby. PLEASE TAKE ONE, the gold script sign said. Paige took all ten and dumped them in the trash can on the way to the elevator.

When the doors opened on the seventh floor, her heart sank. In front of every room was a fresh copy of the *Washington Post*. A few had landed wrong side up, with Travis's goofy mug looking up at her. She flipped them over with her foot as she went to room 705. His paper was already gone.

She knocked once, and K answered. Paige hadn't considered her father had full-time security. "I'm sorry," she said, "I must have the wrong—"

"No, you don't," K said and ushered her in.

Travis was standing in front of the mirror in the back bedroom, unhappy with his morning's first attempt at a Windsor knot. He saw Paige and gave up, leaving the skinny end of the tie dangling a few inches longer than the fat one. He gave her a hug, kissed the top of her head, and pushed her away to size her up. "You look great." He meant it. The Justice Department had let Paige keep her leftist politics, but at least they made her wear a bra. As they hugged, Paige scanned the room for his paper. It was on the bed and appeared unread.

She sat down next to it, planning to swipe it when no one was looking. "So," she said, "we going downstairs for breakfast? I don't have a lot of time."

"Downstairs? Nah, I was thinking of eating here. Hey, K, go find me a couple cups of coffee, will ya?"

K nodded and slipped out the door as Paige recalibrated. "You want to eat in the room?"

"Yeah. Can't beat the view," Travis said. He pulled open the curtains to reveal the White House across Lafayette Square. As he did, she snagged the paper and slipped it into her bag.

"Sounds good," she said. It was probably safer to stay in, she figured. Less chance of someone mentioning the article that way. She knew he would find out soon enough; she was just hoping it would be after she was gone. "How's the room service here?"

"*Room service?* No way. Look at all this food they have here." He showed off a giant cellophane-wrapped basket that came with the suite. "I was going to say we crack open this gourmet popcorn, but it has garlic on it. Yuck." He threw the popcorn in the trash. "Then I thought maybe these cheese and crackers would be good." He held them up for her approval. She was thoroughly confused. "But let's be honest," he went on, "that's not enough food. Not for breakfast, anyway. Then I saw these." Travis held up a tin can and shook it. "Do you know what these are?"

"Nuts?" she asked.

"Yep. Nuts." He popped open the can and took a handful. "Do you like nuts?"

"Uh . . ." She wasn't getting it. "I guess, sure."

"See, I don't just like nuts. I *love* nuts. Cashews, almonds, pistachios, peanuts—which to be fair aren't nuts at all, they're legumes. I even like the occasional filbert. You could probably say I'm nuts about nuts. Heck, I don't know, maybe I *am* nuts."

Now she got it.

Travis smiled, enjoying what he saw as some much-deserved ribbing.

Paige shook her head and started to tear up. "What is wrong with you?"

"Me?" Travis asked.

Paige never enjoyed her father's humor as much as he did. "Why couldn't you just ask me about it? Why couldn't you be sensitive to how I might be feeling?"

"I guess I sort of assumed you'd be feeling bad." He wasn't sure how this had backfired on him.

"Of course I feel bad, but instead of confronting me you turn the whole thing into a joke."

"So you'd prefer me to be confrontational? 'Cause I can do that."

"I want you to treat me like your daughter, like someone you actually cherish. Not some flunky your buddy made you hire."

"Fine," Travis said. "Then let's handle this like adults." However, Travis couldn't help himself. "Oh, before I forget, where's my newspaper?"

Caught, Paige pulled it back out of her bag and slapped it on the coffee table. She was done being civil and headed for the door. "You probably don't care, but I was under the impression the conversation I had with her was off the record, and on top of that I was completely misquoted."

Now Travis did feel bad. Since everything in the article sounded exactly like something she would say, he never once doubted it was true. "You didn't call me nuts?"

"No!" Paige should have stopped herself, but like her father, she couldn't. "I called you an *idiot*!"

Travis tried to stifle his laughter but couldn't.

"Forget it," she said.

She opened the door to the hall as Travis tried to stop her. "Come on, let's just go downstairs."

"I'll get a bagel at work."

She turned to leave and ran straight into K's chest. He lowered one of the coffees like a crane and offered it to her. "Regular okay?" he asked.

"Today? Absolutely." She took it from him and headed back down the hallway.

The governor's black Lincoln headed down Pennsylvania Avenue at fifteen minutes before nine. Travis and Cole rode in back while K sat up front with their driver, a Romanian immigrant who pulled up that morning with a half-eaten cheese wheel in one hand and a two-liter bottle of Canada Dry between his legs. That was all the weirdness K needed to insist on a pat-down and a look under the car's chassis for bombs before hopping aboard. The preliminary report from the NTSB on Governor Allen's car crash was in, and while there was no evidence to suggest the accident was attributable to anything other than a sleepy driver, K wasn't taking any chances. If someone had found something worth killing in a man who stood for nothing like Allen, then a loudmouth like Travis had to be a target.

Damon Cole had been up since five. One of Princeton's selling points was that it was halfway between New York and Philadelphia. Unfortunately, that also meant it was close to neither, and so after an hour's drive to Philly, an hour's wait at the airport, and a thirty-minute commuter flight, Cole would have been better off just driving the hundred eighty miles in his 5 Series Beemer while listening to Bach's Brandenburg Concertos.

Nevertheless, he was in good spirits, sporting a pair of rare black iguana-skinned wingtips that had their origins in the Galápagos Islands. Cole was quick to point out that the reptile in question died of natural causes and was, thanks to him, finally off the prehistoric island and seeing the civilized world. If there was ever a time to look his best, it was today. Politics was about power more than anything else, and this was its epicenter.

Travis, on the other hand, was suspicious of anyone who desperately wanted to be president. After all, no one wanted to be president *less* than George Washington. At the end of the American Revolution, he promptly resigned as interim commander in chief and returned to Mount Vernon. During the first presidential election six years later, Washington didn't campaign at all and told electors he was not interested in the duty. He won anyway, and spent the entire carriage ride from his home in Virginia to the capitol in New York City worrying about living up to expectations and hoping to serve the country "in obedience to its call."

As they pulled to a stop at the North Gate of the White House, Travis realized that Cole hadn't mentioned that morning's *Post* article. Likewise, Cole recognized that Travis hadn't mentioned breakfast with Paige. Between men, sometimes the most sensitive response is the tacit agreement to not talk at all.

The officer on duty held out his hand and stepped from his wooden booth. He was dressed in the standard black pants and short-sleeved white shirt of the White House police force. His hand rested not-so-casually on his holster. "Morning," he said.

Their driver put down his cheese wheel and handed the guard all four of their IDs. "Governor Travis and Professor Damon Cole to see the president."

The officer returned to his booth and lined up the IDs above his keyboard. "Do you have an appointment?"

Travis leaned forward. "Not yet."

Cole stared daggers. "What?"

"You were right," Travis said. "The president is dang hard to get ahold of."

The guard picked up his phone and dialed.

"You're unbelievable. Unbelievable!" Cole said. K turned around in case he needed to be restrained. "I had to reschedule my final lecture of the year for this."

Something about seeing Cole upset made Travis smile. The guy was so unflappable that making him angry was a real achievement. The White House policeman put down the phone and returned the IDs. "I'm sorry, gentlemen, but the president is not currently available. They ask that you call and make an official appointment."

"Surprise, surprise," Cole said, stewing.

Travis rolled down his window and leaned his head out. "I'm sorry, Officer, but could you tell them we're here to discuss the interstate water pipeline?"

The guard glared at Travis.

"Please?" Travis added.

The guard sighed and reached for the phone.

Cole had more to say. "Is my time not valuable to you? You think I've got nothing better to do? My life may look cushy, but between faculty meetings, office hours, grading papers, I'm lucky to only work fifty hours a week. And that's not even counting my own research."

"I know that," Travis said. "Would you still be this angry if we were actually seeing the president?"

"What? I don't know. It would certainly help."

"Good, so then knock it off."

Cole looked out the front window. The heavy black iron gates were swinging open. As the car started to roll forward, Travis waved to the officer, who looked just as surprised as they did. In front of them was nothing but gray asphalt and the most famous house in America.

10

A nervous Mark Ruflowski directed Travis and Cole to "have a seat" in the Red Room. They shared a scarlet Empire-style couch near the fireplace, but the early-nineteenth-century piece wasn't quite made for two, making the duo look like a couple of school kids waiting outside the principal's office. Once Ruffles was gone, Travis was back on his feet and wandering around the room, looking at paintings and pretending to appreciate their historical significance.

Despite its name, the Red Room wasn't always red. Back when James Madison was president, it was yellow. His wife, Dolley, used the space every Wednesday night for get-togethers where she impressed politicians and diplomats with her charm and knowledge of current events. Jackie Kennedy changed it to its current motif, a combination of red satin walls and dark crimson covered furniture. Over the years it had been a breakfast room, a music room, and a place where presidents hosted intimate dinner parties. Bill Clinton's were more intimate than others.

"This sort of seems like an appropriate color for this administration," Travis said, eying the red walls.

Over in the West Wing, back in the Oval Office, Ruffles informed the president of his surprise guests.

"And you sent them away?"

"Actually, they're waiting in the Red Room."

"What?!"

It was a rare hiccup for Ruffles. Scheduling a phone call would have made more sense, but when he heard the reason for Governor Travis's visit, he figured it was dumb to turn him away before finding out exactly what he knew and what he intended to do about it. Now if he could just get Leary to understand this logic.

"He knows about the pipeline," Ruffles said.

"How?"

"Let's play dumb and find out. After all, didn't Sun Tzu say to keep your friends close and your enemies closer?"

"Yes," Leary said, "but I don't think he meant keep them in your living room." He pushed the morning paper across his desk. "You need to read this piece on him in the *Post*." Ruffles had read it. "The guy's a complete wahoo," said Leary. He meant *ya*hoo—a wahoo was a tropical fish—but Ruffles knew that correcting the president, even privately, was ill-advised.

When he threw his name into the hat for president, Leary was the junior senator from Massachusetts, a seat he had filled for less than a year—hardly a power player by D.C. standards. Before that, he had served less than one term in the Massachusetts State Senate. Pre-politics, his résumé was a mishmash of law school positions and nonprofit work. Based on experience, he had no business trying to run the country. He would have been hard-pressed to land a job running his local Outback Steakhouse. Yet his lily-pad career path was genius. He knew that a long political record would only open him up to undue scrutiny over his donors, his votes, and his left-wing ideology. For the first few months of the campaign, he sat back and watched the mud fly between Democratic candidates. By the time the Iowa Caucus arrived, he was the only one without any on his face.

Once he had his party's nomination, he began acting as if he were already president. He met with foreign leaders. He wrote books about himself. Most importantly, he avoided talking specifics. Instead, he spoke of the future. He painted a picture of an America that was devoid of pain and suffering. A place where everyone had all he or she needed and shared his or her bounty with others. He was going to be so amazing that not just America would be changed, the rest of the world would be changed, too, transformed overnight into one giant global body of love. The first time he delivered the speech, women fainted. Veteran reporters wept on camera. One even copped to having tingles run up his inseam.

By the time the election arrived, Michael Leary wasn't merely a candidate for president. He was a messianic figure, sent from on high to save America from two hundred and thirty-two years of inequality, selfishness, and global insensitivity. Every word he spoke was of greater value than gold, destined to be carved in marble and hung on the walls of thousands of Michael Leary elementary schools, middle schools, high schools, post offices, aircraft carriers, and prisons (assuming there would be any need for aircraft carriers or prisons after he was done fixing America). Success had come so quickly that he, too, became a believer in his own mythology. Therefore, for someone to pull him aside and say "you're wrong" was folly, the equivalent of trying to change history as it was happening.

That didn't mean that he had any idea about how to solve this morning's problem. For that he had Ruffles. "Well," his adviser said, wiping his nose with his hanky, "I'm pretty sure Ken Fray's in town. Flew in last night, I believe."

Leary knew where Ruffles was going with this. "What about Slubs?" the president asked. "Slubs" sounded like some misogynistic nickname, but in this case it was the real name of Marjorie Slubs, the humorless director of FEMA.

"You know her. She's always around," said Ruffles. "You want our boys to whip up a speech?"

The president popped some Nicorette. "Might as well. We've got enough pieces in place. What are you going to do with America's favorite new governor?"

The extra three minutes with the president had bought Ruffles enough time to figure that one out, too. "That'll be easy," he said. "It's an Avery Adams special."

Avery Adams was a curvy thirty-year-old White House aide with
blond hair and the special ability to make any man forget exactly
what it was he wanted. Some in the West Wing felt it was her only
skill, but it proved valuable nonetheless.

"I am so sorry to keep you waiting," she said as she arrived in the
Red Room. Her heels clicked on the wood floor before going silent
when she reached the carpet. Her black skirt was one inch shorter
than White House dress code; just long enough to be chalked up as
"close enough" but still short enough to be noticed by every hetero-
sexual male inside 1600 Pennsylvania Avenue.

She put out her hand. "I'm Avery Adams." Travis and Cole shook
hands and followed her lead when she sat. "Whew. What a morning." A few strands of blond slipped from her ponytail and fell across
her cheek. Her guests watched as she tucked them back behind her
diamond-studded ear. It was a good thing the air-conditioning was
blasting or Damon Cole's *gulp* would have been audible to all three
of them.

"So," she focused in on Travis, "congrats on the new job." Exhibit A
on why Avery Adams was always better seen and not heard. "I mean—
obviously—that's probably not the way anyone dreams of becoming
governor."

"I wouldn't say anyone," Travis answered. He had no clue what
he meant by that. He was just trying to stay on the offensive and
not get distracted by counting how many buttons were undone on her
blouse (three). "So does this mean the president's not going to be joining us?"

Avery scrunched her button nose, making it seem like she was
just as disappointed as they were. "Ugh. No, he won't, and I apologize. When he heard you were here, he thought he could rearrange
his schedule and make it work. It just wasn't doable on such short
notice, but he made a point of saying he wants you to come back for
his big Fourth of July barbecue." It was an affront to call that event a

barbecue. The only thing grilled was shrimp. The only beer served was imported. Still, the thought of hanging out at the White House on Independence Day was too much for Cole to resist.

"Sounds fun," he said, proving to be Avery Adams's first kill of the day.

"Miss Adams." Travis was staring at the bridge of her nose now, the result of almost losing his bearings in her Caribbean Sea eyes. "Professor Cole and I came here this morning to discuss what I believe is the unreported construction of a major pipeline in my state. While the federal government can put whatever it likes under its highways, I think we are still owed an explanation of its ultimate purpose."

"Governor, I absolutely agree. That seems like a very reasonable request."

Good. Back on track, Travis thought, narrowing his field of vision even further.

"Unfortunately I just don't have any of that information in front of me," she said.

Not a problem. Just be reasonable. "Well, we'd be happy to wait for you to get it."

"Oh boy, how I *wish* things worked that quickly," she said, laughing. Cole laughed too, fully gone. "But I'll tell you what I'm going to do. The second I leave this room, I am going to put in a formal request with the Department of Transportation. I should have some answers for you in three to four days."

"Three to four *days*?"

"It seems extreme, I know, but we pride ourselves on doing things right around here, and we can't do that unless we have all the information first. That makes sense, doesn't it?"

"Not really," Travis said. "Isn't this the same administration that pledged transparency, then urged Congress to pass gigantic bills before anyone had the opportunity to read them?" If Cole wasn't going to put up a fight, someone had to.

Avery laughed again. "Governor, you're a riot."

Travis looked to Cole for some much-needed support.

"Miss Adams, by chance is there anyone else with whom we could speak about this?" Cole asked, rallying slightly.

"Wow, Professor. I'll try my best not to be hurt by that, but you need to realize how rare it is that guests drop by the White House and are treated with the consideration that you and Governor Travis have been shown this morning." She was good, that was for certain.

"I apologize," Cole said, rolling over.

Geez, Damon, Travis thought. *Why don't you let her scratch your belly while you're at it?*

"Miss Adams," Travis said, "just for clarification, you're saying the president doesn't know anything about this pipeline?"

More laughter. "I can't speak for the president, but for what it's worth, this is all news to me."

Avery closed her still-blank notebook and stood. "Now if you don't hear from me in a couple days, call me. I mean it." She pulled a business card from the pocket of her form-fitting blazer, palming it just a bit so their fingers would touch in the exchange. Not wanting to miss out, Cole asked for one, too.

"Have a safe trip home, Governor. Hope to see you both again soon."

"In July," Cole called out, pathetically.

Mission accomplished, Avery Adams disappeared around the corner and was gone. Her perfume lingered in the Red Room the rest of the morning.

11

"W here to, Governor?" the driver asked as he and Cole drove away from the White House.

"Hay-Ad—"

"Reagan National," Cole interrupted.

"Nice work back there," Travis said.

"Please," said Cole, annoyed at Travis's tone. "What did you want me to do? Chain myself to the staircase and demand answers?"

"I don't know. Maybe you could have grilled Avery Adams instead of looking up her skirt," Travis said.

"What would that have accomplished? She doesn't have any control over there," said Cole.

"Really? Because she sure seemed to control you."

From Cole's perspective, the whole idea of trying to talk to the president was worthless. "He's not beholden to you. Not with the power Washington has," he said. "Anyway, you can't expect to blow up a bridge when all you have is a water balloon."

Travis slipped off his tie, done with the argument. "Well, then"—he pressed his head into the headrest—"crud."

In a perfect world, Travis would do everything on his own. It was a desire borne out of Prosper High's season-ending basketball game against Celina in 1977.

Prosper was so small at the time that Travis's senior class only had fifty-one kids, which meant that any guy who wanted to be a three-sport athlete could pull it off without much effort. Each season brought a unique balance of victory and defeat. Fall was football. Travis was amazing, and so was the team. Travis was all-everything, including 2-A Player of the Year. In his three years on varsity, they'd only lost twice. Spring was baseball. Travis wasn't that great at it, and neither was anyone else, so any sting from their losing record was tempered by the fact they all knew they didn't deserve to win anyway. However, basketball, Travis's winter sport, was an unending source of agony.

Travis was the point guard and the best kid on the team. It didn't matter, though, because everyone else was terrible. No one knew why, but Prosper was a veritable black hole of basketball talent. As a result, if Ben had a bad game, the team had zero shot at winning. If he played well, they had a chance, but it was entirely dependent on the other dunderheads on the team not doing something stupid, which inevitably they did. Someone would find a way to dribble out of bounds. Or into the backcourt. Or just punch another player out of frustration.

If they managed to keep it close right up to the end, it only increased the likelihood that something tragic would happen. Travis's junior year, the team lost a game at the buzzer when the ref noticed Prosper had seven players on the court instead of five. The coach, a decade past retirement, challenged the ref's call with the always clever "So what?"

The 1977 season was especially draining. They came into their last game against the Celina Bobcats with a perfect 0–22 record. Travis wanted to avoid the infamy of a winless season and took every clear shot he had that night. He made enough of them that with forty seconds left, Prosper held a tenuous 62–61 lead and possession of the ball. On the sideline, Travis drew up a plan. "Just give me the ball," he said. Travis took the inbound pass, and since there was no shot clock, he just started dribbling in placc. After a few seconds, Celina realized that Travis had no intention of moving the ball across half-court and began to press. Technically, he had to get the ball across half-court in under ten seconds, but it was the end of an otherwise meaningless game, and Travis figured the refs wouldn't remember to count until the Celina coach started to yell at them to do so.

The one thing he couldn't do was pass it. It was too risky. Instead, as the pressure built, he began to slither around the backcourt. He maneuvered around picks, dribbled through legs. It was inspiring. Graceful. People in the stands, even the ones from Celina, knew they were witnessing something special: a control freak at his finest.

Travis eyed the clock. *Twenty seconds.* The other Prosper players stopped running and put their hands on their hips, just as curious as everyone else to see how this would play out. The five Celina boys were losing their patience and took some meaty swipes at Travis's arms, hoping to foul him, but, a parquet matador, he avoided every one.

Ten seconds. The ref was counting now, and Travis was getting tired. Worst of all, after a few dozen revolutions around the backcourt, things were starting to spin. He was disoriented, and before he knew what had happened, he'd dribbled himself right into a corner. Celina saw the slip-up and converged, zombies in high-tops. The gym was whirling around him, but Travis could still make out the orange numbers on the clock. *Five seconds.* A blur of hands pawed at the ball. He wasn't going to make it. He had to give it up—but to whom? Standing all alone was Jeb Nutting. Jeb was only five-six, but he was the second-best ball handler on the court. Travis heaved it high, over the Celina defenders and right into Jeb's hands. He caught it clean and then, to the shock and horror of every Prosper fan, turned to the nearby basket and shot. The wrong basket. Jeb hadn't made a bucket all season. The ball arced through the air. The fluorescent lights glistened off the brown leather dimples as it spun. Travis screamed, but it was too late.

Swish. Nothing but net. Jeb raised his arms and turned with a grin, braces gleaming, believing he had sealed the team's victory. He had, just not for his team. The buzzer blared, and Celina fans poured onto the court. They grabbed Jeb and hoisted him onto their shoulders, giving him the full hero treatment. He enjoyed it, briefly, until he looked down and didn't recognize a single face beneath him, at which point he looked at the scoreboard and started to cry.

Jeb's parents tried to save him, but it was impossible. The fans carried him out of the gym. They were a half mile to Celina before the Prosper sheriff broke up the crowd and rescued the terrified sixteen-year-old. Travis eventually got over the loss, but relying on others remained a struggle.

The governor's town car negotiated the midmorning traffic at Reagan National and pulled up to the terminal. Cole undid his seat belt and grabbed his attaché case. "Hey," he said, putting one foot on the curb, "we tried."

They had accomplished far more than they thought. At the same moment that Damon Cole was being wanded by TSA agents, President Leary was walking to a podium in the Rose Garden. He was flanked by Ken Fray, secretary of the interior, and Marjorie Slubs. They were instructed to look weary and wan. This was easy for Marjorie since weary and wan was her natural state. Ken Fray, on the other hand, was just back from a ten-day taxpayer-funded "workation" on Maui. No matter how hard he tried, he proved that it's impossible to look grave while sporting a snorkel mask tan line.

"Good morning," Leary began. "Before starting, I'd like to thank Marjorie for being here, as well as Ken. The two of them have worked tirelessly on this crisis as it came to a head over the course of the last forty-eight hours."

Halfway across the country, Hunter Reese was already on the phone to his boss. Travis fumbled with his new technology for a moment before he found the right button. "I did it," Travis said.

"You did what?"

"I answered a cell phone," said Travis.

"Congratulations. Listen, weren't you meeting with the president this morning?" Hunter asked.

"I tried. They stonewalled me. Not sure why."

"I think we're about to find out," Hunter said. "He's giving a speech in the Rose Garden and has already used the word 'crisis.'"

Wonderful. Leary had used "crisis" to justify all sorts of schemes. Passing spending bills, taking over car companies, raising the debt ceiling . . . The whole idea of it was Ruffles's brainchild. When the American people are scared, Ruffles reasoned, they'll agree to almost anything. Time to find out what Leary wanted this time.

"Three weeks ago," the president continued, "with no notice and little fanfare, China and India signed an economic sharing agreement with Brazil and a number of OPEC nations in the Middle East. The centerpiece of that deal was a large-scale purchase of oil futures in those regions. In layman's terms, it means that one, two, or five years down the road, if America needs oil from those regions, it won't be ours to buy. To put it more bluntly, it was an agreement that had the potential to cripple our economy and bring industry to a standstill."

"Wow," Travis mused, listening to the speech on the car radio, "so that makes it equivalent to your first term as president?"

"I chose not to alert the American people of these ramifications right away. I felt it prudent to wait until we could see the agreement in detail, then seek wisdom from experts in the field. We did that, and the consensus was that this action by China and India posed a very real threat to our nation's oil supply, and in turn to our nation as a whole. Couple that with continued tensions in the Middle East driving up oil prices even further, and what we were dealing with was a crisis of the highest order.

"As anyone knows, the stability of our national resources has been in flux for years. And acquiring those resources is a dangerous business. The consequences of past oil spills are still reverberating through the Gulf. Air pollution from reckless natural gas drilling is releasing benzene and causing cancer all across America. Everywhere you turn, the race for resources is contaminating our fresh water and putting innocent Americans at risk.

"Unfortunately, as my administration has pointed out time and again, we're addicted to the stuff. Water . . . gas . . . oil."

Travis laughed. "We're *addicted* to water?" That was a new one.

"In fact, before today is over, the United States will use twenty-one *million* barrels of oil." He paused, wanting that figure to produce some environmental shock and awe. It wouldn't. Among the casualties of the Leary administration was the power of the word "million." The appearance of *trillion*-dollar budget deficits had ensured that. Ken Fray, only half his face on camera, swallowed a yawn. Damn Hawaii jet lag.

"Over the course of my time in office, my administration has done everything possible to change our addictive behavior. We've incentivized people to buy smaller cars and to use public transportation. And thanks to that, we've seen encouraging decreases in overall gasoline use."

Sure have, mused Travis. It also helped that thirteen million people were out of work and had nowhere to drive . . .

"We've also poured more money than ever into research for the use of alternative fuels. In fact, we recently gave a grant to a company in Nebraska that believes it can make fuel from human waste."

"Good Lord," Travis said. "And Chevy thought selling people on the Volt was tough." He was already imagining the marketing meetings. *New from GM . . . the BM!*

"While we intend to continue those policies and believe they are the long-term solution to our energy needs, they cannot solve our current global oil emergency. And so, after having our finest, most educated minds weigh our options, I decided it was necessary to take swift action to secure our resources. This morning, with the full support of FEMA and the Department of the Interior, I put into effect Executive Order 10997, a contingency plan signed by President John F. Kennedy in the event of just such a national emergency.

"The order transfers full authority and control over our fragile natural resources into the stability of government hands. We're calling it the Responsible Resources Act. Under Washington's watchful eye, Americans can rest assured that their oil, gas, and water needs can be better regulated and distributed, bringing less uncertainty and lower costs to the marketplace."

Travis stared at the radio. "You slick son of a bitch." Many on the far left had been looking for a way to take over the oil and gas industry for years. The Brazil/India agreement, while a surprise, proved to be a gift. Like the disastrous Gulf oil spill that had enabled them to ban offshore drilling with little public outcry, this, too, allowed them to mask their coercive actions as mere *re*actions.

"Now, I can already hear my detractors. They're going to try to tell you that 'this is unprecedented!' It's not. If anything, the United States is arriving late to the party. Ninety-five percent of the world's oil reserves are nationalized. Nearly every developed nation in the world centralized control of their resources years ago. Not so long ago Russia bought a five percent stake in British Petroleum while we in Washington sat on the sidelines. These nations all understand what has taken us far too long to figure out, that letting private corporations control our oil and gas is too risky, putting our most basic needs and the safety of the environment in the hands of powerful CEOs who, more often than not, are out for their personal gain rather than the well-being of others.

"My enemies will also try to say this is somehow 'un-American.' To my naysayers, I remind you of the lyrics from that classic folk song: *This land is your land, this land is my land / from California to the New York Island.*

"The principle is so simple that we teach it to our preschoolers. It's called sharing. Yet here we are as grown adults struggling to do just that. Why should California have to spend billions of taxpayer dollars for fresh water when other states have more than they can handle? Why should Iowa never see a penny of oil revenue, while Oklahoma and Texas get nearly all of it? Is it Iowa's fault that glaciers came through ten million years ago and wiped the state clean of all fossil fuels? Of course not. Under the RRA we will return a sense of much-needed balance and fairness to our union. And the extra revenue it provides will allow us to balance our budget, reduce our deficit, and put us on the path to fiscal responsibility.

"Some of the fruits of this decision can be implemented quickly. Thanks to a provision in an earlier piece of legislation, a pipeline bringing water to the Southwest is already close to being operational."

Leary and his team had decided that owning up to its existence was the best way to take the stink off the fact it was buried in a bill supposedly devoted to new banking rules. "Other elements of this may take longer. Just know that in taking these measured steps today, we have every confidence that we've insured ourselves against a national disaster down the road.

"We'll be rolling out more details in the coming hours, days, and weeks. I know you have a lot of questions, but I won't be answering any at this time. I'll leave that to Ken and Marjorie." Ken's shoulders dropped. No one told him he'd have to answer questions.

Reporters leaned in and started to pepper the two cabinet members as Leary turned away. He patted Marjorie on the back and then whispered in Ken's ear, "Mahalo," a subtle reminder that taxpayer vacations always come with strings attached.

Travis sat in the car long after they returned to the hotel. He had K turn off the radio so he could just think in silence. The only positive he could glean was that Avery Adams wouldn't have to bother with that burdensome call to the Department of Transportation. If he took away the fear tactics and the moralizing from on high, what the president was attempting was incredibly simple: He and his cronies were dissolving state water rights and nationalizing the oil and gas industries—and doing it by decree alone.

When Leary nationalized health care, it was a grueling yearlong fight. The public had months to weigh in and express its disdain for the idea. Getting the votes required sweetheart deals and ignoring long-held Senate rules. The bill passed, but at the expense of the seventy-one Democrats who lost their seats in the midterm elections because of it. This time around, Leary had neither the political capital nor the votes to push the RRA through the legislature. True to form, he had found another way to get it done.

This news necessitated a stop at the hotel bar before packing for Texas. Inside the Hay-Adams, Damon Cole was already waiting for him.

Cole had watched the announcement from the Admirals Club. The TV was muted in favor of a Nationals-Cubs day game on the screen next to it. He read the speech as it scrolled across the screen and left the airport before it was over.

"I didn't miss anything, did I?" Cole asked.

"You mean did he end the speech by saying 'just kidding'? No."

Despite all that had happened, it was still only 11:00 A.M., and after some searching they found a bartender in the kitchen drying glasses. Travis ordered a Scotch. Cole wanted a Dr Pepper.

"We've got Coke and Sprite," the bartender said.

"Forget it," said Cole.

The bartender tried again. "Ginger ale?"

"I said *forget it.*"

The only thing rarer on the East Coast than a black, conservative, Ivy League professor was a restaurant or bar that served Dr Pepper. Some grocery stores didn't even carry it. He'd tried all the imitators, of which there were plenty. Mr Pibb (close but not the same), Dr. Skipper (not close), Dr Thunder (no thank you), Dr. Riffic (never again).

"Why'd you come back?" Travis asked.

Cole was busy bending a red bar straw into a triangle. "You ever read William F. Buckley's mission statement from the first issue of *National Review*?"

Cole read through all the back issues of the magazine when he was in high school. Most of them were on microfiche and had to be sent down to his Houston library from a WASPy branch up in Dallas. School was out at 2:50 P.M., and by 3:05 Cole's face was pressed against the gray screen, scrolling through fifteen years of conservative thought.

"It was 1955, and here's Buckley, just twenty-nine years old and the founder of a magazine that America wasn't sure it needed. Most people in the country thought they were alright. We'd won World War II, the economy was booming, we were paying down our debt. The only threat most people were worried about was rock 'n' roll. Buckley knew better.

"He saw the Left taking over universities and rejecting the traditions of our Founders with its own relativist ideas. He saw world leaders clamoring to take authority away from the U.S. and give it to the United Nations. He knew Communism was on the rise, and he knew it was evil. He warned about the coming monopoly of labor unions and their true purpose of pushing socialism on American business. Buckley knew the enemies we were facing. He didn't want to compromise with them. He wanted to defeat them. Because when those enemies won, the virtues and truths of America lost. He wrote in that first issue that his magazine was to stand 'athwart history, yelling Stop, at a time when no one is inclined to do so.'

"I read that and knew that's what I wanted to do with my life. I wanted to put my neck out and not worry that it might get chopped off. I wanted to save my country from itself. But then I came to Princeton. Next thing I knew, I had tenure, and something changed. I had a job for life. I bought a nice house near campus. Suddenly it didn't matter if the world outside was on fire, because I was safe. I didn't change my beliefs, but I changed my purpose.

"When you and I had lunch, I told you America was broken. The sad thing is that I was okay with that. I was happy to diagnose the problem and let someone else fix it. But today, sitting in that airport lounge, I looked around and saw fifty business travelers caring more about two last-place baseball teams than about the fracturing of their own country's ideals. It hit me that America isn't just broken, Ben. It's close to being lost altogether—and that scares the hell out of me."

Travis liked what he heard. "So what are you telling me?" he asked.

"I'm saying I'm ready to yell Stop."

Travis opened his wallet and dropped five bucks on the bar. "Forget Stop," Travis said. "What do you think about secession?"

Cole rolled his eyes. "Ha. Yeah. Good luck with that." Travis didn't laugh. He just stared. The edges of his mouth curled up. Cole knew the look. "Oh no . . ."

It meant that Ben Travis was serious.

12

It was eleven forty-five, and the bar at the Hay-Adams was starting to fill up. To be seen inside the Beltway drinking in public
before noon on a weekday put you in one of two categories. You were
either so powerful that your personal choices, however questionable,
were unassailable (which explained the House minority leader with
the pair of Midori sours in the corner), or your reputation was already so shot that drinking at noon was merely what people expected
of you (which accounted for the lobbyist to the erotic film industry
who was burying his self-loathing in an Amstel Light). Either way, it
wasn't the audience around which Travis or Cole wanted to be caught
discussing revolution and treason. With K leading the way, they
headed down Fifteenth Street toward the National Mall, where saying ridiculous things in public was far more commonplace.

Historically speaking, trying to wrest Texas from the Union wasn't
that ridiculous. No other state had changed hands so many times,
with Texas having been under six different flags in the previous five
hundred years. In 1540, less than fifty years after Christopher Co-
lumbus discovered the New World—and gave it smallpox—Spanish
conquistador Francisco Vásquez de Coronado mustered an army and
crossed the Rio Grande. They had been told of a land of gold and
silver. All they found was Native Americans. One of the first tribes
they stumbled upon was the Caddoans, who were quick to tell the

Spanish they were *teychas,* their native word for "friends." Coronado mistakenly assumed this was their tribe's name and from that point on referred to them as the Tejas people, which was later changed to "Texas."

Spain (Flag #1) would hold Texas for almost three hundred years until Mexico won its independence from the shrinking European power in 1821. Texas was under Mexican rule (Flag #2) until 1836, when American settlers successfully defeated Santa Anna and created the independent Republic of Texas (Flag #3), making it the only state that had also been its own nation. The republic was annexed by the United States (Flag #4) in 1845, only to leave again in 1861 and join the Confederacy (Flag #5) during the Civil War. The sixth flag was France, which technically owned a small piece of Texas between 1685 and 1690, but its colonization attempt was such a disaster that it almost doesn't deserve to be included.

Explorer Robert de LaSalle left France in 1684 with four boats and three hundred settlers. One of the boats—the one carrying most of their provisions—was lost to pirates near Santo Domingo in the Caribbean. It took another three months before the remaining boats arrived on the coast of Texas, which would have been alright except that LaSalle had meant to land at the mouth of the Mississippi, four hundred miles to the east. No longer sure of where they were, he ordered a group of settlers to unload and set up a temporary camp, only to watch from his boat as they were carried off by Karankawa Indians. LaSalle, no doubt feeling a bit guilty at this point, left his ship in order to pursue the Karankawa on foot. When he returned, he discovered that the ship he left had run aground.

Sieur de Beaujeu, LaSalle's naval commander, with whom he had been quarreling since before the unfortunate pirate incident, decided he'd seen enough of Texas and announced he was heading back to France in one of the two remaining boats. He was joined by over a hundred of the original three hundred settlers. La Salle stayed, and within two years, their only remaining boat had sunk, he still hadn't found the Mississippi, and all but fifteen of the original settlers were dead. LaSalle, in a fitting end, was killed by one of his own men.

Worst case, Travis figured, his attempt at nation building had to end up better than the French's.

"I still can't believe we're having this conversation," Cole said as they approached the Mall on foot.

"You think I haven't given this a lot of thought?" Travis asked. Cole raised his eyebrows. To be fair, Leary's plan to take over the energy industry had been public knowledge for no more than ninety minutes, but Travis had been drinking Texas-flavored Kool-Aid for his entire life. Now that he was governor, he was armed with empirical evidence of his state's superiority. "This is totally doable," he said.

"I don't care if it's *doable*! Call me coy, but if the goal here is to trigger a second Civil War, you can count me out."

"The basic fact is that Washington needs us way more than we need *it*. You know how many jobs we've added in the last decade, even with this recession? A million. That's more than every other state—*combined*. Measure it any way you want, we're the strongest state in America. Heck, we're stronger than America. We have more Fortune 500 companies than anyone else. We're sitting on around a quarter of the nation's oil reserves, a third of the natural gas reserves. We have three of the nation's ten biggest cities. For every dollar our taxpayers send to Washington, we only get eighty cents back. We could transfer those taxes to the state's coffers and still give every person a twenty percent tax cut."

"You might want to save some of that for defense—"

"Then there's the infrastructure, which is already in place. *We even have our own electric grid*, which means Washington can't turn the lights off on us."

"Really?" This was news to Cole.

"You bet! It got set up during World War II. The whole state's connected to it. Well, except for El Paso. They'd be screwed, but let's face it, would that be so big a loss?"

Cole had established his position as the killjoy in this debate and saw no reason to ease up now. "The Feds will kill you. And they will kill me. And probably a lot of other people, too."

"Not necessarily. I think we can do this without bloodshed."

Cole knew that peaceful secession had happened, yes, most recently in the Soviet Union in 1989 and again with Czechoslovakia in 1993, but those were the exceptions to the rule.

"Ben, listen to me. The Supreme Court ruled on this after the Civil War. *Texas versus White.* States have no legal right to secede. Five to three."

"Well, of course the Court decided that. What else would you expect? I thought you wrote a book on judicial activism."

"Three, actually, but I think you're—"

"*Three?* I tried the first one. Couldn't get through it. No offense."

He had debated Travis plenty of times, but Cole had never felt so thoroughly steamrolled. It reminded him of the time he made the mistake of going on Bill Maher and found himself on the losing end of a tort reform fight with Florence Henderson.

A vendor pushing an ice cream cart rolled their way. Attached to the handle was a dented silver bell that jingled with every step. Travis stopped. "You want an Italian ice? On me."

Great, Cole thought. *Just what Travis needs—sugar.* Cole declined, as did K, but Travis bought himself a cup of lemon slush and sat down on a bench across from the Washington Monument. The tip of its shadow stopped right at their feet.

"And look," Travis said between licks, "if people get all uppity about us trying to secede, we just argue that Washington, D.C., long ago seceded from *us* . . . figuratively speaking."

With Travis distracted by dessert, Cole saw his opportunity to lure his friend back to the shallow end of the pool. "I'm not saying you don't have some valid points. You do. If there's any state that could pull it off, it's yours."

"*Ours,*" Travis corrected midslurp.

"Right. Fine. Ours. But the problem remains. You're not going to be able to convince enough members of the Texas Legislature that this makes sense."

"Why not?"

"Because no matter how you say it, you will come off sounding crazy."

"I'm not crazy. I'm *passionate!*"

"Which, I hate to break it to you, is usually just a patronizing way of saying 'crazy'!"

Travis flashed back to the media attention he'd received the week before. He was called "passionate" by five different news networks.

"I'm sorry, Ben. I just think we need to set realistic goals. You're not a third-term governor whom everyone knows, loves, and respects. In my opinion, your best bet is a full-on legal assault. First thing tomorrow, we have your attorney general file a brief in federal court, asking for an injunction. Worst case, that will keep the Feds from taking over oil, gas, and water for a few weeks. From there you hire the best lawyers in Texas to fight this all the way. I wouldn't be surprised to see this thing end up in the Supreme Court before it's all over."

"So what? If it ends up in the Supreme Court, we're toast. After Ferraro's mental meltdown, we can forget about winning. The Court's stacked against us."

Even with three boring books on the subject, Cole hated to think that America's judicial system was so impervious to reason and a well-made argument. Still, he knew it was probably true.

Travis could sense he had Cole's ear, if only for a moment. "When I was seven years old, the circus came to Dallas. It set up at Fair Park near I-30. Now, my dad's impatient as all get-out and couldn't be late to anything. The circus doesn't start till noon, but he and I get there at ten. We're so early that there isn't even anyone guarding the entrance, so my dad just shrugs his shoulders and walks in holding my hand. Whole place is still dark and empty except the center ring, where the lion tamer's running through his routine one last time. We just stand in the shadows and watch. The only place I'd ever seen a lion was at the beginning of an MGM movie, and I never realized how big they were. Four hundred and fifty pounds. All muscle. The tamer does all the tricks, sticks his head in its mouth, everything.

And about halfway through I realize there's no cage around the ring. Just a circle of string about three feet high, connected to poles cemented into Yuban coffee cans. That's all that's separating us. When the tamer's done, he puts the lion away. As he's going around picking up his props, my dad goes over to him and asks him what the string's for. The guy says, 'To keep the lion from escaping.' We think he's joking, but he tells us that he spends the first three months with every new cub just using electrified wire. When the lion gets close, he gets zapped. But it's dangerous to use and costs money, so after three months, they turn it off and the lion just assumes it's still charged. Then over time they don't even need the wire anymore."

"The lion's trapped himself," Cole said.

"Which is exactly what's happened to us. The authority of a big central government hinges on everyone buying into the fallacy that states have to bow down to Washington no matter what. We could try to negotiate a middle ground, but then we're just accepting the same premise. I'm not saying we need to secede. I get it. But I am saying that if we don't push hard for something big, we can't expect to really change anything."

Cole absorbed the point. He stared off across the Mall, settling his gaze on the Jefferson Memorial. It gave him an idea. "How about this? What if we get the Texas Legislature to nullify the RRA?"

"Which would mean what exactly?"

"Essentially they'd be saying the law doesn't apply to Texas. Jefferson was a champion of nullification. So was Madison. Said it was one of our basic protections against tyranny."

Travis liked the sound of it, and yet he figured it couldn't be that simple. "I feel a 'but' coming."

Cole smiled. "*But* it's been ruled unconstitutional every time a state's tried it," he said.

"So what makes you think anyone's going to vote for it?"

"I never said they would. Nullification is the legislative equivalent of slapping President Leary in the face."

Travis chuckled and caught a drip of lemon juice racing down his thumb. "Maybe I should just explain it like that. You'd be surprised how many votes we'd get."

"No, no, no," said Cole. "The only way you're going to get a politician to say yes to this is if you make it sound reasonable. The sane option. Rational."

"How am I going to do that?"

Cole considered the question and started laughing, to himself at first and then out loud.

"What?" Travis asked. Being a few steps behind Cole was old hat for him, but he never particularly enjoyed it.

"You know how you're going to do it? The same way you did it to me."

"I don't understand," Travis said.

"You've got to tell them you want to secede."

Travis glared at him. "You're serious."

"Think about it," Cole said. "If someone comes to you wanting to buy your company and you think it's worth eight hundred thousand dollars, you don't ask for eight hundred thousand dollars. You ask for a million and know you'll never get it. That way when the buyer offers eight hundred, you both feel like you've won, and in a way you both have. That's what you need to do. Push for secession and you just might get them to compromise with nullification. It's brilliant, actually. Essentially by playing the nut you're helping the Texas Legislature make a scary decision seem like a safe one."

"You really think that could work?" Travis couldn't believe his absurd idea had been co-opted by Cole and was now being sold back to him as unadulterated genius.

"It's a long shot, but if you're asking for an expert's opinion, that's your best bet." Thoroughly pleased with himself, the professor stretched his legs into the midday sun, clasped his hands behind his head, and closed his eyes.

"And here you made *me* out to be crazy," said Travis.

"Not crazy," Cole said, soaking in the warmth. *"Passionate."*

13

Paige Travis hated running. She hated the unflattering, bulky shoes. She hated the color her face turned, alabaster white except for her cheeks, which resembled the strawberry jelly half of some first-grader's PB&J. She hated never knowing what to do when another runner came the other direction. Often the other person would muster a weak smile and a breathy "hey," and she'd do the same, but by mile two, the whole idea of smiling when the only thing her mouth wanted to do was vomit seemed absurd.

What she did like was the way she felt when her run was over. Not immediately over. Like two hours later, after she'd had the chance to shower, rehydrate, blow-dry her hair, and squeeze into her favorite jeans for one more day.

She ran southwest from Dupont Circle and headed toward George Washington University, a free afternoon ahead of her. Her boss had come to the Department of Justice after a stint with the Centers for Disease Control and never asked for proof that she was really sick. He had too much secret knowledge of deadly viruses to risk it.

Paige wasn't going to be much use at work anyway. She could only think about her dad. His insensitivity was stunning, even after all these years. What made it all the more frustrating was that he couldn't see it. "Maybe you'd have thicker skin if you cut back on the lotion," he once quipped. Bottom line was he had wanted a boy and got a girl. He'd never admitted this, but in her baby book is a picture of him holding her for the first time. In his free hand is a tiny football she'd never seen since.

She ran with a glazed focus on the path in front of her, not noticing that she was nearly doubling her usual running speed. She hit the Rock Creek Park Trail and turned south, paralleling the Potomac. It felt good to move her legs as fast as they could travel. Her clenched fists loosened and her hands pointed straight out like a pair of bayonets cutting through the humidity. She weaved in and around slower runners, tiny clouds of decomposed granite kicking up with each step. By the time she neared the Lincoln Memorial, Paige was free of all her burdens, happy to be nothing more than an object in motion.

Her pace slowed near the Jefferson Memorial. Her muscles, believing they had outrun whatever predator had been chasing them, tightened at the first opportunity. She limped her way back to the Mall, not far from where Travis and Cole had been plotting earlier, and collapsed her body onto a perfect patch of clover.

"Miss Travis?" The gentle voice spoke to her from beyond her closed eyelids. "Oh dear, I've woken her, haven't I?"

Paige squinted toward the sky and made out the outline of a giant red umbrella, lit from behind by the three o'clock sun. Silhouetted in front was a short, suited man in his late seventies, his head covered in a bowler hat. She sat up on her elbows as her pupils raced to dilate and make out his face. As he came into focus, she sat up even straighter.

"Mr. Metzos?"

He smiled and turned to his aide, Mutuku, a handsome and slender Kenyan in a herringbone suit. "She recognizes me? I am flattered."

Anatole Metzos was arguably the world's most successful currency trader and global investor, a self-made man to the tune of eighteen billion dollars. He was born in Austria, but his father was Greek; his family escaped the Nazis and settled in Switzerland during World War II. His father opened an apothecary shop in Rougemont, a hamlet on the invisible border between the German- and French-speaking parts of the country. Anatole mastered both languages and quickly became his father's most valuable employee. At age six, he was mixing medicines and counting pills. Over the course of the war, as different medicines disappeared off the shelves, Anatole witnessed firsthand how market forces could dramatically affect his father's income. At the height of the conflict, prices didn't change daily, they changed by the minute, and Anatole found nothing more thrilling than playing customers off each other for the greatest profit. If he was so fortunate as to have one of the customers speak French and the other German, the added confusion and reliance on Metzos made for an even greater payday.

When he landed at Oxford a decade later, he was stunned to learn that he understood more about business and money than most of his tutors. He finished in three years and was off to America, where, by age thirty, he had his own investment fund and was boasting an annual return of 22 percent, a number that attracted great attention on Wall Street.

Yet he had no real interest in being an investor. He saw himself as a humanitarian, compelled to use his exploding wealth to alter society and create real progress for mankind. "Money is merely zee means, not zee end," he was fond of saying in his thick Austro-German-French accent. Indeed, it was fair to say that if you turned a D.C. liberal upside down and shook him long enough, some of Anatole Metzos's money would fall out. Over the last twenty years, he had donated hundreds of millions of dollars to fund various nonprofit organizations and political campaigns. The centerpiece of it all was the Forward Foundation, which billed itself as the leading progressive think tank in America.

It was through the Forward Foundation that Paige had come to know him. She and her fellow Leary volunteers used the foundation's research throughout the presidential campaign to frame the issues and influence voters. She'd only met him once, at a Yale book signing, but there was no way he remembered that.

"Of course I remember!" he said after Paige recounted the story.

"Well, I don't remember meeting you specifically, but I remember the event. Wonderful crowd that night. Very energized."

"I bought a copy of your book for me and another for my father."

"What did he think?"

"Oh, I'm sure he never even opened it." He had, but only read the first three pages, which was enough to tell him it would make great kindling.

Paige was excited to meet Metzos again, but how he recognized her now was still unclear. "Oh, well, that's easy," he said when she finally asked. "I saw your face on the news not thirty minutes ago. All about the . . . well, you know . . . comments."

Paige had forgotten the drama of her morning. Her shoulders tensed up at the memory. "Oh no. You did? Was it a flattering picture? On second thought, if you were able to recognize me based on how I look now, it couldn't have been very good. It wasn't my Department of Justice ID photo, was it? They wouldn't let me retake even if—"

"It was a lovely picture. I'm sorry about the strife at home. If I may, could I offer some grandfatherly advice?"

"Of course, yes," Paige said, happy for any wisdom that didn't originate from a ranch in Prosper.

"When you're trying to change someone's beliefs, you have two options. You can keep arguing and hope that they eventually see the world the way you do. Or you can simply change the world into what you want—"

"—so they have no choice." Paige smiled.

"Well, someone read my book," Metzos mused. "Very impressive, Miss Travis." He turned to Mutuku and then back to Paige, a simple move that he could only accomplish with ten miniature shuffles of his feet, five each direction. "Listen, it is short notice, but I'm having some friends over for lunch Sunday at my home. I'd love for you to join."

Paige was floored at the thought. "Of course. Yes. I will make myself available."

"Wonderful."

Mutuku handed her a card with Metzos's name and number. "One o'clock. Call for directions."

Paige was glowing, "Thank you, Mr. Metzos."

"You're welcome. We look forward to it. Now come, Mutuku, before this old man melts."

Metzos and Mutuku continued down the Mall. Paige watched until his umbrella disappeared behind the rolling wave of a Japanese tour group.

14

Damon Cole sat behind his new oak desk inside the governor's office and brushed up on the Tenth Amendment. He hadn't told the Princeton administration where he had gone or what he was doing, but he had lined up enough help from sycophantic grad students to pull off the disappearing act. One of them would oversee the administration of his final exams, and another would grade papers. A third had volunteered to overnight-mail a selection of the professor's clothes and shoes, not knowing this was the most tedious of the tasks, involving cedar hangers, bubble wrap, and the placement of silica gel packets in the toe of each shoe to help regulate humidity during air travel.

Travis put Cole's desk a few feet away from his own and told the office that the professor was acting as a senior adviser and not drawing a salary. Hunter Reese wasn't sure where that left him, but either way, the governor was under no contractual obligation to keep him on as chief of staff, a fact he saw no upside in pointing out. He couldn't help but feel threatened. Hunter bought the majority of his clothes from Costco. Actually, his wife bought them. She held them up to her own body and tried to imagine a male, gaunt version of herself. If she liked what she saw, she threw it in the cart alongside five pounds of salmon and a pallet of diapers. He'd gotten used to the fact his clothes often came in pastels and smelled like fish before they'd even been worn.

Hunter poked his head into the office for the umpteenth time, already aware of his diminishing role. "You sure you don't need me for anything, Governor?" he asked.

"I need you to sleep," said Travis, not looking up from his newspaper. "We've got a busy week ahead of us."

"Have a good night," Cole added with a smile, trying to show Hunter that he was not to be feared.

Travis and Cole's day had been bookended by meetings with the Texas attorney general, who'd emerged an hour earlier with a thirty-page brief asking for an injunction against the RRA. Neither Travis nor the attorney general believed it would be fruitful, but if the nullification attempt fell flat, it was at least something. In between, Travis and Cole had been on the phone with nearly every energy company in the state. Altogether the energy complex supported 9.2 million jobs in America with over 2 million of those in Texas. There were the major players like Exxon Mobil, but for every behemoth like that, there were a dozen companies like Chesapeake or Petrohawk, smaller companies that dotted the Texas landscape by the hundreds and were left wondering if some suit from D.C. was already en route to their six wells with a hard hat under one arm and a court order under the other.

The White House had yet to provide details, but Exxon knew what to expect when a government says it wants to nationalize oil. Hugo Chávez had done it to them a few years earlier in the Orinoco River region of Venezuela. If it played out in a similar fashion, the Feds would take over the large-scale operations and management elements while paying off the shareholders and grabbing a majority stake in the companies; somewhere between 60 and 70 percent seemed like a good guess. The energy companies would be "invited" to stay on as minority partners and expected to use their employees to run the operating wells, processing plants, and refineries day to day, something the government didn't have the expertise to do on its own. Of course, these employees wouldn't be allowed to stay nonunion and, in the name of workers' rights and central planning, would be welcomed into the ever-expanding Service Employees International Union, where a portion of their wages would be siphoned off and sent right back to Washington. Exxon Mobil could refuse the government partnership and shut down its rigs and refineries, but in doing so the corporation would be cutting itself off from a major source of revenue, and 30 percent of something would always be better than 100 percent of nothing.

The Texas oil boom didn't hit until 1901, though Native Americans had found petroleum seeping through the dirt for hundreds of years. Unsure of what to do with it, some used it as salves; the really curious ones ate it. By the 1800s, the sludge was seen as a nuisance, not a gold mine. Companies paid to drill for water would strike oil and just keep going. As the turn of the century approached, however, one young Texan was convinced that oil would supplant coal as America's fuel of choice. He also believed he was sitting on the mother lode.

Pattillo Higgins had one arm and no schooling after the fourth grade, but he had plenty of faith, particularly in his unspectacular plot of land on Spindletop Hill. Higgins grew up a troublemaking two-armed kid in Beaumont, a small town in the southeast corner of Texas. His bad reputation caught up with him when the local sheriff's deputy responded to word that the seventeen-year-old Higgins was harassing blacks at the local Baptist church. The sheriff fired a warning shot over Higgins's head, figuring that would scare him off. What he didn't take into consideration was the fact that Higgins was the son of a gunsmith. He returned fire. When the shooting stopped, Higgins had a bullet in his arm and the deputy was dead. Higgins was arrested and charged with murder. Meanwhile, his arm became infected from the wound and ultimately had to be amputated at the elbow. Higgins could very easily have spent the rest of his life in jail—or worse—but he argued that he only fired in self-defense, and the jury believed him.

Higgins left Beaumont and, despite the handicap of having only one good arm, successfully managed to land a job in the logging business on the Louisiana border. While there, he sat in on a Baptist revival meeting and gave his life to Jesus. He was a changed man and decided to flee the seedy lumber industry and return to Beaumont, where he taught Sunday school while starting his own brick company. His kilns ran on oil and gas, and Higgins could sense that the role of these fuels in manufacturing was only going to grow.

He took a trip to Pennsylvania, then the oil capital of the United States, and began studying the characteristics of oil-rich land. Higgins got his hands on every U.S. Geological Survey report he could find and continued his self-education. With each report, he became more and more convinced there was a large untapped reservoir under Beaumont's Sour Hill Mound, a place he would take his Sunday school kids on outings.

With help from a fellow Baptist, Higgins bought half of the hill and formed a partnership with the man who owned the other half. They started to drill. Seven *years* later, they still had nothing. Higgins was the laughingstock of Beaumont and broke, forced to sell his stake in the company. Other partners drilled on, believing, like Higgins, that something was down there.

On January 10, 1901, after they had drilled down more than eleven hundred feet, mud began bubbling up through the hole. It was followed by six tons of well pipe, which shot back out of the hole like missiles and sent workers running. For the next few minutes, all that came out was gas and then, finally, the gusher. A hundred feet in the air, it blew uncapped for nine straight days, at an estimated output of a hundred thousand barrels a day. Those hundred thousand barrels surpassed the combined daily amount of oil produced by every other well in the *entire United States*.

While Higgins didn't have a stake in the gusher, he still owned thirty-three acres in the center of Spindletop. He was quick to cover them with wells and became a millionaire many times over. Within months, the population of Beaumont grew from ten thousand to fifty thousand. In an instant, the world realized that Patillo Higgins was right: Oil was the fuel of the future, Texas was sitting on the mother lode, and everyone was going to want a piece of it.

The federal government had been digging into that pie ever since through heavy taxes at the pump, all the while framing the oil companies as the greedy crooks. As it currently stood, every gallon of gasoline sold in the United States included a hidden tax of almost twenty cents that went directly to the government. If they got their way with the RRA, the Feds would take the whole pie.

Hunter reluctantly waved good night and closed the door behind him. It was just Travis and Cole now, with K picking at the leftovers in the main office bullpen. "I thought he'd never leave," Travis said.

Cole cleared the papers off his makeshift desk as Travis unearthed a crooked stack of photocopies he'd hidden in a drawer earlier in the day. They were color headshots of every sitting member of the Texas Legislature.

Travis and Cole had their plan in place before they'd even landed in Austin. Travis was going to call a special session of the legislature, something only the governor had the authority to do. Pursuant to the Texas Constitution, the governor was required to announce in advance what the purpose would be. Travis would do it under the auspices of needing to name a new lieutenant governor and hoping to find a legislative response to the Responsible Resources Act. It seemed specific enough, but not so specific as to raise Washington's antennae to his real intentions.

"How are we doing this?" Cole asked, looking at the stack.

"Three piles," said Travis. "*Yes, no,* and *not sure.*" Travis had filled the vacancy he left in the senate with a retired baseball coach he'd met through the Rotary, bringing the total membership in the "Lege" back up to a hundred and eighty-one. "We'll need a hundred from the house and twenty-one from the Senate," Cole said.

The state constitution, rewritten after the Civil War in 1876, didn't cover a procedural way to nullify federal law, leaving it in Travis and Cole's hands to decide the fairest way to do it. Gaining approval from two-thirds of each chamber felt like the right start. Two-thirds was the amount needed for any amendment to the Texas Constitution. It was also the same number necessary to put any bill into immediate effect. If they were able to get to a hundred twenty-one votes, few could deny that Texas meant business. From there the Lege would send the proposal to the people at large, where a simple majority of Texans would be enough to make it all official . . . at least in their eyes.

Travis quickly began to sort through the faces on his desk, each of them trying to outsmile the other. "Look at these teeth," he said, holding up one particularly cheery representative from the Fourteenth District. "If Elton John got close to these, he'd try to play 'em."

"You know, George Washington didn't have wooden teeth, by the way," Cole said. "I saw his dentures in a dental museum in Maryland."

"Just think of the more exciting places you could go if you weren't spending all your money on shoes," said Travis, still sorting.

"It was between that and an Orioles game."

"So what were they made of if they weren't wood?"

"The base was ivory, but the teeth themselves were a mix of gold and silver along with human and animal teeth."

Travis threw another picture on the *yes* pile and looked up. "You're telling me the greatest hero in American history had animal teeth?"

"Horse or donkey, most likely. The top and bottom dentures were connected with a spring in the back to make it easier to chew. The curator said the reason Washington didn't smile much wasn't the way his teeth looked, but that he knew they might jump right out of his mouth if he did."

"No way Washington would get elected today," Travis said. "Once Jon Stewart finds out you've got donkey teeth, forget it."

So far, the *yes* pile was outpacing *no* and *not sure*. Cole started to count. If it weren't for a Republican majority in the Texas House and Senate, they wouldn't stand a chance of getting this passed. Texas wasn't always a GOP stronghold, though the elites on the Coasts assumed differently. When Republicans won control of the state senate in 2002, it was the first time they held the majority in both houses since the 1870s. In between, Texas politics had been dominated by heavy-hitting Democrats like Lyndon B. Johnson, Ann Richards, and Lloyd Bentsen, the vice presidential candidate in 1988 who once referred to Texas politics as a contact sport.

Republicans believed that the Democratic dominance in the legislature was more a matter of poorly drawn congressional districts than of their rivals' actual popularity with the people. In 2003, the new senate set out to redraw the districts and make it a fair fight. Fifty-two Democrats in the house saw their electoral future at stake and, rather than vote on the measure, fled authorities and holed themselves up at a Holiday Inn across the border in Ardmore, Oklahoma, denying the house the quorum it needed to pass the redistricting measure. It was all the more reason for Travis to keep the full purpose of the special session under wraps until the house chamber was full and the doors were closed.

After a few passes through the piles and some last-second switching, Travis was ready for a tally. He had ruled out twenty-eight liberal Democrats who he knew wouldn't vote for nullification even if he promised to bulldoze the entire state and cover it with wildflowers and marijuana. In the *yes* pile were the outspoken conservatives, along with the moderate Republicans and Democrats living in the heart of oil and gas country. He also added the self-preservationists: moderates who didn't live anywhere near oil country but had made sharp right turns after the 2010 elections when it became clear that being associated with Leary was no badge of honor. If they were looking for a way to distance themselves from the president, Travis was about to give it to them. Everyone else landed in the *not sure* pile.

"One-oh-six," Cole said. By his completely unscientific method, they were fifteen votes short.

"What? Count again," Travis said.

"I did," said Cole.

Travis was hoping for something in the teens, but one-oh-six . . . Travis grimaced and bit the inside of his cheek. He picked up the *not sure* pile and flipped through it again. He paced slowly to the corner of his office and back, throwing one more on the *yes* pile upon return. He got to the bottom of the stack again and shook his head.

"That's all I can do," he said. "I think one-oh-seven is the most I can guarantee." Travis dropped into his dark leather couch as Cole leaned against the front of his desk and crossed his arms.

"So what are you saying? That's it? You don't even want to try?"

"I still want to try," said Travis, slightly annoyed at the suggestion. "It just means we're going to need some more help."

15

The Limestone County Detention Center in Groesbeck, Texas, was as lovely as you'd imagine. Gunnite walls, pipes running along the ceiling, and gum-stained cement floors broken up by the occasional rusty drain—and this was still in the *public* part of the jail. Travis and K walked ahead of Cole, who was stepping from dry spot to dry spot in a desperate attempt to save his three-thousand-dollar John Lobb wingtips from contacting anything that was, in his own words, "felonious." In front of Travis was Steve Sanchez, head of public relations and a recent addition to the Limestone staff after getting axed from the Texas State Penitentiary at Huntsville for using too many adverbs in prison press releases. Sanchez had a master's in PR and fought the firing, unable to see what might be off-putting about HUNTSVILLE PENITENTIARY EXCITEDLY ANNOUNCES LETHAL INJECTION OF RAPIST TIM COOK.

Sanchez remained miffed about the demotion and hoped a photo op with the new governor in front of the portable trailer he called his office might be the beginning of his own rehabilitation. Travis refused. "The fewer people who know I was here, the better," he said.

"Why *are* we here?" Cole asked.

"I'm meeting a fan," Travis explained. In the week that Travis had been in office, he'd received over five hundred letters and a thousand e-mails. They broke down into five basic categories: generic well-wishers, kids, reasoned critics, angry psychos, and desperate divorcées who hoped Travis was one pornographic photo away from popping the question. He'd added a dozen volunteers (Austin retirees, mostly) to his staff to wade through them all and pull out the gems. When he saw a letter from prison on the top of his must-read pile, his interest was piqued.

They arrived at the long bank of windows and phones where inmates talked with loved ones and lawyers. Each prisoner was outfitted in an orange jumpsuit with white Velcro sneakers. Neck tattoos appeared to be all the rage, with various morbid designs choking inmates like satanic turtlenecks before slipping beneath bleached white undershirts. Cole scanned the dandies on the other side of the glass. "Well, you're certainly attracting America's best and brightest, aren't you?"

"Window four," Sanchez said.

Waiting for them on the other side of the three-inch glass, looking thoroughly out of place, was Adam Wexler. Thanks to a drawn-out puberty and soft features, the nineteen-year-old could still pass for fifteen. At just a hundred and thirty-five pounds, he wore a jumpsuit that came special order from the juvenile facility fifty miles east. The guards kept this fact to themselves, figuring Wexler was enough of a target as it was.

Wexler nodded as Travis sat down, then reached for the phone.

"Thanks for your note," Travis started.

"You're welcome." A few weeks in prison and the kid still had his manners.

"How much of what you wrote is true?"

"All of it."

"Glad to hear it."

"Sorry to interrupt the conjugal visit," Cole said, "but would you mind telling me who this kid is?"

"Oh. Sorry. Adam here is a . . . well"—Travis turned toward the glass—"what's the official charge?"

Wexler licked his lips. He had become addicted to ChapStick in high school, and his lips no longer knew how to moisturize themselves. He was miserable. "I reappropriated objects of cultural heritage."

Cole clarified. "You're a thief."

There was more to it than that. Six and a half months ago, Adam Wexler was a straight-A student at Baylor University in Waco. He was a computer science major with a minor in history. He worked in the library. He played video games till 5:00 A.M. It was a charmed life where the only thing that scared him was the thought of graduating from college a virgin. That all changed when he went home to San Antonio for Christmas. His parents sat him down his first night home and delivered the news. They were broke. His dad had lost his engineering job in the recession and was promised he'd get it back when things turned around. That was three years ago. They were already two semesters behind on tuition, and Baylor wasn't letting them go a third. Barring a miracle, college was over.

Wexler's miracle came in the form of the Baylor University library archives, a basement full of letters, photos, and documents dating back more than two hundred and fifty years. Many of them were gifts to the school. Others had inexplicably landed there over time.

Even though Wexler wasn't allowed back as a student, his library keys still worked.

The first document he swiped, a letter from Franklin D. Roosevelt to Harry S. Truman, sold on eBay for seventeen hundred dollars. The next sold for five grand. A week later, Wexler walked into the Administration Building with ten thousand dollars cash. His entire debt was paid in full within another month.

That was when he should have stopped. Then again, a college kid has got to eat. Not to mention drive a 2011 Mercedes SLS Gullwing. His explanation for the sudden change in wealth depended on who asked. His parents were under the impression he'd sold a business idea to Google. He told attractive coeds he was the heir to the Michelob fortune. No one guessed he was busy committing federal offenses hundreds of times over.

It was so easy to pull off that in time Wexler got sloppy. When he sold a 1750 handwritten Jonathan Edwards sermon to a televangelist in Ocean City, he forgot to scrub the Baylor University label from the back. That was all it took. He was in the middle of a date with a bubbly cheerleader when FBI agents swooped in. He tried to negotiate for three more hours of freedom in exchange for a guilty plea, but his virginity was of no interest to them. So ended the illustrious college career of Adam Wexler.

Travis covered the phone with his hand so he could finally answer Cole. "Adam wrote me because he found a document he thought I'd be interested in."

"A stolen document," Cole said.

"Geez Louise," Travis said. "If it will help you to sleep at night, I'll let you personally return it to Baylor when we're done with it. You'll be a hero. They'll probably offer you a job. Which you'll need, by the way, when this is over."

"Who needs to work?" Cole asked. "I was planning on just collecting unemployment for a hundred weeks."

Travis took his hand off the jail phone. "So you got my attention, Adam. Nice going. Now I just need to know what makes this letter so special."

Wexler licked his lips again, choosing his words carefully. "It's one page. Its message is irrefutable. And once it becomes public knowledge, it could be the nail in the coffin of the progressive movement."

Cole had his ear to the phone, too. "That's nice, kid. But what does it say?"

Adam stared at them through the glass. *How could these two guys be so dense?* "You think that's how this works?"

Travis and Cole stood in the shade near the back door of the penitentiary. The asphalt on the parking lot was starting to seep tar in the midday heat. "Seriously, how can you live somewhere this hot?" Cole asked.

"But it makes October seem so lovely," Travis said.

The heavy door flung open and out tumbled Adam Wexler, duffel bag over his shoulder. He was back in his uniform of choice: khakis, polo shirt, and Top-Siders. "Welcome back," Travis said.

"For now," Wexler said, not stopping. "You said you were going to get me pardoned."

"I thought about it," Travis said, following him to the car, where K was using a long telescoping mirror to finish his now routine bomb check. "But after thinking about it I realized that *A,* you haven't shown me the letter yet, and *B,* stealing historical documents is a federal offense. Only the president can pardon you for that. So instead we posted bail."

"*I* posted the bail," Cole clarified. He was always a stickler for details, but having maxed out his credit card at twenty-five g's, he felt it was worth the clarification. "And you have to be back in three weeks for the trial or else the money's gone forever."

"But hey," Travis said, "if you keep your nose clean, who knows what the president could be talked into once we show off that letter."

Wexler flung his duffle bag in the trunk. "Yeah, well, that's going to be a little tricky."

"Why?"

He turned around slowly to face them. "See, I don't actually *have* the letter."

Travis and Cole didn't understand. The guy who was fresh out twenty-five thousand bucks broke first. "You said you already stole it!"

"I did, but when I was arrested, the Feds cleaned out my room and took all my stuff."

The steel door swung open again behind them as a guard headed for lunch. "Hold that door," Travis called out. He looked at Cole. "What does your paperwork say about returns?"

Wexler backpedaled. "Hang on hang on hang on . . ." He knew he was one gas station away from a fresh tube of ChapStick.

"You lied to us, kid," said Travis.

"Yes, but I can get it back."

"How?"

"It's probably buried in my case file."

"Probably?" Cole asked.

Travis tried to remain calm. "Where is your case file?"

Wexler licked his lips. "Somewhere inside the Department of Justice."

"Wait," Travis said, "that's where my . . ." He saw Wexler smiling and realized he was playing catch-up to him and not the other way around. "Now hold on a second—"

Wexler slammed the trunk closed. "I saw the *Post* article. Cute girl. Looks like you'll be setting us up on a blind date." He walked around the car and ducked into the backseat.

Travis stared at Cole.

"Huh," said Cole.

"Yeah," said Travis.

They stood there for a few more seconds, both of them coming to terms with the fact that they just got conned by a kid with peach fuzz.

16

The governor's car stopped at a dive called Star Stop Pizza Pro, a place that stayed in business solely because it was the only pizza joint in a forty-mile radius.

"What's good here?" Cole asked.

The troll-like man behind the register wiped his nose with his sleeve. "Pizza," he said.

Cole ordered a salad. The three of them spread out over two orange booths and ate in silence. The pizza was awful. The soda was flat. It was still the best meal Wexler had eaten in a month.

"Aren't you guys curious about what the letter says?" he asked, his lips shining from beeswax, menthol, vitamin E, and aloe.

They were curious, but that was of secondary importance to Travis. "I'm not going to put my daughter in harm's way over a piece of paper that we can't even be sure exists."

"That's fine. Your choice. Just let me say this: Have you ever heard Texans say the state has the right to secede whenever it wants?"

Travis and Cole shared a look. Wexler took it as a sign of interest.

"Now, some people say it's in the state's 1845 Annexation Agreement. Others say it's in the Texas Constitution. It's in neither."

"Right," Travis added. "It's a Texas legend. Like Pecos Bill lassoing the moon or Davy Crockett wearing a coonskin cap."

"Somehow I'm guessing our new friend here is about to tell us that it's not," Cole said.

Wexler didn't need any more of a setup than that. "It was the fall of 1864. General Sherman had burned Atlanta and had the Confederates on the run in his March to the Sea. General Grant was closing in on Robert E. Lee in Virginia. Lincoln had just been reelected. Everything seemed"—he searched for a word he thought Travis's generation would appreciate—"*peachy*. The only problem was Texas. Of all the Rebel states, Texas was the farthest from Washington and the hardest to infiltrate. Jefferson Davis had put Colonel Baylor in charge of the frontier beyond Fort Worth, and the guy got so bored doing nothing that he went west, took over the New Mexico territory, and decided to conquer Arizona while he was at it. He was a typical Texan, trying to add land when everyone else was just praying they could hold on to what they already had."

Wexler's history-minor juices were flowing. Cole was silently impressed. The kid knew his stuff. This was a point of pride for Wexler. Early in his criminal career, he decided that if he was going to steal something and make some money off it, the least he could do was be scholarly about it. A positive side effect was that his research convinced buyers that they were dealing with an expert rather than a thief who'd only been out of his braces for three years.

"By the end of 1864, the only part of Texas under the North's control was the water off the Gulf. That was it. They'd made one last attempt the previous spring to take the state, but it didn't go too well. Twenty-five thousand Union troops sat ready to strike in Louisiana, forty miles east of the Texas border. The Confederates could only muster eleven thousand soldiers, cobbled together from a bunch of different regiments. They were outnumbered, but they didn't care. So they attacked, and the Union boys were so surprised that they fled all the way to the Mississippi River. The North never tried again."

"You know that story, Damon?" Travis asked.

"Of course," Cole said, casually picking through his brownish-green salad. "That was under General . . . uh . . . I'm more of a politics guy, but I do know this, uh—"

"Richard Taylor," Wexler said.

"Right, right. Exactly." Cole said. He was steaming. It was the academic equivalent of getting a basketball dunked in your face.

"So by the end of 1864, Lincoln started to realize that even if he got Robert E. Lee to surrender, the nutjobs out in Texas were just going to keep fighting. In fact, the last battle of the Civil War wasn't at Appomattox, it was—"

"Brownsville," Cole interrupted. "It was in Brownsville." Slight redemption.

"Yep. Brownsville. A month after the rest of the Confederates officially gave up. But Lincoln was hoping to avoid this. So in November of 1864 he sent a letter to the Texas governor. A guy named Pendleton Murrah. Big secessionist. Constitution-wise, an originalist. He was such a huge states' rights freak that when Jefferson Davis asked if he was willing to turn the Texas militia into Confederate armies, Murrah told him to suck it."

"I'm sure those were the words he used," Travis said.

"Anyway, Lincoln writes Murrah, and he asks him what would have to happen in order to get Texas to stop fighting. He waits and waits. Doesn't hear anything. Four and a half months later, mid-April, a guy knocks on the door of the White House and asks to speak to the president. No appointment or anything."

"Sounds like someone I know," Cole said, giving Travis a look.

"Back then there wasn't heavy security or even a fence around the White House, and when Lincoln was in town, ordinary people would stop by all the time to ask him for favors or complain about how he was doing his job. School kids would play on the steps out front after school. Kinda nice, actually. But this guy who came to the president is wet and coughing. He's got tuberculosis. Been traveling for weeks. A mess. It's Governor Murrah.

"Murrah knew what to ask for. He wasn't going to ask for an exemption to abolition. That wasn't going to happen. Instead he asked for something simple. A promise. He wanted a guarantee that if the federal government ever deviated from the limited powers of the Constitution that Texas would have the unquestioned authority to put secession to a state vote. Lincoln considered the proposal, then went to his desk and got out a piece of paper and a pen."

A more serious conversation had never taken place inside the Star Stop Pizza Pro.

"That doesn't sound like Lincoln," Travis said.

Cole came to Wexler's defense. "Sure it does. Abraham Lincoln had no interest in a giant federal government. What he was passionate about was the importance of the Union. A 'United' States gave America a strength both at home and abroad that it could never have otherwise."

"Yeah, but he was still opposed to secession in theory," Travis said.

"Who says?" Cole asked. "Was Lincoln against the colonies seceding from Great Britain? Was he against Texas seceding from Mexico thirty years earlier? Of course not. Lincoln believed what the Declaration of Independence said—that whenever any form of government becomes destructive to our unalienable rights, 'it is the right of the people to alter or abolish it and to institute new government.' The difference with the Civil War was that Lincoln didn't believe that the actions of the North were tyrannical. The South didn't make its case, in his opinion. Considering that a desire for slavery was one of the South's biggest arguments for war, I tend to agree with him."

Travis turned his attention back to the kid with cheese hanging from his chin. "You're telling me you've seen this document?" he asked.

"Yes."

"Then how come no one else has?"

Wexler nodded. "That's the other half of the story. So Murrah makes his pitch for this agreement, and Lincoln agrees to it. Murrah can't believe it, to be honest. Lincoln had been so vilified in the South. In the 1860 election that triggered the Civil War, Lincoln didn't get a single vote in Texas—*not one!* But there he was, signing the doc and passing it across the desk to Murrah for approval. Lincoln knew that having some friends in Texas would make Reconstruction a lot easier. They shook hands. Lincoln slipped the paper into his coat and promised Murrah that he would present the agreement to Congress the following week.

"Murrah made one critical mistake, though. On the way out of town, he met with some desperate secessionists, Confederate sympathizers who were still reeling from Lee's surrender the week before. Murrah told them of his deal, hoping they would see it as a good thing for states' rights and a guarantee against future tyranny. One of the men there didn't see it that way."

"John Wilkes Booth," Cole interrupted. He said it with conviction even though it was a guess. A good guess.

Wexler nodded. "Booth refused to believe the war was over. Plus he couldn't stand the idea of any state bending its knee to Lincoln, especially one as powerful as Texas."

"You're saying this is why Booth killed Lincoln?" Travis asked. This was all getting a little nutty.

"Booth had a lot of reasons," Wexler said, "and none of them particularly good. This was another one."

Cole was smart enough to start filling in the blanks before Wexler could do it himself. "It gave him a reason to do it when he did," he said. "If Lincoln brought that agreement to Congress, it would further deflate Booth's fanatical dream of the Confederates rising again."

Wexler took a big sip of soda and continued. "Everyone knows the next part of the story. Booth shoots Lincoln in the back of the head at Ford's Theatre, jumps from the balcony and yells, 'Sic semper tyrannis'—thus always to tyrants—breaks his leg, and escapes on his horse."

"What the hell ever happened to that letter? Someone in the White House had to find it." Travis asked.

Cole smiled. He had the rest figured out. "It was still in Lincoln's coat. Booth stole it before he jumped."

"And since even Lincoln's wife didn't know it was in there, she never knew what he really got. The only mystery for me is how it ended up in the Baylor archives," Wexler said. "I was going through a box of donated books and found an old one on Texas history. I flipped through it to see if it might be something that could fetch a nice price, and the letter fell out of the middle. It crackled as I unfolded it. The signatures all matched, the paper was the right age. It was the real deal."

"What happened to Governor Murrah?" Travis asked.

"That's no mystery. Lincoln was killed, and it became clear that no one, not even Texas, could defeat the North. So Murrah fled. Went to Mexico with the governor of Louisiana and the governor of Missouri. They buried a Confederate flag in the Rio Grande on the way. His tuberculosis only got worse. When the group got to Monterrey, they left him behind. He died a few weeks later. Thirty-nine years old."

Cole was silent with his thoughts. He expected Wexler's story to fall apart under his scrutiny, but it all made sense. It was fantastic in nature, and yet strangely probable. Travis's thoughts went another way, to the fate of Governor Murrah. That was a different time, under different circumstances, but he wondered if he was steering himself toward the same tragic end. If he could get the Lincoln-Murrah agreement, it might be enough to get the nullification votes out of the Lege. Without it . . . well, no need to go there. He needed that letter.

"Hey kid," Travis said, "how can we be sure that no one at the DOJ has already found this thing and destroyed it?"

"We can't," Wexler said, "but scientifically speaking, the slowest-moving species on the planet is humans employed by the United States federal government."

"Eventually someone will find it," Cole said.

"Uh-huh," Travis agreed. "I'd rather it be us."

17

Anatole Metzos's dining room table was round, big enough for a dozen guests at a time, and covered in a burgundy tablecloth that matched the wine, a 1994 Screaming Eagle cabernet known for its creamy finish and pretentious four-thousand-dollar-a-bottle price. The shape of the table was intentional; the host didn't want to make one person feel more or less important than another, though Paige knew that if a meteor dropped on the house and annihilated everyone, her name would be the last one mentioned in the next day's AP story. As the other guests settled into their seats, Paige looked around and couldn't help but feel as though she had hopped out of her Prius and fallen into the opening chapter of an Agatha Christie novel.

Directly across from her was Umbali Njaaga, the secretary-general of the United Nations and the only obese Nigerian on the planet. She couldn't get over the sheer size of his head. When he yawned, he sucked in so much additional air she saw the candles at the center of the table flutter. Next to Njaaga was an elegant woman in her late fifties, bejeweled and exquisitely coiffed with curls upon curls of stiff red hair. She was introduced, without further explanation, as "Countess Antonia." Antonia and her husband were direct heirs to the throne of Czar Nicholas II, and despite the monarchy being toppled almost a hundred years ago by the Bolsheviks, they remained quite bitter about it, refusing to drop their titles in the event the country should give up on capitalism and decide to give the old king-and-queen idea another go.

Metzos was in resort attire on Paige's left, wearing Top-Siders, seersucker pants, and a white Ermenegildo Zegna linen shirt. Next to him was his thirty-two-year-old wife, Stefania, a retired *Sports Illustrated* cover model from Ukraine. She was six feet tall, with straight auburn hair that stretched half that distance. Her bell-bottom pants and halter top matched her bronze skin. When she stood next to her husband, the two of them resembled a mismatched pair of salt and pepper shakers. Rounding out the group, in a full-length dishdasha robe, was Sheikh Assad bin Mahoud Raktoum, a houseguest of Metzos while on holiday from the Abu Dhabi heat.

"And you are?" Countess Antonia had asked as they mingled in the parlor a few minutes earlier. Paige was slightly embarrassed at her lack of status until Metzos interrupted to give her a title of her own.

"This is Paige Travis, unabashed agitator." Metzos winked at Paige as the countess nodded and held out her limp hand.

When everyone was seated, Stefania gripped what looked like a standard garage door opener and pushed the button. There was no noise to be heard, but a second later the service door from the kitchen swung open and a team of uniformed Latin American servants entered with bowls of gazpacho.

"It smells divine," the sheikh said, lowering his nose all the way to the rim of the bowl, then springing back up like one of those hypnotizing novelty dippy birds.

Metzos flagged down a server. "A Coke Light, please," he said to her. She nodded and returned to the kitchen. Metzos had reached that special level of wealth where you can call things by their wrong name and no one will correct you. He called blue jeans "cowboy pants." Rap music was "urban rhyme." Even Jay Leno's name was too much for him to remember. On those rare occasions when he stumbled upon the *Tonight Show*, he would refer to Leno as "that man with the chin."

Metzos had six residences scattered around the globe, but he spent most of his time here on the shore of Cherry Tree Cove, five miles south of Annapolis and an hour's drive east of Washington, D.C. It provided him convenient access to the most influential men and women in the world. He was surely included in that group, a distinction he publicly denied. Privately, on his office desk was a grainy, yellowed picture of himself at age five, a penniless Austrian exile in mismatched socks. He looked at it often, a reminder not of who he was but rather of the powerless person he vowed never again to be.

"Anatole, don't tell me you really paid four thousand dollars a bottle for this," Sheikh Assad said as he spun his glass of Screaming Eagle and watched the tannins run.

"I didn't," Metzos said. "I paid a hundred thousand for three cases."

As lunch progressed, Paige stayed quiet. She didn't feel she could add much to the conversation on overrated St. Bart's restaurants. When the entire table switched to French midconversation, it was an excuse to slip away to the restroom.

She returned to find they had shifted back to English and to a more relatable subject: her.

"Ah, Miss Travis, at last," Metzos said. "The secretary-general is dying to hear your insight on the administration's Responsible Resources Act. As he sees it, you have a few horses in this race."

Paige's mouth went dry. *Umbali Njaaga is waiting for my opinion?* She took a sip of water. "Well," she began, "I'm not going to let the Texan in me cloud the evidence. Resources are historically used as weapons in times of uncertainty. With all the global instability, it just makes sense in America to centralize control of them before things get ugly."

"Oil is up thirty dollars a barrel since the announcement," Njaaga said. "Someone's worried."

"Not I," Sheikh Assad said, raising his glass in a one-person toast to his 25 percent jump in net worth.

"Personally," Paige continued, "I think it's premature to decide what people think. People always prefer the status quo, but that doesn't mean it's in their best interest. Within a few months, I think the price will stabilize and everyone will begin to see the long-term benefits."

Paige picked up her fork and poked her foie gras, unsure of how she'd fared.

"I agree with Miss Travis," Metzos said, patting her hand.

Countess Antonia slipped back into French, and Paige ate her duck liver in happy silence. She'd more than held her own. The moment she was done, Stefania pushed the garage door opener, and the servants swooped in to clear the plates.

Paige and Metzos strolled the grounds of the estate after lunch. It was a rolling piece of land with water on three sides. He had bought the property in 1976, the year he moved to Washington. At the time, it was all grass. Devoid of character, as he saw it. The first thing he did was order a line of Chinese elms to be planted along the water's edge. The landscape architect warned about the sandy soil, but they were still thriving thirty-five years later, outlasting Metzos's first three marriages. Over time he divided the remainder of the yard into different sections, filling it with plants, flowers, and modern art.

The centerpiece of it all was a pair of heavy, square, rusty-looking sculptures, each more than seven feet high and a foot thick. They faced each other, thirty feet of grass in between. Paige knew nothing about modern art, but she recognized the squares as almost identical to ones she'd passed every day on the Yale campus. There was nothing distinctive about the squares themselves, but that was the point. She'd once overheard a campus tour guide explain that the purpose of the work was to draw one's attention to the empty space around the sculptures rather than the sculpture itself.

"Richard Serra?" Paige asked.

"Indeed," Metzos said. "A gift from the artist himself on my seventieth birthday. I told Stefania that when I die, I plan to be buried between them. Amazing, aren't they?" He knocked on one with his knuckle, sending a low *waa-waa-waa* reverberating through the steel.

Metzos set off again through the gardens, and Paige followed. "You know, Miss Travis, I am quite impressed with you. I can't help but feel your talents are being wasted in the Justice Department."

"Thank you, Mr. Metzos, but I've only been out of school a year. A job with the DOJ isn't flashy, but it's a good start."

"My fear is you're just going to languish behind a desk reading . . . *briefs*." He said the word with such pain. "Have you ever considered something more in the public eye? Something in front of the camera?"

Paige blushed. "Well, I . . . I did once pursue acting, but—"

"I thought so. I could tell. Most people your age would have crumbled back there at dinner. Hell, I know five-term senators who can't string two sentences together without slobbering all over themselves. But you were quite good. Quite good."

She beamed. Having Metzos compliment her was like the pope coming up to a new priest after church and saying, "Nice mass."

"Tell you what," Metzos continued, "I'm going to think about this. About *you*. See if I can find a better use for you. Is that alright with you?"

It wasn't technically a job offer. It was a hint of one. By saying yes, all she'd be doing was granting Metzos permission to ponder. "It would be bad manners to say no, wouldn't it?" Paige asked.

She was so caught up in the moment that she hadn't noticed they'd arrived at the pool. It was black bottomed and kidney shaped, resting at the far corner of the yard near the cove. "It's beautiful," she said. The secretary-general treaded water in the deep end while Stefania floated along on a raft, a martini glass in her hand. Both were completely naked.

Before she could think, Metzos stepped out of his boat shoes and started to unbutton his shirt. "Join us, won't you, dear?" Metzos asked. He wiggled down to nothing and dove in headfirst. *Well this just got weird,* she thought. Metzos resurfaced, looking like a distressed buoy in need of barnacle scraping. He turned to Paige.

"I promise it's exhilarating," he said.

She had no idea how to read this situation. Was this just some Euro thing? They were all speaking French at dinner. Then again it could also be a test of her loyalty—Metzos's unique way of finding out just how much she trusted him, and in turn how much he could trust her. Every second she stalled could be sending him silent signals. Paige turned and looked back at the house, fifty yards up the hill. Sheikh Assad was standing on the patio looking down on them, smoke rising from his Marlboro Red.

Shit, she whispered to herself.

"It feels as good as it looks," Stefania said, spinning her raft in a slow circle with her long fingernails.

"Well . . ." Paige was still trying to convince herself that she believed what she was about to say. "When in Rome . . ."

She took a deep breath of warm Chesapeake Bay air and slipped out of her flats.

18

It was almost dark and the governor's office remained a flurry of activity. Wexler and Cole had left on a chartered flight for Washington that morning, shortly before Travis formally announced the legislature's special session and ordered all members of the Texas House and Senate back to Austin by 8:00 A.M. the following day. Wexler was confident that that would be more than enough time to retrieve the letter, but for many senators and representatives, it was a logistical nightmare. The Lege was bound by oath to make every attempt to be there, but one member was on a cruise ship, halfway between Greenland and Iceland. "That doesn't sound like much of a cruise," Travis said. Another senator was scheduled to have a kidney transplant. Travis gently asked the senator's wife if he could talk them into pushing it a day or two, but her answer was drowned out by the noise of the dialysis machine.

As Travis passed through the bullpen, Hunter pulled him aside. "Good news. Looks like we'll have enough for a quorum," he said.

"I don't need a quorum," Travis said. "I need everyone."

"We're working on it," Hunter said. He handed him a freshly stapled doc. It was still warm from the printer. "Here's our latest draft of your speech. I think it's a home run."

"Great. Thanks," said Travis. He didn't care about a single word in that speech, but he had to pretend he did. Travis neared his office and tossed it to his secretary, Fran, sixty-something and motherly. With her buoyant hair and holiday-specific sweaters, she looked like she should be hosting a show on the Food Network. "Slip this to a few press outlets at midnight, no sooner," he said. "Make 'em feel special that they're getting it."

Fran shot out of her chair as Travis reached for the door's round brass handle and turned the knob. "Governor Travis," she said, desperate to stop him. He looked in and saw the back of a bald, tan head. "Speaker of the House Coggins's here to see you," Fran said.

Travis focused on the ring of yellow hair around Coggins's bronzed dome. He looked like Saturn. If only he were really that far away. He toyed with a few opening lines but ditched them in favor of his standby Gabe Coggins greeting. "So," Travis said, slamming the door behind him, "how's my ex-wife?"

This wasn't pathetic. At least that's what Paige had tried to convince herself all afternoon. A lot of girls are set up by their own fathers on blind dates, she thought. It was sweet. By her second appletini, she almost believed it. The deeper truth was that she felt some residual guilt about the *Post* quotes—not that she said those things but that they ended up in print—and agreeing to meet this guy was her self-inflicted penance.

Travis had told her that Wexler was the nephew of a friend in Prosper and new to D.C. In Paige's one conversation with her father, Travis hadn't exactly made him out to be future husband material.

"Have you seen a picture of him?"

"Yeah."

"Is he good-looking?"

"I don't know. Sure."

"Well, if he were a celebrity, who would he be?"

"I don't know any celebrities."

"Anything would help."

"He kind of looks like your cousin Stephanie."

"What?"

"I mean, if she were a guy."

"That doesn't sound very encouraging."

"No, he looks nice. Sweet."

"You want me to be excited about 'sweet'?"

"Hold on, I just got it. Did you ever see *Superman*?"

"He looks like Superman?"

"Oh. No, I was thinking more like Jimmy Olsen."

With nothing else to go by, Paige waited inside Kafe Leopold, a quaint Georgetown eatery, and watched the door for someone in a fedora with the word PRESS sticking out of the hatband. On the off-chance he was wonderful, she looked good. Flat-ironed hair, black fitted dress, three-inch black wedges, and just the right amount of eyeliner to make it all pop.

Adam Wexler came around the corner, shielding himself from the light rain with a blue hoodie sweatshirt. He paired it with stained Dockers and gray Roos running shoes, the kind with a tiny pocket on the side so nerds have a place to hide their allergy medicine.

Oh no, Paige thought, terrified that this was the guy.

Adam walked up to the door and pushed, missing the large-print PULL sticker in the window. The door didn't budge. He tried again with no luck.

Please no . . .

Wexler put his hands to the window and looked in, wondering if maybe he had the wrong place. One of the hosts bounced over and opened it for him.

"Sorry," he said. He scanned the waiting area for Paige without seeing her.

This might not be him, she thought.

Wexler pulled out his cell phone and began texting.

This might not be him.

He hit send. He waited. Paige held her breath. *Buzz.*

Damn.

She looked down at her phone. IM HERE. U?

She slipped her phone into her pocket. Time to dust off the old acting chops and try to enjoy a free dinner, she thought. Little did she know Adam Wexler was about to prove himself worthy of an Oscar of his own.

There were two dominant issues in the previous year's session of the Texas Legislature:

1) Entitlement reform vs. increased property taxes
2) Ben Travis vs. Gabe Coggins

The former affected more Texans. The latter was far more interesting. At the heart of it was the question of whether Speaker of the House Gabe Coggins was a home wrecker. Elements of him certainly fit the mold. He was handsome and fit, though Travis thought he looked ridiculous with those muscles, like that old man with six-pack abs in the back of airplane magazines. When he wasn't in Austin he ran a successful optometry practice in the Houston suburb of Sugar Land. When he wasn't doing either of those things he split his time between the Houston Ballet and the Houston Symphony. Travis labeled him "artsy-fartsy," while the rumor for years was that Gabe Coggins was gay. Yet until he met Kate Travis, he'd done nothing more salacious than accidentally walking out of a Kroger supermarket without paying for a bottle of chardonnay.

There was little debate over what had happened between them. Gabe Coggins made a play for Kate, and twelve months later they were married in the Bahamas by, in Travis's words, "some voodoo priestess." What remained in great dispute was the *when* of it all. Travis was convinced that Coggins was a smooth-talking lothario who had been pursuing Kate since the day Travis announced his desire to run for the state senate. Coggins insisted he hadn't made a move until the couple was publicly separated. Each man felt his honor was on trial and refused to back down. Although they were both Republicans and running for different offices in separate branches of the Texas Legislature, their feud spilled over into each other's election campaigns, thrilling their Democratic opponents and dismaying the Texas Republican Party.

Travis told party officials that he wasn't above admitting when he had been bested by a better man; he just refused to accept that Gabe Coggins represented an upgrade. Both men won their elections anyway, guaranteeing a few years of uncomfortable passes in the halls of the state capitol.

"I have to confess I'm a little offended, Ben."

"And why's that?" said Travis, knowing Coggins was the kind of guy who was offended by almost everything.

"Well, I am the Speaker of the House. I was a little surprised that I had to find out about the special session from my television. I thought I deserved a phone call."

"I'm sorry. I'm pretty sure the terms of my divorce say that I'm not allowed to call your house."

From under Coggins's seat came a tiny *yelp*.

"What was that?"

"That's . . . Rafael," Coggins said.

Travis leaned over. The dog was in one of those rectangular carrying cases with the mesh window in the front. All he could make out was a tiny pink tongue.

"Cute." It was the first time Travis ever wished he owned a pet python.

"Kate's visiting her mother in Minnesota this week. She's not well. I'm on doggie duty."

Travis normally wouldn't have missed such an easy opportunity to make a joke at Coggins's expense, but the news that his own ex-mother-in-law was sick caught him off guard. His memory of her was locked in the past, that of a spirited seventy-three-year-old who would never grow old.

"I'm sorry to hear that," he said. "Is she gonna be okay?"

"Fifty-fifty. It's cancer. They don't know how far along."

"Wow." Two years ago, he would have picked up the phone right then and there, but all the rules had changed. "I'll send her some flowers."

"That'd be nice."

They weren't used to such civility between them. Rafael broke the silence with another yelp from behind Coggins's feet.

"Anyway," Coggins said, "I was hoping you could fill me in a bit more about tomorrow's session. I'm a doctor. I like to be prepared."

Travis needed his vote, but he couldn't help himself. "Are optometrists technically doctors?"

"Yes."

"Even though you don't get the MD on the end?"

"I'm a real doctor, Ben."

He'd had his fun, but he still didn't trust Coggins enough to let him in on the big reveal. "It's all in the press release, Gabe. We need a new lieutenant governor and we need a legislative response to Washington about the RRA. Simple stuff."

"That's pretty vague."

"Is it?"

"Very."

"Look, I can't dictate action in the Lege. You know that. I can only give you guys a push."

"So then you *are* going to ask us to push?"

Travis needed to end this conversation, and quickly. "Tell you what. Let's steal a play from the liberals' playbook and just vote on it so we can find out what's in it."

Coggins spent his entire career looking into people's eyes. When he stared into Travis's, he saw a glint. "I don't know what you're hoping to accomplish, Ben, but just remember that we moderates in the Lege like our governors the same way Kate likes Rafael—well coiffed and neutered."

Adam Wexler was becoming better looking by the second. The more he talked, the less she cared that, yes, he did look like a male version of her cousin Stephanie, and while he might be boyish and awkward, so was Craig Forster, her first high school boyfriend. She dumped him after three weeks, but six years and a few dozen creeps later, Craig Forster was starting to sound pretty darn good.

". . . and that's when I knew I wanted to spend the rest of my life helping those who can't help themselves," Wexler said.

"Me, too," Paige said.

In one short hour, Wexler had crafted quite the bleeding-heart biography. He told Paige he was born in Nicaragua to proud hippie parents who had devoted their own youth to the Peace Corps. He said that they moved to Berkeley when he was ten after his mom was offered a position teaching women's studies. "Thanks to her, I think I understand women even better than I do men."

Paige seemed to be buying it, so he pressed on. His fictional father was a stay-at-home dad, happy to let his fictional mom be the breadwinner. "He was really more a friend than a father," he added, knowing he was dealing with a girl with some daddy issues. Once fictional Adam was off at college, though, his father felt called to a higher purpose and started a nonprofit organization called STOP IT! that works with A-list Hollywood celebrities to raise awareness to a whole list of environmental threats.

"Which ones?" Paige asked, now hanging on every word.

"Gwyneth Paltrow, Natalie Portman, three of the four Baldwin brothers—"

"No, I meant which issues."

"Oh. Gosh." Wexler thought, trying to remember what ridiculous things actors worry about. "Global warming, obviously. And global cooling. It could go either way at this point, that's what's scary. They were also the first group to shed light on butterfly mutation." He said it as if butterfly mutation were now common knowledge— thanks to STOP IT!

"They're mutating?"

"You haven't heard about this? It's frightening stuff. We all know caterpillars change into butterflies, but there's more and more evidence that carbon dioxide levels could be causing some butterflies to change back into caterpillars."

"Come on . . ."

"Oh, absolutely. Look it up. I mean . . ." Wexler looked down, trying to contain his pretend emotions. "Imagine your grandkids growing up in a world without butterflies."

"Terrible," she said.

There was a half-smile on her face as she said it. Not that she didn't feel bad for the butterflies—she did—but it was trumped by her fascination with the boyish suitor sitting across from her. She grabbed her purse and excused herself to the restroom, ready to reapply lipstick.

As she slipped away, Wexler shook the sleeve of his hoodie and out dropped Paige's Department of Justice ID. He had surreptitiously removed it from her wallet while she talked about her burgeoning relationship with Anatole Metzos.

There had been no mention of the skinny-dipping incident. She hadn't told a soul about that yet, worried about her friends' kneejerk response to the fact that she had a job dangled in her face and was asked to get naked thirty seconds later.

The front of Paige's ID had the DOJ seal with her headshot digitally imprinted onto the plastic. He held it up to the candle and saw a hologram of the scales of justice. On the back was a black magnetic strip. *Pretty standard stuff,* he thought. Should be enough to get him where he needed to go. He made eye contact with another guest having a drink in the shadows of a corner booth. It was Damon Cole. Given that Paige hadn't seen Cole in a decade, the corner was overkill, but showing excessive caution was his MO. Wexler held up the ID. Cole gave no visual response but took out his phone and started typing. Wexler's phone buzzed. He read the text. LET'S MOVE, ROMEO.

He was signing the check as Paige returned from the bathroom. It was too dark to notice the fresh lipstick, but the perfume was impossible to miss. It took all the self-control he had to stick to the script that he, Travis, and Cole had agreed upon before they left.

"Listen," he said, "it's getting late. I should probably head back to my apartment. Big meeting tomorrow." He was hoping she wouldn't ask for more details because he couldn't remember what he told her he did for a living.

Paige was hurt. "Oh. Okay." She pushed in her chair, deciding not to sit after all.

"But I'd love to see you again. I'll . . . I'll call you," he said.

"Great. Sure. Whatever."

Paige didn't believe him, and Wexler knew it. He felt sick. Despite the fact that he was completely using her, he liked her. Really liked her. He wondered why it always seemed to play out like this. Every time he was on the verge of conquest, life interrupted.

Cole saw Wexler stalling and started to get nervous. *Just leave, kid.* Wexler moved toward the door with Paige, then stopped.

"Listen . . ." he said.

Cole gritted his teeth. *What are you doing? Walk! Go!*

"This may be sort of crazy, but . . ."

Paige smiled. "What?"

"Nah, it's stupid." He tried to leave. She grabbed his arm.

"Tell me!"

"Well . . . can you give me a tour of the Department of Justice?"

Paige laughed. "Now?"

"Yeah, why not?"

"It's nine thirty."

"You saying there's no justice to be done after five o'clock?"

"No, I mean, we can. It's just . . . you really want to?" No one ever wanted to see where she worked. "I've got to warn you, it's not that exciting."

Wexler placed his hand on her lower back. "Then let's make it exciting."

Paige blushed. This nerd was full of surprises. She stepped toward the door as his arm continued around her back and returned her ID to the open slot of her purse. Cole watched them go, then downed his drink and signaled for the waiter.

19

For the first ninety years of American history, there was no Justice Department; just one lonely attorney general. His official duties were to represent the United States in the Supreme Court and assist the White House and Congress with legal advice when needed. The first three attorney generals combined argued a grand total of six cases in front of the Court. It was literally a part-time job.

The DOJ was founded in 1870, and as the reach of federal law expanded, so did the department. Over the next sixty-five years, dozens of other entities were either created under its banner or grafted into it. There were now so many divisions and subdivisions that only Rain Man could name them all. Many sounded identical, like the Bureau of Justice Assistance and the Bureau of Justice Statistics. Most agencies had since compressed their names into three- or four-letter acronyms, making it the switchboard operators' headache to figure out if a caller was trying to reach the OLC or the OVC. Or the OTJ. Or perhaps the OJDP, OPCL, OIPR, or the OIG.

The department had grown so unwieldy in the last half century that after various cases of internal DOJ misconduct had gone unchecked, the Office of Professional Responsibility (OPR), which exists for the sole purpose of investigating itself, was created. No one could say what would happen in the event that someone inside the OPR committed some form of malfeasance, but one might hope it would create a black hole that would suck up all seven floors and 1.2 million square feet of the Justice Department's Washington head-quarters.

The twelve angry text messages that Cole sent Wexler between the restaurant and the Justice Department headquarters had done their job, and by the time he and Paige arrived, he asked if they could cut out the boring stuff and go straight to her office.

"Don't you want to see the Great Hall?"

"Not really." He was looking for the bank of elevators.

"What about the mosaics? The colors are amazing."

"I'm color-blind, so . . ."

Paige laughed and pulled him by the elbow. "So what? You'll love them. I promise."

"You don't understand. Seeing them would be like playing Beethoven's Fifth for a deaf person. It's cruel."

"I'm sorry. I guess . . . I guess I never thought about it like that."

"It's why I can only watch the first twenty minutes of *Wizard of Oz*. Once Dorothy opens her front door after the twister, it's just too painful." He looked past her, as if making eye contact would trigger a complete emotional breakdown.

She placed her hand on his shoulder. "Let's go to my office."

Paige pushed 5 and filled the awkward elevator silence with a smile. Wexler reapplied his ChapStick and watched intently as the numbers climbed in the mirrored reflection behind her. Halfway between the third and fourth floors, he reached behind his back, felt around for the round emergency STOP button, and yanked. The elevator jolted to a halt.

"Uh-oh," he said.

Paige didn't look the slightest bit worried. "It happens all the time. They redid the system five or six years ago, and now it breaks down more than ever."

Perfect, Wexler thought. He'd found the one person in the world who wasn't panicky over being trapped in an elevator.

"Well, we can't just wait here," he said.

"Why not?"

"At some point we're going to run out of oxygen."

"I think you've seen too many movies. Besides . . . there's no rule that says all we can do in here is wait . . ."

Paige pulled him away from the controls and pressed him against the wall, bringing her lips to his. ChapStick and lipstick congealed into a pink gelatinous blend. Wexler tried to resist. But not really.

Once Coggins and Rafael were gone, Travis picked up his cell phone and dialed Cole for a progress report from Washington.

"Hey, thanks for going all out on the rental car," Cole said before Travis had a chance to even say hello. Cole was parked across the street from the DOJ building in a white Hyundai Accent with cloth seats. "You know, when James Bond went undercover, his cars tended to get fancier."

"James Bond was a spy," Travis pointed out. "He was always undercover. Anyway, a car's a car."

"Really? This one has manual windows. Good thing we're not driving anywhere with a lot of tollbooths."

"Any news from Wexler?"

No good could come of Cole telling Travis he'd decided to continue their mission with his own daughter in tow.

"No word yet, but he's been inside for a while. He must be close."

They were still making out. Wexler didn't know if it had been five minutes or fifty. He just knew that his lips had never felt so moisturized. As much as Wexler was enjoying the moment, he realized he couldn't wait forever. At some point, security was going to notice the stalled elevator flashing on their board and investigate. He separated Paige's lips from his ear and pushed her away.

"Do you smell smoke?"

She stopped and sniffed. "No."

"I do. We can't stay here."

Wexler moved to the elevator doors and forced them apart. As he'd hoped, the lit fourth-floor landing was just peeking out from the top. He tried to pull himself up on his own, but he'd used what little strength he had making out with Paige.

"Push me up and then I'll pull you up after me," he said.

"Are you sure about this?"

"Trust me."

Paige gave him a lift, and he slithered through the gap. Once out, he turned and dropped his skinny arms to pull her up. She grabbed on and waited for a tug. He made a few intentionally lame attempts before giving up. "You're too heavy," he said.

"Thanks a lot," said Paige.

"No, I mean . . . too heavy for me . . . to lift."

"Again, thanks." Wexler promised he'd be back for her and disappeared.

Wexler followed the numbers on the office doors, looking for 4183. The floor was empty at this hour. Somewhere far off he heard a vacuum. Room 4183 belonged to Gary Spawn, the Justice Department attorney who'd been assigned to his case. Wexler had insisted to Travis and Cole that once he got past DOJ security, he wasn't worried about getting into Spawn's office. There were a few secure rooms inside the DOJ, but the office of a middling second-year attorney in the criminal division wouldn't be one of them.

As he speed-walked down the long, empty hall, he peered into the other open offices. The building was in the National Register of Historic Places, but once you pierced the outer layer of art deco, limestone, and half-topless statue of Lady Justice, the place was an Office Depot nightmare.

Room 4183 was no different. Inside the door to the suite were a wooden desk, a flimsy bookshelf, and a black torchiere lamp. He moved past them to Spawn's private office. Locked. *Not a problem,* he thought. Every good assistant keeps a spare key in his or her desk for those occasions when the boss locks himself or herself out. Wexler turned the lamp on low and opened the assistant's top drawer. It could not have been messier. Pens mixed in with Post-its stuck to a topless glue stick. He tried to wade through the mess only to be jabbed by a pushpin hiding beneath a knot of rubber bands. The type A in him desperately wanted to rearrange it. At least to separate the paper clip necklace. If he got caught, maybe that would curry him some favor with the jury. "Yes, my client broke in and stole DOJ evidence, but their offices have never looked better!"

Wexler looked but couldn't find the key. No big surprise under the circumstances. He ran his hand under the desk in case the assistant kept it in the second most obvious spot. He found a few wads of gum, one of which was still squishy and moist. "Ugh," he said, wiping his hand on a yellow legal pad.

He crossed over to Spawn's door and pushed against it with his shoulder. It was thicker than he'd imagined. This wasn't the particleboard kick-it-down-with-your-foot sort of wood, not that he had the quad strength to pull off that move anyway.

He looked at the ceiling and spotted the air-conditioning vent. Paige was right: He'd seen too many movies. Air vents helped Bruce Willis maneuver through Nakatomi Plaza in *Die Hard*. They helped Tom Cruise navigate CIA headquarters in *Mission: Impossible*. It was so successful that he used one again in *Mission: Impossible III*. Off the top of his head, Wexler could remember seeing air vents employed in *Alien, Aliens, Men in Black II, Toy Story 2*, an episode of *Lost*, and too many episodes of *Star Trek* to count. Traveling through them was either complete bull or as natural a mode of transportation as walking.

He dialed one person who'd know for sure. Travis saw the number pop up on his phone, expecting a positive report. "Well?"

"Your company made A/C ducts, right?" Wexler remembered it from the infamous *Post* article.

Travis knew the mere asking of the question was a bad sign. "Yeah . . ."

"Would it hold my weight if I were to climb through one?"

"You realize they were designed to hold air, right?"

"Yeah, but I'm pretty light. One thirty-three tops."

"Still heavier than air."

Wexler hung up. He was looking for a little more optimism than that. It wasn't like he had a lot of options. He closed the outer door to the hall, then stood on the desk and unscrewed the vent with his fingers. This took longer than he imagined. In movies they usually fell open, inviting people inside. He grabbed the sharp metal edge of the tubing and pulled. It creaked under his weight, but it held. *Good to know there's still some truth in Hollywood,* he thought. He scooted through the darkness, an inch at a time, trying to ignore the groans from the strained aluminum around him. After a few more minutes, he reached the vent above Spawn's office. He held up the light from his phone to make sure, spotting a UVA diploma and a new Scotty Cameron putter.

He pushed on the vent, but it wouldn't budge. He pushed harder, popping off one of the screws. He was rearing back to pound on the other side when he was overcome by the shriek of metal scraping against metal and felt the front half of him drop a couple of inches.

"Frick."

The brackets holding the ducts in place could hold him, just not forever. He punched the vent cover one more time. It flipped open just as the brackets gave way. The entire ten-foot stretch of pipe crashed through the paneled ceiling, with Wexler still inside. A cloud of dust and shreds of pink insulation covered the office as he poured out of the tube like a Pringle and slammed chin-first onto Gary Spawn's desk.

Wexler lay on the hard wood, stunned and feeling betrayed by Tom Cruise. There wasn't time to take an inventory of what he'd broken in the fall. He rolled off the desk and hit the lights, then hobbled to a bank of five-drawer file cabinets. Every case was sorted alphabetically from the top drawer down. *Boy,* he thought, *this Gary Spawn is going to be pissed if he ever catches a glimpse inside his assistant's nightmare of a desk.* He found *W* and fingered his way through the files. There was no WEXLER.

He looked around the room. Along the far wall next to a set of bookshelves was a stack of nondescript cardboard file boxes. Each was labeled in Sharpie with the name of a pending case. GORDON, FLEMING, ROBISON, TWAY . . . WEXLER. He tossed aside the lid and pulled his stack of files. Stapled to the front of them was his mug shot. He'd never seen it. Mug shots weren't like school pictures. They didn't get developed and then delivered to your cell in big envelopes with cellophane windows in front. All in all, it was a good one. He didn't look disturbed or drunk. He wasn't smiling. He looked defiant.

He flipped through the rest of the contents as quickly as possible. There were photos of his dorm room from every possible angle. The hard drive from his laptop. Screen grabs of his correspondence with buyers. Photocopies of bank statements. At one point he had two hundred grand in a no-interest checking account. That would be damning. Then again, so would breaking into the Justice Department while out on bail. He kept digging until he came to a white legal-sized envelope. It was sealed with special red-and-white-striped tape, ensuring that Wexler wouldn't be able to open it without forever damaging the package.

Wexler tore it open anyway, reached in, and pulled out a small stack of documents and letters. The signatures at the bottom of each one represented a Who's Who of American history. John F. Kennedy, Mark Twain, Sam Houston, Douglas MacArthur . . . each came with a story. Wexler wasn't scanning the names. He was looking for a color. It was what he remembered most from the first time he saw the Lincoln-Murrah agreement. It was a deep orangey yellow—the color of weak cider—a casualty of a century and a half of exposure to the elements.

The letter was halfway down the stack. A simple note written in Abraham Lincoln's own flowery hand. Pendleton Murrah's signature was next to his. It was shakier than Lincoln's, something Wexler chalked up to a mixture of nerves and illness. The edges of the paper were worn, and there were a few scattered holes, but the document was—

Vrrrrrrr!

Outside Spawn's door, the fourth-floor cleaning lady and her vacuum had arrived at room 4183. She didn't notice the vent above the secretary's desk hanging open. She was in the semiconscious malaise that overtakes workers in any monotonous job. Every day was the same: run the vacuum, empty the trash can, put in a new liner. When she had done that seventy-three times, her night was over. She pulled the master key from her pocket, put it in the lock, and turned.

She opened the door to see Wexler standing on Spawn's desk, surrounded by debris. The vent and pipe still hung from the ceiling. He was holding Spawn's putter over his shoulder and gripping it tightly with both hands, his back to the door.

The cleaning lady snapped awake and screamed.

"Don't come in here!" Wexler warned, waving a hand in her direction without turning around.

"*Qué es esto?!*" she asked, worried that all of her family's post-9/11 fears about her being a terrorist target were about to come to fruition.

"Raccoon!"

It made sense to her, especially seeing the scratches on Wexler's face. She screamed again and slammed the door, leaving Wexler to fend for himself.

Wexler got to the bank of elevators just as one opened, carrying an unamused Paige.

"I'm saved!" he said, looking up at the heavens. He hurried into the elevator and hit the DOOR CLOSE button repeatedly.

"Where were you?" she asked. "Security said you never came down the other elevator."

He fumbled his way through an explanation of what happened. He decided against the other elevator out of fear it, too, would break and settled on the stairs . . . only to get lost trying to find them . . . and when he did find them, the twisting staircase brought on vertigo . . . "It's not important," he summarized. "I'm just glad you're okay." He wiped the sweat from the back of his neck with his hand and gave Paige a kiss on the cheek.

"But what about my office? You wanted to see it."

"I did. Crappy particleboard desk, flimsy bookshelf, torchiere lamp. Stumbled on it when I was lost."

"I like to think it has a little more character than that," Paige said.

Before Wexler could respond, the doors opened onto the first-floor lobby. An armed security guard was waiting for them. He wore navy pants and a white shirt with epaulets. Wexler took quick stock of the various things on his belt. Keys, handcuffs, taser, fifteen-round .40 caliber Glock 22 . . . The more Wexler looked, the more things he saw that could cause significant amounts of pain. "So you found him," the guard said.

"Yep," Paige said. "He got lost."

"I apologize," Wexler said. "I have a terrible sense of direction." To prove it, he pointed in the opposite direction of the exit and asked if that was the way out.

"I'm afraid I'm going to have to ask you to empty your pockets."

"What?" Paige asked. "Why?"

"He was slinking around the fourth floor without a Justice Department employee. I need to screen him."

Paige spoke up in his defense. "But like he said, he was—"

"Now," the guard said.

"Of course. Sure. Not a problem," Wexler said.

Out came his cell phone, wallet, some gum, and the receipt from dinner. The guard wasn't satisfied. He patted him down, starting with the shoulders.

Paige mouthed "I'm sorry" as Wexler faked a "no biggie" eye roll. The guard made it to his Dockers. Something gave him pause, and he zeroed in on the front right pocket.

"I said remove everything from your pockets, son."

"Didn't I? I thought I . . ." Wexler reached in and pulled out a square color photograph. His mug shot. Before turning it around for the guard, he spun it so his thumb was covering his long inmate ID number. "Passport photo," Wexler said.

The guard looked at it for a beat. Then at Wexler. Then back at the photo. "Nice lighting," he said. "You guys have a good night."

"We will," Wexler said, dropping the photo back into his khakis. He put his hand on Paige's shoulder and led her toward the exit.

"Can you believe that guy?" Paige asked once they were safely outside.

"It's okay. When you've been frisked as many times as I have, you tend to get used to it."

Paige gave him a disbelieving smile. "Is that so?"

"Oh yeah," Wexler said, playing along.

"When was the last time you were frisked?"

"About half an hour ago, actually."

"Really."

"Uh-huh. Right in the elevator, in fact."

"I'm sorry to hear that."

"No, don't apologize. She was cute. Very cute, actually."

"You think there's any future there?"

"I don't know. I'm not sure her dad's gonna like me very much."

Paige laughed and slipped her fingers between his as they headed down Ninth Street. "I'm twenty-two years old and my father is a thousand miles from here. I wouldn't worry about him." Try as he did, Wexler couldn't poke a hole in Paige's logic, even while his cell phone continued to buzz in his pocket.

Cole spent his entire night in the Hyundai. It wasn't a car that was made for sleeping. In his opinion, it was barely made for driving. He had lost track of Wexler and Paige when the happy couple left the DOJ headquarters and disappeared into the Farragut Metro station. He hoped that meant Wexler had been successful in the actual reason for the trip, but he didn't know for sure. He texted a few dozen times without any response and tried to convince himself that Wexler and Paige were doing nothing more lascivious than chatting over tea or getting caught up in a cutthroat game of Monopoly. At 5:45 A.M., his phone lit up with a text message from Wexler: C U ON PLANE.

Their chartered jet, courtesy of Travis, sat at Hyde Field, a tiny regional airport fifteen miles southeast of Washington. Every minute that the jet was made to wait was another thousand dollars. Cole had Wexler's tab at fifty-seven grand and counting. The sun was already up, and at this point they'd need to hurry just to make it to Austin before the special session started.

After another eleven thousand dollars, a yellow D.C. cab tore through the airport parking lot. Wexler jumped out. His hair was a moppy brown mess, his collared shirt untucked. There was no security at Hyde Field, and Wexler sprinted across the tarmac and straight onto the plane. Cole signaled to the pilot that they were good to go.

Wexler didn't sit down.

"Do you have fifty bucks?" he asked, out of breath.

Cole glared at him and reached into his back pocket. Sixty-eight thousand *and fifty* dollars.

Wexler returned from paying the cab and collapsed into his seat, huffing and puffing. The copilot pulled up the stairs as the pilot fired up the engines.

"We're going to be late," Cole said.

Wexler ignored him, reaching up to blast the air vent right at his face.

Cole wasn't used to having to fight for the attention of nineteen-year-olds. "What were you doing last night, anyway?"

"Busy not blowing my cover." Wexler pulled the handle near his hip and reclined his seat. With his head all the way back, a fresh hickey could be seen on his neck.

"And the letter? You do actually have it, don't you?"

"Of course." Wexler wouldn't even open his eyes.

"May I see it?"

Wexler grunted, annoyed. Without sitting up, he reached down and pulled off his right shoe. He unzipped the pocket-sized zipper in his Roos. Inside it, folded five times over, was the yellowed piece of paper.

"You wadded up a hundred-and-fifty-year-old document and stuffed it in your shoe?!"

He handed it across the aisle. "Calm down. It's fine."

"Why does it smell like lotion?"

"It's hand cream. I rubbed a little on it so it wouldn't disintegrate when I folded it."

Cole carefully unfolded it and began to read:

14 April, 1865
By issue of executive order, for the express purpose of bringing
much-needed reconciliation between the States and with the
hope of securing lasting prosperity for this Union, I pledge on my
honor this Government's fervent commitment to the Liberty and
Freedom of all American people, and its eternal bond to the
Constitution by which these states were freely grafted together . . .

Cole paused. Wexler hadn't done justice to the lyrical quality of
the document itself. Here was a president who learned to write with
a piece of charcoal for a pen and a shovel as his paper. Over the
course of his life, he only had eighteen months of formal education.
He grew up in a country that didn't have a Department of Education
(and wouldn't until 1980). There was no Harvard, Yale, or Princeton
on his résumé. He didn't need it. He had wisdom and he had virtue,
and those two things trumped everything else.

"This is amazing, Mr. Wexler," he said. "Just . . ." He looked across
the aisle. Wexler was already asleep, one shoe on, one shoe off. Cole
carefully placed the letter in his lap and settled into his leather seat,
feeling very ready to nod off himself. He tried to keep reading but
found he couldn't stay awake. He blamed the Hyundai. Within a few
seconds, he was out. When he and Adam Wexler woke up, twenty
minutes had passed. They were still on the tarmac, the engines were
running, the cabin door was open, and the letter was nowhere to be
found.

20

Ben Travis and Damon Cole stood outside the closed doors of the Texas Senate. Inside, the thirty-one senators were picking a new lieutenant governor. As they waited, Travis was still trying to piece together exactly what happened to the letter.

"So you had it," Travis said.

"Yes," said Cole.

"*Physically* had it."

"Yes."

"But now you don't."

"Correct."

"I still don't understand."

"We believe we were drugged."

"Drugged?"

"Technically, sedated. It's either that or we all just decided to take twenty-minute naps at the same time."

Travis held up his hand. "Hold on, the pilots were drugged, too?"

"Sedated. Yes, and they're not too happy about it. You'll probably be getting a call."

"And you have no idea who stole it?"

"Not really."

"Where was the letter?"

"In my lap," Cole said.

"You didn't think to keep it someplace more secure?"

"I know. In retrospect, we probably should never have taken it out of Wexler's shoe."

"It was in his *shoe*?!"

The gavel banged from inside the chamber, followed by applause. Hunter Reese had been a fly on the wall and was the first one out of the room.

"It's Big Bill," he said.

"Okay," Travis sighed, using the minimal amount of energy to say it. It was about as glowing a response as Big Bill could ever hope to receive at the mention of his name. Big Bill Lewis was the sort of Texan the rest of the country abhorred: big, loud, and obnoxious. The "big" part was apparent on first sight; the other traits were quickly discovered. Based on his diet—pathologically carnivorous—he should have been dead twenty years ago. His sixtieth birthday party wasn't so much a celebration of his life as it was a testament to modern medicine. His blood pressure was regulated with a complicated blend of prescription drugs. He had quarterly angioplasties. His gallbladder was gone, as was half of his right lung. Doctors wanted to go back in and take some more, but he refused. Another surgery would mean another unwanted break from smoking, and then what was the point of even living? His wife sided with Bill, but for selfish reasons. After his last surgery, he nearly blew her up when he snuck a cigarette while still on supplemental oxygen.

From Travis's perspective, the one good thing about Big Bill was that he came from Borger, an oil town in the dead center of the Texas panhandle. It was about as Republican a district as one could find. No one up there could remember the last time a vote was cast for a Democratic president. They even voted for Barry Goldwater in '64 over LBJ. As long as Big Bill stayed alive for the next hour—which was never a guarantee—he would support nullification without even asking for a good reason.

"There y'are, you old sonofabitch!" Big Bill emerged from the chamber, leading the other senators and holding the gavel proudly.

His free hand slapped Travis on the shoulder, causing him to lurch forward as if he'd backed into a charged defibrillator.

"Congratulations, Bill," Travis said.

"Not the way I wanted to get it, not the way I wanted to get it—but I'll sure as hell take it!" Another slap. This time Travis saw it coming and stabilized himself.

Big Bill led the way as they headed toward the house chamber on the far end of the second floor. "Come on, let's do the ol' walk and talk." He'd been drawn to politics after getting hooked on NBC's *The West Wing* and, in a subconscious effort to make life imitate art, loved having his most important political conversations on foot. "Standard setup, that's all you need from me?"

"I don't know if it's standard, but yeah. Five, maybe ten minutes tops," Travis said as they walked around the rotunda. "Call the session to order, give me the floor, I'll say what I need to say, and then it's up to you guys to sort it out."

"I rack 'em. You smack 'em." Big Bill loved talking in idioms, and the more obtuse the better.

"Something like that," Travis said.

A page held the door of the house chamber, allowing Big Bill the pleasure of being first down the center aisle. By his swagger one would have thought he'd been lieutenant governor for years. The rest of the senate followed behind. The group's arrival drew applause from the house members already assembled, who, despite the circumstances, were excited to see everyone again. It had been over a year since the entire Lege was together, and to many, it felt like the first day of school. There were hugs and laughs. Members gave each other grief about how they looked; others came with books or golf clubs they'd borrowed a year before and were finally remembering to return.

Travis, Cole, and Hunter eavesdropped from the doorway.

"Good crowd," Cole said. "Lot of energy."

"You sound like I'm about to go do stand-up." Travis turned to Hunter as Cole cinched his tie and gave the collar of his suit jacket a tug. "How many did we end up getting, anyway?"

"One seventy-four," Hunter said.

Travis was disappointed. "Guess I better give one hell of a speech."

Hunter couldn't understand Travis's paranoia. The proposal Hunter had helped write was so uncontroversial that he was surprised when Travis appeared so smitten by it. It called for a middle ground between the full-on government takeover and the status quo. It respectfully argued for no government interference in energy companies that employ fewer than two hundred people and a greater percentage of profit-sharing with the larger ones. The proposal reminded him of the kind of forward-thinking legislation that his old boss Governor Allen would have loved, and, assuming it passed, Hunter felt it would bring Travis some positive national attention for making Texas look like a team player.

Big Bill slammed his gavel against the podium five times. The house members returned to their assigned seats, and the senators sat in extra chairs that the pages had arranged along the aisles. The chamber oozed Texas history and strength. The desks were all original, made of heavy mahogany, and dated back to the late 1800s. Each one was paired with a leather chair emblazoned in gold with the state seal. The windows were shuttered and stained to match the desks. Simple white pillars held up the empty second-floor balcony, which wrapped around the entire chamber. Every open wall space in between was decorated with framed pictures of past legislatures and portraits of celebrated Texans.

"Mr. Speaker, distinguished members of the legislature"—Big Bill was reading off a script, incapable of sounding so official on his own—"per the Governor's proclamation, under the provisions of Article Four, Section Eight of the Texas Constitution, this special session of the Eighty-second Legislature is officially called to order." He banged the gavel one more time.

"Now, we've already tackled the first issue on the docket, which was filling vacancies in our leadership . . . and may I say I think my fellow senators made a wonderful choice." The crowd laughed. "Of course, that doesn't mean that we're halfway done. What's left is addressing the governor's request to shape a legislative response to President Leary's Responsible Resources Act. I know plenty of you have strong opinions on this. Me, too. But before we dive into all that, Governor Travis is here and has requested the opportunity to speak to all of us. He's spent some time thinking about this, and I know we'll be hospitable and treat him like one of us. Because, let's be honest, two weeks ago, he was." More laughter. The house had already approved Travis's request to forbid public attendance during the session, and it was obvious that a lot of the fake civility followed them out the door.

"So without further ado, I'd like us to give a warm welcome to the forty-eighth governor of the great state of Texas . . . Governor Ben Travis."

The Lege applauded and looked to the back of the chamber. "Don't forget this," Hunter said, handing Travis the hard copy of his statement.

"I'm good," Travis said, passing it back to him.

"But—" Before Hunter could stop him, Travis was en route to the dais. As he made his way down the aisle, senators and representatives put their hands out, wanting a handshake that they could use later as evidence that they were friends with the governor; unless Travis turned into a political liability, as some governors did, in which case they would deny having ever made eye contact with the man. Travis shook a few hands before walking around the high bench at the front of the chamber and climbing the wooden stairs.

Those wretched teleprompters were waiting for him on either side, wanting him to open with the same tired "good morning" and list of "thank yous" that plague political speeches. He didn't care for shout-outs. In the generation of short attention spans, he needed to start strong and grab his colleagues while he had them.

"As we speak, somewhere in the bowels of Washington, a team of overpaid bureaucrats is thinking about Texas and licking their chops." A few sleepy senators sat up straighter. "These are men and women with no experience in the energy industry. Heck, they've never run *any* business. And yet there they are, drooling over corporate audits, employee breakdowns . . . assigning values to companies they've never seen and people they'll never meet. They're probably talking about one of your constituents right now and deciding whether or not he or she gets to keep their job."

Travis wasn't sure that any of this was true—*it was*—or that it was actually taking place now—*it was*—but he knew it was inevitable.

"Ten minutes ago I didn't think I'd have to paint that picture to all of you. Unfortunately, based on the smiles I witnessed in this chamber as I came in, it's apparent that many of you don't grasp the seriousness of our situation. Some of you may not even think there's anything all that wrong with the RRA." Travis scanned the room like a teacher looking for the kid who threw the spit wad. "You also probably didn't think there was anything wrong with the federal takeover of our private banks. Or the federal takeover of all student loans. You might have scratched your head when Congress buried Wall Street in new regulations. Or passed massive bills without reading them. With money we didn't have. Resulting in legislation no one wanted. At the end of the day, though, you saw all of this the same way I did, as isolated incidents brought on by extraordinary circumstances.

"But there's a problem with this. The problem is that at some point, there are too many isolated incidents to keep calling them isolated. At some point we need to see that we're the lobster in Washington's pot, and we're not getting a bath; we're getting boiled."

Travis knew he'd stumbled onto a good line and stopped to let it marinate. He had their attention. That much was obvious. Whether or not they were agreeing with him he could only guess.

"You see, at its core the RRA isn't really about oil. It's not about natural gas. It's not even about water. It's about power and control. It's about taking the hard-earned wealth of Texans and giving it to people they deem more worthy of it.

"Why? Well, I hate to break it to those of you who haven't figured this out yet, but the elites in Washington don't much like us. After all, our success single-handedly proves their incompetence. They believe the only way to achieve meaningful progress is through big government. Through big deficits. High taxes. More regulation.

"And yet we do the opposite. We limit our government. We

balance our budget. We keep our hands off private property. We don't overtax individuals, we don't overtax businesses, and we don't badger anyone with unreasonable rules. The result is a workforce that's growing faster than in any other state. The results are individuals who aren't afraid to take risks. The results are companies that encourage innovation. The result—to steal their favorite word—is progress.

"Now, if we say yes to the RRA, we're letting Washington control an industry that it's destined to destroy. Just look at some of its recent work. In the last four years, the United States Postal Service lost twenty billion dollars. That sounds like a solid business model. What about government-owned Amtrak? It's lost thirteen billion in the last decade. But now we're expected to sit back and believe that all the country's problems will be solved if we allow them to manage the energy industry?

"My fellow Texans, let's not mince words here. This is no government takeover. It's an *invasion of idiots!*" The Lege applauded. So far they were into it.

Travis shook his head and leaned against the dais. The more he talked about the subject, the more aggravated he got. "How did this happen? I'm serious. How did we get here?" He was thinking out loud at this point, no more certain of where he was going than those listening to him. "Were we too trusting? Probably. Too nice? Absolutely. But that wasn't our biggest mistake. Our biggest mistake was forgetting to protect the things that really matter. Things like freedom. Individual responsibility. And . . ."

He stopped midsentence and turned around as if he'd been tapped on the shoulder. He walked toward Gabe Coggins, shooing him away with his hand as he squeezed past his chair.

"Liberty!" Travis said, pointing up toward the most prominent artifact in the whole house chamber. Directly over the Speaker's chair, protected by glass, was the original flag from the Battle of San Jacinto, the decisive battle of the Texas Revolution. It was six feet by six feet and featured Lady Liberty hoisting a sword into the air. Draped over her sword were three words: LIBERTY OR DEATH.

Travis returned to the podium and gripped both sides of it. "No matter what mistakes we've made, the question remains the same: What do we do now? When I became governor, I swore an oath to preserve, protect, and defend the Constitution. Little did I realize that I was taking a vow to defend a document that the powers that be are trying to erase. I can't stop them from doing it in Washington or California or even Oklahoma, but I will stop them from doing it here.

"As you already know, my attorney general has filed paperwork to fight this in federal court. We'll pursue it—but I can tell you right now that we probably won't win. If it's not killed at the district level, it will die in the Supreme Court. Another option is to nullify the RRA and go about our business. It's definitely something to consider. Of course, this administration has made it clear time and again what they do when the public resists their agenda. They do it anyway.

"No, the way I see it, there is only one way to truly protect Texas and preserve the values of this great country: Texas has no choice but to secede."

Travis braced the podium, expecting some sort of explosion. The only sound was that of shocked silence.

"I'm serious," he added. Like a needle to a balloon, the governor's reiteration broke the silence, and at once the chamber erupted in a deafening mix of hoots, boos, whistles, and cheers. Gabe Coggins leaned backward in his chair as the noise hit him like a gust of wind. Bill Lewis fumbled for his gavel and dropped it. He picked it up and hastily banged it on the dais fifteen times over, yelling "Order!" again and again until his one and a half lungs started burning, at which point he sat down and waited for the Lege to regain composure on its own.

Travis held up his hand and leaned into the mike. "The words may be radical," he said, "but the execution of it couldn't be more foundational. I'm not asking for us to pull away from the Constitution; I'm urging us to embrace it anew. The United States Constitution will be our *Republic's* Constitution. The Bill of Rights, *our*

Republic's Bill of Rights. It worked once. It will work again!" More cheers and whistles. "Now, I know there are a lot of questions to be answered and work to be done. But none of that can start without your support. I pray you make the right choice. May God bless Texas, and"—as weird as it now sounded to say—"may God bless the United States of America."

Travis stepped down from the podium as the Lege sat frozen. As he reached the center aisle, a handful of senators began to applaud while the majority remained numb. After all, these were doctors and lawyers and ranchers. They passed state budgets and divvied up tax revenue. None of them expected to be in the position of green-lighting a revolution.

Travis continued down the aisle, anxious to escape. K met him at the rear and accompanied him as he made his way around the south side of the rotunda to his office. Travis sensed the dark pair of eyes watching him as they walked. "What?" asked Travis.

"Best damn speech I ever heard," K said.

Inside his offices, Travis was met with silence. Muted staffers watched him closely, trying to gauge his sanity. They all felt duped, especially Hunter. He was still holding the speech he thought his boss was going to give. The speech he'd told his wife she'd be reading about in the paper the next day. *Mental note,* he thought, *call home . . .*

Travis steamed straight past them all and into his inner office, where Cole and Wexler were waiting, only stopping to call out one last request to Fran. "Try Paige, will you?"

21

The missed call from Austin awakened Paige. She rolled over and looked past her phone to the alarm clock. The red digital numbers blinked at her, triggering a silent panic—9:23. 9:23? 9:23! She was hurrying through the entrance of the Justice Department eighteen minutes later. Her fellow employees stopped and watched as she went. It had to be obvious that she'd had a wild night. She clearly hadn't showered. Her hair was held up in a butterfly clip. "Did I wear this outfit yesterday?" she wondered. *Oh well*, Paige decided. *I'm allowed to have a life.*

Still, she slowed to a walk as she neared her office on the fourth floor. She knew that arriving sweaty and out of breath was the fastest way to admit you've screwed up. Sashay in with a proud "Good morning!", on the other hand, and you never know. That burst of confidence might just plant some doubt in her boss's brain, enough to make him stop and think that maybe she told him she'd be late and he just forgot. Paige had eavesdropped on enough of his personal conversations to know his wife regularly chided him for being a terrible listener.

She flattened her navy skirt with her hands and turned the corner. "Good mor—" That was as far as she got with her ruse. Her boss, a paunchy man in his forties with a fondness for sailing-themed belts, was sitting in her swivel chair, hands in his lap, slowly turning back and forth with the tips of his feet. A man she didn't recognize sat on the edge of her desk. Another leaned against the wall, arms crossed. Everyone looked grim, the kind of faces one was likely to see in the opening moments of an intervention. The man against the wall, sporting a buzz cut, a cheap suit, and rubber-soled shoes, stood up straight and pulled a badge.

"Miss Travis, Agent Ross from the FBI. This is Agent Hoffman. We'd like you to come upstairs."

The White House aide followed the protocol exactly as he'd been trained. He held up the baseball in his right hand, counted to "two Mississippi," then dropped it into the whirring pitching machine. It flew across the tennis court, past the president's slow-moving bat, and stopped with a clink as it hit the chain-link fence, joining a pile of matching balls on the ground around it.

"You sure that was *two* Mississippi?" the president asked.

"Yes, Mr. President."

"I don't know. It felt like you might have dropped it early that time. Don't drop it until you've finished saying the second Mississippi."

"Yes, Mr. President." He grabbed another ball from the bucket and held it up. *One Mississippi, two Mississippi . . .*

Drop.

Whiff.

Clink.

Leary had promised St. Louis Cardinals fans the pleasure of watching him take batting practice with his "favorite" team before the summer was over, and with his approval rating in Missouri tanking—38 percent and dropping—it was decided he should do it sooner rather than later.

Drop.

Whiff.

Clink.

He never considered that hitting a moving baseball might be a challenge for him. It was, and unlike national security or foreign policy or even domestic policy, he couldn't hire someone to make him look good. It would just be him, the ball, and fifty thousand fans armed with video phones.

Drop.

Whiff.

Clink.

Ten minutes into his first cage session, the thought finally crossed his mind that he might come off looking ridiculous. Michael Leary *hated* looking ridiculous. It was why he never wore a bicycle helmet. Or at least he didn't until the first lady made it another one of her pet causes (*"Be a Helmet Hero!"*®) and he had no choice but to strap one on.

Drop.

Whiff.

Clink.

"Maybe increase it to *three* Mississippi," he said, showing off those deft problem-solving skills that 38 percent of Missourians loved.

Ruffles and Avery Adams showed up together. They'd been back and forth on who should be the one to tell Leary what Travis was attempting in Texas. In the end, they decided to do it together, hoping to divide the president's animosity between them.

As expected, Leary didn't take the news well. "What? Why?!"

Ruffles slipped the aluminum bat out of his hands, although if he'd been watching batting practice, he'd have known there was little chance of the president hitting anything. "Travis says it's the only way to stop Washington, something like that."

"The guy's wee-wee'd up, that's all. If he's got a beef, he should use the court system like a civilized human being," Leary said.

"He's trying that, too," Avery said, "but he says they don't stand a chance of winning."

"They don't!"

Leary took an angry sip from his water bottle, then signaled for the White House aide to fire up the pitching machine again. He grabbed the bat back from Ruffles.

Ruffles felt there was a lot more to discuss here. "Do you want to—"

"No, I don't. Wait and see if they have the votes. If they do, then type up the single most frightening statement you guys can come up with. Try to scare them, but keep it vague enough to give us some wiggle room."

"We'll look at the latest UN resolution against Iran," Ruffles said.

"Perfect," Leary said. The aide held up a ball. *One Mississippi* . . . "Now you two better move back. You're about to take a line drive to the head." Ruffles and Avery stepped out of the way and watched.

Drop.

Whiff.

Clink.

Paige knew the gravity of the situation when Agent Ross waved his keycard over a black sensor and pushed the round button for the seventh floor. Her clearance only allowed her to go as high as the fifth. The seventh was where all the top DOJ officials had their offices and where, according to the rumors shared during DOJ intramural softball games, "all the serious shit went down."

Her first impression was that the walls were darker and the marble floors whiter, creating the sensation that she was walking down an Oreo tipped on its end. The only signage was the glowing green EXIT signs at either end of the long hallway. Apparently even in the upper realms of government power one couldn't escape the despotic grip of OSHA. A pair of heavy black doors lay open, and the two agents led Paige inside. Beyond the black doors waited a second set, these metal and without handles. Agent Hoffman looked at the security camera mounted in the corner, and the doors opened from the other side.

The inside was nothing more exciting than a windowless conference room, just one long oval table with a dozen chairs scattered around and a telephone at either end. Until it moved locations in 2009, the obscure room on the seventh floor of the DOJ was the impenetrable home of the Foreign Intelligence Surveillance Court, the highly secretive judicial body created in 1978 with the sole authority to approve or deny government requests to spy on Americans. Few people even knew that the court existed, though its caseload had spiked in the years following 9/11. To this day there were no visitors allowed, no recordings of its proceedings, no announcements of its decisions. It was almost as if FISC didn't exist at all, which was sort of the point.

Once the court moved to D.C.'s federal courthouse, the attorney general hoped to expand his suite and remodel the old FISC room, but the reinforced concrete walls and nine-inch doors were not coming down without some serious amounts of TNT, and so it became the most secure conference room in the world.

At the far end of the conference table was David Velez, the scrappy, fifty-three-year-old attorney general. His glasses rested near the end of his nose. In front of him was a single file that appeared empty. "Have a seat, Miss Travis." He didn't feel the need to introduce himself. He knew Paige walked past his photo twice a day, and if it weren't for having a recognizable face, David Velez wouldn't be here. His legal career had begun twenty years earlier in San Diego when he went into private practice and decided he might be able to attract more clients by advertising on bus benches. His fellow Yale Law grads thought it was beneath him and that kids were just going to draw a mustache on his face. Velez grew his own—neutralizing the threat—and hired a photographer.

The ads showed him sitting at a desk with a phone up to his ear while staring at the camera, deadly serious. Beneath him were the words DAVID VELEZ PUEDE AYUDAR (or DAVID VELEZ CAN HELP in the wealthier neighborhoods). It was ridiculous but effective—here was a lawyer so busy that he couldn't even put down the phone to pose for his own ads!

Once he had clients, Velez established himself as a courtroom killer. His reputation grew as he carved out a niche clientele: people who like to sue businesses with little to no evidence of wrongdoing. He was a class-action magician, able to land multimillion-dollar settlements from fast food chains using only a smudged lunch receipt, an unrelated scientific study, and a misdiagnosed cancer scare. In his eleven years as a San Diego attorney, Velez had driven thirty-four different companies to the brink of bankruptcy and eight of them out of business altogether.

When he decided to run for California attorney general in 1992, he received an abnormally high percentage of Republican votes. Exit polls discovered that the unanticipated support came from small business owners (and their employees) who were willing to do anything to get David Velez to stop practicing law.

After one term in Sacramento, highlighted by overturning four different voter-approved propositions, he left his post and returned to Yale Law as a faculty member. Students discovered Velez was outspoken even by Yale's liberal standards. He thought the Second Amendment's right to bear arms only applied to militias, not private citizens; of course, he didn't care much for militias, either. He regularly defended the rights of American Muslims to practice Sharia law, and he routinely spoke on the importance of American judges elevating international law over the U.S. Constitution when making decisions. Most legal scholars felt that Velez's positions would relegate him to academia, but Leary offered him the job of attorney general, and he took it.

He was the most powerful lawyer in the world, and yet he couldn't use his cell phone in a public place without having some middle-aged Latino spotting him and yelling, "David Velez puede ayudar!"

"So . . ." Velez began.

Paige bit the inside of her cheek.

Velez opened the file and looked at a single sheet of white paper. "You joined the Justice Department in June of last year, currently work under the Director for the Office of the Ombudsperson . . . That's a terrible name for a division, isn't it? We should change that."

"It's a tough acronym," Paige said. "OO. Every time I answer the phone, the person on the other end thinks that something's wrong."

He looked at her, emotionless. He didn't *really* want her opinion.

"Before that you had a stint with the Office of Dispute Resolution."

"Yes."

"I'm glad to see that. Might give you a fighting chance in here."

Paige wasn't loving the mystery of what she'd actually done wrong. "Mr. Velez, would it be possible to give me a little more insight into what this is regarding?"

Velez couldn't help but be thrown. Paige seemed so sincere that either she was the greatest actress in the world or she truly didn't know what was dominating the morning's headlines.

"Miss Travis, are you not aware of what's going on in Texas?"

"With all due respect, sir, my life is in Washington. If I cared about Texas, I would be in Texas."

"I understand, but that wasn't a breezy question about your love of home. I'm asking about your father's attempt to garner a secession vote from the Texas Legislature."

"Excuse me?" The word "secession" traveled through her ears into her brain and then exploded, scattering the letters to the far reaches of her body.

"Surely you heard."

"I didn't hear. I—"

"You didn't hear?"

"No, I . . ."

Velez smiled. "Incredible. Agent Ross, notify the National Science Foundation. We've just discovered a twenty-something American who has successfully avoided all media for more than forty-five minutes. They'll want to run some tests, I'm sure."

"Sir, I normally . . . well, I was up late last night, and then I just got a late start this morning. This is all news to me. It's pretty common knowledge at this point that my father and I don't—"

"We're aware of your history. Still, you have to acknowledge that given the seriousness of his actions, I wouldn't be doing a very good job if I didn't ask. This is a little more egregious than just being behind on his taxes."

"I understand."

Velez looked down at the sheet and then quickly back up. "Just out of curiosity, he's not behind on his taxes, is he?"

"I, uh—I don't . . ."

"Never mind. Not even sure we could get him for that anyway. A third of the people working in the White House haven't paid their taxes. We make an example out of your father, suddenly half the cabinet has to start answering questions."

"Mr. Velez, all I can tell you is that my father and I are different people. With different ideologies. I don't support his views. At times I don't even understand them. Do we share a name? Yes, but nothing else. By all means look for ties or connections between us, but it would be a misuse of your valuable time and the department's resources."

Velez removed his glasses and set them on the table. "Well, it's hard to argue with such zeal," he said. Paige felt the feeling return to her extremities. "Yet let me try anyway."

Velez picked up his glasses and placed them back on the tip of his nose. He casually returned to his sheet of paper. As he read, his index finger acted as a cursor, moving along the page from left to right. After a minute, it stopped. Then, without looking up . . .

"Tell me about Adam Wexler."

22

Travis, Wexler, and Cole were spread out around the governor's office, each of them concealing something in his hands.

"Three sevens," Wexler said, staring down at the numbers on his dollar bill.

"Four threes," Cole said, looking down at his own.

"Four sevens," Travis said.

Wexler eyed Travis, looking for a tell, then kept going. "Five sevens," Wexler said.

"Five sevens?" Travis asked.

Wexler nodded.

"Liar," said Travis and Cole simultaneously.

Wexler flipped around his dollar, showing five sevens on his bill alone. "I've had it since I was ten," he said, smiling. Travis and Cole groaned and begrudgingly handed over Wexler's winnings.

Cole had wanted to watch the debate on the closed-circuit TV, but Travis wouldn't let him, figuring it would only aggravate him. They were already down twelve bucks to the kid when the bell rang in the hall.

"They're voting," Travis said.

"That was quick," Cole said as Wexler flipped on the TV. The motion on the floor was Travis's secession proposal. Technically they would have to get that one out of the way first and then move on to the lesser proposals, the first of which would hopefully be the one they wanted—nullification.

The voting process in the Lege was normally a little chaotic; because the lawmakers were only in session four months every two years, they had to pass a budget and a heap of legislation in a brief period of time. Usually their votes were recorded electronically. If they were close to their desks, they hit one of the built-in buttons. Green meant "aye," red "nay," and white "present but not voting." If they weren't able to get to their desks in time, members signaled their votes, and another member would punch their desks for them.

With only one issue on the agenda and all the time in the world, Gabe Coggins made a motion to take a voice vote instead. He wanted anyone crazy enough to vote with Travis to be forced to say so out loud.

"What a jerk," Travis said. He grabbed a sheet of paper with the names of everyone in the Lege. "How many votes do we want to see on secession?"

"I'd be happy with fifteen or twenty," Cole said, yawning. "Enough to show there could be real support for something less drastic."

The clerk called the names alphabetically. *"Representative Abbott . . ."*

"What do you know about this guy?" Cole asked. The only camera in the chamber was a wide shot, so he was relying on Travis to help add a little color commentary to the proceedings.

"He's a podiatrist from Odessa. Quiet. I say he's probably a soft yes."

"Nay!" he said forcefully. The vote was met with some applause from around the chamber.

"That sounded more like a hard no," said Wexler. Travis wrote a red *N* next to his name.

"Representative Almayo . . ."

"Monica Almayo. From El Paso. Liberal district, likes to be thought of as independent even though she isn't."

"So a nay," said Cole.

"No, she'll vote 'present.' She likes to hedge her bets in case of a presidential run," Travis said.

"*Nay.*"

"In her defense," Wexler said, "you can't become president of the U.S. if your state's no longer in the U.S."

"*Senator Ambrose . . .*"

"Definite no," Travis said.

"*Aye!*"

"We got one!" said Travis, excited it wasn't going to be a shutout. Ambrose's aye brought some boos, but also a good number of cheers.

"*Representative Barry . . .*" Cole looked to Travis.

"Hey, don't look at me. I'm oh-for-three."

"*Aye!*"

Cole was encouraged. "This is good," he said. "Now we've got a little credibility, a base that—"

"*Representative Beckman . . .*"

"*Aye.*"

"—we can build on and use for the next—"

"*Representative Bernd . . .*"

"—proposal. Even if we only end up with—"

"*Aye!*"

"—a couple votes, it's still—"

"*Senator Blake . . .*"

"*Aye!*"

Cole stopped. "Alright, what the heck?"

"Just relax, Professor," Travis said. "The early part of our alphabet leans right. There are plenty of moderates out there."

After the seventh straight aye, Cole started clearing his throat unconsciously. He was nervous, the same tell he had playing liar's poker. He had to get up and walk. Each vote of support that followed was like twisting an invisible key in his back, making him march back and forth a little more quickly across the room.

"*Representative Cass . . .*" "*Aye.*" "*Representative Chalke . . .*" "*Aye.*" "*Senator Clayton . . .*" "*Aye!*"

Gabe Coggins was panting by the time the clerk got to him. *"Nayyyyyyyy!"* he said when his name was called. He really dragged it out too, using every last *y* to cast aspersions on the integrity of the members who dared to vote otherwise. Cole's spirits brightened. Votes like this hinged on momentum, and how the other members reacted to their own Speaker would reveal a lot.

"Representative Coosey . . ." Cole and Wexler eyed Travis again.

"Well,"—he hated bursting Cole's bubble—"if those other guys voted yes, then—"

"Aye!!!" Coosey roared, holding a finger up into the air so there would be no confusion.

Wexler leaned in toward the TV. "I don't think that's his index finger."

Coosey's support began another run of passionate ayes, each of which was followed by cheers and whistles.

"Oh no," Cole said. "No no no no no . . ." He had never actually considered that secession could pass. He had barely considered that nullification would pass. His mistake was assuming that members of the Texas Legislature were like politicians everywhere else, where being in Congress is a full-time job and self-preservation is the driving force behind most decisions. Most members of the Lege only cared about *Texas* preservation, and once Travis made his case, it was a simple matter of deciding if they believed they could win—and there's where reason stopped being a factor, because Texans, independent of the situation, always believe they'll win.

After ten more minutes, Cole asked where they stood, having lost track of how close they were to the supermajority required to pass it. Travis made a quick tally and scribbled down the current total. Only when he saw the numbers in print did the reality of what was happening hit him. He stared at the paper for a moment, then turned it around for Cole and Wexler to see; *93 ayes, 12 nays.* It was a landslide.

"Whoops," Travis said. He said it with such a lightness, it was as if he were responsible for nothing more serious than over-microwaving some soup.

"Oh dear God," Cole said. "What did we do?"

"Just imagine how many votes we would have gotten if we had the letter," said Wexler.

Travis stopped counting and watched the rest unfold on TV while Cole fell onto the couch and held a pillow over his face, hoping that if he couldn't hear the rest of the ayes then maybe they wouldn't count. He'd need more than a pillow to drown out the governor's staff. As the Lege neared the magic hundred and twenty-one votes needed to send the matter on to the people, each vote was met with an ever-increasing gasp of horror from those on the other side of Travis's door.

Cole pulled the pillow off just long enough to berate Travis. "This is all your fault, I hope you realize that."

"Me?" Travis asked. "What about *you*?"

"I didn't tell them to secede, you did!"

"But you told me to do it. You said they'd never go for it!"

"Yes, but I never thought you'd be so convincing!"

"What else did you expect? I'm in business. I sell product. Today I was selling secession!"

"What was all that talk about the U.S. Constitution is *our* Constitution? The Bill of Rights is *our* Bill of Rights?"

"I thought it was good."

"It was good," Wexler added, munching on a chip.

"It was *too* good!" said Cole. "You were supposed to sound psycho. Instead you made the whole thing sound simple and easy!"

"Maybe because it is!"

Outside their door, the staff went silent. On the TV, the members of the Lege were cheering and patting each other on the back. They had the votes.

Coggins couldn't bear to hear one more aye and moved to have the clerk count the rest electronically. The motion was seconded and the remaining votes were tallied in a matter of seconds. The red electronic screen above the Speaker displayed the final count. AYES = 131 NAYS = 43. Big Bill repeated the results and banged the gavel. The motion was passed. The session was over.

All that remained was the fallout.

23

Attorney General David Velez saw no need to forward Paige's case to the DOJ's Office of Professional Responsibility (or to the DOJ's Professional Responsibility Advisory Office, which was entirely different, though he couldn't explain how). Instead, he suggested paid leave. Velez willingly admitted that he couldn't prove Paige knew anything of her father's plan. He also couldn't prove that she knew her date was breaking the terms of his bail in order to steal something—as for what, no one knew—out of his own case file. He suspected Paige didn't know, mostly because she turned green and asked for water upon learning Wexler's true identity. Still, in the name of national-security-slash-public-perception, he couldn't let her stay. She made it easy on him. She quit.

Her first call was to Anatole Metzos. Metzos offered her a position over the phone, doubled her salary, and encouraged her to take a few weeks off first. He gave her a choice of his various properties as vacation spots, though he felt it best to avoid his nature reserve outside Nairobi, what with it being elephant mating season and all. "All night long it sounds like the New York Philharmonic tuning itself," he said. Paige didn't want a vacation. She wanted to start that afternoon.

The headquarters for the Forward Foundation was only a stone's throw from the White House, an appropriate distance since many current Forward Foundation staffers had in fact thrown rocks at it during past Republican administrations. It was three stories of polished red granite with the foundation logo—two giant italicized *F*'s leaning forward—chiseled into the front. It hadn't always been known as the Forward Foundation, however. For its initial three months of existence, it was called Forward United, only to be changed when the higher-ups began to worry that the giant *F U* out front was too confrontational.

Metzos's aide, Mutuku, met Paige out front as her car pulled up. Her new boss didn't like the idea of her mixing with the hoi polloi, insisting she let him provide her with a car and driver. "Good afternoon, Miss Travis," Mutuku said, holding an umbrella over the open car door despite the lack of either rain or sun. "Mr. Metzos has asked to see you first thing upon arrival."

The lobby was bright and cheery, its interior walls lined with large-format color photos of Anatole Metzos in various candid moments. Laughing with African orphans. Carrying the Olympic Torch. Slow dancing cheek to cheek with Teresa Heinz Kerry at the Democratic National Convention. Flying over some unidentifiable natural disaster in an Apache helicopter, his hand pressed against the glass, a lone tear appearing from under his Louis Vuitton sunglasses.

Inside the elevator, Mutuku pushed a button and the doors closed. Paige grabbed for a rail when she felt herself dropping instead of rising. Mutuku smiled. Hers was the typical reaction. "Mr. Metzos says he gets more done the darker and colder it is."

The doors opened on level B2 to a lavish, but frigid, subterranean suite. The decor was a tasteful mix of things that Metzos had collected over the years. The rugs were hand woven in Iran; the forty-seven-inch brass gong was from Burma, the tapestries from Italy. His sultry blond secretary came from France, though her taste was a little more questionable. She wore a beige pencil skirt and a low-cut sleeveless silk blouse that provided two more reminders of the room's fifty-five-degree temperature.

"*Bon après-midi*, Brianne," Mutuku said. She held her smile, frozen like the rest of her, as Mutuku and Paige walked past.

Metzos's office was tucked in the suite's far corner, beyond the well-stocked kitchen and a sitting area upholstered entirely in fur from big game that Metzos had personally shot. He stood in the doorway, arms held out high as though he were awaiting a hug from a giant. "Welcome to my cave," he said. Paige continued toward him as Mutuku peeled off and took a seat on what was once a wildebeest.

The inside of Metzos's office was stark. The lack of windows meant plenty more wall space, but he feared the distraction of clutter, choosing instead to leave the gray walls bare. Except for his Herman Miller chair, the rest of his furniture (a desk, a bookshelf, an end table, and a pair of guest chairs) was all 1950s early-NASA brushed steel. Paige sat in the cushionless straight-back chair opposite the desk and shot up briefly as the bite of cold metal raced up her unsuspecting thighs.

"I like it," she said, following her breath with her eyes.

"I'm not the only one who sees the value in a cold office," Metzos said. "The humorist with the gap in his teeth"—David Letterman—"has his theater turned down to *fifty* before every show. Says it keeps the audience more alert." She looked at her arms. Goose bumps.

Metzos took his seat behind the desk and finished a Danish. When all that was left was the crumbs, he folded his paper towel like a half-pipe and poured the remaining bits into his open mouth. He unfolded the towel and fed it into the shredder next to his desk, watching with a look of quiet satisfaction as it got sliced into long strips and fell to the bottom of the plastic can.

"I love that sound," he said. "That *verrrrrrp*. The more I work, the more that machine *verrrrps*. Around here that's the sound of progress." He leaned back and cracked the seal on an ice-cold bottle of Fiji water.

"Have you ever tried Fiji?" he asked.

"I think so."

"Then you haven't tried Fiji. If you'd tried Fiji, you would have remembered Fiji." The comment didn't leave her a lot of room to argue. He leaned forward. "Brianne, bring me another Fiji!"

Brianne brought in a second Fiji bottle, half the size of Metzos's. Paige twisted off the cap on the square plastic container and lifted the bottle to her lips.

"Ah! No, not yet," he said. "Smell the cap."

"Really?"

"*Smell the cap.*"

She held the inside of it up to her nose and took a whiff. "I don't smell a thing."

"Exactly!" Metzos was delighted. "At lunch I want you to go smell an Arrowhead cap. It smells like death."

Paige was finally given permission to drink. It was smooth, almost buttery.

"Makes your bones quiver, doesn't it?" he asked. Paige's bones were quivering, but not from the water.

"Delicious," she said.

"You taste that and then you wonder . . . how does a company like Poland Spring even stay in business?"

Out of small talk, Metzos opened his top desk drawer. He pulled out a white piece of paper and slid it across the desk for Paige to read. It had that day's date at the top and a list of handwritten names beneath it, numbered from one to twenty. There was no subject or header. Just names.

"What is this?" Paige asked.

"As you know, the Forward Foundation is the heart and soul of the modern progressive movement, but I prefer to let the well-paid people upstairs work on public policy and that sort of thing. It's important. It just doesn't excite me. I like to focus on targets."

"Targets?"

"Enemies, Miss Travis. We all have them—and the sad truth is that the more good you do in the world, the more enemies you attract. Some say we should ignore them, and I understand that position. By acknowledging them, you're giving them the attention they crave. But I don't simply want to shine a light on them. I want to confront them, and in doing so, whenever possible, to sterilize them."

Metzos updated the list every day, based on his inner barometer of the latest world events. It was a bizarre collection of both the obvious and the unexpected. Radio host Walt Thompson was first and had held that spot for seven straight years. Fox News was #2. The

Tea Party as a whole was third. The Marks (Levin/Steyn) were inexplicably paired together and tied for fourth.

Paige scanned the list and stopped when she got to #5. "Ronald Reagan?"

"I know, I know," said Metzos, "he's been dead since 2004. But he's still beloved. Still referenced. Still influential. If I could find old photos of him kicking a dog, I'd pay handsomely for them." Paige moved her way down the list, hit #7, and stopped again.

"Number seven?" Metzos asked with a grin, knowing just where she was. "*Ben Travis*. Until today, no one had ever entered my list inside the top ten. Palin showed up at number twelve and went as high as number three, but your father eclipsed that this morning. Quite an achievement, really."

It stung to see his name there, even if he had set her up on a date with an accused felon. She put the piece of paper back on his desk.

"You look confused, Miss Travis."

"No, just . . . trying to understand how this affects what you want me to do for the foundation."

"It doesn't affect it. It *defines* it. I expect you to learn everything about these people. Their strengths, their weaknesses, what they eat, where they holiday, how much they tip their waiters."

"And then?"

"And then, as opportunities present themselves, you go out as the face of the Forward Foundation and—using your knowledge and charm—eradicate them . . . politically speaking, of course. You may have thought you left the stage behind at Yale, but frankly I think this is the role you were born to play."

"Oh, but still, I'd be using the foundation's positions as a—"

"The foundation gets you on the couch and in front of the camera. Our positions are secondary. When you go on with that bearded gnome"—Wolf Blitzer—"I want you to be thinking of this list. When you're sitting around that oval table with those tarts"—*The View*—"you're doing the same. And when MSNBC is lobbing softballs . . ." Metzos picked up the list and shook it.

"Even my father?"

"*Especially* your father."

Paige nodded. She got it, but Metzos sensed some reluctance.

"Miss Travis, I haven't asked, but I suspect you were drawn to politics because you wanted to make a difference."

Paige nodded. It was true, though hearing him say it out loud made it sound corny.

"Now, you may go on to work for important campaigns or push for meaningful legislation, but trust me when I say that you're never going to get another opportunity where the stakes are so clear. Our movement is on the verge of accomplishing great things in this country. Think of all your dreams for what government can be and what government can do. A fractured nation puts all of that at risk."

"You really believe I'm the right person?"

"Your mere presence endangers all the people on my list, especially your father. By simply aligning with us, you're helping to discredit him. Then factor in the fact that you're young, smart, attractive, polished . . . Compared to you, your father can't help but appear old, out of touch, demented, heartless."

"That's not much of a stretch," Paige said.

"Of course it's not—and who better to convince people of that than his very own daughter?"

Ben Travis had his feet up on the windowsill, just listening. Down below, a swarm of protesters had been at it for hours, taking turns banging on drums and yelling into megaphones. High above, three different news helicopters circled the capitol. Cole lifted his head temporarily off the couch to make sure Travis hadn't abandoned him, then returned to the fetal position.

The first protesters had gathered within minutes of the news of the secession vote. A handful came with handmade signs calling for Travis and the Lege to resign en masse. From his second-floor window, the governor made out one that read TRAVIS = TRAVISTY!

Inside the office, everything was quiet. The phone lines had crashed minutes after the vote became public and weren't expected to be up for

another hour. Travis watched ten minutes of cable news coverage, but
Cole made him turn it off. The governor had had visitors, including
Big Bill, but decided it was best to stop all of them at the door until
they had an idea of what to do with the tsunami they'd created. Travis had spent most of the day just thinking and listening to the tor-
tured noises emanating from Cole's knotted stomach.

Wexler knocked and let himself in. He had a fry dangling from
his mouth and was carrying a stack of printed-out news articles and
reactions from around the globe.

"Ah, good. Here we go," Travis said, spinning around to face him.

"You really want to do this?" Cole asked.

"We've got to know what people are saying," said Travis.

Wexler sat down across from Travis and set the pile in his lap.
"Where would you like me to start?"

"White House?" Travis suggested.

"Why do you do this to me?" asked Cole.

"Something tells me you were one of those kids who spent ten
minutes pulling off a Band-Aid," said Travis. He looked at Wexler
and nodded the signal to go ahead.

Wexler started to read. "'The president condemns Governor Ben
Travis and the Texas Legislature for their willful disregard of the
law, lack of civility, and for letting their grossly un-American views
threaten the freedom of so many patriotic and peaceful Texans.'"

Travis looked at Cole. "How am I threatening the freedom of Texans exactly?"

Wexler continued. "'Federal law does not recognize or condone
secession in any form. The president orders the state of Texas to re-
scind the proposal immediately or risk being prosecuted to the full
extent of federal law.'"

"Alright," Travis said. "Tell them that considering the way they
handpick which federal laws to enforce, that seems a little vague."

Wexler started to write down the response.

"Ben . . ." Cole said. He was hoping for an easy fix, not a counter-
attack.

"I'm serious," Travis said. "They sue one state for trying to enforce federal immigration laws, then ignore another when they announce they're not going to enforce drug laws. Congressional kickbacks go without prosecution. The president thumbs his nose at the confirmation process in Congress and just appoints people to high-level positions. I mean, Cole, you're the one who first told me this—a republic only works when it has laws and borders, and right now we've got neither. These guys are a joke."

Wexler finished jotting it down on a spiral notepad and moved on. "Did you see the Drudge Report?"

He had.

SECESSION, Y'ALL!

screamed the headline, typed out in 50-point Arial so that even those readers who were legally blind could make out the text.

"Got anything from the *New York Times?*" asked Travis. "I don't suppose I'm getting any love there."

Wexler dug till he found the *Times* and started reading its lead editorial. "'Texans have always been known for their healthy egos. But braggadocio broke new ground this morning in Austin, where Governor Ben Travis coaxed a deluded Texas Legislature into believing that secession was not only legal, but sensible. It is either a testament to Travis's genius or evidence of their mutual naïveté. The editors of this paper are convinced it is the latter, and can only imagine the land speed record that will be set as the governor finishes his ephemeral political journey from unknown to bozo.'"

"Lovely," Cole said.

"Was that end part supposed to rhyme?" asked Wexler.

"No," said Travis. "You think so?"

"It doesn't," Wexler said.

"No, it doesn't work at all," Travis said. "Hero to zero would have been better."

"Yeah, but then the *New York Times* would have had to accept the notion that anyone ever thought you were a hero," said Wexler.

"That's true."

"Do you want to respond?" asked Wexler.

"No thanks. Don't want to give them the satisfaction. Keep going."

Wexler flipped and flipped. "Well, the rest are mostly like that one, just with less pretentious words."

"Come on, there have to be some positive responses?"

"Uh, yeah," Wexler said. "One."

"Well, why are you sitting on it?" said Cole. "I'm dying here."

"Okay . . ." Wexler pulled it from the stack and paused a moment before reading. "'I congratulate Governor Travis on his bravery in standing up to the Washington tyrants. He is an example to freedom fighters everywhere. He has won the first battle, and I believe that with God's help he can win the war.'"

"That's nice," said Travis.

"Uh-huh," Wexler said.

"Who's it from?" Cole asked. He was suspicious.

Wexler shifted in his seat. "I think we should focus on the *spirit* of the message versus—"

"Who's it from?"

"Fidel Castro."

Perfect, Travis thought. Somehow in trying to stoke the flames of foundational American values, the only outside support they'd gained was from an unrepentant Communist.

"Nothing from the Oklahoma governor yet?" Cole asked.

"Not yet."

"What about the Dallas Tea Party?" asked Travis.

"No."

Travis stood up and started pacing. He always thought better that way; most men did. It was why football coaches roamed the sidelines and male lawyers burned holes in the courtroom carpet. As he walked past Wexler, he spotted something unusual on the side of his neck. "What is that?"

"Where?"

"On your neck."

"Huh? Oh, I don't know." Wexler pretended to brush it off like a pesky fly.

"Is that a hickey?"

Cole sat up straight. Finally some drama he could stomach.

"I don't know what you're talking about," Wexler said.

"On your neck. There's a hickey, and I can only think of two ways you got it. One, from wrestling a vacuum. Two, from my daughter."

"Hey, I was sedated for twenty minutes. There's no telling what those creeps did to me."

"Why were you making out with her?"

"You wanted me to do whatever I had to get that letter!"

"And . . ."

"And I got it."

"And then you lost it!"

"No, *Cole* lost it! I was sedated!"

"So was I!" Cole said, springing to life.

The three of them faced off in a triangle, the drama of the day having taken its toll. "You know what," Travis said, "it's fine. It really is." They couldn't afford to be derailed by infighting. "The measure passed, and trying to undo it is only going to make things worse. Right now we just have to regroup and figure out a plan." Cole and Wexler nodded without speaking. "Kid, call Hunter in here, will ya?" Wexler ignored the request and nervously restacked his papers. "Wexler?"

Cole put two and two together. "Hunter quit."

Wexler was happy he didn't have to say it himself. However, now that the news was out, he was ready to dish. "He said he was worried about his future."

The news pushed Travis back over the edge. "*His* future? What about our future? What about our kids' future?"

"A few other people quit, too," Wexler said.

"How many?" asked Cole.

"I don't know. A few."

Travis walked to the door. He opened it to discover the rest of the office was empty, except for K, who was sitting against the outside door playing video games on his iPhone. He looked up at them and waved.

"That's more than a few!" said Travis.

"Okay, yeah," said Wexler.

"That's basically everybody!"

"Well . . . yes."

Travis returned to his window and looked down at the protesters. They were showing no signs of stopping. The painful symphony had even added a vuvuzela horn someone had brought back from the World Cup.

"Let's call it a day," Cole said. "Give everyone a break. Including the protesters. We'll start fresh tomorrow."

Cole called in K, who walked them through the plan. They would take his private elevator all the way to the basement, where the governor's two Suburbans were in a secure garage. They'd send the first one out to get mobbed, and then they'd slip out the service entrance ninety seconds later. Two minutes after that they'd be home.

Cole began gathering up their things as K radioed the drivers.

"That's sort of weak, though, isn't it?" Travis asked.

"What are you talking about?" asked Cole.

"Sneaking away. That's the sort of thing you do when you're guilty of doing something wrong, which we're not. If people are this riled up, they'll be back the next day and the day after that. Which means the press will, too. Maybe they deserve to be heard."

"We have heard them. All day," Wexler said. "From what I've gathered, the issue they're most passionate about is kicking your ass."

"I'm going out there," Travis said. "Answer a few questions, help 'em see I'm not some monster. That sort of thing."

K wasn't one to interject himself into official state business, but from a safety perspective this made as much sense as letting your toddler be a dry-cleaning bag for Halloween. "These aren't your 1960s hippie protesters, Governor," he said. "There may be a handful in there like that, but the majority of them are thugs that the unions have paid to just come and be angry."

"And ironically, not even paid particularly well," Cole said.

"Three minutes," Travis said.

The governor rolled up his sleeves as he and K walked toward the south exit of the capitol. A pair of Texas state troopers—brown pants, brown shirts, cowboy hats—stood just inside. Five more were lined up on the outside. The bright lights of handheld news cameras lit their faces as reporters stood inside the police barricades and filed reports for the evening news.

The troopers on the inside couldn't believe who was coming their way and raised their eyebrows. "I know, I know," K said.

Travis was immediately swarmed by microphones and cameras. Cindi Patti, Channel 13 ABC Houston, was in the middle of them. "Governor Travis, Cindi Patti, Channel 13 ABC Houston, when did you decide to pursue secession?"

"Not a good time, Cindi," he said. K tried to push them aside, but Cindi Patti was battle tested.

"Have you heard from the president?"

"No, but it took him four months to decide how many troops to send to Afghanistan. I'm giving him six months before he figures out what to do with Texas."

Travis patted Cindi gently on the shoulder and turned away from the lights. K pushed through the throng and up to the police lines as Travis drafted behind him. Thirty officers in full riot gear—helmets, masks, batons, shields, body armor—had been keeping the mob of about four hundred at bay for over three hours and, like K, would have preferred that Travis hadn't dropped by to say hello.

"There he is!" one of the protesters yelled.

The crowd took his arrival as evidence that they were winning and let him have it. He was greeted with a chorus of whistles and

R-rated obscenities. The guy on the vuvuzela went nuts, blasting a hundred twenty-seven decibels into Travis's eardrum.

K was right, Travis thought, this didn't feel like the typical Austin liberal crowd. Most of the protesters were outfitted in matching purple T-shirts. On the front were yellow fists, the favorite icon of the Socialist Workers Party. On the back . . . well, Travis couldn't see the back since every single person was currently facing him and screaming.

Travis signaled for them to be quiet so he could talk. They refused, many of them opting to give him the finger instead. Near the front was a protester with a megaphone. Travis pointed at it and signaled that he'd like to borrow it.

The protester held up the megaphone and used it to tell Travis to go to hell.

"Just for a minute," Travis said, holding up a finger.

"Nazi pig!" The crowd cheered in agreement, despite the glaring lack of historical parallels.

This isn't working, Travis thought.

The voices drowned out the megaphone and started to surge forward. The police muscled up and pushed back, triggering cries of police brutality.

"Let's get out of here, chief," K said.

Someone a few rows back ripped the wooden stake from a sign and heaved it at a cop. He saw it coming and stepped back, causing a purple-shirted protester to fall through the line. Before the protester could get to his feet, he took a billy club to the shoulder and fell back to the ground in a heap.

"Hey!" Travis yelled, rushing forward to protect him. He'd only taken a few steps when an empty bottle smashed against his own face. The crowd cheered as Travis fell sideways, his head landing hard against one of the granite steps. The noise around him grew distant, pulling away from him like a wave that had pushed him underwater. He knew from his football days that he was losing consciousness. He tasted something warm and salty and then, just as he was blacking out, felt the unmistakable sensation of being carried away in the muscled arms of a large Hawaiian.

24

Travis regained consciousness in the ambulance, though given the rate at which they were speeding and the tightness of their turns, he would have preferred if they'd knocked him back out again. The driver wasn't driving so fast because of the actual injury—it was a fairly standard Stage 3 concussion with facial lacerations—but because of the victim. If Travis had been some drunk UT student they scraped off the sidewalk outside the Jackalope, the two EMTs would have taken their sweet time, maybe even stopping at Chick-fil-A for some nuggets on the way.

Instead, he was swarmed by medical personnel the moment they pulled up to the ER at Brackenridge Hospital. Someone wrapped a blood pressure cuff around his arm and began squeezing. A nurse cut off his shirt while another glued a heart monitor to his chest. Once they'd placed him in a room with uniformed police at the door, the hospital's top physicians huddled in the corner to consult on treatment. They were all in agreement: five stitches, a CAT scan, Tylenol, and plenty of sleep.

The sleep turned out to be the hard part. Travis found that he could only do it in ten-minute increments. He'd fall asleep dizzy, wake up with a headache, have five or ten alert minutes, and then repeat the cycle all over again. "PCS," the four doctors said in unison when he complained about it. "PCS" sounded much better than "post-concussion syndrome" and far less scary than "shell shock," which is what it used to be called. It happened to 25 percent of concussion victims, with headache, dizziness, fatigue, and insomnia being the most common symptoms. Of course, that described most men in their fifties. There was no treatment for it other than time.

"Usually it goes away in a day," Doctor #1 said.

"Or a week," said Doctor #2.

"Sometimes a month," said Doctor #3.

Doctor #4 didn't want to be left out. "Occasionally a year."

"Good thing there're only four of you," Travis said.

The next morning, with the stitches in place and fresh off his latest ten-minute nap, Travis assembled the entire executive branch, which now consisted of only him, Damon Cole, and Adam Wexler.

"Do I dare ask for a new update?" Travis inquired as Cole and Wexler tiptoed in.

"Forget about that. How are you feeling?" asked Cole.

"Geez, it's that bad, huh?" Travis grabbed the remote and tried to raise the bed. It stopped with his head still reclined at a thirty-degree angle, perfect for a teeth cleaning or sunbathing but annoying when trying to run a state he'd left in turmoil.

The public takedown of Travis hadn't done much for their cause. It gave the mainstream media another twelve hours to get in front of the story without a word from the man who started it all. In a twenty-four-hour news cycle, that much one-sided reporting was often fatal. The polls were proving it. *USA Today* was reporting that Travis had the support of just 28 percent of Texans and just 8 percent nationally.

Cole led with the bad poll numbers; Wexler moved on to other damaging news. "Some senator from San Antonio has been getting a lot of face time on the news. He said your speech was 'tinged with racism.'"

"What?! That's absurd!" Irritability was another common PCS symptom. "What did the people who voted for it say?"

"They called him a liar, but the media's been painting them as racist, too," said Cole. Travis pushed the remote again, trying in vain to get another few degrees out of that bed.

"Let's be fair," said Wexler. "You did say the word 'secede.'"

"So?" asked Travis.

"It's a loaded word," Cole said. "It makes people uncomfortable. Looking back, we probably should have just invented a different term for it to avoid the whole issue. Like 'evacuate.' That might have worked better."

Travis's dizziness was returning. "Use whatever word you want, it's not racist. Why don't we put out a transcript of my speech and let the people decide?"

"I tried, but it doesn't exist," Wexler said. "Per your request, the press wasn't allowed in the chamber."

"Damn," Travis said. He'd done that to allow squeamish Lege voters to speak their mind, not give his opponents a blank check to make up their own version of what happened.

"If you had a rough draft of your speech, we could try to re-create it," Cole said.

"It was off the cuff, Damon! I was in the moment. That was the whole point." The room was spinning.

Cole crossed his legs. "In retrospect, we probably—"

Travis shot him a look, cutting him off. The five stitches above Travis's eye made him look far more menacing than usual. "What about video? They must have that."

"It was streaming, but not recorded," Wexler said. "Again . . . per your request."

The heart monitor began to flash its number in red as Travis's ticker hit 90 beats per minute. He laid his head back on his pillow and closed his eyes, angry but now barely awake. "So . . . let's summarize, shall we? I'm a crazy racist—and there's no evidence to say otherwise."

"Yes," said Cole. "Basically everything that actually happened yesterday has been left up to the imagination."

"Well, not everything," said Wexler. "Channel 13 did get a clear shot of you getting nailed in the head. Went viral and everything."

Travis couldn't take any more. His heart rate monitor hit 110, triggering an alarm. A pair of roly-poly nurses ran in, expecting to see Travis clutching his chest and gripping a rosary.

"Code Blue!" one of them screamed back into the hall.

"I'm . . . fine," Travis said. "Just . . . tired."

It wasn't that reassuring. The head nurse didn't know where to start. "Who put his bed up?!" she yelled at no one and everyone. "Helen, find the cuff. The *cuff*!" Helen dropped to all fours to find his missing blood pressure cuff while the head nurse reclined Travis's bed. "I'm still under here!" Helen screamed as the governor came down on top of her.

Doctors #1 through #4 hurried into the room and ignored the chaos of the nurses, locking their eyes on Travis's monitor: 95 . . . 82 . . . 76 . . . 68 . . . 65 . . . 65 . . . 65. They waited another thirty seconds until they were sure the numbers had leveled off, then turned to their patient's guests. "Maybe it would be best . . ."

Cole and Wexler took the hint and were gone before they finished the sentence.

The staff at Brackenridge Hospital was more than happy to release Governor Travis into Damon Cole's care. They couldn't fix the shell shock, and they couldn't explain the heart scare, so better to have him sign three inches of paperwork promising not to sue and let him be on his way than take the chance of being known as "the hospital that killed Ben Travis."

Travis had the hospital inform the press that he was headed to his ranch for a few days of doctor-recommended R&R, but he made sure they didn't make the announcement until he was gone. He was in his own bed by six that night. He slept better, not great, and was up by five. He popped some extra-strength Tylenol, poured a mug of black coffee, and lumbered out to the porch to find Gene, his suntanned, hippophobic ranch hand. In his boss's absence, Gene had worked up the courage to walk and feed the horses but still wasn't ready to ride them. "Welcome back, Mr. Governor," he said.

"Howdy, Gene," Travis said.

"Nice cut you got there," he said. "Gonna leave a nasty scar, huh?"

"Nah, the doctors say it's gonna heal up alright."

"Nope. That'll scar. You can tell by the edges." He held up a finger and made a vertical zigzag, likening Travis's forehead to the Marianas Trench. As a participant in more than twenty bar fights, Gene prided himself on his wound knowledge.

"Well, I guess we'll just have to wait and see, then," said Travis.

"You can wait all you want. I already see." Gene put his head down and went back to sanding the porch railing as Travis settled into a rocking chair. "So what next?" Gene asked, not looking up.

"What do you mean, what next?" said Travis.

"You got the Lege on your side," Gene said. "What next?"

It was the question he'd been avoiding since he blacked out. "I don't know, Gene. It's not much fun being a piñata."

"Boo-hoo," Gene said.

"Excuse me?"

"I heard you take the oath. There was nothing in there about only doing the job until it got too hard. The way I see it, you can't stop now."

"You haven't seen the polls, Gene. I'm despised. And I'm not going to force something on people that they don't want. That's how Leary operates, not me."

"You know why they take polls? Because people's minds are always changing. One day they love you, next day they hate you. One day they like Doritos. The next day, Tostitos."

"It's hard to come back from crazy."

"That's just the catfish talking. All mouth, no brain. Anyway, that's why you've got to show them something. That you're different. You talk and people will listen."

"Who's gonna listen?"

"I will."

"You don't even vote!"

"I would for this!" Gene said. "Two or three times if I have to."

Travis decided not to go into the nuances of the democratic process.

"Well, thanks, Gene. I appreciate your advice." He tried to change the subject. "Porch is looking good."

It was a brush-off and Gene knew it. "Governor, I know my job is to shovel manure and dig your ditches, but I'm not going to shut up because, well, I'm a Texan and I can't help it."

Travis sighed. "Sorry. Go ahead."

"Now, the way I see it you only got two options. You keep going. Or you quit. But if you quit, what are you trying to save? Even if you do nothing but sit here and count sunsets, your career's shot. Texas is about to be sucked dry. That teenage thief of yours is headed to prison forever. And Paige don't want nothing to do with you. If you want that to be your legacy, I can't stop you. But as far as exit strategies go, yours is shit."

Travis waited on the porch until exactly 8:04 A.M. and dialed the number. He still had it in his cell phone's memory, and it was easy to find since it was the only one that started with 212. The line was busy. He tried again. Busy. He wasn't surprised. After twenty minutes of nonstop calling, it rang through and a woman answered.

"*Walt Thompson Radio Show.*"

"This is Governor Ben Travis. Calling for Walt."

"Oh . . . o-kay." The call screener looked at the caller ID and saw it was coming from a cell phone in Texas, but that was hardly proof he was who he said he was. With fifteen million listeners a week, she was used to prank calls and pretty good at sniffing them out.

"Governor Travis, do you have a specific message you'd like me to pass along to Walt?"

"Sure. Tell him he got me into this mess and I'm pissed."

She put Travis on hold, then relayed the message to Walt, who, upon hearing it, let loose a phlegmy cough-slash-laugh and snuffed out his Davidoff cigar in an official *Walt Thompson Radio Show* ashtray, available at waltthompsonradioshow.com for the unbeatable price of $12.99. "Put him on the board," he said.

Walt waited until the bottom of the hour before bringing him on, then spent another five minutes building up the suspense surrounding his surprise guest before finally patching Travis through. "Welcome to *The Walt Thompson Radio Show* for the very first time . . . Governor Ben Travis. Governor, thanks for joining us."

"You're welcome, Walt."

"You've had quite a couple days. How are you feeling?"

"Other than the Frankenstein stitches on my head, I'm doing okay. I'm still waiting for my flowers from you though."

"Huk-huk-huk," Walt cough-laughed again. "Yes, well, Top Flowers is always my choice for the freshest bouquets at the most affordable prices. Simply enter the word 'Walt' in the referral box at checkout and . . ."

Travis couldn't believe it. He was turning his call into a freakin' plug? He stifled his postconcussion irritability, knowing he needed Walt right now far more than Walt needed him.

"So, Governor, you've been up, you've been down, over and now *out* . . . *huk-huk-huk* . . . the question everybody wants to know is, are you *in*? And I guess by that I mean, is this for real? Or was the secession vote purely symbolic as some have suggested?"

Travis took a breath. There was no backpedaling from this. "It's not symbolic, Walt. This is happening. And in a week from tomorrow, the people of Texas get to decide if they think it's a good idea or a terrible one."

Walt sat up straight and pulled the microphone closer. "Whoa. Well, okay then." He, like many people, had already written Travis off as a punch line. "Although if we believe the numbers, right now you're not even close."

"You're right. Eight days isn't much time. But between now and then I'm going to lay out exactly why I believe what I believe. I'm going to explain how we got here. And I'm going to explain how a free Texas will work—and I sincerely believe that it *will* work."

"Governor, what makes you think that President Leary is so understanding that he's going to just let Texas go?"

"If I can only convince Texans this makes sense, you're probably right. Leary won't have it. But if I can convince a majority of

Americans that we have the right to do this, and that every state threatened by tyranny does, I think he'd have to consider the ramifications of trying to stop us. The last time Leary thought he knew better than the people, it cost his party the House. Pretty sure this would cost him the presidency."

"So, a little over a week to turn public approval nationwide in your favor? Good luck."

"Well, see, that's where you come in, Walt."

"Now hold on . . . *huk-huk-huk* . . ."

"Twenty minutes a show. Every day till the vote. It's Thursday so let's try it for two days. If your ratings don't spike because of it, you don't have to have me back on Monday. Simple."

Walt didn't like anyone else being the pitchman other than himself. "Now, Governor, if you've been a loyal listener, you'd know that no one appreciates profit as much as I do, but you'd also know I'm not going to genuflect on the altar of any one politician."

"I'm not asking you to genuflect, Walt. In fact, there's nothing I'd enjoy more than for you to challenge me on anything I say. If you think I'm wrong, tell me."

Walt clipped the end off a new cigar and weighed the offer. He decided that it was safer for the time being to change the subject. "Governor, I'd rather use our time to ask you about the unsavory accusations out there concerning what you did or did not say in the Texas House chamber yesterday. Specifically the racism charge—"

"That's easy, Walt. They're lying."

"So you didn't say—"

"They're lying. And to be honest, I don't fully understand why. That's for other people to figure out. I don't have the ability to look into people's souls. What I do know, and you'll agree with me here, is that the system is broken. Unfortunately, the most anyone wants to do is talk about reforms. But we're so far beyond reforms right now. I wish we weren't. I wish someone could push us back on the road and off we'd go. If that were the case, you better believe that Texas would be there pushing. But the car's totaled, Walt, and you don't start fixing it by pounding out the dents. You go back and you get an engine that works."

"That's right." Walt was glad to hear Travis making sense. He lit his cigar and leaned back in his chair to watch the smoke disappear. He knew this was good radio.

"We know what that engine is," Travis continued. "It was the one our Founders drew up for us. It was a response to the heavy hand of the British government. It had limited powers, low taxes, and relied on local communities and governments to take care of their own problems. Washington was supposed to be the last line of defense. Now it's the first stop on the gravy train. The whole hierarchy has been turned upside down. And hey, I'm no fool. I know this country's a heck of a lot bigger and more complicated than it was in the eighteenth century. But we're making a mistake in assuming our government was ever intended to grow along with it."

Walt puffed away, seeing no reason to interrupt.

"You still there, Walt?"

"Loving every second of it, Governor."

"Alright, good. Now listen, my opponents might agree that we have problems, but they don't like our solutions. They say we need new ideas. Well, I don't see why we need new ideas when the old ones worked. Their ideas, on the other hand, have failed every time they've been tried. Central planning always results in a big government getting bigger and high taxes getting higher, and eventually they swallow the peace and prosperity they claimed to protect! Look at Greece. Or France. Or Japan. Or the Soviet Union. You name a failed empire and you'll find a big government in its ruins. No thanks. I like the government Thomas Jefferson gave me. The one George Washington fought for. That's the government that Texas agreed to. One that rewards success and doesn't shackle opportunity. Not the one we've got today."

"Which leads us back to secession . . ."

Travis looked and saw Cole standing on the other side of the screen door, still in his pajamas, wide-eyed and worried about who

Travis was talking to in his condition. "You know, Walt, I'm not really comfortable with that term."

"No?"

"Think of it more like . . . an evacuation."

Huk-huk-huk-huk-huk-huk . . . Score one for Cole. They were fifteen seconds away from a hard commercial break; just enough time for Walt to compose himself and squeeze in one last question.

"So, Governor Travis, for the record, then, is it safe to say that you're *not* crazy?"

Travis could hear the bumper music building in the background. It was Billy Joel's "You May Be Right." He smiled, knowing where they were going, and decided to play along.

"Walt, I'm from Texas. We're all a little crazy."

Walt *huk-huk-huk*'ed, snuck in a pitch for P. F. Chang's, and asked the governor to call in again tomorrow. As Travis hung up, the Piano Man was just getting to the chorus: *You may be right / I may be crazy / but it just may be a lunatic you're looking for* . . .

25

The presidential motorcade sped west through West Hollywood, clocking sixty miles an hour on closed-off Santa Monica Boulevard, a street where commuters often felt lucky just to be outpacing pedestrians. End to end the line of vehicles stretched four city blocks and had successfully clogged rush hour traffic throughout Los Angeles. The breakdown of it all read like an annoying Christmas song: twelve squad cars flashing, eleven Secret Service men glaring, ten black Suburbans, nine pooled reporters, eight undercover coppers, seven motorcycle officers, six communications vans, fiiiiiive on-call chefs . . .

Right in the center was the presidential limousine, a.k.a the Beast. Its doors were armor plated and eight inches thick. Standard equipment included night-vision cameras, pump-action shotguns, and three units of the president's blood in case of emergency. At eight miles a gallon, the 6.5-liter diesel engine was slightly more fuel efficient than a Carnival cruise ship. The taxpayer tab for the eight-hour trip to Los Angeles and back was four million dollars, but Leary was confident it would be worth it once the public had a chance to see his interview that night with Conan O'Brien.

"Your best sit-down ever," Ruffles said while clicking through his BlackBerry.

The president was fighting fire with fire. Travis's second appearance on Walt Thompson's show that morning had netted Walt his biggest ratings in ten years and bumped the number of Texans in favor of secession from 28 percent to 39. The national sentiment about it saw a big bump, too, a fact Leary took as an affront to what he saw as his exclusive ability to use the popular media to move the needle. In response, his *Conan* would air tonight, his *Face the Nation* interview Sunday morning, and, as luck would have it, his voicing of himself for an episode of *The Simpsons* on Sunday night.

"Better than Travis?" Leary asked after stewing a bit.

"What?"

"Was I better than Travis would have been?"

It wasn't beneath Ruffles to make up answers to hypotheticals. "Oh sure. You bet."

"You're holding something back," Leary said.

"Am I? No, you were great. The audience loved you."

"What did I do wrong?"

"Nothing," said Ruffles. He knew the president wouldn't relent until he said something. "I just think . . . in the future . . . it's best to not try and explain the intricacies of the Federal Reserve system to an audience of stoned twenty-year-olds."

Leary grumbled a nonresponse while he watched Beverly Hills fly by in a blur. He had never battled self-doubt before, but ever since the crushing midterms, less and less was making sense to him. "Why is he so popular, anyway?" he asked.

"Who?" Ruffles asked. "Conan? Because he's funny without being threatening."

"Not Conan, *Travis*."

"Oh." Ruffles had been in the political game his entire life. He started as a junior staffer to the mayor of Boston, a job that found him dunking the mayor's head in a sink of cold water most Monday mornings. Like nearly all of the cabinet and White House staff, he'd never held a job in the private sector. While he didn't have many marketable skills, he had grown adept at knowing what people liked and why. "Travis is simple," he said after giving it some thought.

"Uncluttered. There's no second layer there. No real skeletons, unfortunately. He is what he is and people are either going to like him or they won't."

Leary nodded. It made sense. "So how do we shut him up?" he asked.

"If I were you?"

"Yes."

"If I were you, I wouldn't try to shut him up," said Ruffles. "You stay out of it. No need to make yourself look small."

"Then let's silence Walt Thompson," the president said.

"Under what pretense?"

Leary could think of three or four reasons. He led with the most damning. "How about aiding and abetting an enemy of the United States?"

Ruffles grinned. "I like that."

"Good," Leary said. "Then call the FBI. Have them pay Walt Thompson a little visit."

"Welcome back, Governor!"

Travis nearly tumbled back into the hall at the sight of his secretary, Fran. There wasn't anything particularly scary about her—though her stars-and-stripes sweater was an odd choice, all things considered—it was the fact he and Cole thought they were returning to an abandoned office.

"Welcome back to you, too," he said.

Travis had said it to make a point, but Fran laughed at the jab as if she were sitting front row at a Don Rickles concert and had just been called a hockey puck. In her eyes, that was a safer response than telling the governor the truth, which was that she went home two days ago like the rest of the office only to be reminded by her livid husband that she only had three more months until she qualified for her full retirement. He didn't give a damn what she thought about secession; that pension was going to pay the mortgage on their two-bedroom in Fort Myers.

Travis steadied himself and stepped into the office. Any sudden movement like the one he'd just experienced triggered a fresh bout of dizziness, so he took it slowly. His headache wasn't gone either, but thinking about it wasn't going to make it go away. He moved past Fran to find dozens of bouquets of flowers and enough helium balloons to lift the dome off the capitol.

"Somebody die?" Travis asked, taking it all in.

"You. Almost," said Cole.

Travis picked one bouquet at random and pulled out the card. He read it once to himself then a second time out loud. "'Don't screw this up. Sincerely, Sue.'"

Cole thought about it for a moment. "Who's Sue?"

"Beats me," Travis said.

"There's more in your office," Fran said. "Five or six dozen from Walt Thompson himself."

Travis spotted one of the deserted desks. It was completely covered in a mountain of mail, like the one dumped on the judge's bench at the end of *Miracle on 34th Street*.

"What the heck is that?"

"Came yesterday," Fran said. "I haven't sorted it yet."

"No kidding," said Travis.

"You also have a slew of messages," said Fran. She flipped through her notepad. "I'm still getting caught up, but the governors of Oklahoma and Louisiana heard you on Walt yesterday and today. They're offering their help if you need it."

Travis and Cole shared a look of surprise. They weren't used to good news. "Fantastic," Travis said. "Tell them I'll call later."

Fran wasn't done. "And Mike McKill called. Three times, actually."

Travis couldn't imagine this was true. "The actual Mike McKill?"

Part martial artist, part gunslinger, Mike McKill was Hollywood's highest-paid actor for sixteen months between the fall of 1991 and spring of 1993. In that brief stretch, he made a staggering ten movies, all with roughly the same plot but set in different countries. The box office was strong for the first three, but in time the public grew wise to the fact that McKill was phoning in his performance and cashing in on their ignorance. He was Chuck Norris without the chops (karate or acting), and his loyal audience turned against him, sending his last three movies, for which he received ten million dollars apiece, directly to video. He hadn't been heard from since, not that anyone was complaining.

"Ugh, he's terrible," Cole said.

"Hold on," Travis said. "Did you ever see *Blood Storm*?"

"No," said Cole.

"What about *Pistol Whipped*?"

"No," said Cole.

"So how can you say he's terrible?"

"How can you say the names of those two movies and argue that he's anything but?" Cole was a movie snob, making a point of seeing every Oscar-nominated film each year in order to sound intelligent at Princeton holiday parties. Travis also contended that Cole was the only black man in America who had seen every Woody Allen movie ever made.

"Anyway," Fran said, "Mike McKill says he's a big fan of yours. He'd really love to talk."

"Okay, well, not now," said Travis. "I'm supposed to meet with Big Bill. Let me know when he gets here."

From inside Travis's office came a response that bore through the oak door like a high-powered drill. "I'm here, ya big idiot. And you're five minutes late!"

26

Like seemingly every important structure built in nineteenth-century America, the governor's mansion in Austin was designed in the Greek Revival style of architecture, fronted by six white thirty-foot-tall columns. It was square in shape, two stories, with just eight main rooms; opulent by 1856 standards, but quaint when compared to many of the McMansions that hugged the hillsides above Lake Austin.

There had been changes to the mansion over the years, a bigger kitchen, larger family room, but never a petition to start over. There was too much history. Visitors could still see the filled-in nail holes on the railing of the main staircase where former governor James Hogg once hammered tacks to keep his children from sliding down the banister. Until the mansion was damaged by an arsonist a few years back, it had been the oldest continuously occupied residence west of the Mississippi.

None of that made the basement smell any better, which was where Adam Wexler had been banished. It was a dank maze of pipes—some hot, some cold—with just enough lightbulbs to illuminate a third of it, leaving Wexler to guess about what was occupying the other two-thirds. From what he could tell, his bed and desk were surrounded by an antique chalkboard, abandoned Christmas decorations, carpet cleaners, Ball jars full of blackened strawberry preserves, and some still unidentified nocturnal creature. On his first journey into the darkness, he found an old Ping-Pong table and challenged K to a game. The first time a ball hit the net, the ancient string disintegrated into a puff of dust. After ten minutes, all that remained was the two posts on either end.

Wexler wasn't down there by choice. Travis sent him there, partly as punishment for making out with his daughter while on official state business and partly to keep him hidden in the event the Feds came knocking. It also turned out to be a nice quiet spot for Wexler to get some work done. With Travis busy yukking it up with Walt, Wexler was employing his computer savvy to spread Travis's messages online. So far Travis had a hundred thousand people following him on Twitter and three hundred thousand fans on Facebook. Travis didn't know what either of those things meant but took Wexler's word for it that it was impressive.

Travis was more concerned about tracking down the missing Lincoln letter. That wasn't going to be quite as easy as expanding the governor's social network. The crew of the plane had gone quiet after meeting with lawyers and was readying a lawsuit, though none of them had decided exactly who they were suing and why. Wexler was left to do his own ruminating, and hadn't gotten very far.

There were no eyewitnesses and no evidence. That wasn't a good starting place. The only lead was the fact that the culprit somehow knew Wexler had the letter in his possession that night. Wexler never told Paige what he had hidden in his shoe, and both Travis and Cole insisted they hadn't told anyone either. That only left one more avenue for Wexler to pursue.

The governor's mansion had been the last stop for the FedEx truck the previous night, delivering Travis an overnight envelope. He took one look at the contents and knew it had to be for Wexler. Inside was a four-inch stack of rewritable DVDs, unmarked and held together with a pair of brown rubber bands. A gift from Wexler's old college roommate.

When the FBI swooped in on Wexler a few months earlier, they took everything he had. It wasn't a delicate job. They more or less pulled every drawer out of his desk and dumped the contents into boxes. Watching his computer be carted away by meatheads in black gloves was almost as painful as the perp walk he had to endure across the Baylor campus.

Like any true nerd, Wexler had a special relationship with his computer. He talked about it the way his father discussed muscle cars. The operating system was the engine. The RAM was the horsepower. When he was bored, he'd open it up and tinker with the motherboard, add some more memory, put it back together, and see what new tricks it could do. It held his files, his creations, his life.

Which was why he always made backups and sent them to friends.

As everyone in the mansion upstairs went to sleep, Wexler began feeding the stack of disks into the computer one at a time. Travis had procured for him an Apple Mac Pro from the IT department at the capitol. It was okay, not great. He would have preferred something with a bit more kick, but it would do. As he transferred data, his hands danced across the keys. He trashed what was useless, organized the rest. The fan in the back of the CPU spun like mad. By 4:00 A.M., he had his entire network—the one the FBI thought they had dismantled—up and running again.

Wexler had sold his historical documents through HeritageTreasures.com, a Web site he'd built, which claimed to be "America's most trusted resource for historical artifacts, according to *US News & World Report.*" It gave him enough legitimacy that buyers on the up-and-up felt confident dealing with him. Those who suspected they were dealing with black market goods didn't care either way. They just wanted their stuff and their anonymity.

The Lincoln agreement had only been listed for a day when he was arrested. He was purposefully vague about the details, figuring that the $250,000 opening bid price implied that this was no Lincoln grocery list he was selling. He remembered that traffic was brisk to his site that day, but no one bid or even e-mailed wanting more details. True collectors knew that looking eager only drove prices higher.

With his operation back online, Wexler searched through stored logs and found the analytics on that day's visitors to the site. He filtered out the ones to the Lincoln page. There were some outliers, a random click from Manitoba, a visit from a Kenyan, that sort of thing, but the majority were based on the East Coast. New York and D.C. He sniffed around a little more. According to the network configuration, most of the visits weren't from home computers. They were from offices. The potential buyers were either wasting time at work—no shocker there—or endeavoring to get this document *was* their work. The next step was taking all the IP addresses he'd found and connecting them to specific street addresses. This took another hour. Once he'd compiled a list, he did a routine Google search to see who or what lined up with each location. When he was finished, he was left with a mishmash of people, corporations, and organizations:

Elevate International
Students for a Peaceable Planet
Dr. John Hays—Dentist—Oklahoma City, OK
The AACWR (American Association of
    Civil War Reenactors)
All 4 One
Collective Ascent
Daughters of the American Revolution
Global United
Don Batie—Professor—Chico, CA
ODD (Organization for the Determined Democrat)
En-Game Inc.

There was no "aha!" name in the bunch. He could see the historical motive for the Daughters of the American Revolution, but he couldn't imagine any of them cinching her pearls and then hijacking a private jet over it. Wexler wanted to rule out the harmless Civil War reenactors, but he couldn't discount their passion for the subject matter.

He set those aside and focused on the less familiar names. Global United clicked on the Lincoln letter seventeen times over a two-hour period. Elevate International had done so twelve times. ODD had been there six times during that stretch. Same with Collective Ascent. En-Game Inc., Students for a Peaceable Planet, and All 4 One had all made visits as well. It was a tight bunch of data.

Why these nonprofits had any interest in this letter was puzzling. One existed to fight voter disenfranchisement. Another devoted itself to improving education standards. He perused each Web site for hours, filling his head with inane platitudes on collective salvation and social justice, which, based on each nonprofit's specific policies, seemed to really mean the exchange of American prosperity for global parity.

"This is all the same drivel," Wexler muttered, resting his cheek on the palm of his hand as his eyes sagged. He stopped scrolling and raised his head. *All the same* . . .

Back to Google he went, typing in the most overly specific search request he'd ever attempted: "Global United"+"Elevate International"+ "ODD"+"Collective Ascent"+"Students for a Peaceable Planet"+"All 4 One." He clicked SEARCH and netted just a single result.

It was an August 2006 article from the *Nation* magazine entitled "The Rising Tide." The piece was all about the upcoming midterm elections and the "exciting tools" at the disposal of the left. Central to their efforts were "expanding opportunities to use tax-exempt 501(c)3 organizations to generate grassroots excitement for candidates and causes." The article went on to list all of the nonprofits Wexler had found along with many others, all of whom the article was proud to say took their seed money from the same munificent benefactor: Anatole Metzos.

Wexler spotted a yellow rotary phone hanging on the wall—no way he was going to use his trackable cell phone—and picked up the receiver. Wexler had never used a rotary phone before and was amazed that his ancestors had put up with them for as long as they did. He stuck his index finger through the 1 hole and traced a dusty clockwise circle as he spun the dial.

Paige was in line at the Starbucks down the street from the Forward Foundation and picked up on the second ring. "Hello?"

"Paige, it's Adam Wexler."

She pulled the phone away from her ear and took note of the Texas number. "Please tell me I'm your one phone call from prison," she said. "I want to fully savor the thrill of hanging up on you."

He loved how quick she was; just like her dad. "I'm not in prison," he said. "Not yet at least. Listen, I know you're busy, but I was hoping—"

"A tall hazelnut latte, please," she said.

"Excuse me?" asked Wexler.

"Sorry, go ahead."

"I was hoping you had some time to talk and—"

She squeezed her phone between her chin and shoulder as she pulled four dollars from her wallet. "Are you asking me out again? Because I'm not sure how you'll top the last date."

"Are you crazy? I'm not asking you out."

"Good-bye, Adam." Paige moved to hang up.

"Don't trust Metzos," he blurted, hoping to get it in before the click on the other end. Paige didn't respond, but she didn't push the red button. "I know you like him and think he's a saint," Wexler continued. "I bet he smells like cinnamon and rum."

"He doesn't," she said. He smelled like *cocoa* and rum.

"My point is, I don't think he's so pure. He may be a lot worse, actually."

"I understand," she said. "So really, he's a lot like you."

Wexler nodded on the other end. "That's fair. I know I haven't done much to earn your trust—"

"Ya think?" she said, moving to the back corner of the coffee shop. "Except for your name, literally everything you told me that night was a lie."

"That's"—he tried to switch hands with the phone but got caught up in the coiled yellow cord—"not true."

"Oh really? So you're saying you really *do* sleep at a soup kitchen to keep yourself grounded?"

"Well . . . no. That was a lie."

"Uh-huh. And I don't even have to ask about butterfly mutation. I looked it up the other day. Doesn't exist."

"It doesn't? That's good news. For the butterflies, I mean."

"So what was true, Adam?"

Wexler had told some whoppers that night. When he finally landed on something, he hesitated to say it, knowing it would produce an extreme response of one kind or another.

"The fact that I liked you," he said.

He waited for Paige's response. This time, she did hang up.

Big Bill was wearing his favorite black Stetson and calfskin boots. His wide hips formed a tight seal with the sides of Travis's leather chair. Travis closed his door and walked around the back of his desk, passing another row of bouquets on the way.

"Sorry about disappearing for a few days there," Travis said. "Wasn't my intention. Anyway, now I'm back and ready to . . ." Travis could tell that Bill wasn't looking at him. Not directly, at least.

"Ouch," Bill said. It was the first time he'd seen Travis's forehead. The gash was healing but still red and tender. The end of the stitches hung from the bottom of it, just long enough so Travis could see it out of the corner of his eye.

"Oh. Yeah. Nice one, huh?" Travis said, touching it gently with his hand.

"Rattled you good, huh?"

"Yeah. Still feeling it, actually."

"Still? Give me the symptoms."

"Nothing crazy. Dizzy, got a headache . . . can't really sleep. Just not myself, that's all. It's called postconcussion syndrome or something. Another few days, I'll be fine."

"Well, now hold on. What do they got you on?"

"Just some Tylenol."

"*Tylenol?* No no no." After fifteen surgeries, standard drugs had been rendered powerless to Big Bill, and he assumed everyone else had built up the same tolerances. "You need something stronger," he said.

He pulled his leather bag onto his lap and started to dig through it. Beneath his papers was a miniature pharmacy. Pills, creams, an EpiPen. He was ready for any medical emergency that might befall him.

"Thanks, Bill, but that's really not—"

"What do you want, Governor? You want some Vicodin? Oxycontin?" Bill held up a white container of pills and read the small print. "It expired a few months ago, but that doesn't mean anything. Just the FDA helping drug companies make more money." He shook it to make sure there were still some pills left and threw it to Travis, who caught it against his will.

"I don't think so, Bill."

"Sorry, I thought you said had PCS, not PMS."

"Cute," Travis said.

"You know where I'd be if I only took what my doctor prescribed? Dead."

Travis popped the top and looked inside at the round yellow pills.

"And you're going to need more than one," Bill said. "I'd start with two or three, really take that concussion by the balls, you know what I'm saying?"

Travis couldn't believe this guy. "Why stop at three? Let's start with eight or nine and then just see what happens. 'Course, I'm going to need something to wash down all those pills." Travis leaned around Bill and yelled out his door. "Fran, could you bring in my flask, please? Thank you."

Big Bill was buying Travis's performance. "You sound like a man who's done this before."

"I'm joking, Bill. I don't want this junk." He tossed the pills back toward his confused lieutenant governor. The bottle bounced off his rubbery chest and disappeared back into his bag.

"Make your jokes. That's fine," Bill said. "I'm trying to help you. That's my constitutional duty. I just think you need something."

"Yes, I need something. I need sleep, and hopefully I'll get some when this is all sorted out. Now, let me tell you where we are with all this—"

There was a tepid knock on the door, and Fran stepped in. "Here you go, Governor." Somehow she had actually found a flask.

"Where'd that come from?" he asked.

"Don't you want it?"

"Whose is it?"

"It was Governor Allen's. He kept it in the cabinet near the hall. He'd always take a swig before a big speech. I figured someone told you."

"Nope."

"Oh." She looked at the flask, then back at Travis. "Do you still want it?"

"No thanks, Fran. Send it to his wife."

"Yes, Governor." She turned to leave and almost had the door closed when Travis stopped her.

"Hey, Fran? On second thought, put it back in the cabinet. We might just need it before we're done."

27

President Leary took his seat at the head of the White House
Situation Room's dark-stained conference table and waited in
silence. Filling out the other black leather seats were a serious-
looking Ruffles, the always sexy Avery Adams, Attorney General
David Velez, and Vice President Crudders (he wasn't invited per se,
but the group ran into him on their way downstairs and no one
knew what to say). The Situation Room was the most state-of-the-
art spot in the entire White House. All four walls were covered in
flat-screen TVs. Its advanced videoconferencing technology allowed
the president to speak with any world leader face-to-face in a matter
of seconds. Battles were planned here. Wars were won. The speakers
above their heads crackled to life. Leary took a steadying breath. As
far as anyone was willing to admit, it was the first time any of them
had ever listened to *The Walt Thompson Radio Show*.

As requested by Ruffles, the FBI had warned Walt over the
weekend about the risk of having Travis back on as a guest. According to an agent involved, Walt laughed off the threat, forcing David
Velez to follow up with a personal phone call of his own. Walt
insisted that he got the message, but they wanted to hear it for themselves. Walt's intro music filled the room. It was a bouncy melody, but
the lyrics were serious sounding—something about flags and eagles
and rockets. Ruffles caught himself tapping his foot and stopped.

"There's no picture," the vice president said, staring at the main flat-screen against the back wall.

"It's a radio show, Hank," Leary said, knowing this was the first of many dumb questions he'd have to field today.

"Actually," Avery said, "I think he has streaming video if you want to do that."

"See?" Crudders said.

"Fine," said Leary. He looked at the spectacled White House techie sitting behind a computer in the corner. "Pull up the video, will you?"

The techie pushed a few buttons. All six flat-screens lit up with Walt Thompson's Web page. It was a blinding attack of red, white, and blue. They watched on the screens as the aide's mouse searched in vain for the link.

"There," David Velez said, pointing at the tab marked WATCH LIVE. Those old San Diego TV ads were true: *David Velez puede ayudar!*

The techie, too far from Velez and unable to see where he was pointing, moved the pointer in the opposite direction.

"No, down . . . down!" Velez said. The room joined in as they tried to help the aide find what they could plainly see. "Now left . . . keep going . . . farther . . . too far . . . back . . . a little higher . . . stop!"

He found it and clicked. The next page delivered the bad news. *I'm sorry, Walt Thompson Live is only available to premium Walt Thompson subscribers. JOIN TODAY!*

"What the hell does that mean?" Leary asked.

"It means we have to become a member to watch it," Ruffles said.

"That's ridiculous," Leary said.

"How much is it?" Crudders asked, taking out his wallet.

The techie read the fine print. "Nineteen ninety-five a year."

"No problem. Here's a twenty," the vice president said, tossing it magnanimously across the table to Ruffles.

Ruffles thought about strangling him. There was no Secret Service down here. He could probably get in a couple of good shots before someone ran in and pinned him to the ground.

"Forget it. Let's just listen," Leary said.

Travis and Cole believed that today's show was the most critical and had used the weekend to prepare. Day 1 set the tone and hit the major issues, showing Walt's listeners that Travis wasn't a nut but a guy who loved America and the ideals of its founding. Day 2 was focused on the failure of big government. The giant truth of it all was that government doesn't exist to create wealth. It's not simply that it shouldn't; it *can't*. It could create jobs for people, but those new salaries would have to be paid by the taxpayers. It could print money, but as the last few years had shown, that would only devalue currency, which was the equivalent of *destroying* wealth. The more it tinkered, the sicker the country grew.

Travis and Cole felt they had done a sufficient job talking about the problem. Day 3 needed to be about the solution. Walt's senior producer called Travis in advance to say that they'd be ditching Walt's opening monologue to go with the governor at the top of the show. Travis had no problem with that and was on the line and waiting at 8:04.

"Welcome to another magical three hours with the smartest man in the Milky Way, I am Walt Thompson, armed with the truth . . . and therefore always dangerous. As you all know, throughout the end of last week we were joined by Texas governor Ben Travis. But not today. I've had my hand slapped, ladies and gentleman, by no less than the FBI and the attorney general himself. The Mustached Muchacho as we call him here."

Back in the Situation Room, the vice president chuckled.

"No, there will be no Ben Travis today—but that doesn't mean we won't talk Texas. Because you want to talk about it, and so do I. And the one issue that has continued to bug me is, how is Texas going to pull this off? I'm talking *after* seceding. Can a new republic really survive? Or will it wither away into some continental Cuba? I have some thoughts, but rather than continue with my traditional twelve minutes of orgasmic wisdom and wit, I want to speak to an expert"—Travis's line clicked in—"someone who knows the issues inside and out. Welcome to the show, renowned Texas expert *Ten Bravis*. Welcome, Ten."

Travis stifled a laugh. "Howdy, Walt. Glad to be here."

The mood in the Situation Room turned incendiary. "You fat prick," Ruffles murmured. David Velez looked at the president for direction.

"What?" Leary asked. "*Do* something."

"Okay," Velez said, "it's just . . ."

"It's just what?"

"Well, I mean, technically I don't know how we can *prove* that's Ben Travis."

"It's not Ben Travis," the vice president said. "It's *Ten Bravis*. Am I the only one listening here?"

The president ignored the imbecile next to him. "Just do it, Velez. We'll figure out after the fact how to make it legal."

As David Velez shuffled to the nearest phone, renowned Texas expert Ten Bravis was in the midst of explaining the viability of a Texas currency. "Once our state is on its own, it would immediately become the tenth wealthiest nation in the world based on GDP. To give you an idea of where that would put us, Canada would be number eleven. So I'm not particularly worried about our people having faith in our currency. It's going to look a lot healthier than the dollar." Travis wasn't missing a beat.

"What about national security? Texas is going to have a large target on its back. You've got Mexico right there, Cuba, maybe even Venezuela . . . Who's to say someone won't try to take you down once the U.S. is gone?"

"They might," Travis agreed, "but we have two of the biggest army bases in the country, Fort Hood and Fort Bliss. We'll buy the bases and everything in them off the U.S. for a fair price. Might even give them oil and gas in trade. We've got the Texas State Guard, which only answers to me. We've got the Texas Army National Guard and Air National Guard, which are highly trained. I assume we'll have some support from nearby states. We've also got the Texas Rangers at our disposal—and I don't mean the baseball team, though those guys are pretty tough, too. All told I'd put our boys up against just about anyone."

Walt was skeptical. "Don't forget the border. You've got over twelve hundred miles just on the Mexico side alone."

"That's right, Walt. It's a big border, and we're going to protect it. Unlike the president, we believe in borders and don't see how we can pretend to be secure without them."

"What's your solution to the immigration problem?" Walt asked.

"We don't have an immigration problem, Walt. We have an *illegal* immigration problem. There's a difference. Our plan is a little un-orthodox, but I think it could work. The day after Texas peacefully breaks off, we're going to secure the holes in our border and make an announcement. Every immigrant who's here illegally will have thirty days to register with the republic. If they don't register by then and we find them, they're out."

"Sounds a little Gestapo-ish so far," Walt said.

"You and I have to register with the government, Walt," Travis said. "I don't think it's asking too much for immigrants to identify themselves like you and I do. But bear with me. Once they register, then they'll have a year of probationary citizenship. If at the end of that year, they've worked, paid all their taxes, and haven't been con-victed of any felonies, they'll be made full citizens of the Republic of Texas with all the rights that come with it."

"Amnesty," Walt said.

"One time only," Travis said.

Travis kept on going until the bottom of the hour. It was a home run. He'd hit every point that he and Cole had outlined. He was rational and well-spoken, approaching magnetic at times. There was just one small issue. No one in America had heard anything past the first sixty seconds.

President Leary leaned back in his chair in the Situation Room with a contented smile on his face and his eyes closed. Everyone else had returned upstairs, off to other tasks, but he wanted to stay and enjoy the sound. It was the beautiful noise of nothing but static.

28

Anatole Metzos thought long and hard about the best place to break the story. He needed a sizable audience, which immediately ruled out CNN and MSNBC. Fox News would be perfect, but he was worried that they'd ask too many questions. A network morning show would be ideal. Something with a high demo of Republican women. Polls revealed Travis had made most of his gains there. Metzos knew that if he could turn the ladies back against him, Travis was done, and so was the Texas secession movement.

"Welcome to *Today,* I'm Ann Curry, a hot day here in New York City, and week two of the fallout between Texas and the federal government over the president's Responsible Resources Act. Under new threats from Washington and with pressure mounting around the country, some polls"—all polls—"are showing that support for the controversial Texas secession vote may be surging." NBC brass had sent out a memo making sure that no one took the bait of calling it an "evacuation." "As they have been since the saga began. NBC reporters are on the ground in Austin with all the latest developments. But first, a disturbing revelation concerning the unlikely leader of the Texas secession movement, Governor Ben Travis. For that we go to Natalie Morales behind the news desk."

"Good morning, Ann. A troubling new audiotape has surfaced which has law enforcement officials asking questions and is certain to threaten the credibility of the Texas governor. Obtained exclusively by *Today*, the tape appears to catch Governor Travis talking with an unidentified individual and admitting to not only being mentally unstable but also to using painkillers, perhaps Vicodin or Oxycontin, to ease his pain. According to sources, Governor Travis does not have a legal prescription for either drug, a crime that is a felony in Texas . . ."

A production assistant popped her head into the greenroom. "We're ready for you, Miss Travis."

Paige was wearing a trim black suit with heels and a gray blouse. Funeral attire. She'd already thrown up once in her dressing room. It was nerves, and not about being in front of the camera. Like the president, she'd been all over TV in the last few days. This was different. Her other appearances had been centered on the nonexistent legal case for secession and the security risk of a divided America. Wonkish stuff. Her familial connection to Travis was implied but never dealt with directly. This morning's appearance would be all-out character assassination. She followed the production assistant through the winding halls to her comfy seat on the set. Anatole Metzos only had two stipulations for the interview: Matt Lauer and soft lighting.

As she settled down, Matt took the seat next to her and adjusted his earpiece. He smiled warmly at Paige as the audiotape in question was just finishing up.

". . . *What do you want, Governor? You want some Vicodin? Oxycontin?" "I need something . . . Let's start with eight or nine and then just see what happens. 'Course, I'm going to need something to wash down all those pills. Fran, could you bring in my flask, please?"*

"The governor has no criminal record of drug or alcohol abuse," Morales continued, "though former classmates tell *Today* that Travis drank heavily at times during his college years. Given the seriousness of these charges, we expect a statement from the governor shortly. Until then, let's throw it over to our own Matt Lauer with a special guest who hopes to shed more light on the instability of Texas's divisive leader."

A stagehand pointed at Lauer as the camera in front of him lit up with a red light.

"Thank you, Ann. Over the past week, Texas governor Ben Travis has captured the attention of many Americans. Polarizing, bold, but, as we're learning, perhaps tormented in a way few people know. Paige Travis is the associate director of domestic policy for the Forward Foundation and, more importantly, daughter of Ben Travis. Thank you for joining us, Paige."

"Thank you, Matt."

"Your rift with your father has been well documented at this point. Still, I can't imagine it's easy to hear something like this."

"Of course not. I love my father. I always will. I . . ." Her voice started to warble. She never expected to be this emotional.

Matt nudged the Kleenex a little closer. "Tell me how you felt when you first heard that audio."

"Sad. Disappointed . . ."

Matt suggested another adjective. "Surprised . . ."

"Yes and no," Paige said.

"Talk about that," Matt said. The gentle lighting and fatherly presence of Matt Lauer was working just as Metzos had hoped. Paige was starting to forget where she was. At Yale, she'd tried and failed to get the hang of Method acting, where the goal is to literally become the character you're playing. Turns out it's rather easy when the person you're asked to play is yourself.

"My parents separated right after he was elected to the senate," Paige said. "My mother was tired of being invisible and rightly so. He wasn't good to her. Didn't cherish her despite all she'd done for him. What made it especially sad was that he couldn't see that. If anything, he felt he was the one who'd been betrayed."

"He doesn't seem very grounded in reality," Matt said.

"He's an acquired taste. That's the simplest way to say it."

"So how did that separation and then divorce affect him?"

"He was stunned. He's a successful businessman who's used to getting what he wants, but this blindsided him. He retreated to his ranch for a month. Wouldn't return my calls. Those who served with him in the senate would tell you, he was more or less a zombie."

"To an outsider, this sounds a bit like depression."

"I believe that's clearly what it was, Matt."

"Did he ever receive medical attention for it?"

"It was my understanding that he did. He was prescribed something. Whether he ever took it or is still on it today, I don't know, but his behavior of late has obviously been erratic, even for him. So while I'm shocked to hear this tape, it obviously fits with some of the ups and downs one would expect from a person who's battling some of those demons."

"Are you and your father currently speaking with each other?"

Paige's eyes welled up with tears. The director yelped in his ear, *"Ten seconds."* Matt used most of that time to let the moment linger. *"Eight, seven, six . . ."*

"It's complicated," Paige said, keeping it together.

Matt put his hand on Paige's knee as she dabbed her eyes. "Paige Travis, thank you for opening up to us." He looked at the camera. "It's twelve minutes past the hour . . . on *Today.*"

K tore through Travis's office, not sure what he was looking for but figuring he'd know when he found it. Travis was trying to help, too, but his progress was impeded by his rants.

"This is unbelievable!" Travis said. "Truly unbelievable!" He picked up a cushion on the couch, looked under it, and threw it back down. He'd been a mess since he found out the FCC killed Walt's show, but this had him reeling in a way that even Cole had never seen. "Who the hell had access to this place?!" Travis yelled.

Cole stood in the doorway. "A lot of people, unfortunately," he said. "After you got knocked out, the office was basically abandoned for two whole days."

"There must be security camera footage, then," K said.

"Yes," said Travis. "Tell Fran to call someone and get the footage." He pulled open his desk drawer and pushed some pens around.

K intervened. "Governor, could you please just not touch anything? If there's any remaining evidence here, I'd rather you not . . . defile it."

Travis put his hands in the air as if he were under arrest and retreated to the center of the room. "So it could have been pretty much anyone is what we're saying."

Fran stuck her head in the door. "Mike McKill's on the phone again."

"Not now!" Cole and Travis said in unison.

Fran turned to leave and bumped right into Big Bill. He announced his arrival appropriately. "What a bunch of bull snot!" He looked awful, which was saying something for a guy who had been pronounced legally dead on two separate occasions. "They're gonna figure out it's me on that tape, you realize that, don't you? Just a matter of time! And then it's good-bye Bill!"

Cole didn't have patience for one more person's drama. "Don't take this personally, Bill, but no one gives a crap about you right now. They're trying to take Travis down any way they can. That's all they care about."

K was still searching. He'd checked under the desk and up along the track lighting in the ceiling. His attention turned to the flowers on the windowsill behind Travis's chair.

"At least they had to doctor the tape to make you sound bad," Big Bill said to Travis. "I sounded like scum without them having to rearrange one damn word!" Big Bill returned to the bullpen in search of Governor Allen's flask.

Travis looked back at K, who seemed to have homed in on something. "Whatcha got?" Travis asked.

K didn't answer, just signaled for the room to stop talking. He rolled up his sleeve, revealing his massive OU tattoo, and reached past the red carnations. He pulled out a flat transmitter, rectangular in shape and smaller than a dime. It had a two-inch black antenna coming off one end and a wire on the other end that connected to a standard 9-volt battery, strong enough to transmit the signal a thousand feet or more.

Big Bill was back with the flask. "Is that a bomb? Is that a bomb?!"

K pulled the battery off the connector.

"A bug," K said.

"In the flowers?" Big Bill took a swig and laughed. "Brilliant." The compliment drew stares from Cole and Travis. "Hey, you've got to admit, that is pretty smart."

"Who sent the flowers?" Cole asked.

K pulled the card out of the envelope. He read it and passed it to Travis. Travis shook his head in disbelief. He remembered back to last week, when Gabe Coggins was up in arms about not receiving a personal call from Travis about the special session. This call would more than make up for it.

Travis started with Coggins's optometry office, but his secretary said he had already gone home for the day, a piece of information Travis felt—at only 10:00 A.M.—said volumes about either his work ethic or his lack of patients. He moved on to his cell phone, but it went to voice mail. *This is Dr. Gabe Coggins . . .* Travis hung up before the beep. He wanted the satisfaction of hearing Gabe's reaction to being caught live and in person. He dialed his home number.

"Hello." It was a woman. Travis had been so focused on his villain that he forgot there was a 50 percent chance his ex-wife might answer. Travis hadn't spoken with Kate in six months. He'd seen her at a few senate parties and had successfully looked through her, even though it pained him to do so. "Hello?" she said again. If there were such a thing as a perfect voice, hers would be it. A little breathy, Kate always sounded like she'd just woken up from a long nap on a tropical beach. He used to love to hear her read to Paige. The world of every book sounded more magical when she was describing it.

"Hi, Kate. It's, uh, Ben . . . Travis."

"Hi, Ben Travis," she said. Kate could always read his mind, and some part of him felt as if she should know why he had called. *This must be about the secret transmitter in the flowers. Let me get my evil husband for you.* Something like that. "Can I . . . help you?" So far she was playing dumb.

"I'd like to speak with Gabe, please."

"Sure," she said.

It was over too fast. Travis didn't want her to go. He needed to say something to keep her on the phone. "By the way, that's a real winner you got there, Kate."

"Excuse me?" It wasn't his best moment.

"I mean . . . do you ever wake up in the morning, roll over in bed, and say, 'My God, what was I thinking?'"

"No, Ben, I don't," Kate said. "Do you?"

She didn't wait for him to respond. She put him on hold. Travis realized too late that inquiring about her sick mom might have been a more congenial area for conversation.

After thirty seconds, the line clicked on. "What was that all about, Ben?" Coggins asked. "Kate just walked into my study crying and—"

"You know what, Gabe, drop the act. I don't have time. I'm calling to let you know that I know what you did. You probably thought you'd never get caught, but you did. You did, and you're going down."

Travis's rebuke was met with silence. It felt good to finally nail him on something. This was probably just the beginning. Travis wondered what other illegal activities Coggins had been up to. Drug running? Human trafficking? His mind swirled with the possibilities . . .

"Ben, I have no idea what you're talking about," Coggins said.

Travis laughed. He couldn't believe that was his best retort.

"We found it, Gabe. *The bug.*"

More silence. Now that the boom had been lowered, Travis figured Gabe was scrambling to come up with a more convincing counterargument.

"What bug?" Gabe asked.

"In the flowers, Gabe! The carnations. Which, since we're on the topic, thanks for going all out on that bouquet. That must have set you back, what, eight bucks? The only reason my guy spotted the transmitter was because they were already starting to wilt."

Travis was savoring every second of this phone call. He felt like Sherlock Holmes, taunting his suspect while at the same time proving his guilt.

"Ben, I don't know how else to say this, but . . . well . . . I didn't send you flowers," Coggins said.

Travis's smile drooped. "What do you mean? I'm looking at them right now."

"Don't get me wrong," he said. "I believe you have flowers with my name on them, but all I'm saying is they didn't come from me."

This time the silence fell on Travis's end of the call. In his rush to judgment, he had overlooked the fact that while the bouquet might have come with Gabe's name on it, nothing about it truly proved he sent them. Short of a blood, urine, semen, or hair sample haphazardly included with the flowers, Travis had nothing. He put down the phone and picked up the small rectangular card that had been clipped to a forked plastic holder and flipped it over, hoping to find it stamped by the florist. It was blank.

Gabe had been browbeaten and was now being ignored. "Ben?" His voice came from the receiver of the governor's forgotten phone.

Travis picked it back up. "Yes, Gabe?"

"We about done here?" he asked.

"Yes, Gabe."

The arms, head, and shoulders of Travis's secretary, Fran, were buried in the ten-gallon plastic recycling bin, rummaging for discarded florist delivery slips. One foot was on the ground, the other in the air, and Travis watched knowing that, as if she were a sedan teetering on the edge of a cliff, it would take only the smallest accidental transfer of weight to send her entire body into the paper abyss.

When she emerged, she was empty-handed. Her face was flushed. "Nothing?" Travis asked.

"They must have been delivered before we'd all returned to work," said Fran, readjusting her stirrup pants.

Cole wasn't ready to let their prime suspect off the hook. "How can we be so sure that Coggins wasn't lying to you?"

"He wasn't lying," Travis said. "If you're committing that crime, you wouldn't put your own name on that card. Gabe Coggins isn't an idiot." Explaining this out loud made Travis feel like even more of a boob for falling for the ruse in the first place.

"I think that's the nicest thing I've ever heard you say about him," K said from inside Travis's office. He was double-checking the rest of the bouquets.

In the fifteen minutes since he'd hung up the phone, Travis had moved beyond the whodunit aspect of it all. Instead, he just felt remorse. It was Travis's father who told him before he left for college that you can get all of the people to like you some of the time and some of the people to like you all of the time, but you can't expect all of the people to like you all of the time. It made sense to Travis. It was why he was never scared at the thought of making the occasional enemy. Still, he couldn't help but notice that he'd made enemies out of his wife and only child, and perhaps he shouldn't shrug that off without a little more self-reflection.

"Am I that difficult?" Travis asked, looking at Cole.

Cole was puzzled, and not by the sudden change in conversation. "What are you talking about?"

"Simple question. I'm just asking if I can be a pain and not fully realize it."

"Travis," Cole said, "you're attempting to secede from the United States of America, an act no prominent American leader has seriously attempted in a hundred and fifty years. You're doing it despite warnings against it from the highest levels of the federal government. Despite the fact you're having your name dragged through the dirt twenty-four hours a day by the mainstream media. And despite some very real threats against your own life."

Travis flopped into Fran's chair. "So, in other words, *yes*." The latest secession poll was lying on Fran's desk. The *Today* show bombshell had taken its toll. After swelling to 41 percent nationally, the newest numbers showed support for Texas secession was back down to a flaccid 32 percent support.

"I can't believe they found people to say I drank too much in college," Travis fumed.

"Are you claiming you didn't?" asked Cole. "Because I seem to remember—"

"That's not the point!"

Travis appraised the situation. "I need to get back on Walt's show tomorrow," he said.

"Walt Thompson can't help you anymore," Cole said.

"Geez, Cole, he has like fifteen million listeners—"

"Yeah. Fifteen million listeners who already like you. You squeezed everything you could out of him."

"But thirty-two percent? When I started at twenty-eight? I don't need an investment banker to tell me that's not much of a yield."

"It doesn't matter. His lawyers said the two of you can't communicate. One more offense, the FCC could strip him of his license forever. He'll be done."

"All because the White House doesn't like me."

"No, because you're an *enemy of the State*," said Cole.

"Not *this* state. Not a lot of states."

"State with a capital *S*. Which is the only one the FCC cares about."

"Yeah, yeah . . ." Travis stood up and caught K's eye, signaling his desire to leave with a quick flick of his index finger toward the door.

"Where are you going?" Cole asked.

"Back to the mansion."

"To do what?"

"Not sure yet."

"Will you tell me when you know?"

Travis paused, giving the question some thought. "Probably not."

K tapped the front pocket of his pants, making sure he still had the Suburban keys, and led Travis out the door. Before it was closed, Cole felt obligated to comment on the moment.

"In case you don't realize it, this is you being difficult."

29

Travis opened the creaky door to the mansion's basement and felt his way through the dark to the bottom. The white glow of the monitor lit up Wexler, asleep at his desk. And why not, it was almost noon.

"Hey there."

Wexler popped his head up and pretended to be typing. "Oh. Hi. Just . . . doing my thing."

"I love what you've done with the place. There's a nice Anne Frank feel to it."

"Really?" Wexler asked. "I was actually going for more of a postapocalyptic vibe."

Travis looked for another chair but couldn't find one. He took a seat on Wexler's bed. It was a mess of rumpled sheets.

"Sorry about Walt," Wexler said, turning around to face him.

"Did you see the *Today* show?" said Travis.

"I wasn't going to mention that one."

"Listen," Travis said, "I need to get a message out on the, uh, Inter . . . web."

"O-kay." Wexler spun back around in his chair to face the computer. "Like a typed message or—"

"A video. You can do that, right?"

"Sure. We can do it with my phone," Wexler said. He stood up and started turning on a few more lights.

"I need a lot of people to see it," said Travis.

"No problem." Wexler grabbed his chair and set it against one of the brick walls. "I'll tape it, edit it, put it on your Web site. The FCC shut down your Facebook page, but they can't figure out how to crack the badass firewall I attached to your main site. It's been sort of fun watching them try."

"No, I need you to get this video up on all the news Web sites," Travis said. He pulled the chair back to Wexler with his foot. "And we're not filming it down here. It'll look like I'm starring in an Al Jazeera hostage video."

"Whatever you want," Wexler said. "I'll e-mail it out to all the majors just to be sure they see it."

"Yeah, see, that's the problem. They're not going to show anyone this. Not on their own. Whatever heat the Feds put on Walt Thompson to stop featuring me has been put on them, too."

"Alright . . ." Wexler sat back down. "But then I'm not sure what you're asking. You're saying you want *me* to put this video on their Web sites for you."

"Can't you do that? Like slip it in there without them knowing or something?"

Wexler was having flashbacks to the day his grandmother bought a computer and tried to talk into the mouse. "Hold on. You want me to hack into all the major news servers—which is illegal, mind you—and embed your video?"

"If that's what it's called, yeah."

"What makes you think I have that capability?"

Travis shrugged. "Don't you?"

The simple part was recording the video. That only took ten minutes. Wexler spent the next ten *hours* unpacking code and filtering encryptions at what he felt were the nine biggest news sites in

America: DrudgeReport.com, Yahoo.com, FoxNews.com, CNN
.com, ABCNews.com, NBCNews.com, NYTimes.com, WSJ.com,
and Breitbart.com. The video would also be posted at Baylor.edu. It
wasn't a news site, but since he already knew how to hack into it from
his abbreviated college days, he figured what the heck.

If he could pull it off, the video would go live at 11:00 P.M. Eastern Time, when nationwide Internet usage typically peaked. Travis
didn't want the video buried in the content. He wanted it to be the
only content. From a hacker's perspective, that approach would be
easier. Once Wexler was in, there would be no blending of computer
codes. He would just remove theirs and put in his. It was a cut-and-
paste job on a nuclear level.

The unanswerable question was how long the link would stick.
Wexler could only guarantee three to four minutes at the most.
There were too many IT nerds who were paid six figures to make
sure this sort of thing never happened, or when it did, to undo it as
quickly as possible. If it held for five minutes, though, it was safe to
assume the video would be seen twenty million times, maybe more.

At nine o'clock Central Time, the basement door opened. Wexler
had cracked eight of the sites and was working on the ninth. A pyra-
mid of empty Dr Pepper cans was piled on the edge of his desk.
Travis's bare feet appeared first, followed by the end of his plaid pa-
jama bottoms. He stopped halfway down the stairs and leaned
through the railing.

"Good night, nerd," he said.

Wexler looked over, his eyes red from staring at code. "You're going to bed?"

"Yeah," Travis said. "Not all of us get to take naps at noon."

"But we're only an hour away . . ."

"Hey, if you're depending on me at this point, we're all screwed,"
Travis said. He turned back and headed for bed.

"This is gonna work, Governor," Wexler called out.

"I know," Travis said, as his feet disappeared up the stairs.

"Ben . . . Ben . . ." Travis woke up to see Cole looking down at him. Travis had tried the four-post California king bed his first night in the mansion and found its size too depressing for just one person. Every night since, he had fallen asleep on the comfy couch in his upstairs living room, his feet dangling over the far end.

Cole was backlit by the light coming through the double doors out to the hall. Travis looked at the clock. It was only ten thirty-five. "What's wrong?" Travis asked.

"They're taking Wexler," he said.

"Who is?"

"The FBI. They found him."

The Feds had been after Wexler since it came to their attention that one of their prisoners out on bail had crossed state lines and stolen something—though no one knew what exactly—from his own case file at the Department of Justice. Once they found out who posted the bail, it wasn't much of a leap to suspect that Adam Wexler was holed up at the governor's mansion. Still, they needed more than a guess to secure a search warrant. An anonymous call from a female employee at the Forward Foundation did the trick.

Travis rolled out of bed and made for the stairs. He was downstairs in time to see Wexler being led out the back door of the mansion, a blue-jacketed agent on each arm. The night staff huddled in the kitchen and watched the drama wide-eyed through the windows as Travis followed the Feds out the door in his bare feet.

"Wexler!" Travis called. The kid turned and gave Travis a pointed stare. He was trying to relay some message to him without words. Travis knew what it meant.

Wexler hadn't finished the job.

When the last unmarked car was gone and the gates of the mansion were closed, Travis headed straight for the basement.

"Where did the FBI find him?" he called out.

"Living room," K said. "He heard the commotion and came upstairs. He didn't even put up a fight."

"Good," Travis said, heading belowground. Cole had successfully avoided the basement until now. He covered his nose and mouth with his cashmere sweater, sure that this subterranean den was the Carlsbad Caverns of black mold. "Why did you put him down here, anyway?" he asked.

"Penance," Travis said. He walked to the computer and jiggled the mouse. The monitor lit up, revealing window upon window of unreadable computer gibberish.

"Define 'penance,'" Cole said.

"Holy crap," K said.

Travis stared at the jumble of numbers and letters on the screen. "You told me that fifteen million Walt Thompson listeners weren't enough. That I needed to widen my audience. Wexler was trying to help me do that."

Cole leaned in closer. A few keywords jumped out. "Drudge . . . Yahoo . . . CNN . . . What is all this?"

"Hacking . . . embedding . . . we were gonna go live at 11:00 P.M. Eastern." Travis said coolly. "I'd explain it all to you, but it's pretty technical. You wouldn't understand."

"And you do?" Cole asked.

Travis dropped the act. "Not a clue," he said. He stared at the code for a few seconds, hoping that it would rouse some unused part of his brain and suddenly make sense to him. It didn't. "You don't know anything about this stuff, do you, K?"

K shook his head. "My friends and I beat up all the kids we knew who were good at this," he said.

"Dang it," Travis said. He backed toward Wexler's bed and started to sit. The sight of it gave him a start and he shot back up.

"What? What's wrong?" Cole asked. Ever since they found the bug in the bouquet, he'd been on edge, wondering what nefarious things were hiding in other everyday objects.

"His bed's made," Travis said.

"So?" asked Cole.

"When was the last time that kid ever made a bed?" Travis turned around and stared at the blue comforter, lying flat against the mattress. With one motion, he picked it up by the corner and yanked it back. Underneath was the antique chalkboard that had been hanging on the wall at the bottom of the stairs. Scribbled in frenzied handwriting with white chalk was a short message:

Open Apple A. Open Apple V. Return. Repeat.

"They're instructions," Travis said. "Okay, everybody spread out and look for some apples."

"These aren't instructions," Cole said. "It's a riddle. Something Wexler thought only we would understand."

"Okay," Travis said. He started to think out loud. "Apple A . . . apple . . . apple . . . fruit of knowledge . . . keeps the doctor away . . ."

K looked over their shoulders, read the hidden note, and chuckled. "That's not a riddle. Those are keystrokes."

"What do you mean?" Travis asked.

"For the computer," said K. "'Open Apple A' is 'Select all.' 'Open Apple V' is 'Paste.'"

"What's 'Return'?" Travis wondered.

"The button that says 'Return' on it," K said, trying and failing to not sound patronizing.

"I thought you didn't know anything about computers," Cole said.

"I don't," he said.

Travis felt exonerated. "Like I said. Instructions."

Travis moved to the computer and took a seat. He looked at his watch. It was ten minutes till eleven on the East Coast. Close enough. The first window was CNN's. K pointed at the keyboard. "Hold down that button and then hit a," he said. Travis did it, highlighting the whole page. "Now hold it down again and hit v." The code was instantly replaced with an entirely different set of gobbledygook. "Now RETURN," K said. Travis pressed it and the entire window disappeared off the screen.

"Where'd it go?" Cole asked.

"Hopefully into a few million households," Travis said with a smile.

He repeated the steps nine more times. When he finished the last one, all that was left was Wexler's blank computer desktop. "We did it," Travis said.

"Now that we have, can you tell me exactly what we did?" Cole asked.

"It would be more fun to show you," he said. He stood up and offered his bodyguard the chair. "K, open the interweb for us."

Paige was doing her normal end-of-the-night online rounds. She found it was a good way to ease herself into sleep. She started with the most conservative Web sites and headed left, always ending with the soothing voices of her comrades at the Daily Kos. By eleven o'clock, she had already been to WorldNetDaily, HotAir, and Townhall. She was happy to see that their enthusiasm for Travis was becoming a bit more tempered. Next up was Fox News, but before she clicked through, she made sure that her volume was muted. The last time she went to the site her cat, Delano, heard Sean Hannity's voice and hid under the dresser for two days.

Paige and Delano were greeted with something far scarier. The entire Fox News Web site was blanketed in a rippled Texas flag. At the center of the page was a black rectangle. She double-checked the URL. She was at the right place. Out of the black appeared her father, suited up, warmly lit, salt-and-pepper hair slicked to the right. One of the mansion's maids had lent some of her touch-up to the cause, dulling the red around Travis's stitches. He was sitting in a comfortable leather chair in the corner of his first-floor living room. Out the window, between the elms, the state capitol rose into the clear Austin sky.

"Oh no . . ." Paige said. When she realized Travis was speaking, she turned up the volume.

". . . evening, America. My name's Ben Travis, and I'm the governor of the great state of Texas." Delano stopped licking himself and listened. "A lot has been said and written about me in the last week or so. Most of it is false. And all because I've dared to stand in Washington's way and say 'enough.' I've been labeled a racist without evidence. I've been called crazy. Groups that claim to be peace-loving have called for my head, and as you can see by my stitches, some have taken that call quite literally. But I got back up, I kept talking, and many of you started to listen. And then I was silenced. Somehow our government thinks it's right to give unapologetic terrorists public venues to vent their anger at the United States, and yet when I say what I believe with the intention of preserving America, my freedoms and liberties are stripped away.

"I said *most* all of the allegations against me have been false. Not all. No, I'm not addicted to drugs. For those who need proof, I'm happy to provide it in whatever manner you prefer. But I have been a poor husband. An insensitive father. An occasional jackass. My wife and daughter deserved my best, and all too often they didn't get it. And yes, in the wake of my divorce, I was a mess. My daughter's allegations on the *Today* show were right: My doctor said I was depressed. A shrink said it was a midlife crisis. I told them both I was just out of sorts. I imagine most of us have been there. Maybe it's when you lost a job you thought was secure. Or when you realize someone you care about is not coming back. When everything you thought you knew to be true turned out to be wrong. That's where I was. Right up until a couple weeks ago. But when I took the oath of office, my former chief of staff, Hunter Reese, told me that if I were going to be the face of Texas, it couldn't be a depressing one. And so . . . I left that Ben Travis behind.

"Or at least I thought I did. You see, I'm not without flaws. Sometimes I speak before I think. My daughter would tell you that sometimes I never even get around to the thinking part. But, my fellow Americans, I have indeed thought about my actions regarding Texas. I have fallen asleep with the Declaration of Independence and I have woken up with the Constitution. I have searched the writings of our greatest Americans. If you are among those who believe that Washington has the right to do what it wants without a check on that power from the states, then it's not only Ben Travis who disagrees with you. So does Ben *Franklin* . . . and Thomas Jefferson . . . and George Washington . . . and Abraham Lincoln.

"This isn't the first time Texas has been in this position. The last time we found ourselves on the verge of a secession vote, Sam Houston, our great Texas governor, stood up and bravely tried to stop it. He said, 'What is there that is free that we have not got? Are our rights invaded and no government ready to protect us? No. Are our institutions wrested from us and others foreign to our taste forced upon us? No. Is the right of free speech, a free press, or free suffrage taken from us? Has our property been taken from us and the government failed to interpose . . . ? No, none of these . . . Whence then this clamor about disunion . . . Are we to sell reality for a phantom?' In the last hundred fifty years, the answers to nearly all those questions have turned from *no* to *yes*. And that abusive government he spoke of as a phantom has become a reality.

"So you see, there can be no happy middle here. There is no compromise to be had. It's a question of principle. And on that, I won't cave. The stakes are too high. To borrow a line from Ronald Reagan, 'If we lose freedom here, there's no place to escape to.' So, in the event that we receive the support of the people of Texas in three days, we will leave. And we'll do so peacefully. This is not a declaration of war; it's a declaration of liberty. If you're a Texan, I humbly ask you for your support. If you're not, well . . . it's not too late to move. We'd love to have you. I thank you for listening. God bless Texas, and yes, may God bless the United States of America."

The video faded to black. Before it stopped, Adam Wexler snuck in one last trick, a voice-over he'd recorded himself in his best Austro-German-French accent: "I'm Anatole Metzos and I approve of this message."

Paige couldn't help but laugh. It was the only reaction she hadn't experienced over the course of her father's three-minute speech. She had started off shocked, then moved on to anger. For most of the middle part, she was tearing up. In the end, she felt guilt. She clicked over to the Drudge Report to see if they had picked up the story. The same Texas flag background popped up, followed by Ben Travis.

"Good evening, America," he began once again.

"No way," she said. She clicked on CNN.

"Good evening, America—"

NBC News . . .

"Good evening, America—"

ABC News . . .

"Good evening, America—"

"How in the world did they do this?" she wondered aloud. The FBI, when notified of the stunt a few minutes later, asked Adam Wexler the same question.

"Easy," Wexler said. "Open Apple A. Open Apple V. Return. Repeat."

30

Anatole Metzos summoned Paige to the Forward Foundation headquarters, knowing he need not give any other explanation. She brought a scarf and wrapped it around her as she stepped off the elevator. Metzos's entire floor was dark except for the light coming from under his distant office door. She shuffled past Brianne's desk, avoiding the gong and suit of armor on the way.

Through the crack she heard the tag of Travis's video repeating over and over. "I'm Anatole Metzos and I approve of this message." Pause. "I'm Anatole Metzos and I approve of this message." Pause. "I'm Anatole Metzos and I approve of this message." She knocked. "I'm Anatole Metz—"

"Come in." Hearing the two voices back to back like that, Paige was even more impressed with Wexler's impression.

She found Metzos slumped behind his desk in a purple Izod shirt. An empty tumbler sat on the edge of his desk. "Here's tomorrow's list," he said, skipping the small talk and sliding the piece of paper across his desk. He stared at her, sullen.

She looked at the list and nodded. Ben Travis had risen all the way to #1. "You don't seem very disappointed," he said.

"I'm not disappointed. It makes sense."

Metzos walked to a closed steel cabinet against the wall and pulled out a half-empty bottle of Glenfiddich. "Not disappointed in him, disappointed in *yourself*."

Paige was caught off guard by the attack. "What do you mean?"

He filled up his glass halfway. His hand shook as he poured. "You've failed. It's important you realize that," he said.

"Excuse me?"

"I said you failed," Metzos repeated.

"How? I've done everything you've asked of me since I started."

Metzos returned the bottle and slammed the cabinet shut, causing her to flinch in her seat. "If you had done *everything* I asked, your father would not be where he is! You were supposed to ruin him!" Metzos emptied his tumbler in one sip and turned to face the blank gray wall, looking out a window that wasn't there.

Paige peered through his door toward the blackness of the suite. If Mutuku was out there somewhere, she couldn't see him. "Maybe the best thing for us to do is get some sleep and then talk again tomorrow," she said.

Metzos wheeled around. "Don't treat me like some babbling grandparent you abandoned in a convalescent home, Miss Travis."

"I'm not—"

"Without me, you'd have nothing right now. Without me, you'd *be* nothing! I recognized your value when no one else did."

She wanted to chalk up his behavior to a combination of old age and alcohol, but Wexler's words of warning from his phone call were pinging around her brain. Just for safety, she reached into the pocket of her sweatshirt and felt around for her sharpest key, gripping the handle of it between her thumb and forefinger. "Good night, Mr. Metzos."

Paige slipped into the black. She was halfway to the light of the open elevator when Metzos called out. "They're trying to pull you away, aren't they?" he asked. She stopped in the darkness. He couldn't see her, but he could hear her breathing and knew she had stopped. "I thought so." Metzos laughed, admiring his own intuition. "You must admit that it's curious. How your father only tries to make amends when his political life is on the line. It's sad, really. I can't help but wonder how many times he has hurt you before and never said a thing . . . how many times he's made you feel irrational . . . how many times you felt unheard . . . invisible . . . misunderstood. How many times have you cried yourself to sleep, Paige?" She held in the tears, not wanting Metzos to know he was getting to her. "Don't be duped, Miss Travis. He hasn't changed. When you're my age you'll realize that people *don't*—no matter how much you wish it to be true."

The president was playing golf, and everyone in the West Wing knew this would ruin his round. This wasn't Leary's typical Sunday, Tuesday, or Thursday round of golf. This was Pine Valley. Leary had been trying to get on America's most revered private course since he took the oath of office. He thought it would be easy, a simple matter of calling the club and introducing himself. The great complication, he discovered, was that club rules dictated that any guest must play with a member, and that every member of Pine Valley was a staunch Republican who hated his guts.

Leary finally caught a break when his secretary of agriculture was kicked in the head by a horse at the Iowa State Fair, opening up a spot for a Pine Valley Republican in his cabinet. They would have to tee off before sunrise, play as a twosome, and be gone before the regular late-morning crowd arrived, but Leary didn't mind. He would have played the course at midnight with a glow-in-the-dark ball if that were his only option.

The president saw it was the White House calling and answered with an angry whisper. "What?"

"It's Avery Adams—"

Leary shushed her before she could finish. Pine Valley had a strict ban on cell phones, and women weren't allowed on the course unless it was after 2:00 P.M. on Sunday, making this a possible double whammy that he feared could be grounds for his immediate dismissal from the property. Pine Valley didn't understand the concept of preferential treatment. Golf legend Jack Nicklaus stopped in to play the New Jersey course while on his honeymoon in 1960 and was informed upon arriving with his wife that the club was open to men only. Nicklaus weighed the options, and had a friend drive his bride around the perimeter of the club for four hours while he went and played.

"Yes, *Mr.* Adams," the president whispered, hoping to buy some clemency lest his caddy decide to tattle on his infraction.

Avery blew past the unexplained gender reassignment. "We just received the numbers from last night's cyber coup," she said.

"And . . . ?"

"Fifty-six percent."

"Fifty-six percent?!" Leary screamed. A pair of white-tailed deer bolted into the trees. "In Texas?!"

Avery took to whispering now, hoping to lure Leary back into a sense of calm. "No, that's the, um . . . national number, Mr. President."

"Fifty-six *nationally*! Are you effing kidding me?! Tell me you are effing kidding me!"

"People like him and they like what he's saying," Avery said. "That's a powerful one-two."

"That's what I don't understand. How can people like what he's saying? *We* are the ones trying to help them. Why can't they see that?"

"Well, I think the unemployment numbers aren't good, and the debt is obviously—"

"This is what change looks like!" Leary yelled. It was the double-edged sword of Leary's first campaign slogan. On the one hand, it was so wonderfully vague that voters on both sides of the aisle could make it stand for whatever they wanted. The rub was that when Leary's true agenda—untethered big government—took shape after the election, almost everyone was disappointed to discover that his change bore little resemblance to their own romanticized version of it. "How many days do we have till Texas is supposed to vote?" Leary asked.

"Three," Avery said.

"Okay, then, what do we do here, Mr. Adams?"

The president had never directly asked her for guidance before—he always went through Ruffles first—but his chief of staff was off getting a crown replaced and Leary was desperate to be off the phone, a coalescence that left her with more influence than she'd ever had in her three years of working at the White House.

"I think you should meet with Governor Travis," she said.

"You do?"

"Yes, Mr. President. As you know, I've met him."

The president had forgotten that she was the one sent to dispatch Travis when he came to the White House a few weeks back. "That's right. What did you think about him?"

"I think he's no match for you, sir," she said quickly. Leary stood up taller upon hearing her say it. "You're more intelligent, you're more eloquent, you understand the complexities of the issue . . ."

"Doesn't sound like it's even going to be a fair fight," Leary said.

"You'll pulverize him," Avery said.

Leary couldn't wipe the smug look off his face, not even when he spotted the head pro of Pine Valley speeding toward him in a golf cart, shaking his finger. "Fine, Miss Adams," Leary said, whispering again. "Set it up."

Anatole Metzos was barely conscious. The bottle of Glenfiddich was empty and rested at his feet. His cell phone buzzed and scooted a half inch across his desk. Paige watched him sleep from the doorway. She had popped in a few times already that morning, and the only things that had changed were the position of his phone and size of the puddle of drool around his mouth.

Paige wasn't going to wait any longer. She walked silently across his carpet and placed her letter of resignation on his desk near his head. Where she would go from here she didn't know. There were worse things to have to fall back on than a bachelor's degree from Yale. She turned to leave, and Metzos's phone buzzed again. It continued its slow creep, reached the far edge of his desk, and disappeared over the side like a barrel going over a waterfall. It landed in his trash can without a noise, cushioned by a few days of shredded paper.

Paige turned back to rescue the phone. She knew that if she didn't, Metzos would waste the first hour after he woke looking for it. She set it on top of her letter and spotted the waiting text message: *WE CAN STILL FIX THIS.* It was from a 512 number. Austin.

She looked out toward the reception area, where a steaming cup of tea sat on Brianne's desk. Paige wanted to walk away; to just be done. Her idealized notion of progressive politics was already feeling fragile. She feared that she was one body blow away from peeling the Kerry/Edwards sticker off her snowboard. One right hook away from thumbing through Dick Cheney's memoirs. One anesthetizing uppercut away from being open-minded about Sarah Palin. She could feel every friend, every professor, every colleague she ever had screaming through her subconscious, telling her to set Metzos's phone on the desk and leave. It was the same enlightened chorus that had convinced her that the floundering Keynesian policies of the last three and a half years had failed only because they didn't go far enough; the gentrified voices that brushed aside the notion that the dying progressive democracies of Western Europe were harbingers of America's own demise; elitist spirits begging her not to look beyond the *New York Times* editorial page.

She had always liked to think of herself as a rebel. She had certainly been one in Texas. Now, however, she stood convicted of the fact that here in Washington, she had become the establishment. She was exactly what she once would have questioned. None of this meant she had to denounce NPR or join the Tea Party. It just meant she had to call that 512 number.

She slithered over to Brianne's vacant desk and dialed. The call nearly went to voice mail before it was answered on the fourth ring. "Yes," a male voice said. *Well, that's not helpful,* Paige thought. She was hoping for someone who answered the phone like her aunt— *"This is Peg Parsons!"*—of course Aunt Peg was way too forthcoming with all personal information. She opened last year's Christmas newsletter with a detailed account of her botched hysterectomy.

"Anybody there?" the man asked. Paige recognized the gruff voice but couldn't put a face to it. Hearing Brianne's bagel pop up from the toaster in the kitchen, she decided to pull out the French accent she'd used when she played Elmire in a particularly awful high school adaptation of *Tartuffe*. "Escuse, I'm calling from Monsieur Metzos's office. Such a busy day. I've quite forgotten whom I dialed . . ."

"Oh," the voice said. He paused before saying anything else, as if he, too, were questioning the identity of the person on the other end. Paige decided not to say anything else either, lest he was one word away from discovering she was a fraud. After a few more seconds, he broke. "It's Bill Lewis, darlin'."

"Oh. Yes . . . of course," Paige said, trying to keep her wits about her. "Monsieur Metzos wanted me to apologize and tell you he'll be calling you shortly."

"Fine," Big Bill said. Brianne turned the corner as Paige hung up.

"Who was that?" Brianne asked.

"No one," said Paige. "Just checking on . . . um . . . hey, is that blueberry?"

"Oh, yes," Brianne said.

"Looks good," Paige said, putting an end to the gripping conversation. She excused herself and returned to Metzos's office. He hadn't moved. She wanted more answers. She reached down and opened his side desk drawer. It slid with precision like a pair of skates on a freshly Zamboni'd rink. There were no files, just an untouched stack of white paper embossed with an *FF*. She squeezed between his chair and the wall and opened the drawer on the other side. Stationery. How could a man with so much paper have no paper trail? She set the phone back on the center of this desk and spotted his trash can, filled with a few days' worth of shreds.

It had been a decade since Paige had stuffed her bra, not that she hadn't considered it a time or two since. With Brianne busy dunking her tea, Paige went to work, packing a pound of possible evidence inside her blouse. By the time she was finished, she looked like a scarecrow, strips of paper escaping from between buttons. She wedged them in best she could and tried to give it all some vague booblike form. Despite her effort, the left one was far bigger than the right. As she worked on balancing them out, Metzos began to stir. She abandoned her self-augmentation and grabbed his cell phone one last time, setting it at the bottom of his empty trash can. If it took him an hour to find it, good, she thought. She needed as much of a head start as she could get.

Travis and Cole were already in the office. They found it far more fun to do transition-of-power planning now that it appeared a transition of power might actually happen. Cole had a giant list of things they'd need to know in advance. They had been through most of the big ones, but there were a few incidentals he hadn't solved yet. Travis cut him off with a worry of his own.

"What do we do about the Cowboys?" Travis asked.

"What cowboys?" said Cole.

"The *Dallas* Cowboys," said Travis. "I'm not worried about losing our baseball teams. The Major Leagues already have a Canadian team. But the NFL . . . I don't know. I wouldn't put it past the Redskins to find a way to ban us from the league."

"So what? It's just football," Cole said, eyeing his sheet of paper with twenty far more pressing issues.

"Geez, you have been in New Jersey a long time," Travis said. Cole sighed, conceded the indiscretion, and added the future of the Dallas Cowboys to his list.

The pair had been in an ebullient mood all morning, and it began thanks to an unlikely source: the *Austin American–Statesman.* The paper had been slipped under Travis's bedroom door by the mansion staff. The headline had shouted at him as he rolled off his favorite couch:

TRAVIS TRICKS . . . AND TREATS!

Travis had never received such a chummy headline from the *Statesman,* but in a bit of good fortune, the regular night editor at the paper was out with a gout flare and the backup editor had food poisoning. Third in line was a closet Austin Tea Party Patriot who had seen a rare opportunity to bolster the cause and took it. Over breakfast, Cole argued that the headline wasn't biased at all.

"Why not?" Travis had asked.

"Because it's true!"

Other than Wexler not being around to see it, the cyber coup had been a total success. Both Rasmussen and Gallup were calling it the biggest day-to-day jump in support the pollsters had ever recorded. The Web sites that had been targeted pretended to be livid about it in public but were secretly giddy that they'd been deemed worthy of such select sabotage. Each one had seen at least a 40 percent bump in traffic because of it, long after the video had been discovered. Once the video was removed, people who had missed it or who wanted to see it again ended up at Travis's official Web site, where visitors could not only watch the famous video but could also listen to all of the governor's other appearances on the Walt Thompson show and read about Texas's simple plan for self-governance. The site had received nine million hits in ten hours.

Fran knocked on the open door and delivered the next round of pleasant news. "The White House is on line one," she said, smiling.

"Wow," Cole said, raising his eyebrows.

"What do you think this is about?" Travis asked.

"Has to be good," said Cole. "The only time this president meets with his enemies is after he's done or said something incredibly stupid."

Travis tried to guess the purpose of the call. "What if they offer me a trade: Wexler for Texas?" Last they heard he was being transported to a federal holding facility near D.C. while awaiting trial.

"Look, I like the kid and all, but I don't even think he'd want you to take that deal."

Travis put the call on speaker for Cole's enjoyment. "This is Governor Travis, how can I help you?"

"Governor, this is Mark Ruflowski, White House chief of staff."

"Hi there, Mark. How the heck are ya?"

Ruffles wasn't about to say it, but he was pissed. He had only been gone from the White House for a few hours and returned from the relative calm of dental work to find that the president was asking to meet with his chief rival and, thanks to the persuasiveness of Avery Adams, would not be talked out of it.

"I'm calling on behalf of the president," Ruffles said. "He would like to meet with you at the White House at your earliest possible convenience."

"Sure, Mark. I'd love to. How's next week sometime?" Travis smiled, knowing this was not the answer Ruffles was hoping to receive.

"Uh, well . . . I'm sure the president would like to do it sooner than that. Can you meet tomorrow?"

"Hmm . . ." Travis flipped through his notepad as if he were looking at his calendar for the next few days. "Oh, Mark, boy, that's going to be hard for me to pull off, what with us seceding and all."

"It needs to be tomorrow. In Washington. How's noon?"

"Mark, again, I appreciate the effort, but that's just not going to be possible."

"Governor Travis, it's important you understand that the president is reaching out with an olive branch here. It might look bad for you to turn down the meeting, don't you agree?"

Travis shrugged at Cole, willing to take the risk, but Cole nodded forcefully. You can't turn down the president of the United States. "Okay, Mark, tomorrow at noon, then."

"Wonderful. I'll tell the president."

"Oh, but Mark—"

"Yes?"

"I can't do it in Washington."

"No?"

"No, I'm sorry, I can't," Travis said.

"The president was very specific about the Washington part." Leary didn't care so much about that, but Ruffles was hell-bent on at least making Travis come to them.

"I understand where you're coming from, Mark, and I'm not

insinuating that he is any less busy than I am. I mean, heck, I was there just a few weeks ago trying to see him, and he was . . . well, I forget, what was he doing again?" Travis was making the most of his leverage.

Ruffles fumbled. "Oh . . . that was the day he was . . . speaking at the, um, National . . . Bureau . . . of American . . ."

"It doesn't matter, Mark. That's not the point." It *was* the point. "Just let the president know I'll meet him at the Cotton Gin Cafe at noon."

"I'm sorry, the where?"

"Cotton Gin Cafe. In Prosper. It's a few doors down from Maggie's dress shop." He could hear Ruffles digging for a pen.

". . . Maggie's Dress Shop . . ."

"I'm pretty sure that's what it's called. Bottom line is that it's a shop that sells dresses and the lady who owns it is named Maggie."

"Ah." He heard Ruffles scribble out what he'd written. "Is there an address?" He was keeping his cool, but just barely.

"It's basically the only restaurant in Prosper," said Travis. "Just ask anyone on the street and they'll point the way."

"Governor, this may be fine, but just know that we have to clear everything through Secret Service first. See if there are any security concerns regarding the location."

"Security concerns? I can answer that one for you. It's a nonissue. Pretty much everyone there will be carrying a gun."

"I beg your pardon?"

"Guns. Firearms. Some won't even be concealed. And that's good for your guys, because no one would be dumb enough to try something there. If someone did, he'd end up with a head full of lead."

"Well, that's . . . good to know, Governor. Tomorrow then . . . Cotton Gin Cafe."

"High noon," Travis added. He hung up the phone and grinned triumphantly at Cole.

"I can't believe he agreed to that," Cole said.

"I can," said Travis, "and you know why?"

Cole shook his head.

"We're winning," Travis said.

Paige waited in the reception area of the *Washington Post* with a canvas grocery bag on her lap and a complimentary copy of that morning's paper in her hands. The *Post*, like every other paper in America, was anorexic. Every time she picked one up it was a little lighter than the time before.

Aubrey Garza approached from the newsroom with trepidation. She was pretty but plain, figuring that she was a decade away from being famous enough for her picture to run alongside her articles. When the time came she'd worry about finding the perfect lip liner to match her short coffee-colored hair. Until then, she was happy in Chuck Taylor Converses and T-shirts with ironic sayings. Today's choice: MY THERAPIST THINKS YOU'RE THE PROBLEM.

The only contact she'd had from Paige since the *Post* ran her hit piece on Travis a while back was a very brief phone message, which consisted of an exasperated Paige mumbling the word "itch"— though likely something worse—while trying to hang up. She was glad the big receptionist was working today, just in case this reunion turned into a catfight.

Paige lowered the paper and faked a smile. "Hey, stranger."

"Hi," Aubrey said.

Paige folded the paper neatly—not hard to do with only twelve pages—and tossed it on the open seat next to her. "In the interest of time," Paige began, "I'm not even going to bring up the article. No matter how betrayed and used I felt, I'm not even going there. Was it evil for you to do that to a close friend? Obviously. Was it spineless for you to not even reach out and apologize after what I assume was a tsunami of guilt rolled over you? Yes. But that's a topic for another day. Agreed?"

"Well . . ." Aubrey didn't want to swallow the premise that easily.

"Just agree. Because I'm about to offer you the story of the year."

"*Me?*"

"I know. *You.* What does that say about the current state of mainstream journalism when, even after you did what you did, I still trust you more than any of the other reporters in town?"

The only reason Aubrey had torpedoed Paige was out of fear of losing her job. The *Post* had fired thirty people since she started four months ago and warned of more to come. If she wanted to stay, she had to deliver.

"What's the story?" Aubrey asked.

"Hopefully, the answer to that question is in this bag." She opened the bag and held it up. Aubrey peered inside to see hundreds of pieces of shredded paper Paige had taken from Metzos's office.

"Confetti."

"*Evidence.*"

"Of what?"

"I'm not sure."

"You're not sure?"

"That's why I need you."

Aubrey put her hands on her hips, exposing a quarter inch of olive skin at her waist. "Paige, I want to help you. I do. But I can't leave the newsroom. Not today. If I walk away and there's nothing in that bag but scraps, I lose my job."

"There *is* something," said Paige. "I can feel it."

"Good," Aubrey said. "Let me know when you can see it."

31

Travis let K drive him to Prosper early the next morning. He wanted to bone up on random Texas history on the way to impress President Leary.

"Did you know the first Frito was fried in Texas?" Travis asked, his eyes stuck in a book.

"Huh," K said. He estimated it was his hundredth "huh" since they left Austin.

"And did you know the word 'maverick' came from Samuel Maverick, a Texas rancher who refused to brand his calves?"

"Huh."

"And did you realize that it's farther from El Paso to Texarkana than it is from Texarkana to Chicago?"

"Wow," K said, ecstatic to see the exit for Prosper off Highway 289.

The town of Prosper was born in 1902 when the St. Louis, San Francisco, and Texas Railway needed a stop in the agricultural region of North Texas. By the mid-1980s, the town had barely grown at all and was home to just eleven businesses and a population that had topped off near a thousand. In the last decade, however, thousands of Dallas suburbanites had discovered the town and made it their own. Even so, downtown Prosper remained one story high and half a block long. Just when it seemed to be getting started, it ended.

On one side were the town bank and a lawn maintenance company. On the other, sharing a weathered brick facade that looked older than the Alamo, were a men's Baptist retreat center, the Prosper Police Department, and the Cotton Gin Cafe.

The largest thing in downtown Prosper was the street. Aptly named Broadway, it was so wide that cars parked perpendicular to the curb on both sides, which still left plenty of room in between for even the biggest pickups in Texas to make a U-turn.

It was only eleven thirty when Travis and K parked. Travis was like his father in this regard. The more important the event, the earlier he left. "We could keep driving around for a bit if you want," Travis said, flipping through the end of his book.

"No," K said, worried that if he heard one more fact about the Rio Grande he'd be tempted to cross it and never come back.

Judging by the number of open parking spots on Broadway, no one in Prosper cared that the president of the United States was making his inaugural visit. The town was just as drowsy as on any other blazing afternoon in early June.

Travis and K stepped onto the sidewalk and took seats on the wooden bench in front of the restaurant. Travis had been torn about what to wear. If he wore a suit into the Cotton Gin, someone would cut his tie off with a pair of scissors. If he wore jeans, he might be accused of disrespecting the presidency. He split the difference and went with khakis, boots, and his best blue dress shirt, sleeves rolled up and open at the collar.

"No sign of Secret Service yet, huh?" Travis asked, looking around the quiet street.

"Look again," K said. He nodded toward the roof above Lawn Tech, where a sniper sat munching on a sandwich.

"Impressive," Travis said. "What else do you see that I don't?"

K didn't hesitate. "There's some lady in a blue sweater standing in the window of the lawn place across the street. There's a plane at ten o'clock, about three thousand feet, heading south. The front right tire of that Dodge Ram is a little flat. But all I really care about is that guy staring at you in the black Ford Expedition with the windows down."

Three cars away, a middle-aged man with dark shades and a black ball cap pulled down tight was indeed fixated on Travis. Seeing he'd been spotted, he rolled up the windows and stepped out. K had his hand on his gun and the safety off . . . just in case. The stranger stepped onto the sidewalk and gave a militant wave. "Governor!" he said.

"You know this guy?" K asked.

"I don't think so," Travis said, a bit nervous himself.

K stood up and stepped in front of Travis. "Can I help you?"

"Oh, I get it," the guy said, a bit offended, but not in the least bit intimidated. "What are you going to do? Shoot me?"

"If I have to," K said.

"That won't be necessary," the guy said, playing it cool. He went to pat K on the back but never got the chance. K lowered his shoulder into the man's chin and sent him wobbling backward toward the sidewalk. K caught him before his head hit the ground, spun him around in midair, and pinned him to the sidewalk with his knee, all in one fluid motion. The sharpshooter on top of Turley Insurance Services craned his head and kept chewing, appreciating the free show.

"Who the hell do you think you are?" K asked in disbelief at this guy's moxie.

"Mike McKill," he grunted, "and that was one hell of a move." Travis and K looked at each other before leaning over to get a better look at his face, still pressed to the cement. The hat and sunglasses had made it harder to recognize him, but the most effective part of the disguise was the fact that after almost twenty years away from Hollywood, he looked nothing like Mike McKill.

His bulging muscles were nonexistent. His famous bronzed skin was saggy, pale with sun spots, and covered in a visible sheen of SPF 50. McKill had always been on the short side, but every pound he put on in the last two decades created the visual effect of pulling him even closer to the ground; so much so that if Travis had been forced to guess what celebrity he was, his first guess would have been Danny DeVito.

"Nice to meet you," Travis said. "I know it may not seem like it now, but . . . I'm a big fan."

K helped McKill over to the bench while Travis sent a Cotton Gin waitress to fetch some ice from the kitchen. In McKill's defense, he had tried on six different occasions to reach Travis by phone, but none of his calls was returned. When he heard on the news that Travis was having a powwow with the president in Prosper, he hopped in his King Air turboprop and flew himself northeast from his private airstrip in Brownwood.

"You sure you're okay?" Travis asked, watching McKill's chin turn purple.

"Please," McKill said. "If you're not bleeding, you're not alive." He spoke with a brooding staccato rhythm, every phrase pressed to produce the maximum tension.

"I love that movie," Travis said. "*Battle Scars,* right?" McKill had the habit of stealing liberally from the dialogue of his past films without knowing it.

McKill shook his head in disdain. "Hollywood . . . it's a fickle town. One minute you're 1992's *People* Magazine Sexiest Man of the Year, and the next, you're excited about getting a call from the casting director at *Dancing with the Stars.*"

"You got asked to do *Dancing with the Stars?*" K said. McKill gave K an embarrassed look. Apparently he hadn't.

"The truth is that town wanted me to fail," he continued. "I was too extreme. I didn't play by their rules. They told me I had to join the Screen Actors Guild; I said no. They tried to get me to renounce my membership in the NRA; I said no. When they told me to stop calling Bill Clinton a fascist pig, I called *them* fascist pigs. So toward the end, the studio just stopped promoting my films. *Variety* wouldn't even review 'em. I don't expect you to understand the entertainment industry, but you can make the best movies of all time and if no one knows they exist, you're not going to make a dime." Travis had seen those films. They were not the best movies of all time. "So I left. Took the money and ran. Bought a plane and a huge big piece of land where no one could find me."

"Good for you," Travis said.

"Yep. Lined the entire place with guns and ammo."

"Oh," said Travis, hoping McKill meant that figuratively.

The waitress returned with the ice. McKill waved her off and kept talking. "See, I knew this day was coming. And to think they called me crazy—can you believe that?" Travis gave no reaction, but McKill had lived alone for so long that he didn't need another person to carry on a two-way conversation. "Yep. They did. But I knew the Feds were moving in on us. I knew they'd come for Texas eventually. That's why I'm here. That's why I've been stalking you."

"You've been stalking me?" Travis asked. K was ready to pin McKill back to the ground should the situation call for it.

"Governor, I've been waiting eighteen years to find my next project. This is it. I'm all yours." McKill put his right hand to his head and gave Travis an earnest salute.

As much as celebrity endorsements can help a cause, Travis was certain that a bloated, paranoid Mike McKill was not the best choice to increase his credibility. "I appreciate that, Mike," Travis said. "I mean, I definitely need as much support as possible, but from a PR perspective, I think we're in pretty good—" Travis didn't finish the sentence. Mike McKill was laughing at him. It was his trademark laugh. Low and constant like a Harley waiting at a stoplight. "What's so funny?"

McKill composed himself. "Governor, you can't really believe you've got this won, can you? There's gonna be a fight. A fight that will make the standoff between Admiral Skyler and Dirk Dawson's boys look like a kindergarten field trip."

Travis was puzzled by the historical reference, then realized McKill was pulling it from the climax of one of his movies that went straight to VHS. "Okay, fine," Travis said, "and should that happen, what exactly would your role be?"

"Whatever you need. Hired gun. Weapons expert. Spy. I once

spent three weeks training with Navy SEALs. I don't want to brag, but there's not much I haven't done."

Yes, on film, Travis thought, *and often with the aid of a professional stuntman.* He caught a quick glimpse of an amused K. "Well, look," he said, "I'm gonna mull this one over."

"Of course," McKill said. "Mull. Strategize. Take a few days."

"I've already got your number, so . . ."

McKill looked uneasy. "Actually, I wouldn't call. Not now. I mean, we've been seen in public together. They'll be listening."

"Okay . . ."

"E-mail's probably out, too. Same reason," McKill said. "I'm gonna give you an address in Brownwood." He took out a scrap of paper and jotted down the info. "You need me, this is how you find me." He looked both ways, then handed the paper to Travis. "Just don't come after dark. It's best not to sneak up on me." Travis opened the paper and looked at it.

SETH JOSEPHSON
135 County Road 464
Brownwood, TX 76801

"Who's Seth Josephson?" Travis asked.

"That's me. Mike McKill is just a stage name."

"Really?" Travis asked, feigning surprise.

K's phone buzzed. He pulled it out of his pocket and stole a glance. "Five minutes away," he said to Travis.

McKill was back on his feet. "I guess that's my cue, Governor." He shook Travis's hand and nodded at K. "See you boys at the gates of Hades." They watched him as he waddled back to his SUV.

K waited until he was out of earshot. "What movie was that from?" he asked.

"Heat Packer 2," Travis said.

"Geez, I didn't know they made a second one," said K.

"They shouldn't have," said Travis.

The floor of Paige's apartment looked like a ticker tape parade thrown by someone with OCD. Strips of paper covered every flat surface, but all were facing the same direction in neat, orderly lines. Delano, her cat, scratched at the bathroom door, angry that so much shredded paper was going unbatted. After throwing out all the bits of napkin and Kleenex, Paige organized the rest by color, then by thickness. Beyond that there wasn't much science to it. It was pure trial and error, matching up fonts and numbers and handwriting. When she had four or five strips in a row, she slapped a piece of Scotch tape on them.

Paige had worked through the night without finding anything of note. Much of it was worthless: a subscription slip that had fallen out of *Mother Jones* magazine, a handwritten receipt from Mutuku for two cases of Fiji water, a graphic love letter from Metzos's super-model wife, Stefania. While the things Stefania described were certainly life-threatening to a man of Metzos's age, they were hardly enough to warrant congressional hearings.

There were downloaded news articles and transcripts of speeches from the White House, not a surprise considering Metzos rarely watched TV. There were some interoffice memos, all banal. A half-dozen while-you-were-outs from Brianne, but none of the names raised any suspicions. Paige was down to only a few dozen unaccounted-for strips, and the only thing the shreds proved beyond a reasonable doubt was that Anatole Metzos probably didn't need a paper shredder.

She pressed on anyway, masochism replacing curiosity as the driving force behind the task. She taped a few more strips together, reassembling an 8½" by 11" piece of paper that Metzos had used to play tic-tac-toe against himself, and flipped it over as was her routine to see what, if anything, was coming together on the other side.

There were only a few words to read on each line, but they grabbed her attention.

```
6.4 WH    National S
```

```
              ISTRIBUTION**
         EXAS—G.T. a "lone nu

         ovement easily contain

         y swift Fed response.
                —Few ready-to-f
                —Control of com
                —XX thousand tr

                —No sign of sup
```

Paige searched the remaining strips for size 12 Courier and pieced it together. Having been at this for almost twenty-four hours, she was like a machine, spinning strips around and moving them back and forth until letters become words and words became sentences. She cross-checked her work by making sure the *X*'s and *O*'s on the tic-tac-toe side lined up as well. She slapped on the final piece of tape, turned it back over, and read it from the top.

```
6.4 WH    National Security Briefing
```

```
**FOR IMMEDIATE DISTRIBUTION**
  1. TEXAS - G.T. a "lone nut." Assessed threat:
     MINIMAL.
     Movement easily contained with/without G.T.
     but must be met
     by swift Fed response.
                —Few ready-to-fight TX/G.T. loyalists
                —Control of communication lines vital
                —XX thousand troops within XX hours
                 of border
                —No signs of support from OK, AR, LA
```

It appeared to be the agenda—or at least part of it—for the President's Daily Brief (PDB). It didn't matter where the president was, not a day went by when he didn't have his PDB. Every meeting was initiated and run by the director of national intelligence for the CIA and consisted of a global rundown on the latest American security threats and the various tools at the president's disposal to fight them.

There wasn't much decoding to do. "G.T." was obviously Governor Travis. The line about troop levels was ambiguous. With those two exceptions, it was a transparent report, and as of two days ago, the CIA didn't seem too worried about Texas's chances for victory, especially if Washington showed some muscle.

It wasn't the details of the brief that concerned her. It was the fact Metzos had access to them at all. What was said in PDBs was top secret, never to be shared except at the discretion of the president himself. If President Leary was willingly passing national intelligence to an outside individual with no government oversight, it was unsettling. If someone else was leaking it to Metzos without the president's permission, it was criminal.

The Cotton Gin Cafe only had nine tables. Some square, some round, and never in the same configuration two days running. You ordered off the giant whiteboard at the front, you filled your own foam cup of soda, and the Heinz ketchup and French's mustard were waiting for you on the table.

"Fine dining," K said as he took in the scene.

A pair of camera crews were camped out near the kitchen and already rolling. Five Secret Service–approved photographers were with them, snapping away as Travis sized up the afternoon clientele. Travis grabbed a passing waitress. "Hey, Ginny, who are these people?" he asked. Except for the staff, he didn't recognize a single one. They were young, beautiful, and diverse. It was as though they'd been kidnapped from a Gap ad.

"Oh," she said, replacing her pencil behind her ear. "They were brought in on a bus an hour ago from Dallas. Guess the president was worried about the local yokels."

"How about that?" Travis said. "The turd's trying to neutralize the home field advantage."

Outside the restaurant, a line of black cars pulled up. The Beast, miniature American flags waving from its hood, stopped in the middle of Broadway and idled. Secret Service poured from the other vehicles and fanned out along the street to secure the area. One of them, an intimidating white guy with a prominent brow and shaved head, was the first to enter the restaurant. He walked with his left shoulder visibly lower than the right, a high school wrestling injury whose only side effect was that when he walked, he looked like he was trying to turn left but couldn't. The Secret Service listed it as an attribute on his initial evaluation since it made his movements harder to predict. He saw the governor and nodded.

"Governor, I'm Agent Dermis."

"Howdy."

"Beg your pardon?" Travis might as well have been speaking in tongues.

"Howdy," Travis repeated.

"Oh. Yes. Howdy to you, too," Dermis said. "I just want to go over the plan."

"Of course," said Travis.

"The president is going to walk through the front door behind me, and the two of you will shake hands right about where we're standing now. From there you and the president will walk and sit at that table over there." He pointed to a square one in the corner. "You'll talk, eat lunch . . . we're estimating twenty minutes beginning to end. Sound good?"

Travis was a bit thrown. "Well, we have to order at the front. That's how it works here."

"We know how it works, governor. We made special arrangements with the management for you to order at the table. It will be simpler that way."

Agent Dermis didn't give Travis the opportunity to discuss it further. He turned and faced the street. Travis figured it was a signal, because the moment he did another agent opened the passenger door of the limo.

President Leary had also had questions about proper attire for the lunch. He'd even brought different options in case he saw Travis through the tinted window and decided that a change was in order. Ruffles said it was important he look both presidential and relatable. The long-sleeved dress shirt was never in question, but when the limo door opened, the president was just zipping up his most comfortable blue jeans (relatable) pressed with a crease down the front of each designer leg (presidential).

Leary hopped onto the sidewalk with some pep and strode into the Cotton Gin Cafe as Agent Dermis held the door. The patrons stopped eating and applauded as cameras rolled. Some snapped photos with their phones. *How much are these kids getting paid?* Travis wondered. Leary waved warmly and made his way toward Travis as the camera shutters clicked.

"Michael Leary. Pleasure to meet you, Governor."

They shook hands. Firm on both ends. Another wave of flashes. "Welcome to Prosper, Mr. President," Travis said.

"Beautiful country out here, isn't it, Governor? Just heavenly."

"If your idea of heaven is hot, flat, and brown," Travis said.

Agent Dermis gently put one hand on the president's back and stretched the other one toward their assigned table. Leary started to head toward his seat.

"Actually, what do you say we order first?" Travis asked, leaving Leary behind.

The president stopped to look at Agent Dermis, then back at Travis, who was widening his lead. "Sure," Leary said, changing direction and heading toward the register.

K consoled Agent Dermis as they trailed. "If it makes you feel any better, he doesn't listen to me either."

Leary crossed his arms and tried to make sense of the handwritten menu as photographers scooted around them and kept snapping. The kitchen staff abandoned their duties for a closer look. A ponytailed girl in a green Cotton Gin T-shirt waited starry-eyed behind the counter.

"Mr. President," Travis said, "I know you're busy thinking, but do you know Cassie Johnson, by chance?"

Leary was still looking up. "Is she on the House Armed Services Committee?"

"Boy, I don't think so," said Travis. He looked at the girl behind the register. "Cassie, you're not on the House Armed Services Committee, are you?" The photographers and the kitchen staff all laughed.

Leary looked down from the menu and realized the joke was on him. He joined in the laughter, then tried to cover his gaffe. "My bad, my bad. President Michael Leary. Nice to meet you." She shook his hand. "So Cassie, tell me, everything looks good. What should I get?"

"I'll answer that," Travis said. Leary wished he wouldn't. "If you don't get the chicken fried steak, you're an idiot."

"Is that so?" the president asked.

"Tell him, Cassie," Travis said.

"It's our specialty," said Cassie.

"Specialty, huh? I guess I can't argue with that," said Leary. He could sense the first lady shaking her head in judgment from a thousand miles away.

"Make it two," said Travis.

She pushed a button on the register. "You want fries?"

"I don't know," the president said. "What kind of oil are they prepared in?"

Cassie paused for a beat. She'd never been asked that question before. "Hot," she explained. Another wave of laughter from the kitchen staff.

"Great," Leary said, not about to be skewered a second time. "It just so happens that's my favorite kind."

They filled up their soda cups and sat on opposite sides of the brown table. Per Secret Service orders, the photographers and cameramen stayed out of earshot. Seeing as the steaks wouldn't be ready for a few more minutes, Travis saw no reason to put off the real purpose for their get-together. "So what's on your mind, Mr. President?"

Travis folded his hands on the table. It was uneven, and when he did, the table tilted slightly in his direction. Leary, fearing that this might be some local form of one-upmanship, put his hands on the table and pressed down slightly, forcing the table to lean back toward him.

"Governor, as you probably know, it's been a century and a half since a state tried to leave the Union. And it's not because states haven't had gripes with the federal government. They have. Some state is always mad about something. Yet in every case, the state and the federal government have found a way through it—a solution that both sides can agree upon as fair. I'm here because I believe you and I can find one for Texas."

"I don't take our call to evacuate the Union lightly, Mr. President." Travis spotted the smallest of sneers on Leary's face when he said the word "evacuate." "This isn't a game to me. It's a big deal."

"Good," Leary said. He said it but he didn't mean it. In a perfect scenario, Travis would have already broken down under the pressure and confessed that he was doing all this out of boredom or to impress some woman. "The way I see it, we just have a communication problem. Like you, I want what's best for the people of Texas. Perhaps where I fell short was not explaining that clearly enough."

Travis had heard this rhetoric before from the president. He never believed it was his ideas that were unpopular with the American people; it was merely the way he presented them. "Then by all means," Travis said, "explain how taking private property away from the citizens of your strongest state in order to pay for the fiscal buffoonery of the citizens in your weakest states is a victory for Texas." He knew Cole would be proud of him for forcing the president to define his terms.

"I'd be glad to," the president said. He had done some law school teaching and always enjoyed the chance to enlighten his wayward students. "Since I know you're a businessman, for this argument, let's imagine the government's a business."

246 ★ Bob Smiley

"That *will* take some imagination," Travis said. It was hard to envision a scenario where a business could stay afloat while carrying fifteen trillion dollars in debt.

"And let's say you're the boss," the president continued. "You have fifty employees. Now, some of them are outstanding. They show up on time. They work hard. They make the greatest number of products with the fewest errors. But there are a few that are struggling. Maybe one of them has some extra mouths to feed at home. Or maybe one has a bad back that prevents him or her from working as many hours as the good employee does. But as the boss, you know that if those struggling employees could have a little bit of the money you might have paid to the good employees, the strugglers could turn things around. They could go to the doctor and get their backs fixed. They could get those kids off to college or into jobs. A few years down the road, that struggling employee might be your *best* employee. And that could make the company even stronger than it was before. So strong, in fact, that those good employees might even get a raise. To me, that sounds like a pretty fair deal. It's a win-win. But Governor, with the way you talk, if you were the boss, you'd get rid of those little guys and let them suffer all alone. That's just not something I can defend." The president took a sip from his Diet Coke and leaned back in his chair. The table tilted back to Travis. "Now, you tell *me* where that analogy falls apart."

Travis thought about it for a second, trying in vain to make sense of the logic. "Look, Mr. President, I know you're far more educated than I am, and you have a bunch of degrees from hoity-toity universities that would have laughed at my high school transcript, but I'm pretty sure your analogy falls apart right at the beginning. I mean, I can't even buy the basic premise of it."

Leary was irked. "How so?"

"Well, correct me if I'm wrong, but as I understand it, the states in this country don't work for you. You work for *them*. They formed the Union, not the other way around. So really, if it were a business *you'd* be the employee and you'd have fifty bosses. And if that were the case, I don't imagine your super-successful boss would appreciate your taking some of his property and giving it to one of the less successful bosses without getting his approval. In fact, I'm pretty sure if you tried it, he'd call the police and have you arrested for stealing."

"I think you're reaching, Governor."

"Now, Mr. President, I'm not saying there's not a legal route for you to do some of the things you want. The Founders gave you that option. Get it passed through Congress and then get two-thirds of the states to agree that it makes sense." Leary stared at him blankly. "I'm talking about a constitutional amend—"

"I know what a constitutional amendment is, Governor Travis."

"I'm sorry. Of course you do. Now, I'll be honest. If you were to get one of those passed, you'd be taking a lot of the wind out of our sails. Unfortunately, you don't have that. You're operating on a decree based upon an executive order that none of your fifty bosses ever had the opportunity to approve. So you'll have to forgive me for not exactly loving the idea."

Ginny arrived with the chicken fried steaks and the two baskets of fries lined up on her forearm. "Here y'are," she said, tossing them down with no great affection. "Holler if y'all need something."

Leary reached for a fry. "Whoa whoa," Travis said. "Aren't we going to pray?" Travis didn't pray in public all that often but couldn't resist the chance to tweak Leary.

"Of course," the president said. He put his hands together and bowed his head. Even though he'd skipped the last three National Prayer Breakfasts, it wasn't like he'd forgotten how it's done.

"Dear Lord," Travis began, "thank you for this meal and thank you for the blessing of bringing President Leary to Prosper today. I pray for the president, Lord. I pray for his protection and I pray that you would bless him as he makes decisions. And on this particular issue, Lord, I pray that he would see the error of his ways and the hardness of his heart." Leary gritted his teeth and hoped the video camera mikes weren't picking any of this up. "I pray that he would remember that while Jesus and his followers did share all of their possessions with each other, that they did it because they wanted to

and not because the Roman government made them. And I pray for me, Lord, for strength and courage and wisdom. And of course, God bless Texas. Amen." Travis looked up and smiled innocently. "Dig in!"

The prayer had killed what was left of Leary's appetite. He didn't even want to look at the food. "Governor, I'd like to suggest a compromise."

"I'm listening," Travis said.

"You should know that I promised some of my people I wouldn't do this, but I'm going to. If it will make it easier for you to say yes, I am willing to amend the RRA. Here's my proposal. First, we'll drop the water provision. We won't even touch it."

"But you built the giant pipeline . . ."

"It's yours. No questions asked. As for the rest of the act, we'll delay the full implementation for three years. We'll stagger it. Do it in little pieces. We'll start with oil. See what you think of our operation. If you don't like the way it's playing out, we'll work together to find a better solution. As anyone can tell you, I'm always open to hearing other ideas."

Travis dabbed his face with a napkin. "Okay, let me make sure I understand. We keep the water," he said.

"Right."

"Even though it was already ours to begin with."

"Well—"

"And then you're still going to do all the other stuff, just not all at once."

"Yes," said the president, "and if you have a problem with that—"

"Right, I almost forgot. If I have a problem with that, I can let you know."

"Exactly." It made sense to Leary.

"Okay, well, in that case, consider this lunch me letting you know I have a problem with that."

"But you haven't even given us a chance to—"

"When was the last time the federal government ever gave back private property that it took from someone? When was the last time the federal government ended a program that wasn't working? Or made real cuts in half-baked programs that cost far more than any-one estimated? Your side doesn't have a good track record on this, Mr. President!"

K, standing a few feet behind Travis with his hands clasped in front, stole a quick glance at Agent Dermis, trying to gauge how unusual it was to see someone take the president to the mat like this. Dermis was focused on Travis, a telling gesture that answered K's question.

Travis picked up a french fry and fed it into his mouth like a log going into a wood chipper before he continued. "I'll be honest. On some bizarre level, I admire what I believe is your unbridled opti-mism in government intervention in our lives, Mr. President. What's scary is how, in order to think that way, you have to look past a thousand different examples of government screwing things up in a thousand irreparable ways."

Leary hadn't had a single bite but was still going to need a full heart workup from his cardiologist when he returned to Washing-ton. "I'm sorry to see your resistance, Governor. I really am. I was hoping to show the American people some true bipartisanship here."

"Were you really?" Travis asked. "Because it seems like biparti-sanship in your view means that people like me agree to the majority of your proposals and never the other way around. When *you* say no, you call it 'standing on principle.' Consider me doing the same."

The president didn't intend to leave Texas empty-handed. He pushed his basket away so that he could lean in close and talk qui-etly. The table tilted back to him. "Governor. What will it take to make you happy? There's not a lot that I don't have the power to do."

"I'm sorry," Travis said, "are you offering me a bribe?" He said it a little louder than necessary.

"Of course not!" Leary gasped. "I'm . . . simply telling you that I . . . am a very powerful man."

"I never said you weren't."

From point-blank range, Travis could see the freckles on Leary's forehead beading with sweat. "Do you not think that I'm tough enough to stand up to you, Governor?"

Travis resisted the temptation to say what he was thinking—but not for very long. "Let's be fair, you did crease your Calvin Klein jeans," Travis said.

"Go to hell," the president said. He pushed himself away from his table and stood up. "Of course, it is a hundred and twelve degrees outside. Maybe this is hell."

The president stormed out of the restaurant with Agent Dermis following closely behind. It all happened so fast that the crowd missed its cue, not applauding until after he was gone, which made it seem like even more of a victory for the governor. The presidential limo had already turned around and was pointed toward Dallas. Leary jumped in the backseat as Dermis closed the door. Within twenty seconds, the entire entourage was out of sight.

The seat fillers lined up near the door to sign a confidentiality agreement and receive their promised hundred and twenty-five dollars before heading for the bus parked around the corner. K waited until they had cleared out, then joined Travis at the table and helped himself to the president's unwanted chicken fried steak. Travis chuckled, but not at K.

"Well, that seems appropriate," Travis said.

"What?" asked K.

Travis held up a slip of paper. "Looks like Washington stuck me with the bill."

32

The president's motorcade drove straight onto the tarmac at Love Field. Love Field was the preferred airport for Dallas travelers who wanted to avoid the crush of traffic around the much bigger DFW, an airport so mammoth that commuter planes often spent more time taxiing to their gate than they had spent in the air. Today their roles had been reversed, with all flights in and out of Love grounded as the tower waited for Air Force One—along with its companion air force cargo plane carrying the Beast, the Suburbans, and the communication vans—to go wheels up and leave Dallas airspace.

Ruffles had never left the 747 and was waiting for Leary at the top of the steps. "Well?"

"Nothing," said Leary, walking right past him and down the jumbo jet's center aisle. "Total waste of time."

"Did you offer him—"

"Wouldn't take it. Said he's standing on principle." Leary untucked his dress shirt from the crisply pressed jeans.

Ruffles scratched his ear with his pen. "So then we need to come up with a way to make the governor believe he's standing on principle without giving him anything he wants."

"Forget it," Leary said. "He doesn't think I have the guts to really put up a fight. I'm going to call his bluff." Leary sat down, took the pen out of Ruffles's hand, and reached for a pad of paper.

"What are you doing?"

"Leading," Leary said, making up bullet points as they came to him.

The thought of it made Leary uncomfortable. "How about we get some other folks on the phone," Ruffles said. "Each can weigh in, and we can talk through some options." He started to scroll through his BlackBerry. Leary took that away from him as well.

"I'm a big boy, Ruffles," the president said. "Put your feet up. Take a nap. This might be your last chance to get some sleep for a few days."

"May I at least have my phone back?"

"Take a nap," the president repeated without looking up.

Ruffles stood in the aisle and watched as the president continued to jot down thoughts as they came to him. When he tried to sneak a peek, Leary covered up his work with his arm.

"Mr. President, I think it would at least be prudent for us to—"

"That's an order," Leary said, breaking out some commander-in-chief lingo.

The attendant pulled the door of Air Force One shut and smiled pointedly toward Ruffles. Air Force One–speak for "Sit down." Ruffles picked a seat and reclined it as far as it would go. He turned his head to the side and looked out at Love Field as the president's plane edged onto the runway. When the jet left the ground, he closed his eyes, but he only pretended to sleep.

Aubrey Garza searched the empty reception area. She spotted Paige waving from the sidewalk and pushed through the double doors. Both girls looked a bit more haggard than they had the day before. Aubrey was wearing the same jeans and Converses but had changed T-shirts. Today's selection: HONK IF YOU HATE LOUD NOISES.

"I take it you found something in those scraps," Aubrey said.

Paige started to answer but was interrupted by a passing taxi driver who read her friend's shirt and laid on his horn. "Sorry," Aubrey said, "probably not the best shirt to wear outside. What did you find?"

"I've got a few things. Not sure how they're related. Maybe they're not. First has to do with Bill Lewis."

"The lieutenant governor," said Aubrey, making sure they were discussing the same person.

"Right," said Paige. "It seems he's been reaching out to Anatole Metzos. Don't exactly know why. In any case, I think it's safe to assume they worked together to trap my dad—and me—with the *Today* show tape."

"You have any physical evidence?"

"I know Bill has sent text messages. Plus I talked to him on the phone. He didn't know it was me."

Aubrey's head bobbed left and right as she thought. "Might be something there . . . entrapping the governor for political gain . . . but the story probably won't have legs considering your dad is likely to be charged with sedition and treason before this is all over. What else?"

Paige pulled the salvaged PDB agenda from her purse. A rubber hair band was stuck to the end of one of the many pieces of tape holding the whole thing together. Paige peeled it away as she passed the pieced-together document to Aubrey. "You ever seen one of these before?" she asked, knowing that Aubrey hadn't. Even Julian Assange couldn't get this. Aubrey took it and started reading. She stopped after reading the header.

"This isn't a setup, is it?" Aubrey couldn't help but wonder if Paige was leading her down a rabbit hole. "Retaliation for . . . you know."

"I'm not making this up, Aubrey. I wouldn't do that. Not to a friend."

Aubrey nodded, regret filling her face. "I know." She went back to the doc. Paige watched as her eyes darted across the page. "Pretty crazy, huh? Just sitting in his trash can waiting to be found."

"This isn't right," Aubrey said.

"I know. The question is who's feeding Metzos this info and why."

"No," said Aubrey. "I mean this information isn't right. I can take you upstairs and show you fifty different polls taken over the course of the last week, and none of them supports this."

"What do you mean?" Paige moved so she could see what Aubrey was talking about.

"It says there are 'few ready-to-fight' Texans. Even before your dad crashed the Web the other night, every internal report showed a hundred thousand Texans were ready to do whatever it took to hold off the Feds. I mean, geez, you're from Dallas. You know how many Texans own guns?"

"That's true." Paige nodded, remembering the year her middle school made the first day of deer hunting season an official holiday.

"And this line about no support from Oklahoma, Louisiana, and Arkansas . . ."

"Yeah . . ."

"Bogus. Look at this date. June fourth. The governors of Oklahoma and Louisiana spoke out the day before then and pledged to help Texas however your dad wanted."

"I don't understand," Paige said. "Why would someone send Anatole Metzos a phony PDB agenda?"

"I don't think anyone did."

"Of course someone did! How else would he—"

"Paige, stop. Look at the double x's where it talks about troop levels. That info wasn't left out because it was classified. It was because he didn't know the numbers."

Paige wasn't following. "Aubrey, why wouldn't the national director of intelligence for the CIA be able to get those numbers?"

"I'm not talking about him. I'm talking about Metzos." Paige let Aubrey's theory settle in her brain. Ever since she had taped it together, she had been operating under the assumption that Metzos was on the receiving end of the PDB.

"You think Metzos was the one sending this?" Paige said.

"Don't you?" asked Aubrey.

Paige took the PDB from her hand and held it up toward the sky.

Through the ink and tape she could see the embossed *FF* on the paper.

"I do now," said Paige.

Long before he landed at Andrews Air Force Base, the president finalized his plan and personally relayed it to his staff in Washington.

"This is the President. Number one: I will be speaking immediately upon arrival, and I expect Press Secretary Kurtz to alert the media. Number two: I will need a standard podium with the presidential seal and a microphone—no teleprompter—and I want them placed directly at the base of the airplane stairs. Number three: I want a tie. Blue. *Royal* blue. Not midnight blue. Don't try to tell me they're the same color because they're not." He hung up the phone on Air Force One with authority. He understood why Travis enjoyed the whole going-with-your-gut thing. So far it was very empowering.

It was 6:00 P.M. on the dot when he stepped off the plane, walked down the stairs, and stepped up to the podium he had ordered. It was 6:05 before the deafening noise from the four jet engines subsided enough for him to speak. Ruffles had tried to explain that there was a reason they don't put the podium right next to the plane, but the president rather seemed to relish holding up his hand like some sultan, silencing his chief of staff.

"Good evening," Leary said. He looked in the direction of the teleprompter's normal location and saw only reporters. "As you, um, know . . ." He could function, but was still shaky, like someone who only goes skiing once every five years. ". . . I had lunch earlier today with the Governor of Texas in the town of . . ." He drew a blank. ". . . his birth." *Great,* Ruffles thought, *make him sound like Jesus.* "I came with an open mind and the sincerest of hopes that we could find some common ground. Unfortunately, the governor had a different mindset. He came to . . ." Leary cursed himself silently. He had walked right into having to say the name of the mystery city a second time. Was it Progress? Not likely. Profit. Promise . . . *Prosper*! "He came to Prosper looking for a fight. And to my great disappointment, the governor was not only combative, but he was also rude, lacking the civilized demeanor I would have hoped to see from a figure whom so many have put on such a pedestal.

"It was clear right away that he was not looking to work together to find a solution that was good for all Americans. It was obvious that what he truly wants is division. If he pursues it, it will come at a price.

"To that end, I have drafted a contingency plan in the event that the people of Texas vote in favor of secession. First and foremost, I will use the power of my office to begin a series of severe sanctions against the state. The most punishing element of this will be the implementation of a massive trade embargo, banning all American-made products from crossing into the state. Secondly, I will call for an immediate embargo on all travel to and from Texas. Other than American military personnel, there will be no exceptions. And third, as a final punishment for all Texans who choose to stay, I will be suspending all Social Security and Medicare benefits until the state renounces its secession claim and shores up its allegiance with the other forty-nine states.

"Let there be no mistake: I take no joy in doing this. But every good parent must discipline, and so it is my duty to rein in Texas. Should Texas stand down, so will I. If they choose to continue along this course, then it will certainly be a grim future for the Lone Star State. For their sakes, I urge Texan voters to think twice before voting yes on secession. Thank you."

Leary grabbed his yellow legal pad off the podium and strode to his waiting limo. For the first time in a year, he felt invincible. Once safely inside the Beast, he *un*furrowed his brow and flung the pad on the seat across from him in celebration as he sat down next to Ruffles. "Hot damn, Ruflowski! Now, *that* is how you do it!"

"Well done, Mr. President," Ruffles said.

As far as President Leary was concerned, he had just put the bully in bully pulpit.

Travis and K had driven back to Austin without stopping, arriving in time to catch Leary's remarks on the tiny TV set in the mansion's kitchen. Travis turned the viewing into a sport, interrupting the president repeatedly to scoff and heckle. Cole, by contrast, watched on the large TV upstairs, absorbing the details and stoically considering the ramifications.

"Well, that was something," Travis said when they ran into each other on the stairs. "Talk about a drama queen." He tried to keep walking up, but Cole wouldn't let him.

"*That's* your response to what he wants to do?" Cole asked. "That was serious stuff, Ben."

"It would be serious—if he were really going to do it. Which he's not. He doesn't have it in him." Travis was pooped and continued up the stairs, forcing Cole to follow.

"How do you know?" Cole asked, not ready to trust Travis's instincts without a little more evidence.

"I was a quarterback," said Travis. "I knew before the ball was even hiked which guys really wanted to sack me and which ones were using all their energy on their snarl." Travis reached his living room and kicked off his boots as he headed toward the bathroom.

"Well, clearly you said something to tick him off," said Cole.

"I don't remember. I was trying to enjoy my lunch."

"He said you were rude."

"*Me?*"

"What did you say, Ben?"

Travis splashed some water on his face and returned from the bathroom. "Fine. I . . . may have made fun of the fact someone creased his jeans."

"You made fun of his pants?!" To someone who cared as much about fashion as Cole, this slight seemed especially egregious.

"Now hold on," Travis said. "Don't take it out of context." Travis spread out on his couch and jammed a hard square pillow under his head.

"I'm sorry," Cole said. For the sake of Texas, he wanted Travis to be on the winning end of this argument. "What was the context?"

Travis crossed his legs, closed his eyes and thought for a moment, then remembered. "He asked me whether I thought he was tough or not . . ."

"Okay . . ."

"Well, rather than give him a long explanation of why I think he's a wuss, I thought it would be simpler to direct his attention to the womanly way he was wearing his jeans."

"That's actually *worse* in context. You realize that, don't you?"

There was a knock on the door as K walked in. "Bill Lewis here to see you."

"Ugh," said Travis, knowing this would be another impediment to sleep. "Go ahead and send him—"

Per usual, Big Bill was already there. "And here I thought you boys would be quivering down in the bomb shelter by now," he said as he lumbered around the corner. He smelled like beef-scented cologne.

"Good," Cole said. "We need another opinion. What do you think, Bill? You think the president was serious?"

"Hell yes, he was." Bill braced himself against the wall and twisted his back. It cracked like a muffled firecracker. "He's not going to let us leave. And if we try, he'll cripple us."

"I don't know," Travis said. "It's one thing to do it to Cuba, but the manpower he'd need to pull off a real blockade here . . . I'll believe it when I see it."

"I think if you wait two more days, you will," Bill said.

"Nah," Travis said, gaining confidence in his opinion. "Anyway, with how Washington has destroyed the economy, nearly everything we need is made in China anyway. If the price to leave the Union is the fact I can't brush with some Tom's of Maine toothpaste, oh well."

"Geez, Governor," Bill said, "no offense, but come on now. We did our part. We sent 'em a message. Scared the poop out of 'em, too. But enough already."

"I agree," Cole said.

"But we haven't changed anything!"

"They will change," Big Bill said. "I know it."

"Please." Travis was unmoved.

"I'm serious," Big Bill said. He moved to the edge of the couch and attempted his version of a whisper. "I talked to some people—off the record—this afternoon. Everyone in Washington knows you're the real deal. They know you're not a nut. They told me if you go to D.C. and plead your case, there's a very good chance they'll let Texas opt out of the RRA."

"Who told you that?"

Big Bill shook his head. "I promised I wouldn't say."

"I just had lunch with the president four hours ago, Bill. Letting us opt out was never on the table."

"I'm just telling you what I heard," Bill said.

Travis and Cole eyed each other. The ability to opt out of the RRA was all they'd wanted originally. It was the equivalent of straight nullification. "Tell you what," Travis said. "I'll sleep on it."

"Good," said Cole, feeling some encouragement.

Travis settled back on the couch. "Just don't sleep on it too long," Bill said, "or you're liable to wake up with some marine's nine-millimeter up your schnoz."

Travis didn't answer. He killed the nearby lamp with his hand, leaving Big Bill and Cole in the dark. Just the way he liked it.

33

Cole had been up late researching the history of trade embargos and their effects. The good news was that they were historically difficult to enforce and often did more harm to the country issuing the embargo than to the country being punished. One of the largest attempts in history was Napoleon Bonaparte's Continental System of 1806, devised with the goal of crippling Great Britain's economy by banning shipment of all goods to and from the British Isles. However, when the French failed to make up for the loss of sales to Britain with increased sales of their own, the Atlantic port cities of France fell into depression. By 1813, the overall value of French exports was down by more than a third. Even the United States' embargo against Cuba wasn't really a success. It sped up the island nation's decline into poverty, but it still never achieved its expressed goal of convincing Fidel Castro to embrace capitalism.

Cole woke up at seven and searched the mansion, anxious to share his research with Travis. The only person he found was Minda, the mansion's fifty-something Filipino cook, working on a casserole in the kitchen. "Minda, have you seen the governor?"

"Yes! On TV. He was very good," she said. She went back to grating cheese.

"Wait, what?"

"Yeah, he going early for TV."

"Well . . . what . . . what did he say?"

"Oh, ju know . . . about Texas . . . an' how ees so great . . . talking tings like dat. You be proud," Minda explained.

As promised, Travis had slept on it. Because he went to bed at 6:00 P.M., he was done sleeping by 2:00 A.M. He was on the phone at four, and by seven, his response was ready for general consumption. He called a few reporters, dragged a podium into the governor's reception room of the capitol, and was good to go.

"Good morning from Texas," he had begun. "As the country knows, tomorrow is our state's much-anticipated vote to reclaim our independence. It's a vote that is supported by an overwhelming percentage of Texans and a majority of Americans at large. I appreciated President Leary's willingness to visit Prosper yesterday and share a chicken fried steak. Unfortunately, he didn't stay long enough to eat it. As the president said in his comments last night, he and I did not see eye to eye. But I never asked for a fight. As I have always contended, it is the desire of Texas to leave the Union peacefully and without incident. Last night, the president made it clear that he has other designs. He likened us to misbehaving children needing to be punished. It's ironic since the most recent group of people to be soundly spanked in this country was the president and his party during the last election. Well, we Texans do not intend to be disciplined for protecting ourselves from a thoroughly *un*disciplined federal behemoth.

"We also don't like to be threatened. As far as I'm concerned, Washington can keep their Social Security and Medicare benefits. Both of those institutions are on the verge of being bankrupt anyway, and I have every confidence our state treasury will be able to support its citizens in need. However, I am concerned about the president promising a trade embargo against Texas in the event that tomorrow's vote passes. To put my response in poker terms, I would like to see that threat and raise it, so to speak. You see, in the president's haste, he failed to consider the value of Texas products to the rest of the country. There's no need to list them all. Two will suffice. This morning I have spoken with the major oil and gas suppliers based in Texas, and in the event tomorrow's popular vote passes, they have agreed to shut down the various pipelines that carry oil and gas out of Texas to ninety-five percent of the United States. I didn't order them to do it. I gave them the choice. By our estimate, once those pipelines are fully drained, America would suffer an almost total shutdown of reliable supply in a matter of weeks.

"If President Leary decides to back off his threats and lets Texas be the peaceful neighbor that it wants to be, then I'm sure those energy companies would be glad to have a conversation about their future relationship with the remaining United States. That seems like the logical solution. Of course, as we Americans have been reminded time and again, what makes sense to the majority of us rarely makes sense to this president. For everyone's sake, we hope that he makes the wise choice and pulls back the embargo. Thank you, and may God bless Texas."

Damon Cole showed up twenty minutes later, having read the transcript of Travis's speech on his phone during the walk over. Travis was clicking away with his computer mouse but still managed to get in the first word when he saw Cole crossing through the bullpen.

"I just woke up and thought about it," said Travis. "I thought that any federal government with a president who would so coldly target one of its states and its people like that . . . that's not a government the people of Texas can trust. Even if they let us nullify the nationalization of oil and gas, so what? Will we have to threaten to secede anytime they propose something we don't like? We can't live like that. You're not angry, are you?"

Cole placed both hands on the far side of Travis's desk, like a sprinter setting his hands on the starting line. "It was brilliant," he said.

Travis lit up upon hearing the professor's praise. "Yeah?"

"*Yeah,*" said Cole. "I mean, what can they do? You basically just cut through their femoral artery. And I love the fact that—" Cole noticed the reflection of Travis's computer in the window behind him. "Are you playing *solitaire?*"

"Hey, give me a break. I've already logged six hours of work this morning."

Cole let it go. He was more curious about how Travis convinced the oil companies to agree to the shutoff.

"I asked," Travis said, placing the queen of hearts on top of a black king with his mouse. "If you know anything about business, it's that money goes where there's the least resistance. They knew that if they stuck with me and we won, they'd pay lower taxes on their product and have more freedom to drill in the Gulf. That would mean more money for their employees, higher stock prices for their investors, and what they might lose in sales to the U.S. they would more than make up with sales to other countries. Once each guy knew that his rivals all felt the same way, it was done."

"I'm amazed they can turn the pipelines off so quickly," Cole said. "Just like that . . . and it stops."

"Oh. Psshh." Travis waved off Cole with his free hand. "No, it'll take them weeks."

"But you said . . ."

"I said they would shut them down," Travis said. "*Which is true.* For that to happen, though, technicians have to drive out to all the Podunk corners of Texas near the border, find the right substations, and turn off the right valves. There are hundreds of them."

"And you don't think the White House knows this?" Cole said.

"*You* didn't," said Travis. Enough said. Travis closed his game of solitaire. "So tell me honestly, Cole: What do you think President Leary's up to right now?"

"Who knows. I'd like to think he's working on a concession speech."

"Me, too," said Travis. "But prideful as he is, he's probably out on the South Lawn drilling for oil."

The president and his advisers were back in the Situation Room. No one had spoken a word. Leary was wearing cargo shorts, a golf shirt, and a visor with the presidential seal on it. He had been halfway to Congressional CC when the call came in. He hadn't changed out of his golf spikes and was tearing up the navy carpet beneath him as he walked in a counterclockwise circle around the surfboard-shaped table.

On his fourth lap he noticed that he was leaving a trail of fuzz and stopped dead. "Damn it," he muttered. There was nothing he could do about it now. He set off again, making another three laps around the table as everyone waited patiently with hands folded. On lap eight he scanned the people around the table. "Where's the secretary of state?"

"She's on a goodwill trip to Central Africa," an aide said.

"Of course she is," Leary said. She'd been mulling a last-minute primary challenge to Leary and had made a conscious effort to never be seen at his side.

Two more laps. There was no debate that the president's attempt to channel his "inner Travis" had been a resounding failure. Political commentators on both sides couldn't believe what a giant miscalculation Leary had made.

"I can't be the only one who didn't see this coming, right?" The table swapped looks. Each of them had seen flaws in the president's plan. "Well, thanks," he said, feeling the heat of judgment. "It would have been nice if someone had warned me about the possibility this might happen before it actually did. I thought I made this clear early on—I'm not here to surround myself with yes-men." There was no response. *"Hello??"*

"Yes, Mr. President," they answered in chorus.

He looked to Avery Adams. "What's been the reaction out there, Miss Adams?"

"Not good," Avery said. "The poll numbers aren't budging, and outside of Texas there's some definite panic. Traders are talking about nine-dollar gas by the end of the week. Not surprisingly, most stations are seeing lines around the corner."

"What about the market?" Leary asked.

Avery checked her phone. "Dow's off eight fifty," she said. A few of the president's aides groaned. A year's worth of gains gone. That hurt Leary as much as anything else. Even with every other economic indicator reeking of doom, he had always been able to point to the stock market as a sign of strength.

"So what does everybody think?" Leary asked. "Do we let them go? Wait for them to fail and come back begging to be let back in? If we can keep them out through November, that would take away, what, thirty-eight potential electoral votes from the Republican nominee?"

Attorney General David Velez cleared his throat. "Mr. President, if I may . . . I think there are two risks there. The primary one is that other states see it can be done and follow suit. That's basically what happened to the Soviet Union. You can't very easily let one state go and then try to tell another that it can't. Even if that state doesn't have the leverage that Texas has, you won't have any credibility."

"What's the other risk?" the president asked.

Velez was reluctant to say it, but someone had to point out the obvious. "The other risk is that Texas thrives." It had been the great unmentionable since this started. Forget all the other issues in play; this was the ultimate fear. "It's no secret that Texas leaders would govern with an ideology that would be in direct opposition to ours. If they flourish and we shrink, the progressive movement is done."

"They won't flourish, Velez," Leary said. "They need us. They just don't realize they need us."

Ruffles took the attorney general's side. "It may not matter, Mr. President. Forget the result of the vote in Texas. The simple fact you're *allowing* them to vote shows you've lost the upper hand. If they go to the polls, it will pass. Once that happens, there's little controlling what happens next. Like the attorney general said, most of the scenarios aren't good. In all of them, you lose in November. Worst case, your entire agenda—and I mean *everything*—could be reversed or repealed once you're gone. There will be no passing the torch to future presidents. Your ideology will be sniffed out. Mocked. Marginalized. Then buried in the desert like toxic waste. A whole generation will come and go before anyone has the courage to dig it up, repackage it, and try again. That would be your legacy. And it would be a tragedy. All because you let one state trounce you while you possessed all the power necessary to stop it."

President Leary had given plenty of thought to life after Washington. He wanted to be one of those ex-presidents who spends his life playing in celebrity golf tournaments and being fawned over like Bill Clinton; not like Richard Nixon, who more or less hid out for twenty years until he died. If Leary's legacy turned out to be the global repudiation of everything in which he believed, it would be the ultimate insult. The right would hate him for having tried it, and the left would hate him for having failed. In essence, he would have triangulated himself.

"Well, aren't you two just buckets of Christmas cheer," Leary said.

"You asked to know the possibilities," Ruffles said.

The president started another series of laps around the table. He was counting his options. After a dozen laps, he gave up. He could only come up with one.

Ben Travis hadn't moved all morning. His office phone was near his right hand and his cell phone was near his left. Fran had been instructed to hold all calls except for the one that really mattered. As the day wore on, his pulse quickened every time the phone rang, but it was noon and there was still no official response from the White House.

"Turn on the boob tube!" Big Bill bellowed as he barged into the governor's office. Cole unmuted the TV just as Fox News cut to the Oval Office. The president sat behind his desk. He had traded the golf attire for a suit and his faded visor for his red dome.

"Good afternoon. At 8:00 A.M. Eastern Time this morning, the United States was attacked."

"*We were?*" Travis knew he'd been focused on Texas, but—"Oh wait, I get it," he said, catching on to how Leary was framing this.

"By threatening to cut off America's fuel supply, the state of Texas has decided to strike directly at the engine of our economy."

"What about *green jobs*?" Travis snarked. "I thought *that* was the heart of our economy."

Cole couldn't handle it. "If you keep talking over him like this, I'm going in the other room," he said.

"Sorry," Travis said. "No more."

"In an economic sense, this was very much an act of war," Leary said.

Travis couldn't help himself. "What about in a *war* sense? Shouldn't that be . . ." Cole stood up and went to the bullpen, leaving Travis alone with Big Bill.

"The United States will not allow itself to be so brazenly attacked." Leary continued. "As commander in chief, the security of our citizens is my highest concern, and I will defend them. Therefore, as of 1:00 P.M. Eastern Standard Time, we have commenced preliminary military action against the State of Texas. Per my orders, the FAA has grounded all air travel to and from the state. Out at sea, the USS *Farragut* is currently sailing toward Galveston from Florida. On the ground, twenty thousand reserve and National Guard troops are mobilizing, and many are already in transit from various bases around the country in order to secure the borders."

Cole had no trouble hearing Travis from the other room: "*Secure the borders?!* Since when does he know how to do that?"

"We expect most major roads and highways into and out of the state to be closed within twelve hours. As for the troops based inside the state of Texas, they are awaiting my further instructions. The governor of Texas has until midnight Washington time to *cancel* his state's reckless and unconstitutional vote of secession and guarantee that his state's fuel pipelines remain open. If he ignores this request, I will take further steps to secure the safety of our natural resources. To Governor Travis and the minority of radical Texans loyal to the secession movement, know this is not an empty threat. To quote our cherished Constitution—"

"Cherished since when?"

"—'and secure the blessings of liberty to ourselves and our posterity.' Thank you. God bless you, and may God bless America." For nearly four years, the president had been trying to project an image of strength to a world that thought of him as a disappointing lightweight. What could be stronger than pledging the use of military force against his own citizens?

Travis reached for the remote and turned off the TV. Big Bill stood in anticipation of Travis's reaction. Cole returned for the same reason. Fran stayed at her desk but craned her neck to hear. Travis wasn't sure what to say about the president's announcement. All he knew was that it was the worst concession speech he'd ever heard.

34

Aubrey Garza huddled in her cubicle with Paige as the rest of the newsroom buzzed from the president's pseudo-declaration of war. It was the only topic that sold more newspapers than sex, and the *Post* had been covering the brinkmanship between Texas and Washington from every angle for the last week.

"A few of those things Leary said sounded familiar, didn't they?" Aubrey asked.

"Uh-huh," Paige said. As Metzos's shredded PDB memo had suggested, Leary was trying to react swiftly, he was moving troops to the border, and he was doing his best to make Travis look like a lone aggressor versus the head of a real movement.

The girls were pressed together inside the gray three-sided workspace, unable to roll anywhere without causing a paper avalanche. They had spent the last two hours leafing through tax returns and taking turns shaking each other awake. It had been nearly twenty-four hours since they started. When they began digging the day before, all they had was a hypothesis and two questions: *Metzos is setting the agenda. Why? And how?*

Their research had started by listening to a nine-hour exposé Walt Thompson had run on the man a year before that was largely ignored by the mainstream media. They were impressed with his show, though they could have done without Walt's snarky attitude and annoying ads for tankless water heaters. Walt documented Metzos's secret history of shorting different world currencies—betting that they would lose value. His bets were so large that they caused other investors to follow suit, which succeeded in devaluing the currencies and had netted Anatole Metzos billions of dollars over the last two decades.

Metzos then used those profits to set up his web of organizations. Adam Wexler had connected the dots to a handful of them, but Walt Thompson had uncovered more than that. Aubrey printed the list from Walt's Web site and ran to retrieve it before anyone else in the newsroom saw where she was going for source material. She and Paige both thought it would fit on one page. It took thirty. All told, over five hundred different left-wing groups traced their origins back to Metzos or were partially supported by his benevolence.

He was a man obsessed with power and money but had both in no short supply. Paige could attest to the fact he had no other hobbies. If Anatole Metzos was helping to set the agenda, it may have been for no grander reason than simply that he was a megalomaniac who enjoyed the challenge.

How he'd pulled it off was murkier. It required collusion on the inside. Without proof of that, all their research equaled just a conspiracy theory and a PDB agenda that Metzos would deny ever having seen.

Paige asked how hard it was to acquire a list of everyone who worked for the president. Aubrey had the answer in seconds. The White House, as part of its annual report to Congress, was legally required to submit a list of employees along with their salaries. The most recent report listed four hundred sixty employees totaling forty-one million dollars.

Paige scanned the monitor quickly. "Print that out, too," she said.

The *Post* newsroom cleared out as the next day's edition headed to the printer. Aubrey and Paige stayed in the cubicle, pouring over the White House list and x-ing out all the low-level staff—cooks, maids, plumbers, gardeners. That left a hundred forty West Wing employees plus the twenty-one cabinet members.

They split the list in two and went to separate computers, researching the employment history of each name and narrowing the group down to those who had worked for Metzos or one of his groups before coming to Leary.

By sunup, they had it down to thirty employees, scattered across every field, from tax policy to speechwriting to Homeland Security. The plan had been to nap until 9:00 A.M., but once Travis announced the oil shutoff at eight, sleep wasn't an option. They divided the list again, and spread out across Washington to visit the headquarters of a dozen different 501(c)(3)s.

Every nonprofit 501(c)(3) organization, whether it be liberal, conservative, or nonpartisan, is obligated to file an annual report with the IRS. Those reports must be made available, no questions asked, to anyone who wants to see them; few people ever make the request. Aubrey went to the Forward Foundation, figuring it wouldn't take long for Metzos to hear that Paige had dropped in to inspect their books. They regrouped a few hours later, having cleared a forest in their pursuit of the truth. Their eyes were bloodshot from lack of sleep and from staring at the blue light of photocopiers all morning.

After an hour of coming up empty, Paige found something. "Hey," she said.

"I'm awake," Aubrey said.

"This is weird. Listen to this, David Velez was a senior fellow at the Forward Foundation from 2005 through 2008."

"That's not weird."

"No, but listen." Paige jumped from page to page, making sure her information was correct. "In 2005, they paid him forty-five thousand dollars. In 2006, fifty thousand." She dug through her stack.

"So what?" Aubrey asked. "He ran the Yale Law School while being a fellow at FF. A lot of people do that kind of stuff."

"I'm not done. In 2007, he made fifty-five thousand. And then . . . in 2008 . . ." She held up the page so Aubrey could see it. "Seven hundred and fifty thousand dollars."

"Whoa. Wait. What?"

"Uh-huh."

Aubrey took the report from her and looked at the attorney general's six-figure number up close. It was so innocent looking on the page. "Well, that certainly didn't come up in his confirmation hearings."

"The hearings were in early December," said Paige. "Metzos could have paid him after he knew Velez had the job."

"Damn," Aubrey said. "When I left my last job to come here, my old boss gave me a five-dollar gift card to Starbucks."

"Here," Paige said, handing Aubrey the 2008 return for Elevate International.

"Who am I looking for?"

"Find Lee Kurtz's salary," Paige said. "Okay," she continued, "in 2006, the future White House press secretary made fifteen thousand dollars a year as a public relations consultant. In 2007 . . . he made twenty-five. And in 2008?"

"Eight hundred thousand dollars," Aubrey said.

"Eight hundred thousand dollars?!" Paige gripped the edge of the desk to steady herself. "As a public relations consultant for a nonprofit organization dedicated to, and I quote, 'creating tomorrow's leaders . . . today.'"

"To be fair, that sounds exactly like what Metzos was doing by paying him eight hundred grand."

"Unreal," Paige said. She flipped two more reports onto Aubrey's lap.

"Who's next?"

"Ruflowski," Paige said.

"Okay, let's see . . . 2006, working part-time as an adviser to"— she flipped back to the front page to see what this one was called— "Generation Now, he made ten thousand dollars." She grabbed the other report. "In 2007 . . . twelve thousand."

"And in 2008 . . . how about a drumroll, Aubs?" Aubrey patted her hands on her jeans. "One point three million."

"Holy shit!" Aubrey said.

"Guess 2008 was a good year to be a part-time adviser," Paige said.

They nearly laughed, but knew that none of this was funny. Anatole Metzos had bought more than the president's ear. He controlled the most influential people inside Leary's administration, men and women who shaped the national agenda and saw that it was carried out.

"This still doesn't account for Bill Lewis being involved," Paige said. "He's about as far away from the left wing as you can get."

"Doesn't matter. Some criminals are driven by some higher purpose that makes perfect sense to them. They have some twisted logic where the ends justify the means. Then there are guys like Big Bill Lewis."

"And what is he?"

"A crook. All they want is money and power. Metzos can give Bill Lewis money, and if your dad goes down, he's got the power."

Paige wondered if there was a chance that Leary didn't know about any of this. It seemed impossible, but if he didn't . . . She swept her water bottle off the desk and into the recycling bin and flung her empty bag over her shoulder.

Aubrey was startled. "Where are you going?"

"To call my dad."

"But the story . . ." Aubrey was anxious to write. This exposé could be her Pulitzer.

"Start without me. Just wait until I give the go-ahead to run anything."

"Why not call him from your cell phone?"

"Someone could be listening."

Aubrey picked up her office phone and handed it to her. "Call him from here."

Paige backed away from it like a five-year-old being asked to pet a snake. "No."

Aubrey hung it up. "Sorry. I get it. Do what you have to do. I'll wait."

"You sure?"

"Yes." Paige held her look. "Yes," Aubrey reiterated.

Paige nodded. She believed her. Before she left, she wanted to clear up one element of all this that remained baffling. "How were we the first ones to find all this, Aubs?"

"What do you mean?"

"I mean it wasn't easy to uncover . . . but it wasn't impossible. How could we be the first ones?"

The answer was an indictment against her whole field. "Because we were the first ones to look."

Big Bill poured a few green pills into his mouth and swallowed them without water. "I'm not going to say I told you," he said to Travis, "but . . . ah hell, *yes* I am. *I told you!* I told you to back off these guys and you didn't. *You poked the bear.*" He held out the label-less orange container toward Travis and Cole as though he were offering them a breath mint. "Xanax?"

Travis shook his head. "No thanks," said Cole.

"I didn't think Leary had it in him," Travis said. "It just doesn't line up with the guy. Are we really supposed to believe that at midnight tonight troops are going to kick down the door of the capitol and haul us away if we don't cancel the vote? That's crazy, right?"

"That's what I took away from it," Big Bill said, "and frankly, I think we'll be lucky if all they do is arrest us."

The possibility that this could disintegrate into war had been Cole's great fear from the beginning, but as the only scholar of the group, he felt a duty to mention what the law said on the matter. "Technically, Ben, the president can't send troops into a state for law enforcement purposes without congressional approval."

"Really?" Travis asked.

"Posse Comitatus Act, 1878," Cole said. He saw Big Bill giving him a snide look. "I read a lot of books."

"So you think this might just be posturing?" said Travis.

"I hope so," Cole said. There was no way Congress could convene by midnight. Even if it could, there was zero chance that a Republican House would support martial law in one of its most Republican states.

Travis patted his hands on his desk as though he were playing an invisible set of bongo drums. If this was nothing more than a game of chicken, he hated to blink when Leary was the one whose eyes were starting to tear up.

"Well," Travis said, "as much as I'd love to just wait him out and make him stew, we're gonna look pretty dumb if he's not bluffing."

"Which is why you should back down," Big Bill said. "Be the bigger man and go to Washington. You'll be a national hero, Governor, I mean it. Heck, four years from now you could be president." Bill knew, however, that it wouldn't play out like that. The moment Travis left Texas soil, the lieutenant governor would become acting governor, and Bill had every intention of bowing to Washington, leaving Ben Travis to face sedition charges that had already been drawn up by the attorney general.

"I'm not backing down, Bill. Not yet," Travis said.

Big Bill threw up his arms. "What the heck is *wrong* with you?" He thought he was getting somewhere.

"I just want to talk to some other governors," Travis said. "See where we stand. Put together a plan. Make sure we're all on the same page going forward. Just in case we can't work out a solution."

Cole was fine with making Leary stew, but the notion of colluding with other states sounded like war. "You promised we could do this without bloodshed."

"Just in case," Travis repeated. "If the law were truly enough to stop them, we wouldn't even be in this situation."

Big Bill had heard enough. "Don't make this some damn philosophical crusade, Governor."

"You voted for this," Travis reminded him.

"I wanted to support you."

"And *now?*"

"There are real lives at stake here. Including your own. Be stubborn all you want about taxes and spending. I don't give a crap. But don't be stubborn about this."

"Why *not* this?!"

"Because it's suicide!" Big Bill yelled. The outburst brought K into the room. He eyed the lieutenant governor. Bill's nostrils flared as his carotid artery tap-danced beneath the surface of his neck. He spotted K and wiped his brow with his sleeve.

"We cool?" K asked.

"Never better," Big Bill said, dabbing his upper lip.

"Escort the lieutenant governor back to his office," Travis said.

"Gladly," said K.

The president had just flipped on the news from Texas when Ruffles popped his head into the Oval Office to tell him that his lunch guest was here.

"What lunch guest?"

"This month's student, Mr. President."

"We didn't cancel that?"

"No one told us to."

"Crap."

At the first lady's insistence, the president had made a campaign promise to invite one lucky elementary school student from every state to eat lunch with him in the Oval Office before his first term was complete. The response was so positive that once elected, the administration turned it into a Willy Wonka sort of contest, hiding one winning ticket per state inside specially marked packages of energy-efficient compact fluorescent lightbulbs. What the administration didn't foresee was that there would be such a mad rush of kids opening packages to see if they'd won that hundreds of CFLs were dropped and shattered in the process, scattering liquid mercury and poisoning a few dozen American families who naively thought they could clean up a broken lightbulb without needing hazmat suits. After consulting with the attorney general, President Leary announced that he would be inviting not only the fifty winners for lunch but also any and all kids or family members who had been poisoned along the way.

"Is this a real one or a mercury one?" the president asked. The mercury ones were such downers.

"A real one, sir."

"Oh. Good. Then we can order swordfish for lunch."

Seven-year-old JP, a towhead with a bowl haircut and shoes that lit up in green with each step, entered attached to the leg of his father, JP Sr. The elder JP looked like a lumberjack minus the ax, wearing jeans, a plaid shirt, and his best work boots.

"Welcome to the White House," the president said, turning on the charm. "And what's your name?"

"J-J-J-JP," the first-grader stuttered.

"Sorry. He's a little scared," JP Sr. said.

"Scared? Of *me*?" The president squatted down to put himself at JP Jr.'s eye level. "Nothing to be afraid of, little guy. My job is actually to keep *you* safe. I'm like a superhero in a suit. Did your daddy tell you that?" JP Jr. shook his head. "Oh sure. They give me all kinds of super-duper weapons for it, too. They even give me a *magic suitcase*." JP peeked out at the mention of magic. "That's right. And inside that magic suitcase are special magic codes that I can use to send missiles anywhere I want."

"Anywhere?" JP Jr. asked. His eyes were the size of golf balls.

"Anywhere. *Anytime*," Leary said. At this revelation, the president's special guest started to convulse and then broke down into full-blown tears.

"Oh . . . oh dear . . . there there . . ." The president patted him on the head and stood back up to face JP Sr. "Boy. Sensitive kid, huh?"

"Not really," JP Sr. said. "We're from Texas."

Needless to say, it was an awkward lunch. The second that JP (Jr. and Sr.) were gone, Leary called for Ruffles. When Ruffles arrived a few minutes later, Leary was nowhere to be seen.

"Mr. President?"

"Down here," Leary replied from somewhere in front of his desk, blocked from sight by the Oval Office couches.

Ruffles walked over to find the president flat on his back, on the carpet, staring up at the ceiling. "Are you okay, sir?"

"It's an angry bird, isn't it, Ruffles?"

"What bird, sir?" Initially Ruffles thought Leary had lain down on his own, but now he was wondering whether he had fallen and hit his head.

"The eagle, Ruffles." Leary pointed up to the rarely noticed presidential seal engraved into the ceiling.

"Oh." Ruffles felt somewhat relieved. "Well, it is a bird of prey, sir. Eagles are not supposed to be very friendly."

"This is true," the president said.

Ruffles decided to skip ahead. "Mr. President, is there something else bothering you?"

"I can't do this, Ruffles," he said.

"Yes, you can. It's the right thing to do. Anyone here will tell you the same thing."

Leary shook his head, not yet convinced. "No president has ordered federal troops to fire on fellow Americans since Lincoln."

"And they put him on the penny," Ruffles pointed out. "First time the U.S. had ever put a president's face on a piece of money."

"What if I just call him? Meet him partway on this?"

"Call Travis? No," Ruffles said. "Mr. President, the governor knows what's in play here. You could not have been more clear. Besides, it's only been an hour and a half. Give him a little more time for reality to sink in. We'll hear from him."

"What if we don't?"

"Well . . . then he's made his choice."

Paige sped south on I-95 until she was beyond Springfield, Virginia, then exited at the first rest stop and looked for a pay phone. She was too paranoid to trust any phone in D.C. but felt certain that the filthy blue one inside a Virginia Roy Rogers was not of great interest to the Feds.

The TVs that hung above her head reported the latest news from Texas. With only a few hours remaining before the border lockdown, the roads were clogged—but, as the cameras from news helicopters were capturing, the interstates were more jammed coming *in* than going *out*. Motor homes, pickup trucks, SUVs, and minivans honked their way south as they passed Priuses and Smart Cars traveling north. "Who are these people?" a panicky CNN host wondered when confronted with the footage. "*Where* did they come from? *Where* are they going? One can't help but wonder if perhaps what we're seeing is—who knows—maybe a coordinated effort by right-wing militants to converge on Texas and create a new republic of hate?"

Paige pulled herself away from the coverage and picked up the receiver. She waited for the dial tone, then punched in the number on the calling card that she'd bought at the gas station next door. When the recording asked for the number she wished to dial, she slipped off her shoe, where—like Adam Wexler—she had stashed all her most pertinent numbers in a flattened piece of notebook paper. She dialed her father's office and waited. "Pick up," she whispered. It didn't even ring.

Rrrr—daaa—dee. I'm sorry. The number you have called is unavailable or is no longer in service. Figuring her nerves had caused her to misdial, she hung up and started over. *Rrrr—daaa—dee. I'm sorry. The number—*

She moved on to Travis's cell phone, hoping that she had just written down the other number incorrectly. This number rang, but only once. *Rrrr—daaa—dee. I'm sorry . . .*

"No," she whispered. She tried one more time. *Rrrr—daaa—dee—* "No!" She took the blue receiver and pounded it against the metal numbers as the robotic female operator repeated the bad news ad infinitum.

Neither Travis nor Cole had any military experience. As the two of them scribbled out a hastily conceived plan, both recognized—without ever acknowledging it out loud—that they had little idea what they were doing. At least Travis had run a business. He knew how to manage people and divvy up resources. He was able to differentiate between the essential and the dispensable. The main difference between business and war, as Travis saw it, was the objective; instead of focusing on making money, the focus was on not getting killed. For now, that basic understanding would have to suffice.

There were three elements that Travis and Cole believed—or rather guessed—would be critical to victory. The first was holding Galveston. If they lost control over the refineries and ports, they were finished. Travis would ready the Texas National Guard and Texas Air Guard and at the first whiff of battle send half of them south. He'd divide the other half among the four major cities in an effort to keep the peace.

The second key element was Travis himself. That was Cole's theory, anyway. "Without you, the movement doesn't have a figurehead," he said. "It'll either sputter out or roll into chaos. Either one plays into Washington's hands."

"I thought you didn't have any military experience," Travis said.

"I don't, I've just read *Julius Caesar* a time or two," he said.

At Cole's insistence, Travis would take the smaller Texas *State* Guard—a distinct branch of the Texas Military Forces without any federal ties—and give them the job of protecting the capitol and the men and women inside it.

The last element was something that Travis and Cole quickly realized they couldn't control on their own. They needed to neutralize Fort Hood. It was the country's largest army base, home to more than forty-five thousand soldiers, four hundred tanks, four hundred Bradley fighting vehicles, two hundred artillery pieces, and enough live ammunition to keep shooting for years without stopping. It was also right between Austin and Dallas, perfectly positioned to cut off supplies and scuttle any real chance of victory.

Travis had told Walt that Texas would buy Fort Hood and all that was in it off the Feds, but he recognized now this had been wishful thinking. Washington wasn't going to just give up such a strategic base, no matter how much oil the new republic was ready to offer. If they were going to wrest control of the base away from Washington, it would have to happen from the inside.

"Any chance you've read *Mutiny on the Bounty* lately?" Travis asked.

"Not since I was ten," said Cole.

"Well, I could be wrong, but I've got to believe there've been some grumblings already inside Fort Hood about all this," Travis said.

"You think?" asked Cole. He was glad that Travis's brain was still spinning. His was mush.

"You know what percent of the entire armed forces hail from Texas? Eleven."

"That seems too high," Cole said.

"It's not. I read it on the drive to Prosper."

"In a book?"

"*Yes*, in a book," Travis said. "*Texas Trivia*. K's borrowing it or else I would show you." K was borrowing it, but only so Travis would stop reading it out loud.

"If that's true, that's a pretty high number," Cole conceded.

"I know it is. Can't imagine those guys are oiling their guns and getting too psyched up about being asked to go take out Grandma."

Cole's brain was sparking again. He didn't know the military, but he understood the mind. "We need to find a way to capitalize on that," he said. "Any idea how many soldiers are from Oklahoma?"

"Probably a few percent," Travis said.

"I'll bet it's the same with Arkansas and Louisiana."

Travis was catching up with Cole. "The governor of Florida's supporting me."

"There's another, what, seven or eight percent?" Cole asked.

"Sounds about right," Travis said.

Cole started to jot down some states and numbers. "Ben, if you lump enough states together in this, suddenly you don't need a mutiny; you already have the majority."

"We can't expect too many states to pledge their troops."

"They don't have to pledge their troops. They just have to publicly express their support. That alone might do it. It would just alienate the soldiers even more from the elites in Washington."

"I hear ya," said Travis.

"And take a look at where the major military bases are in this country," said Cole. "There was a time when they were spread all over the Northeast. Most of those are long gone. They've been sold, built over, turned into museums. Now the most active bases are in Texas, Oklahoma, Kansas, Georgia, North Carolina, Tennessee, *two* in Kentucky—"

"For as much as the elites on the coasts like to make fun of us simpletons in flyover country, they sure are putting an awful lot of dependence on the Red States for their safety and protection," Travis said. He pushed himself out of his chair and walked to the doorway. "Fran, get me the governors of Oklahoma and Arkansas, please. And Louisiana."

"Sure." She picked up the phone and scrolled through their contacts.

"Oh, and Kansas," Travis said.

"Got it," Fran said.

"Try Kentucky and Alabama while you're at it!" Cole called from the other room.

Fran punched a few buttons before she stopped. She pulled the phone away from her ear and placed it on the desk, then reached behind the base and started to fiddle with the cord.

"What's the problem?"

"Nothing, it's just . . . the line's not working."

Travis took the phone from her and hung it up. "Don't try to fix it, just use another one. We've got ten in here."

Fran shuffled to another desk as Travis traipsed behind. She picked up the receiver. "Dead," she said.

"Forget it. Just give me the numbers, I'll call." Travis pulled out his cell phone to see NO SERVICE displayed in the top left corner of the screen. "Great. Everyone, check your phones, will ya?"

K looked at his phone and shook his head. "Nothing," Cole said, appearing in the bullpen. Fran went to check with the other offices down the hall. She returned looking grim.

"The entire capitol's been zapped," she said. "Phones, e-mails . . . everything."

Travis clicked on Fran's computer. "She's right. Network's down."

"It's not just down," Cole said. "We've been cut off."

"It sort of makes you wonder how the president is going to reach us, huh?" asked Travis.

"No," said Cole. "I think this means he doesn't *want* to reach us."

35

The president slumped on his couch and watched the news. It was midafternoon and MSNBC was reporting live from the Oklahoma/Texas border on I-35 as the 1st Battalion of the 18th Infantry arrived from Fort Riley in Kansas. The troops poured out of a camouflaged transport vehicle like armed ants. A growing mass of Texans was there to greet them on the other side of the invisible line. They hadn't waited for the troops to seal off the border; they'd already done it themselves, using their parked pickups and horse trailers to make a roadblock that stretched beyond the pavement for fifty yards in both directions. A wide shot revealed dozens more trucks moving into position to extend it even farther.

"Oh my God," Leary said.

The reporter on the scene was going down the line, interviewing Texans. She stopped to talk to a stumpy twenty-something man with Wrangler jeans and a bulge in his bottom lip. He had just parked his truck in the dirt and was pulling a six-pack of beer from the back. "Sir, Jennifer Roberts, MSNBC, may I ask you a couple questions?"

"Goathead," he said.

"Excuse me?" She held the microphone closer to his mouth.

"Goathead," he repeated.

She pressed her finger against her earpiece. "I'm sorry, I admit I'm having trouble—"

"Go. Ahead," he said, leaving plenty of dead air between the two words.

"Oh. Yes. Sorry. Good. I was curious to know what brought you out here this afternoon?"

The man took in the wild scene around him. "Why the hell not?" he asked. "I got some beer. Gonna meet some new folks. And if necessary, kick some ass." He reached back into his truck and took out his hunting rifle and a loose box of ammo.

"Oh. Wow. Okay. So . . . *wow* . . ." Jennifer Roberts hadn't seen a gun up close since she interviewed the rapper 50 Cent for a *Dateline* holiday special. "So you are ready and willing to defend yourself is what you're saying?"

"Ma'am, I adhere to the same three maxims of the Texas Rangers: Never wear a gun unless you know how to use it. Never draw it unless you intend to fire. Never shoot except to kill."

President Leary couldn't take any more. He reached for the remote and muted the TV. As he did, he saw Avery Adams pass by in the hallway. "No calls?" he asked, leaning back in his cushion, unaware that someone in Washington had authorized a communication shutdown in Austin.

Avery double-checked with the president's secretary, then shook her head. "Sorry."

He waved thanks and turned back to the TV. Jennifer Roberts had moved on from the boor with the beer and was now chatting with an elderly woman on a walker wearing a holster. He decided to leave it on mute and checked his watch. Eight hours until midnight.

The IT Department at the state capitol hoped to have things up and running within the hour, treating the downed network as if it were part of a routine system crash. It was far from it. The blackout went beyond the capitol, encompassing a fifty-mile radius around Austin. The coordinated effort necessitated the shutdown of certain satellites under the command of the FCC, the targeted use of Homeland Security's Internet kill switch, and the employment of jamming equipment operated by U.S. military planes, which had gone unnoticed as they circled Texas at high altitudes.

With no way to communicate and safety a growing concern, Travis sent Fran home to be with her husband. The only thing she was accomplishing was making all of them more nervous. They tried to watch the news with her, but she couldn't go ten seconds without muttering a prayer or a de-motivational phrase like "this is bad."

Fran was right, of course. Shop owners were boarding up windows. Grocery stores and Walmarts were being picked clean. Fort Hood was on high alert. The army blockade appeared to be going forward as promised and on schedule. Everywhere U.S. soldiers popped up, Texans met them on the other side. Locals had plugged up I-20 outside Waskom and Highway 75 near Denison. The El Paso chapter of the Tea Party Patriots set up lawn chairs across all six lanes of I-10. They came by car, by truck, even by horseback.

Travis handed Cole and K some leftover tacos and two bottles of Lone Star beer from the office fridge. Cole grabbed his without pulling his gaze from the TV. "Tell me that I'm not about to be responsible for starting a civil war," he said.

"No one's shooting yet," Travis said, joining the two of them on the bullpen couch.

"So we're down to 'yet,'" Cole said.

"Polls open in fifteen hours . . ."

"That's a long time for a standoff," Cole said.

Travis looked at Cole. "You don't think we'll make it, do you?" He wasn't accusatory about it. He was worried, too.

"It's not going to take much," Cole said. He spoke slowly, letting his fear overtake him. "All you need is a trigger-happy local with one too many drinks . . . the backfire of an old truck . . . some idiot yelling 'Pow!' . . . that's all that would have to happen, and then—"

BANG BANG BANG! Someone pounded against the outer office door. Cole dropped his beer and K pulled his gun. He ordered Travis and Cole to hide, then bent down and looked through the tiny horizontal slit under the door. He saw the bottom half inch of a pair of red women's flats. Not the steel-toed army boots he was expecting.

He unlocked the door and pulled it open an inch. "Yes?" he asked.

"I need to see the governor," she said. She wore a black fitted tank top with a zip-up white sweatshirt and jeans. Her short brown hair was pulled back with a cranberry clip. She looked familiar, but K didn't know why. He sniffed the air. It was a scent he'd caught a time or two at the ranch in Prosper. Lavender orange blossom.

"You must be Kate Coggins," he said. "It's a pleasure."

Gabe had been parking the car and showed up in time to slip through the open door before K closed it and reset the lock.

"Where is he?" Gabe wondered, looking around the empty office.

K wasn't sure. "Uh . . . Governor? You can come on out." The knob on the storage closet door turned, and Travis stepped over a box of printer paper, followed by Cole.

"Well, now that looks heroic," Kate said.

Travis was startled to see her. "Hi." He fixed his hair and rubbed his hands along his cheeks in the hope it would remove some of his scruff. "We thought you were the, uh . . ."

"Bad guys," said Cole.

Kate smiled. "Nice to see you again, Damon. It's been too long," she said.

"You, too."

"Love the loafers."

They were his Tanino Crisci's. "Russian reindeer leather," he said, enjoying the temporary distraction from reality.

Kate turned her attention back to Travis. "We just drove in from Houston. I got a call from Paige. She tried to call you, but—"

"The lines are down," Travis said. "I'm guessing the Feds cut 'em. Or fried 'em." He didn't know what the twenty-first-century equivalent of it was. "Is she okay?"

Kate held Travis's gaze with her own. "She found something."

Everyone was too tense to sit. Kate flipped through her notes. She had jotted some of them while on the phone with Paige and the rest as Gabe sped toward Austin. To someone who didn't know better, they appeared to be a jumbled mess. Notes were scribbled right side up, upside down, and diagonally, and there were arrows, dozens of them, leading from one page to another and back again, connecting half-thoughts and third-thoughts and quarter-thoughts as they'd collided into revelations.

Her high school teachers always said Kate had the intelligence and athleticism to be an astronaut. Even as a girl, though, she knew she wanted a husband and a family. So she decided she would use her gifts to be the world's greatest wife and mother. There was nothing she couldn't learn to cook well. No stain she couldn't find a way to remove. Travis had shielded himself from thinking about how good he had had it, knowing that exploring that notion would lead to a level of regret from which he couldn't easily recover.

"What you got?" Travis asked, conscious of the clock.

She gripped both sides of her notepad. "Are you familiar with Anatole Metzos?"

"Sure," said Travis. "Paige's crusty old boss. Walt Thompson calls him spooky."

"Only if you consider buying the allegiance of President Leary's most important advisers spooky," Kate said.

"And Bill Lewis," Gabe added.

"Whoa," said Travis. He said it softer than he wanted, given that the person in question always seemed to be within earshot.

"Right now she and a friend at the *Post* have been able to link Metzos money to Mark Ruflowski . . . Lee Kurtz . . . David Velez . . ." Kate looked up from the list. "The attorney general."

Travis and Cole nodded, a bit in shock upon hearing her name names.

"There's probably more," Kate said.

"More?" said Travis. "That's plenty. Does Paige have any guess what the endgame is here?"

"She wasn't sure, but right now all the focus is on getting the RRA up and running as quickly as possible. For sure ahead of the election in November."

Cole had caught a few hours of Walt Thompson's nine-hour ex-posé on Metzos while driving between New Jersey and Vermont to go skiing. He had been entertained, but he hadn't been too worried. Until now. "He's trying to break us," Cole said.

"What do you mean, 'us'?" Travis said.

"Capitalism. America as we know it. Metzos is a classic leftist. The difference between him and your typical tweed-coated liberal arts professor is that Metzos actually has the means—and appar-ently now the connections—to make his left-wing utopia a reality."

"So what would that look like?" Kate asked.

"Total governmental control over everyone and everything," said Cole.

"Ah yes," Travis said, "progress."

"That may be true," Gabe said, "but that doesn't sound like some-thing Bill Lewis would sign on to, even on his worst day."

"What does Bill do for a living out in Borger?" Cole asked.

"He owns wells," said Gabe. "Natural gas. A ton of them. A lot of drilling equipment, too."

"Well, there you go," said Cole, acting as if the logic should be apparent to all of them.

"But according to the RRA, he's gonna lose a big stake in all of that," said Travis.

"Will he?" asked Cole. "Look at every massive piece of legislation that's come through Congress in the last three and a half years. Each one has been sprinkled with sweetheart deals for certain people or corporations to whom the left owes a favor. I'll venture to say that when we finally see the language in the RRA—which Met-zos presumably has say over—it will include an incentive to drive up demand for natural gas, netting Bill a lot more money overnight, or a waiver that allows him to keep everything he has. It will probably contain both."

"No wonder Ruffles and Big Bill wanted me to go to Washing-ton," Travis said. "Once I leave the state, that dipstick becomes the boss. By the time I would have landed on the East Coast, there wouldn't have even been a deal for me to negotiate."

"Bill would have pulled the plug," Gabe said.

"Instead," said Cole, "now that Metzos realizes you're not going to back down, he had the Feds kill the phone lines. He must have figured that winning a war outright will give Washington more power than negotiating peace."

"Well, thanks for cheering us up," Travis said to Kate. "What else did Paige say?"

"That's not enough for you?" Kate asked.

"She didn't mention anything about a Lincoln letter?" Travis hoped that maybe in all Paige's sleuthing she had unearthed that as well.

"A what?" Kate asked.

"Lincoln letter? Abraham Lincoln?" Kate returned a blank stare. "Nothing?"

"No."

Not convinced, Travis peeked over Kate's shoulder to look at her notepad. He was the only one besides her with the ability to decipher it. "You sure?" he asked.

Kate flipped the notepad back to its cover with a quick snap. "I think I would have remembered something like that," she said, no more willing to put up with Travis's crap now than she had been in the final months of their marriage.

"I'm sorry," Travis said, meaning it. "This is huge." He gave her a look of gratitude.

Cole had been tuning them out. He was doing what he did best; he was thinking. "Does the president know about any of this?" he asked, rejoining the conversation.

"That's partly why Paige called," Kate said. "As best she can tell, the president's being fleeced and doesn't know it."

That last detail was all Travis and Cole needed to hear. In perfect synchronization, each looked at his watch. It was three thirty. Four thirty in Washington. "I need to talk to Leary," Travis said.

"Why not call a press conference?" Gabe asked. "Take him down that way."

"No," Travis and Cole said simultaneously.

"That would look desperate," said Travis. "Like we couldn't beat Washington on our own and had to go digging for dirt instead. If we're going to go that route, we might as well call Gloria Allred and have her sitting next to us."

"Besides," Cole said, "part of our leverage here is that we know about Metzos and the rest of the world doesn't. It could be worth a lot to Leary to let him get ahead of the story rather than be swallowed by it."

"So then call him," said Kate.

"We'd need to drive out of the city and find a phone that works," said Travis. "Even then, do we really think Metzos's gatekeepers will let me speak to the president?"

"You mean Metzos's puppet? Not a chance," said Cole. "If Metzos wants to further destabilize America, then he wants a fight."

"I guess that's probably true," Gabe admitted. He pursed his lips. "These guys never want to waste a crisis, do they?" Travis stopped and stared at him. He couldn't believe those words came from the mouth of Gabe Coggins. Gabe looked uncomfortable with the sudden attention from the governor. "I listened to you on Walt Thompson this past week," he confessed. "What can I say? You made some good points."

Travis eased Gabe with a wry smile. "Well, what the hell took you so long?" he asked. The two men chuckled. It was strange for the rest of the group to see the bitter enemies share a moment. It reminded Cole of the brief stretch in the mid-1970s when ABC forced Hanna-Barbera to make Tom and Jerry friends.

K broke it up. "Governor, what if we could get you to D.C. before midnight?"

"That would be great," said Travis, "but it ain't gonna happen."

K persisted. "Say we could. Say there's a way to get you in front of the president."

"Without Big Bill finding out we're gone?"

"Right," said K.

"The entire Texas border is protected airspace right now," said Cole. "No pilot in their right mind would try to fly us to Washington."

"That's okay," K said. "I happen to know a pilot who's not in his right mind."

Travis tilted his head. "What are you talking about?"

K was smiling. "Seth Josephson," he said.

Travis was still perplexed. "Seth Josephson? Who's—" He interrupted himself and started to laugh when he remembered.

"What?" asked Cole.

"Well," said Travis, ignoring Cole's worried look, "he does have a plane."

"Uh-huh," said K.

"And, as you said, he *is* crazy," Travis added.

"Definitely," said K. Travis reached into his wallet and searched for the folded-up address he'd been handed outside the Cotton Gin Cafe.

"Hold on, hold on," Cole said. "Could someone please tell me who Seth Josephson is?"

"Sorry, Professor," said K. "You probably know him by his stage name."

"I do?"

"Oh yes," said Travis, "and if he can get you, me, and K to Washington safely, I'm going to make you watch every movie he's ever made."

36

Mike McKill lived in Brownwood, the dead center of Texas. In a smaller state, this would mean you're close to everything. Here, it was the opposite. Two hours to Austin. Three hours to Dallas. Four to Midland. The distance was why McKill kept a plane, even though he rarely had a reason to go anywhere, much less a person longing to see him.

Travis had left Gabe Coggins in charge. He had listened intently as Travis talked through the different scenarios that might play out over the course of the night and how to proceed. Gabe asked the right questions, his instincts were good, and he promised to stay out of sight. To throw Big Bill off the scent, Travis and Cole had poked their heads into his office on their way out of the capitol and told him that they were moving operations to the mansion out of safety concerns. Gabe sent Kate back to their home in Sugar Land—with a pair of troopers in tow—and took up his position behind Travis's desk. As Travis pulled the locked office door closed behind him, he had to admit that—*dang it*—Gabe Cogins looked convincingly stalwart.

K ignored every speed limit and every stop sign on the way, just about emptying the tank in Travis's F-150 but making it to Brownwood in an hour and twenty-five minutes. Cole sat in the middle seat, one leg on either side of the gearshift, and held his breath every time K slammed the transmission from third into fourth. They made a pit stop in town to let Travis make three collect calls on a pay phone. One was to Paige, telling her to look for them in front of the north gate of the White House sometime after 11:00 P.M. The others were to MSNBC and the Golf Channel—the only two channels the president ever watched—guaranteeing both the highest ratings in the network's history if they were waiting next to Paige with cameras rolling. He didn't tip what was happening, but should he be rebuffed, it would be captured live on camera, making Leary look like the warmonger, not Travis. There were plenty of holes in the idea, but it was the best he and Cole could come up with while going ninety-five miles an hour through Texas Hill Country.

A few miles past Brownwood, they came to County Road 464. K turned right and began looking for addresses.

"We should be close," Cole said.

"What's the number again?" asked K.

"There it is," said Travis, pointing off to the right. He didn't need to see the name and number on the mailbox. He only needed to see the gate. It was nine feet high, steel, and crudely made, as if McKill had soldered the whole thing together out of melted-down Buicks. There was a camera positioned on either side of it pointed down and protected by thick glass. A dense impassable hedge ran along the Route 11 side of the property. On the other side of the hedge, not visible until they got closer, was a fence topped with barbed wire. Just so there was no misunderstanding, a metal NO TRESSPASSING sign was bolted to the gate.

"I mean, seriously," Cole said, "who does this guy think is that desperate to get to him?"

"Tonight? *Us*," Travis said.

After pulling off the highway and up to the gate, K stepped out and looked for the call button to let Mike/Seth know they were there. He couldn't see one, so Travis and Cole joined in the search. They ran their hands along the gate, singeing them on the steel that had been baking in the sun all afternoon.

"FedEx must love delivering to this place," Cole said, shaking out his fingers.

Travis was about to lean on the horn when McKill's voice spoke from some unseen speaker. "Yes?"

Travis turned and spoke in the general direction of the voice. "Mike, it's Governor Ben Travis. We, uh . . . we need your help."

The gate opened slowly and without a sound. Travis, Cole, and K hopped back into the truck and had just started to drive through when McKill himself appeared from around the other side. He had pulled it open by hand. He held up his palm to stop them, a command they took seriously since his hand was also holding a large-caliber semiautomatic weapon. He was wearing his standard uniform from most of his films: combat boots, camouflage cargo pants, and a gratuitously tight white T-shirt. The T-shirt had a noticeable red stain on the front. Twenty years ago it would have been chalked up to the blood of a vanquished foe. This time around it was marinara sauce from a conquered chicken parm.

Before even saying hello, McKill walked to the bed of the truck and used the butt of his gun to snoop around, as if there might be a half-dozen ninjas lying in wait. Satisfied that they were alone, he returned to the open window on the passenger side and leaned in. "So . . ." He gave Cole a long once-over before continuing. "Who we killing?"

"If everything goes according to plan, no one," Travis said.

"Oh." McKill was disappointed to hear it.

"But we need you to fly us to Washington," Travis said. "Tonight."

"What time do you need to be there?"

"We need to be on the ground no later than eleven."

McKill looked at his watch. It was huge, like a silver-coated hamburger patty. He read the giant digital numbers and scoffed.

"Is there a problem?" Cole said.

McKill backed away from the car and crossed his arms. "Let me get this straight," he began. "First, you want me to load the federal government's most reviled man into my plane and cross a border that, as we speak, Washington is monitoring more closely than Pyongyang watches the DMZ. To accomplish that, I will have to fly

with the transponder off, without a flight plan, off the airways, using pilotage and dead reckoning, below radar coverage, the whole
time hoping not to be midaired by a regional jet or some weekend
warrior who won't know to be looking out the window for a ghost-
ship King Air."

Travis tried to save it. "Well—"

"*Then*"—McKill was only half done—"if we survive, I'll have to
go a thousand *more* miles, in the dark, evading every Class B, Class
C, Class D, and Class God-knows-what-else airspace along the way
so no one asks any questions. Of course, upon reaching Washington, D.C., there will be no avoiding controlled airspace, since the
whole damn place is controlled airspace. At which point the FAA will
not so kindly ask me who the hell I am, where I came from, where
I'm going, and why in shit's name my transponder is turned off! And
on top of all that, you expect me to accomplish this in *four* hours,
when the normal flight time between here and Washington in a
King Air 350 would be *five*. *That's* what you're asking?"

Cole and K looked to the governor. "Are you saying you don't
want to do it?" Travis asked.

McKill leaned back into the open passenger window, the end of
his dangling gun grazing Cole's chin. "Oh, I'm going to do it, Governor. I just want all of you to recognize what a badass I am when I
pull it off!" He walked around to the bumper of the truck, grabbed
the tailgate, and, after a few failed attempts, jumped in the back.

"You've got to give him credit," Travis said, "the man commands
your attention."

There was no time for a tour of the house, which was a shame since
McKill once described the interior to *People* magazine as "a cross
between a Buddhist temple and the original Starship *Enterprise*."
Instead, they went straight to the hangar off the back porch.

"Well, there she is," McKill said as they rounded the corner.

Travis froze. McKill's plane looked like it had been batted out of the air by King Kong. There was hail damage to the exterior, knicked props, a broken landing light . . .

"You've got to be kidding me," Travis said.

Cole rubbed his hand along one of the bald tires. "Is this thing even airworthy, McKill?"

McKill walked toward his sprawling mess of a workbench. "Technically? *No.* But that's just a paperwork thing. Trust me. She'll get us there." He yanked a ratchet set off the wall and slapped it into K's palm. "We only need four seats. Lose the rest." If they were going to take an hour off their flight time without needing to refuel, they needed to be lighter. McKill moved to the cargo hold and started dumping the contents. Out came two duffel bags of weapons, a case of ammo, water jugs, Christmas lights, and an unused set of Hogan irons in a leather bag. He found an old red fuel canister, sniffed the contents to make sure it was indeed jet fuel, and poured what was left into the topped-off gas tank.

Once he was done making the plane lighter, he moved on to his passengers. "If you don't need it, don't bring it," McKill said. "No keys, no wallets, no unnecessary clothes, just an ID to help them identify the bodies. *Kidding!* But seriously, empty your pockets."

Travis, Cole, and K did as they were told, leaving their belongings on a rusty chair. When they finished, McKill looked at the pile, then sized up Cole. Without asking permission, he slipped off the professor's Hermès tie in one deft move and dropped it onto the oil-stained cement.

"Better," McKill said. He turned away from Cole and walked under the wings to do one final inspection.

"But . . . we're going to the White House," Cole protested.

"Blazer, too," McKill said, pulling the wood chocks from around the tires.

Cole looked to Travis for some support. "Keep talking," Travis said. "I'd love to see you meet the president in nothing but boxer shorts and a pair of black socks."

"You laugh," Cole said, "but that's a recurring nightmare of mine."

He took off his jacket, folded it neatly, and set it gently on top of the heap.

Flying unnoticed by radar was a technological impossibility in a plane made of metal. If someone wanted to see it, they could. McKill's goal, then, was to give air traffic controllers no reasons to look for it. The only way to do that was to fly VFR (visual flight rules), without a flight plan. In turn, there would be no help from ATC to see and avoid solid objects: other aircraft, radio towers, terrain. It was up to McKill to know where he was and what might be around him. If he flew too high, too close to an airport, too near a city, or in the vicinity of an MOA (military operations area), ATC was bound to discover him and start tracking the flight. Maybe even scramble fighters if they clipped the wrong airspace.

The first three hundred miles were routine. It was a cloudless sky, the sun was still up, and they flew east, splitting the difference between Dallas to the north and Fort Hood to the south. K and Cole sat in back, tasked with keeping a lookout for other aircraft. Travis sat up front in the copilot seat, following their progress on a sectional chart, and was excited to hear McKill reminisce about his Hollywood past. Twenty years ago this would have been torture for McKill, but he'd been a punch line for so long that he enjoyed the chance to share his experiences with someone who wasn't there just to make fun of him. Still, before they'd reached Waco, Travis was desperate to change seats.

"It was my idea to do that love scene on top of the submarine," McKill said, staring straight ahead. It had been forty minutes since Travis had uttered a word. "Not many people know that. The director thought it was too much, what with the movie set in the Arctic Sea and all, but I told him: 'How many people watched Burt Lancaster and Deborah Kerr roll around on the beach in *From Here to Eternity* and thought about all the saltwater going up their noses? Or all the sand collecting in his skivvies? Zero. That's how many.' The truth is that as long as the passion is there, you can have characters pretty much make love anywhere and an audience will go along with it. And Lancaster, hell, you know what he got for doing it? His first Oscar nomination. That's why I always say, you've got to take risks."

Travis looked back at Cole, hoping for some sympathy.

McKill continued undeterred. "Of course, that was before the Oscars became as political as they are now. It's not enough to have a good performance. Nope. You got to say the right things *off* camera, too. My manager said that I was on the short list to get a Best Actor nom for *Pistol Whipped,* but the Academy decided to punish me for introducing Dan Quayle at a campaign rally . . ."

Travis couldn't take it anymore. He turned back to Cole, who was fully reclined in his seat and listening to Mahler's Fourth on the iPod he had snuck aboard the plane. Travis waved at him to get his attention. "You want to swap spots for a bit?"

"I'm good," Cole said, waving off the request. He had only eavesdropped once on their conversation and heard McKill listing the D-list actresses he had bedded.

One turn around a water tower that said HUBBARD told McKill that they were approaching the Arkansas border. That was a welcome relief since it gave McKill something else to do besides talk about himself. He snatched the chart off Travis's lap and studied it. "There," he said, pointing to a spot north of I-30. "That's our crossing point." It was a deserted spot north of Texarkana. They'd fly over the tiny town of DeKalb, and after that there would be nothing but fields for miles until they crossed the Red River. McKill adjusted his course slightly and turned on his transponder, the electronic beacon that would tell ATC and commercial aircraft who they were and where they were.

"What are you doing?" Travis asked.

"I'm turning the TCAS on for just a second. It'll send out our position and altitude, but I want to see what else is out here." The display instantly revealed a white square ten miles out up at 23,000 feet. "Well, hello there," McKill said.

"What is it?" asked Travis.

McKill twisted a knob. "It's twenty thousand feet above us, but it looks like it's shadowing our course. Moving slowly. Probably an E-3," he said.

The E-3 was the air force's premier communications aircraft, distinguishable by its large rotating saucer centered above the fuselage. It was a flying radar dish, capable of detecting planes, missiles, and bad weather for hundreds of miles. It was also helping to jam communications in and out of Austin.

"Can we circle around until he's gone?" Travis asked.

McKill turned the transponder back off. "Not if you want to make it to Washington by midnight."

"So then we chance it? Hope they're not watching?"

"We could," said McKill, "but assuming they're looking for planes, they won't miss us."

"Well, that doesn't leave us with much," said Travis.

"Sure it does," said McKill. "We'll just have to convince 'em we're not a plane."

He took a quick glance at the chart, then nudged the yoke forward. The propellers rotated faster with the sudden increase in airspeed, causing them to howl. Cole was yanked from his calm and rushed to put his seat up as they descended. When the King Air hit 1,000 feet, McKill leveled off and pressed his face against the window.

"What are you looking for?" asked Travis.

"A road," said McKill. He pulled his head away, leaving a circle of condensation on the window.

He slowed the King Air and dropped another five hundred feet. The terrain below was flat, fields of grass and cotton lined with towering oaks.

"Are we landing?" Cole asked from the back.

"I'm sorry, are we disturbing you?" Travis sniped.

McKill looked out the window again and spotted his target—Highway 8, a lonely two-lane road and the only way across the Red River for ten miles in either direction. He maneuvered the plane till they were paralleling it, a few hundred feet up.

"Is this low enough?" Travis wondered.

"Nope," said McKill. He steadied the plane, eased off the power, and dropped between the two lines of trees. There was no more than ten feet of wiggle room on either side. He kept dropping until they were just high enough off the ground to miss hitting the occasional road sign. Travis felt like the pair of tweezers from the board game Operation, waiting to be zapped. Even K looked scared. It was darker beneath the tree line, and McKill flipped on the wing lights, erasing the long shadows and illuminating the yellow reflectors in the middle of the highway. He narrowed his focus and put all his energy into keeping the strip of yellow bumps centered in line with his right knee.

"Have you done this before?" Travis asked, holding on tight.

"Only in front of a green screen," McKill admitted.

They tore down the open highway at a hundred and thirty miles per hour. Signs passed too quickly to even be read. Cars on both sides careened off the road and onto the shoulders. Up ahead, the road curved slightly to the right.

"Get ready to turn," Travis said.

"I see it," McKill said.

He banked the plane gingerly through the chute. They emerged from one turn and into another.

"Now left!" Travis yelled.

McKill banked the other way. He overcontrolled slightly, and his left wing dipped more than he wanted and decapitated a family of mailboxes, scattering bills and Bed Bath & Beyond coupons across the highway. The road straightened back out, leaving a straight half-mile shot to the river and Arkansas on the other side. Through the dusk they could see a dozen different vehicles stopped on the bridge. Campers with their awnings out. Someone with tongs manning a Coleman grill. A border-crossing cookout.

"It's a party," McKill said.

"Try not to crash it," said Travis.

The King Air buzzed through the festivities, snuffing out the barbecue with prop wash as they went. Beyond it, standing guard over the other half of the bridge, was a jeep full of terrified army privates. They dove for cover, triggering a cheer from the Texans on the other side. As the King Air continued east on Highway 8, the soldier behind the wheel reached for his radio to call in the attack.

"A plane, a plane!" He sounded like Tattoo from *Fantasy Island*.

It took a few seconds for a communications officer to respond. His voice crackled with static. "Soldier, please identify yourself and your position, over."

"Private Kelly, sir . . . 24th Infantry . . . on Highway 8 . . . over!"

"You said a plane? Over."

"Yes, sir. Nearly ran us over. Over."

There was a long pause. "Private, I thought you said it was a plane."

By the time the details were sorted out, it was too late to do anything about it. No one had caught the tail number, the sun had set, and the King Air had vanished into the darkness.

It was a thousand miles, as the crow flies, from the Arkansas border to Washington, D.C. However, since their bird was made of radar-reflective aluminum and their antics over the Red River had every FAA suit keen on finding out to whom the King Air belonged, Travis and company couldn't afford to take a straight shot to the nation's capitol. The first locale to avoid along the way was the Pine Bluff Arsenal in central Arkansas, one of nine army installations in the country that, until recently, housed chemical weapons. It was the sort of place that might get testy about an unidentified plane overhead. They wisely turned north. When they neared Little Rock, they turned east. They stayed to the south of Memphis and Knoxville. From there they followed the Appalachian Trail toward Maryland, skirting the Radford Army Ammunition Plant in Virginia and the peaks of the Blue Ridge Mountains, which crept up on the King Air in the dark before disappearing again. McKill didn't seem worried by them, but Travis watched the altimeter go from 8,000 to 2,000 and back again a few dozen times, trying to trust the confusing jumble of symbols on the charts that said the highest peak in the range topped out near 6,600 feet. It was pushing 11:00 P.M. local time when they saw the lights of D.C. glowing in the distance.

The airspace around Washington, D.C., was the most protected in the country. In the aftermath of 9/11, any pilot who planned on flying within sixty miles of the nation's capital was required by law to prefile a flight plan in order to enter the area. The ATC operated under the call sign Potomac Approach, and if a controller picked up any sense that a pilot was a rookie or not interested in following instructions to the letter, he had no qualms about telling him—not asking him—to steer clear of D.C. altogether.

Mike McKill's King Air had eaten up so much time zigzagging across the South that the original hope of landing in Virginia and then having a taxi drive them the rest of the way was no longer a possibility. If they wanted to make it in time, they needed to land closer. McKill searched the sectional chart for a closer airstrip that would do the job.

He settled on Lee Airport, a small private strip thirty miles east of the White House, just south of Annapolis. It was far enough from downtown D.C. to avoid the ire of Potomac Approach, but close enough that they could be at the North Gate of the White House by eleven thirty.

They descended through the clouds from 10,500 feet and flew straight up the Chesapeake Bay. The moon was out, lighting up a fleet of commercial fishing boats racing toward Baltimore with their holds full of crab. The King Air banked left, a path that took them unwittingly right over Anatole Metzos's estate on Cherry Tree Cove.

McKill pulled a lever with a little plastic wheel on the end of it. Travis felt the clunk of the landing gear open under his feet and searched the ground ahead of them. "I don't see any runway lights," Travis said.

"That's 'cause I haven't turned them on yet," McKill said. With the tower at Lee Airport closed for the night, responsibility for runway lighting passed to the incoming pilots, who could control them by tuning to the local traffic advisory frequency and clicking their microphone. Three clicks for low light. Five for medium. Seven for high. McKill clicked his radio mike three times and waited.

"Nothing happened," Travis said.

"No kidding," McKill said. He tried again, going with five clicks this time. Still no lights. "Maybe I got the wrong frequency. Tell me what the chart says for the CTAF at Lee Airport."

Travis looked at him blankly.

McKill was short on patience. "*Lee Airport*. K-A-N-P. CTAF. What's it say?"

"Forget the chart," Travis said, "I don't even know what *you're* saying."

"Never mind." McKill swiped it off Travis's lap. "Grab the yoke a sec, will ya?" Travis didn't know how to do that either, but McKill didn't seem to care. He let go of the yoke and flicked on the overhead cabin light to read the chart. Travis grabbed the matching yoke in front of him. The King Air pitched up and down violently.

McKill dropped the chart in irritation. "Hey-hey! Relax the death grip," he said. "Hold it between your thumb and your index finger, like a teacup. It's a flying machine, not a truck."

Cole called from the back, "What the hell is going on up there?"

Travis looked back with a proud grin. "I'm flying!"

"You're what?!" K yelped.

Studying the chart in the dim light, McKill could see that Route 2 bordered the airport to the south. He spotted the lights from the fast food joints in the distance, but beyond it was black except for the faint white-green-white flash from the rotating airport beacon. McKill tried his mike a few more times in vain. "Alright, my controls," he said. He took hold of his yoke and the ride smoothed out.

"Why isn't it working?" asked Travis.

"Some airports have a curfew. They don't let planes land after ten or eleven at night," McKill said. "We must have just missed the window."

Cole leaned forward in his seat. "But we know it's there. Our plane has lights. Can't we land in the dark?"

McKill looked back at Cole. "You ever gone cliff diving at night, Professor?"

"Why would I do that?" asked Cole.

"Exactly," said McKill. He pulled in the landing gear. "Find me another airport, Governor."

They continued west toward Freeway Airport, fourteen miles closer to the city. They were sneaking up on a sleeping bear, but so far no one had noticed them. Five miles out, an alarm beeped as something on the instrument panel flashed. McKill silenced it without looking.

"What was that?" Cole asked from the back.

"Nothing," said McKill.

Travis looked at the flashing light in question. FUEL. "McKill, are we—"

"Yes." McKill knew that flying high speed at a low altitude with three passengers all the way to D.C. would be asking a lot from one tank. The light had been on since Virginia. "Doesn't matter anyway," McKill added. "We're here." Just as at Lee Airport, down came the landing gear. McKill clicked his microphone five more times. Just as at Lee, there was no response from the ground.

"What time is their cutoff?" Travis hoped.

McKill had checked this in advance. "They don't have one," he said. He pulled in the landing gear again and banked to the north.

Cole wedged his way into the cockpit. "Why aren't we landing?"

"Someone doesn't want us to," said McKill. He ran his finger over the creases in the sectional chart, pausing at airports as he came to them. "I bet every little airport around here's going to be the same," he said.

K unbuckled his belt and joined in the discussion. "Can we go closer to Baltimore? If we go further out, there has to be a runway—"

"Too far," McKill snapped. They were out of both time and fuel.

"Any reason it has to be a runway?" Travis mused.

McKill looked at Travis and could see he wasn't joking. "Nope," McKill said. "It just has to be flat, lit up, and at least twenty-five hundred feet long."

Cole held up his hand. "I'll go on the record and say I would prefer a runway."

"You thinking I-95?" K asked.

Travis shook his head. "If we're gonna cause a commotion when we land, we might as well touch down as close to our destination as possible."

"You want to Sully Sullenberger it in the Potomac?" McKill suggested. Travis shook his head.

"The Mall," said Cole. He wasn't suggesting it; he was simply reading his friend's twisted mind.

McKill considered the implications while Travis began folding up the chart, his mind already made up.

"We could be on the ground, in, what, fifteen minutes?" Travis asked.

"Ten, but it's pretty risky," McKill said.

"I know," Travis said, "but as a beloved Hollywood icon once told me, you've got to take risks."

McKill nodded, inspired by his own wisdom. Cole wasn't as sure. "I think we're a little too locked in on this midnight deadline. There's no guarantee Leary's going to do something right away."

"That's a pretty dangerous assumption," said Travis. "Anyway, it's irrelevant since apparently Leary doesn't know half the stuff that's going on around him to begin with. He might not give the green light at midnight, but someone else could."

"If we pull this off, you guys could practically run to the White House," said McKill.

"What if we *don't* pull it off?" Cole asked.

They all knew what it meant, but no one wanted to say it. McKill flipped through his mental catalog of motivational one-liners and settled on one from a movie that was so bad, bootleggers in Hong Kong wouldn't even sell pirated copies of it on the street.

"'If' isn't in my vocabulary," he said.

Without another word, he rolled the King Air into a steep bank, heading west. Cole scrambled back to his seat from the cockpit as McKill pushed the power levers forward. The plane shuddered under the strain. An unfamiliar sound of rushing air and a buffeting ran through the airframe.

McKill scanned the dials. "What the hell?"

Travis pointed to the lever that controls the flaps. "Don't these things need to be up?" They'd ascended and descended so many times that he'd begun to pick up the routine.

"Oh. Good catch," said McKill. He'd left the flaps in the landing position. He raised them and the plane sped up. Travis looked back at the others, beaming.

His moment was interrupted by the beep of the fuel alarm, which McKill silenced as before. With nothing else to do, Travis watched his pilot. McKill was expressionless, adjusting knobs and dials with precision. Travis had pegged the guy as nothing more than a lonely kook, desperate to feel relevant again, but operating with the fate of Texas in his hands, he seemed more at ease than ever.

They were eleven miles from the Mall and approaching fast when ATC introduced themselves on the emergency frequency. "Attention unidentified aircraft heading two seven zero, this is Potomac Approach, broadcasting on one twenty-one point five. You have entered restricted airspace. Turn to a heading of zero niner zero immediately, and contact Andrews Air Force Base Tower now on frequency one one eight point four. Acknowledge with an IDENT."

McKill reached for his headset. Travis shot him a look. "What are you doing?"

"Hopefully buying us another thirty seconds," he said. "Roger, Potomac, sorry about that. This is King Air November-Four-Seven-Two-Whiskey-Tango. We are having some electrical problems up here. We're negative transponder. Both nav radios are out. Frankly, I'm a little turned around up here. Hoping you can direct us to a suitable runway for an emergency landing."

"Roger, King Air Two-Whiskey-Tango. Head to zero eight five. Vectors visual approach, runway one zero, Baltimore/Washington Airport."

"Roger, Approach. Heading to zero eight five." McKill held the wheel steady. Air traffic control gave them ten seconds of grace.

"King Air-Two-Whiskey-Tango, I don't show you in a turn."

"Roger. Having issues with our directional gyro now, too. Chang-ing course to zero eight five." McKill opened the throttle even more, breaking another federal aviation regulation, which stated that all flights within thirty miles of Washington could fly no faster than 180 knots.

Air traffic control was well aware of it. "King Air Two-Whiskey-Tango, say your speed."

"Yeah, we're slowing," McKill said. He took off his headset, rubbed his ears, and looked at Travis. "Three minutes."

Travis had failed calculus, but he wasn't that bad at math. "You just said ten minutes *two* minutes ago," he said.

"I know. Three minutes until we have company."

Andrews Air Force Base was only a few miles off their left wing. President Leary appreciated it first and foremost for its fifty-four holes of championship golf. It also happened to be the home of the 121st Fighter Squadron, which existed primarily to defend Wash-ington, D.C., from lunatics who wanted to land their King Air tur-boprops on the National Mall. It took the two F-16 pilots two minutes to go from the leather couch on base to their cockpit and just one minute to go from the runway to having visual contact with King Air N472WT.

K spotted them first. "Someone's coming," he said.

"I got 'em," McKill said. He turned over his shoulder and watched as they flew up behind him. "Wow. F-16s. Beautiful planes, aren't they?"

Travis wanted to remind McKill that the fighter jets were not there to escort them safely to their destination. "You might want to—"

"Oh, and look," McKill said, interrupting, "Block 30 models. Bet-ter radar, precision night attack capability. Kinda long in the tooth, but they'll get the job done—"

"King Air November-Four-Seven-Two-Whiskey-Tango, this is the United States Air Force. Lower your gear and change course immedi-ately, or you will be fired upon. No further warning."

McKill eased off the throttle. They drew in closer. "I flew in one once. A D-model. Nineteen . . . what was it . . . ninety? Maybe ninety-one. They've got that great bubble canopy where you can see everything. Three hundred and sixty degrees. And it was the first fighter built to withstand nine g's. *Nine!* The most they ever did with me was four, but that was plenty."

"Mike," Travis said, trying to snap him out of it.

He quieted the engines even more and kept talking. "It's also one of the only planes that becomes more stable the faster it goes. It's actually easier to control when it's supersonic than when it's just cruising along. It sounds dumb, but it counteracts that with this amazing fly-by-wire system that uses electronic impulses to keep the jet stable no matter what. Full disclosure, I don't really understand how it works—"

Cole saw the planes a mere fifty feet behind them and tried again. "Mike!"

"Yes, they are works of art. No doubt about it. But for all of that, they do have one giant weakness when compared to mine. They can't fly as slowly as I can." McKill pushed the propeller pitch control forward, raised the flaps, and started adding power. The King Air was now in slow flight—almost stalling—and the F-16s, unable to hold their position, shot ahead of it, one on either side. The jets baked McKill and his passengers with a wave of heat as they passed.

"WHOA!" they all yelled.

"I don't think that's going to work twice," Travis said.

"Which is why I'm not planning on being here when they come back," McKill said. He pulled back power on both engines and re-aligned the nose of the turboprop with the narrow strip of green grass three miles ahead. The King Air started to shake under the strain. "Hang in there, beautiful," he said.

The F-16s banked in opposite directions, carving circles through the night sky as they rushed to regroup for a second pass.

"Let's get on the ground, Mike," K said, watching the plane to the south finish its arc.

"Not yet," McKill said under his breath.

The fighters were back in a tight formation. "They're on us!" K said.

"Not yet," he repeated.

He waited until he heard the first 20 mm shell from the M-61 Vulcan cannon hit the tail of the plane, obliterating the sheet metal as though it were made of Kleenex. The second McKill heard the hard firecracker snap of metal on metal, he pushed in the yoke with all the remaining strength his sweaty, doughy, fifty-something frame could muster. The tail absorbed a few more rounds before the plane gave in to gravity and fell into a steep, vertical dive.

The F-16s saw the King Air's accelerated descent toward the Mall and pulled up to watch the rest from a safe distance.

The King Air wasn't made for aerial acrobatics, but Mike McKill was. He corkscrewed toward the ground at a thirty-degree pitch as his three passengers gripped their armrests and prayed their pilot knew what he was doing. They were only twelve hundred feet from the ground when Travis looked out the window and found himself staring straight at the Statue of Freedom on top of the Capitol Dome.

"PULL UP!" Travis yelled.

"Hell no. We're playing dead!" McKill said, his eyes jumping between the cockpit window and his altimeter. In Mike McKill's mind, their dive was meant to give the appearance that he and his passengers had been successfully shot out of the sky. And given the current condition of the plane's tail, that was effectively what had happened.

At nine hundred feet, McKill lowered the landing gear and began a firm but gentle continuous pull on the yoke. At first, nothing happened. "Come on, pumpkin," he begged. He kept pulling, and the nose willed itself up slowly. The stall warning horn began to wail. McKill let the nose drop just a touch to keep airflow over the wings. They slowed a little, but with only two hundred feet to go, it was still way too fast. McKill raised the nose again to bleed off some speed. Travis looked behind him. K was staring straight ahead. Cole had his eyes closed. At fifty feet, McKill was out of the dive and over grass, but the nose was too high to see in front of them. The horn was still blaring. They were fifteen feet off the ground when the wings suddenly lost all lift and the King Air fell the rest of the way to the Mall.

"HANG ON!" McKill screamed, in case anyone on the plane was distracted by the in-flight magazine.

The plane slammed nose up into the grass. The landing gear snapped off on impact, leaving McKill with only the tattered remains of the rudder to steer the King Air as it hurtled out of control down the Mall. Late-night tourists and homeless people scattered as the plane ripped past them at over a hundred miles an hour, propellers chewing up the turf as they went.

They were losing speed, but not very quickly. A few hundred feet ahead was Fourteenth Street, the four-lane road that cut through the Mall, and just beyond that, the Washington Monument. Mike McKill didn't much want to use it as a backstop. He spotted a pair of parked cars along Fourteenth and gripped the wheel.

"Range Rover or Volt?" he asked.

"WHAT?!" responded Travis.

"You want to blow up or be electrocuted?"

"How about neither!"

"Range Rover or Volt!" McKill repeated.

"Well, obviously the Volt!"

Mike willed the plane to the left, T-boning the Volt. The subcompact disintegrated in forty-one thousand dollars' worth of sparks as the plane smashed through it. The impact slowed the plane and sent it spinning. Every three seconds Travis saw the Washington Monument out the window, and each time it was a little bit closer. On the fifth spin smoke filled the cabin and there was nothing left for him to do except hold his breath and hope.

A few feet from the base of the giant marble obelisk, the spinning stopped. The plane hissed and groaned before tipping onto one wing. Travis opened his eyes, not knowing who was dead and who was alive. Mike McKill was the first to speak.

"Ta-da."

"Everybody okay back there?" Travis asked.

"Define 'okay,'" Cole said.

K kicked open the door to let out the smoke. As the cabin cleared, their trail of destruction became visible out McKill's window, highlighted by the flattened Volt and the long brown trench they'd dug that spanned the length of the Mall.

"Well, so much for not announcing your arrival," McKill said. He looked at Travis, who was nursing a few sizable scrapes on his face. "You gonna be okay?" he asked.

Travis wiped the blood on his shirt. "I think so," he said.

"If you need a good plastic surgeon, let me know."

"I'll manage," Travis said. "Thanks for the lift, Mike."

"No," McKill said. "Call me Seth."

"Really?"

McKill considered his offer. "Never mind. Call me Mike."

K jumped out first, followed by Cole. Travis dropped last. A half mile dead north was the White House. They had just started to run when two men in powder blue shirts popped out from behind the Washington Monument.

"*FREEZE!*" they yelled, shaky guns drawn.

The pair of night-duty guards had watched the plane tumble toward them and took cover behind the 555-foot-tall monument, figuring that if that couldn't protect them, nothing would. Operating on instinct, K reached inside his jacket.

"No," Travis said, stopping him short. Against his will, he put his hands in the air. From every direction, they could hear the sound of police approaching.

So much for the Golf Channel exclusive.

37

Big Bill cinched his bolo tie and brushed his teeth with the side of his index finger. He could hear the pool of reporters gathering outside his office, waiting for him to make a statement. He practiced a smile in the mirror and then caught himself. They were expecting him to be somber.

He grabbed his brown jacket with the calfskin elbow patches off the back of his chair and slipped it on just as the phone rang for the first time since that morning. It startled him, only because he had grown accustomed to the quiet. His secretary, June, called to him from outside his door.

"Anatole Metzos."

Big Bill shooed her away and closed the door behind her. He picked up the phone and pushed the flashing yellow light. "That little weasel thought he could slip past us, didn't he, Metzy?"

Metzos laughed. Big Bill had known Anatole Metzos for less than a week, first hearing from him in the aftermath of the secession vote in the Lege, but they had talked enough times since for Bill to pick up on a lightness in the old man's voice that he'd never heard before. "Yes, he did try to slip past us," Metzos conceded. "Thankfully, the news director at MSNBC is one of mine."

"Remind me to send her a box of Texas prime."

"Just a box? When we're done, you'll be able to send her a whole herd."

Bill popped a few aspirin and crunched them in his mouth like M&M's. "So we're good, then, huh?"

"Yes," said Metzos. "I'm leaving shortly to congratulate him personally."

"Well look at you, ya big shooter." June knocked on Big Bill's closed door. "They're ready for me, Metzy."

"Carry on," Metzos said, "and congratulations, *Governor.*"

Big Bill smiled again. He liked the sound of that.

Anatole Metzos followed the bubbles as they rose from the bottom of his champagne glass. There must have been hundreds of them, liberating themselves from below and shooting to the surface with a frenzied recklessness, desperate to reach the atmosphere and once again mingle safely in anonymity with their fellow gases. Metzos allowed a few dozen more to escape, then swallowed the rest in one giant, merciless gulp.

"Splendid," Metzos said, passing the empty glass to Mutuku, who stowed it in the wood-paneled door as their town car headed west toward the White House.

After weeks of turmoil, Anatole Metzos was finally at peace. Travis was finally behind him. In another few years, he hoped to say the same about capitalism itself. Yes, it had brought him a level of wealth his ten-year-old self could never have fathomed, but as he saw it, his experience was the exception to the rule. The trail blazed by just one successful, self-made man was littered with the corpses of a thousand imitators armed with mediocre talent.

As Metzos saw it, the Founding Fathers were right, but only for a time. The republic they shaped was the necessary lily pad to carry America away from British rule. Now it had run its course. Time had shown Metzos that the masses were not made for self-governance. He had seen it play out on Wall Street and on Main Street. True freedom, as he understood it, only led to greed, poverty, and chaos.

What society needed was strict parameters and benevolent leaders blessed with the wisdom and intelligence to redistribute wealth for the collective salvation of the whole.

Metzos watched American liberals try to legislate economic equality for decades, failing at every turn. He came to believe that even in the wealthiest nation on earth, there was only so much a government could accomplish through taxes. It needed something more. *Oil*. Once it controlled its own oil, it had a continuous revenue stream, capable of meeting the basic needs of every citizen. Once the government had its own revenue stream, it was no longer encumbered by anything or anyone. It was free to operate as it wanted, beholden to no one, and a government that was free to operate as it wanted could finally create a society of real hope and lasting change. America needed the RRA. From Metzos's perspective, the only shame of it all was that not enough people knew that he had anything to do with it.

Still, Metzos wouldn't let the world's underappreciation of him subtract from the weight of his victory. He asked Mutuku for a second glass of champagne and chose not to savor it. He downed it, relishing the sensation of hundreds of bubbles sliding down his tongue and disappearing into the blackness of his throat.

The FBI was having difficulty sealing off the entire crime scene, which stretched almost a mile from end to end. "We're gonna need more tape!" someone yelled. In under ten minutes, every federal law enforcement division had arrived, even those who had no jurisdictional reason to be there. The owner of the obliterated Volt had shown up, too, and was searching for his iPad amid the scattered glass and plastic. Dueling female reporters jumped out of moving news vans, visions of Peabody Awards dancing in their heads, and ran to the Washington Monument with a microphone in one hand and their heels in the other, each hoping to lay claim to the coveted title of "First on the Scene."

It was an inglorious sight. The plane was crumpled and smoking from both ends. Its two propellers were a hundred yards down the Mall, tossed aside like a kid's flip-flops on the way to the ocean. Travis was facedown in the freshly fertilized grass, hands bound behind his back with plastic handcuffs. His conspirators were lined up next to him.

"Sorry, fellas," McKill said, his voice muffled a bit by the Bermuda.

Travis blew a blade of grass away from his lip. "Stop it. You did everything right."

"I have a question, though," Cole said. "You waited to dive until they started firing at us, right?"

"You got it," said McKill. "I needed them to think their aim was so perfect they took us out with one shot. It was the only way they'd leave us alone."

"No, I understand all that," said Cole, "but what if they'd fired a missile at us instead of their guns?"

"Huh." McKill hadn't considered that possibility. He lifted his head and stuck his chin in the dirt in order to look at what remained of his plane. "Yeah, that would have been bad."

They lay in shame for fifteen minutes until a pair of poorly polished loafers with thick rubber soles stopped in front of Travis's face.

"Welcome to Washington, Governor." Travis looked up to see Agent Dermis, the tough Secret Service agent with one shoulder lower than the other. "How was your flight?"

"The landing was a little rough," Travis said.

Agent Dermis eyed some Capitol policemen. "Load 'em up, will ya?"

The four of them were plucked off the grass and pushed into a nearby Suburban. Another passenger was already waiting inside. Her eyes were puffy and red.

"Paige . . ." Travis said.

"I was standing in front of the White House like you told me. In retrospect, that was probably not the ideal spot for a covert rendezvous with a wanted man," she said.

Travis joined her in the first row of seats. "I'm sorry."

"It's okay," she said.

"No, it's not. I shouldn't have brought you into this."

"Stop. I brought myself into this, not you," she said.

Cole, K, and McKill squished into the back row as a second agent joined Dermis up front. They didn't wait for their passengers to get settled. They peeled away from the Mall, two squad cars leading and another two behind, all with sirens blaring.

Cole leaned forward until his head rested on the back of Travis's seat. Travis turned and looked his friend up and down. Cole's ear was bleeding, but he couldn't tell from where. His pearl white dress shirt was sooty and torn by shattered glass. Both of his cufflinks were long gone. He looked like an overdressed chimney sweep.

"Just think," Travis said, "you could be sitting on a tropical beach right now, reading missives from the Cato Institute about forgotten Supreme Court rulings."

"Joke all you want," Cole groaned, "but Leary hasn't made good on his promise to close Guantánamo yet. You and I might end up there doing just that."

Without warning, the Suburban made a sharp left turn off Constitution Avenue, sending its unbuckled passengers flying. The two squad cars in front kept going. The two behind gave chase. Agent Dermis gunned it down an empty side street, keeping an eye on his rearview mirror.

"What the hell you guys doing?" McKill asked. He wasn't sure his body could weather two crashes in one night.

Neither agent answered. On they zoomed, ignoring red lights as they passed through E Street, F Street, and G Street. When they'd put enough distance between themselves and the Capitol Police, Dermis made another tight turn and stopped in an alley, killing his headlights.

He turned to face Travis. The other agent watched the side mirrors. "Why are you here, Governor?"

The rest of the car looked at Travis. The professor of constitutional law filled the silence. "I think he'll exercise his right to remain silent until his lawyer is present, thank you," Cole said.

"Settle down, Cole," Travis said. "Agent Dermis isn't going to do anything. Not with this many witnesses." Travis looked to him for reassurance. "Right?"

Dermis was noncommittal, but Travis knew his situation couldn't get much worse. "I . . . *we* . . . have some information on Anatole Metzos. We think the president would find it enlightening. We were hoping to speak about it with him in private."

"Information," Dermis said. "That's a little vague."

Travis eyed Paige. She nodded for him to continue. "We have evidence that Anatole Metzos has infiltrated the executive branch with people who are loyal to him first and the Constitution a distant second."

"You have evidence?" Dermis asked. He seemed skeptical.

"It's in my bag," Paige said. "Check it out for yourself if you want."

The other agent looked down at his feet, where he and Dermis had stowed Paige's bag after she'd been taken into custody. A short stack of papers peeked out of a notebook. He began to reach for it, but Dermis grabbed his hand and stopped him. "No," Dermis said.

Without another word, Dermis flipped on the headlights and accelerated back down the alley. The Suburban sped through Washington, taking lefts and rights at random. Travis had never gotten a feel for the layout of the city. There were just enough traffic circles and diagonal streets to completely confound his sense of direction. After two more rights, one traffic circle, and another left, they pulled up to a dimly lit, nondescript guard house shrouded in oak trees. The guard waved at the Suburban as the gate went up.

"Unbelievable," Cole said.

"What is this place?" Travis leaned over for a better look.

"Where do you think?" Cole asked.

Just off to his left was the South Lawn fountain. On the right, bathed in yellow energy-efficient light, stood the White House.

The Suburban continued up the giant circle toward the South Entrance. "Hold on a second," Travis said. "What's going on?"

Agent Dermis looked at Travis in his mirror, revealing the slightest hint of a smile. "Let's just say we're big fans, Governor."

The other agent chimed in. "Undercover patriots, if you will."

"Walt Thompson wanted to make sure to say hello," said Dermis.

Travis remembered Walt Thompson boasting about his connections "deep inside" the White House during their initial phone call at the Driskill in Austin. He had been so untrusting of Walt at the time that he'd forgotten all about it.

"You're the ones who tipped off Walt about the pipeline," Travis said.

"No, not us, Governor," Dermis said. "Her."

They looked out the right side of the SUV. Waiting for them in the driveway was Avery Adams.

Cole sat up straight. His misery vanished. He was beaming. "I knew there was a reason I liked her," he said.

38

A very Adams moved surprisingly fast in her three-inch heels. She sounded like a metronome as she clicked and clacked toward the West Wing. Agent Dermis tromped along behind the group, his left shoulder drooping extra low after a long night. The West Wing was quiet, but not because it was empty. Every adviser, staffer, and intern was gathered around flat-screens as the details of Travis's crash landing and apprehension continued to unfold. MSN-BC's running caption was SHAMEFUL SURRENDER. It made the governor's arrival in their midst all the more surreal.

"Howdy," Travis said, nodding kindly at the slack-jawed workers. He rolled his wrists as he walked, anxious to get the feeling back in his uncuffed hands.

Cole caught up to Avery. "Alright, I have to know. Were you aware of the pipeline when we dropped in to see the president a few weeks ago?"

"Of course."

"So you lied to us." Cole wasn't angry, only curious. Not even that curious. He was just looking for an excuse to talk to her.

"Yes. Sorry," Avery said. "The president had already decided to make it official. There was nothing to gain by me coming clean."

"I don't know about that. You would have gained my undying respect and admiration."

"For some reason I think I already had it."

Avery reached the closed door to the Oval Office and pushed on through. A production crew was doing the final sound check before the president went live to announce the peaceful reconciliation with Interim Governor Lewis and the state of Texas. Behind the desk, Leary was running through the teleprompter one last time as a makeup artist took the shine off his forehead.

Avery squeezed between the cameramen and the gaffer—they didn't protest—and over to Leary. "Mr. President, I'm afraid I need you to delay the speech."

"Miss Adams, I'm afraid I have to say no."

The director called out from behind the camera, "Thirty seconds, Mr. President."

"It's about Governor Travis," Avery said.

"What about him?" Leary asked. He grabbed his lips and pinched them a few times, a trick he'd learned from Michael Dukakis to help increase blood flow to the mouth before speaking.

Before Avery could answer, Ruffles appeared and interrupted them both. "Why the hell is Ben Travis here?"

"He's *here*?" Leary looked past the camera to see Travis and company waiting patiently at the door. Mike McKill gave a friendly wave. Leary returned it, albeit with a much less friendly one.

"The governor and his team have some information that the Secret Service and I believe the president needs to hear," Avery said.

"Is that Mike McKill?" Leary asked.

"Yes, I believe so," she said.

"Why is he here?"

"That I can't explain."

"Give the speech, Mr. President," said Ruffles. "This country is anxious for a resolution. We can deal with Travis later."

"Fifteen seconds, Mr. President!" The members of the crew took their positions. They were going to be ready even if the president wasn't.

"I think you owe it to the American people to hear them out, sir," Avery said.

"No, they're waiting for him to act," said Ruffles. *"Read the speech."*

"Ten seconds! Nine . . . eight . . . seven . . ."

The teleprompter jumped to the beginning of the speech. The first line pulsed. *Good evening, America . . .*

". . . six . . . five . . . four . . ."

The president looked past the crew to Travis. The governor's right arm resembled a hot dog that had been left on the grill for too long. His left arm looked like it had been scrubbed with a wire brush. His hands were folded together at his waist and his head was down. He seemed to be praying.

Leary didn't know whether it was the lapsed Presbyterian in him or just his God-given bleeding heart, but in that moment, he felt a distant twinge of sympathy for Travis.

". . . three . . . two . . ."

Leary signaled to the director. "Hold up," he said. "Let's cut."

The crew cleared out at the president's request, leaving the equipment behind. Aides picked up the two Oval Office couches and swiveled them until they faced the president's desk. Travis and Paige took one couch, K and Cole the other. Mike McKill, despite his protests, waited in the hall. Avery Adams took her place against the wall next to Ruffles and Agent Dermis. The president stayed right where he had been, behind his desk. He folded his arms across his chest and considered his strategy. Last time he and the governor had met, he let Travis control things from the start. He wasn't about to make that mistake again.

"Impressive team, Travis. A professor, a movie star . . . put your daughter in a red plaid shirt and we'll have half the characters from *Gilligan's Island.*"

"With all due respect, Mr. President, we'd like to cut right to the chase," Travis said.

There he goes, Leary thought. He wished Travis came with an OFF switch. "Now hold on, Governor," Leary said. "You're on my turf this time, and in here I decide what I want to talk about and when."

"Of course. I'm sorry, Mr. President."

"Good." Leary was glad to see Travis's submission. Unfortunately, there wasn't anything else he wanted to talk about. "Okay, so tell me why you're here."

"Mr. President, my daughter, Paige, has been working with a reporter at the *Washington Post*, researching the relationship between this administration and Anatole Metzos—"

"I'm going to stop you again, Governor." Leary was proud of himself. He felt like the steer wrestler he'd seen in a dreary PETA video his wife had made him sit through. "I want you to be careful about what you say here. Mr. Metzos is a constant supporter of this administration. He's an internationally recognized humanitarian. He's a decorated citizen. A national treasure. He's also a good friend. As far as our relationship goes, yes, it's close. Deservedly so." *Game, set, match,* Leary thought.

"In that case," Travis said, "I suppose everything we're about to say is stuff you already know. If you prefer, we can just have the *Post* run the story as is, and I'll tell the editors that you've signed off on its validity." Travis turned to Paige. "Would that work for you?"

"Absolutely," said Paige. "They're just waiting for the green light before going to print with it."

Leary wasn't an idiot. He knew Travis was using reverse psychology. He would go one better and use reverse *reverse* psychology. "Fine with me," said Leary.

Ruffles pushed himself away from the wall. "Well . . . okay, now just . . . everyone, settle down. Mr. President, I don't think it's wise to sign off on something we haven't read."

Leary looked at Ruffles, perturbed. "Fine." He directed his attention back to Travis. "*Quickly,*" he said.

Travis passed the floor to Paige. "Mr. President, we have every reason to believe that Mr. Metzos plays an integral role in your administration, and not simply as a friend. We have evidence that he is directly steering specific policy decisions—including the RRA—according to his will, not yours, and certainly not according to the will of the people."

"That's absurd," Ruffles said.

"It's no surprise that Mr. Ruflowski would say that. The only way Mr. Metzos has been able to succeed is through a powerful Washington network that answers to him," Paige said. "Mr. Ruflowski is a large piece of that network."

"I have known Mr. Ruflowski for fifteen years, Miss Travis, and neither he nor I appreciate the scurrilous charges."

"I'm sure Agent Dermis would be happy to show them out, Mr. President," said Ruffles.

"Without even seeing our evidence?" Paige asked.

"Leave it for our lawyers," Leary said.

Ruffles nodded to Agent Dermis, who begrudgingly walked toward the president's guests. "Sorry," he said as he signaled for them to stand.

Paige, like her father, was not easily silenced. "Mr. President, I devoted an entire summer to your campaign. I fund-raised for you. I supported you monetarily and gave you my vote. I did so because I believed in your promise of transparency and integrity. Don't make a fool out of me, sir."

Paige grabbed a packet of neatly organized, well-marked photocopies and held them out for the president to see.

Leary growled and beckoned to it with his outstretched hand. "Alright, alright." Agent Dermis took the pages and passed them to the weary president. Paige took her extra copies and handed one to Cole and one to Travis. "Tell me what I'm looking at here," Leary said.

"These are IRS reports, Mr. President. From 501(c)(3)s. Nonprofits. They have to file them every year, but no one really bothers to read them. Including the IRS. I've broken down the numbers beginning on page two. It appears that after a few years of modest income, Mr. Ruflowski received over a million dollars from Generation Now in the wake of your election, all while still being billed as a part-time adviser."

"There's no law against that, Miss Travis," the president said. "If Mr. Metzos wanted to pay him that much, that's up to Mr. Metzos."

Travis had to butt in here. "Mr. President, wasn't it you who said that at some point, people have made enough money?"

Paige moved to the next page, sensing that her window of opportunity was closing. "On page three you'll see a similar jump in compensation for the attorney general. On page four you'll see the breakdown for your press secretary. Page five is your national security adviser. There are more, but those were the most egregious examples."

"I'm sorry, Miss Travis, but being well compensated does not equal collusion."

"You're right, Mr. President. Which is why I'd like to draw your attention to page seven."

The president flipped pages until he came to the reassembled PDB agenda. "What's this?"

"It's your PDB agenda from last week, sir."

"How did you get a copy of this?"

"The question is, How did Anatole Metzos get a copy of it? Turns out it was in his trash. Typed on his paper. He wrote it."

Leary went silent and turned to the next page.

"Those are speeches, Mr. President." After Paige had left the *Post* newsroom for the pay phone in Virginia, Aubrey had gone back through the pile of other taped-up documents and realized there was more there that Paige had missed. "When I saw these, I assumed they were transcripts of speeches you'd already given. My contact at the *Post* compared them to the actual speeches you delivered and discovered they matched, but only in bits and pieces. I've pasted them side by side so you could compare them, sir." Leary's eyes darted back and forth between the two. "We believe these are rough drafts that Metzos was slipping to a speechwriter on the inside," Paige concluded.

The president shook his head. It was so simple that even the vice president could have understood it. Travis placed a hand on Paige's knee and gave her two quick pats.

"Conspiracy theories and fabulous fiction," Ruffles said.

"Shut up," Leary said.

Paige pressed on. "The one thing we haven't been able to delve into at this time is Mr. Metzos's finances, but we presume that when we do, we'll discover not only that he has made quite a bit of money off your agenda so far, but also that he is leveraged to make quite a bit more once the RRA is fully implemented."

President Leary put his elbows on the desk and pretended to read, using his hands to shield his face from everyone in the office. Every part of this was news to him. It just didn't make any sense. Yes, he leaned on his advisers and speechwriters, but so do all presidents. It wasn't like he hadn't vetted each one. He had. Ruffles had helped him. *Oh, but . . .* He realized the flaw in his thinking.

"Dermis," the president said, calling the agent to his side. Leary turned away from the group and spoke directly into Dermis's ear. "Lock this place down, will you? And find a good place for Ruffles."

Dermis nodded and walked toward the president's chief of staff. "This way, Mr. Ruflowski." Ruffles didn't put up a fight. He had seen Dermis take out too many Code Pink protesters to make that mistake.

Those who remained waited on the president. "Miss Adams, some water, please," Leary said. She nodded and opened a hidden cabinet filled with drinks. Cole took note as she opened it. No Dr Pepper.

She delivered the ice water. He took a sip, followed by a deep breath as he tried to compose himself as best he could. "Please tell me that's it."

"It's all I have, Mr. President," Paige said.

Cole, on the other hand, wasn't sure they'd have an opportunity like this again and didn't want to leave any card unplayed. He cleared his throat and piped up. "We also had a historical document, Mr. President."

"Oh jeez . . ." Leary said, bracing himself.

"An agreement signed between Abraham Lincoln and Texas governor Pendleton Murrah on the eve of Lincoln's assassination in 1865. Something that, as far as we know, never saw the light of day. We think it might be relevant to resolving the larger issue of states' rights."

Leary sighed. *Great,* he thought. *So now Lincoln's against me, too.* He took another gulp of water and looked to dodge the whole thing. "Professor Cole, I would have thought you, of all people here, would be a little wary of states' rights."

The president had picked the wrong occasion to press Damon Cole's buttons (two of which were missing, in fact). He was exhausted, bleeding, and fed up. "Because I'm black, you mean," Cole said.

"I'm just saying—"

"With all due respect, Mr. President, I think the modern-day attempt to link racism to states' rights is a specious argument at best. By that logic, then, your belief in a powerful central government would be enough to warrant me calling you a pro-genocide Nazi demagogue, but I don't suppose you're comfortable with that moniker."

"Professor, I didn't mean—"

"Yes, you didn't mean me, specifically. Of course. But *in general,* people who argue on behalf of states' rights are racist."

"Please don't put words in my mouth, Professor."

"I couldn't possibly do that, Mr. President. Not while your foot's in there."

"Wow," Travis whispered under his breath.

Cole wasn't finished. "The Tenth Amendment, lest you forget, sir, says that all powers not delegated to the United States are reserved to the individual states or to the people. It was proposed by James Madison to be included with the Bill of Rights, and when he did so, many of his fellow members of Congress didn't see the point of it. It simply stated something everyone already agreed upon. He might as well have added an amendment stating that the sky was blue. Now, all these years later, you and many others would like to believe that Washington is the supreme law of the land, whereas the Founders knew that the power of the states would someday prove to be a vital check on tyranny. So, without belaboring the point any more than I already have, I would ask that you don't marginalize adherents of a constitutionally valid point of view solely because they stand in direct opposition to your constitutionally *invalid* point of view."

Avery Adams smiled, having realized Damon Cole had this in him. Travis whistled. He thought he had only done so in his head, but when Paige elbowed him in the side, he realized he had done so out loud. The president tried to pretend he hadn't been cudgeled. "So did you say you *had* this letter or you *have it*, Professor?"

"We *had* it, Mr. President," Travis said, stepping back in, "and then we lost it."

Leary crunched on a piece of ice. "Just tell me what it said, Governor."

"Me? See, that's part of the problem. I never saw it," Travis said. He looked at Paige. "Did you?"

"When would I have seen that?"

"With Wexler."

"I don't even know what you're talking about," she said.

"*Adam* Wexler."

"I know Adam Wexler, but we never talked about a Lincoln letter."

"No, of course not," Travis said. "You were too busy—" Paige opened her eyes so wide that Travis thought lasers were about to shoot out of them. "Never mind," he said, backing away. "Mr. President, I think the only one here who physically saw it was Professor Cole. You remember what it said, Cole?"

"Not verbatim, unfortunately, but it was a beautiful document. If I may paraphrase—"

A voice rose from behind him. *"By issue of executive order . . ."* The three Texans on the couch plus K turned to see Anatole Metzos. He had made it through security before the president's lockdown was put into effect. Even then, security might not have stopped him. He was on the permanent list and had made so many trips to 1600 Pennsylvania Avenue in the last three years that he passed through the White House gates and bypassed the metal detectors with nothing more than a wave and a smile. That smile vanished when Metzos reached for the Oval Office door and heard the voices of Ben and Paige Travis.

He stood at attention, a rapt audience before him, and recited from memory. " *. . . for the express purpose of bringing much-needed* *reconciliation between the States and with the hope of securing lasting prosperity for this Union, I pledge on my honor this Government's fervent commitment to the Liberty and Freedom of all American people, and its eternal bond to the Constitution by which these States were freely grafted together. Should that bond be perverted, either by tyranny or indifference, it is within each State's Rights to throw off those chains and pursue its own course. Just as no man should be enslaved by a master, neither should any freeman be enslaved by Government.* Signed, Abraham Lincoln, President. Pendleton Murrah, Witness."

Leary couldn't believe it. "This thing really exists?"

Metzos walked between the two couches toward the center of the office. "Yes. Or, perhaps more appropriately, it *did*. I destroyed it. Only after I memorized it, of course. I suppose that's the eternal student in me."

"That was a piece of history," Cole said.

"It was a headache," said Metzos.

"Why would you do something like that?" Paige asked.

Metzos looked at Paige, dumbfounded. "Would you have preferred that I'd given it to you?"

Before he had read the hit piece on the new Texas governor in the *Washington Post*, Anatole Metzos had never heard of Paige Travis. Once he discovered the child of a new enemy was a registered Democrat and an ardent supporter of President Leary, Metzos saw the opportunity to exploit a fractured father-daughter relationship for the good of his personal agenda. He and Mutuku had spent an entire morning trying and failing to "bump into" Paige, only succeeding when she went for a midday run and fell asleep in the middle of the National Mall.

The lunch they shared at his estate was also prearranged; so was the skinny-dipping. As Paige had surmised, it was a test. While she was busy passing with flying colors, Mutuku was driving back from Dupont Circle, where he had concealed a few bugs in her studio apartment. Before she left Cherry Tree Cove, he'd hidden another in her wallet.

"How did you steal it, anyway?" Travis asked. It felt irrelevant to everyone else, but Travis knew that the next time he spoke with Adam Wexler—even if it was through three-inch glass—the kid would want to know.

"I'm the son of a druggist," Metzos said, settling onto the high arm of K and Cole's couch. "When I first started working in my father's shop, I was too short to see over the counter. I remember sitting Indian-style on the wood floor, barefoot, mixing medicines with a mortar and pestle. I used to love listening to my father as he rattled off the complicated name of each drug. Hydrochlorothiazide . . . methylprednisolone . . . acetylsalicylic acid . . . In time, I learned to pronounce them, too. It became our own special tongue, a language that only he and I shared—"

"You know what? Never mind," Travis said, realizing all he'd done was give Metzos a platform to ramble about his salad days.

"I used trihalomethane, Governor. It comes from seaweed. Nowadays it's used mostly as a solvent or to kill maggots. You probably know it as chloroform. It's still a perfectly safe anesthetic, as long as one knows how to dilute it properly. Which of course I do."

"I think I would have remembered someone covering my face with a wet rag," Cole said.

"Which is why Mutuku soaked a pair of bath towels in my mixture and stuffed them into the jet's intake vents after you went aboard. Once the boy arrived, the crew sealed the door, and the toxicity level rose according to plan. Governor, I must thank you for choosing such a quaint airport. It's rare to find one these days where Mutuku can come and go with such ease."

Cole didn't buy it. "You didn't want us sedated, you wanted us dead."

"You're thinking a little too highly of yourself, Professor," Metzos said with a smile.

"That plane was circulating air through the cabin for over an hour before Wexler showed up. If he arrives on time, we're blacking out at thirty thousand feet."

"I'm sorry, but I'm not going to dignify a murder accusation with a response," Metzos said.

The president stared at his mentor with anger and disappointment. "You're going to prison, Anatole," he said.

Metzos remained undeterred. "Don't be absurd. The next four years are critical. We've talked about this. You need my knowledge. You need my financial backing. If you want to slap me on the wrist for stealing the letter, so be it, but—"

"I know about the bribes," Leary said.

Metzos tried to smile the way he had when Cole accused him of attempted murder, but his heavy gray mouth turned down instead of up. "Can we talk in private, perhaps?"

"No," Travis said, butting in.

"Mr. President," Metzos said, now visibly shaking, "you're jeopardizing everything. I beg you to—"

"That's enough," Leary said.

Metzos's darting eyes bounced around the room as if he were following a fly. "What's ironic is that you wouldn't even be sitting here if it weren't for me."

"Just stop," Leary said.

"I picked you," Metzos said.

"Stop!" Leary repeated.

"Eight years ago. A lowly state senator with perfect hair. Your inexperience should have made you unfit for such a high office, but I sold that naïveté to the American people as the tonic for all their ills. I made them believe that you were one of them. A blank canvas. Of course, I knew you weren't. After all, I'd been shaping you for years. It's very difficult to influence a man when he is already prosperous, but I found you when you still had nothing. By the time you were elected, you were controlled so well that you didn't even know you were being controlled. Even now as I say it, you don't really believe it. Do you?"

Leary didn't want to hear this. "You're a senile old man," he responded.

"Old? Yes. Senile? Hardly."

Cole spoke up. "You made sure that distinction went to Justice Ferraro." Cole had connected Metzos's pharmaceutical knowledge with the early retirement of the Supreme Court justice and concluded that it had all the markings of Metzos's handiwork. "What magic compound does it take to drive a perfectly healthy man crazy, Metzos? Did you slip the pesticides into his Diet Coke or his nondairy creamer?"

"My money's on the creamer," Travis said, joining in.

"Enough," Metzos muttered.

They knew he was cracking. "And that car crash in Texas," Travis continued, "that couldn't have just been an accident, could it?"

"Why do I suspect someone at the NTSB made sure it was?" asked Paige.

Travis continued to push. "Of course, that doesn't answer the question of why he killed Governor Allen and Lieutenant Governor Rice to begin with."

"That's easy," Cole continued. "Allen was probably getting cold feet about the RRA."

"Uh-huh," said Travis, "he was probably starting to worry that being aligned with liberals on every issue might cost him another term. Just a theory, of course."

"Enough!" Metzos screamed.

Cole knew they were warm. "That still doesn't explain Rice. He was a proud Democrat. Unless he was turning away, too? Geez, has it gotten so bad for the left that they're scaring off their own?"

"He wasn't supposed to be in the limo," Metzos muttered softly under his breath.

Travis and Cole eyed each other for a moment. "I'm sorry, could you—" Travis said.

"Rice wasn't supposed to be in the limo!" Metzos exclaimed.

"Jesus," Leary said. He meant it as both a swear and a prayer.

"We can still fix things, Michael. We can fix them," Metzos said, wobbling a bit from his spot on the arm of the couch. "We're so close. The world needs me . . ."

"We're through," Leary said. He stood up when he said it, lending some finality to the proceedings.

Metzos looked at the president with eyes that were turning glassy.

Michael Leary was his prodigy. His masterpiece. He wasn't going to see it turn against him. "Fine," he said, "but then so are you."

He fumbled for something inside the breast pocket of his coat, then brandished a small nineteenth-century French Ordnance revolver, holding it close to his chest where only the president could see. Leary was not of a mind to notice the craftsmanship, but it was a beautiful weapon. Metzos's father had bought it off a member of the French Resistance after World War II. Dangling from the butt of it was a sturdy pewter ring, an adornment that harked back to an era when men hung their guns on a nail next to their coat and their keys.

Like most criminals, Metzos had no permit; he had never taken a safety course. He carried the revolver for self-defense, without ever having fired it. The old man pulled the hammer back with his arthritic thumb and aimed in the general vicinity of the president. Leary, sensing he had one brief opportunity to save himself, grabbed the personalized Louisville Slugger bat by his feet and swung toward Anatole Metzos's hand with his best batting practice swing.

Whiff.

As Metzos slipped his index finger around the trigger and began to pull, Leary abandoned his fight instinct and resorted to flight, diving back over his antebellum desk. Before Metzos could fire, another shot rang out behind him. Agent Dermis. Metzos slid off the couch like a buttered pancake off a plate. As he fell, the dull silver barrel of his gun turned away from the president and tilted toward the Texans. Travis covered Paige. K covered Travis. Cole covered Cole. Drifting out of consciousness, Metzos pulled the trigger, no longer aware of his surroundings.

Cole screamed when the bullet hit him. The next sound was Agent Dermis deflating Metzos with a heavy thud as the agent's two hundred and twelve pounds buried the septuagenarian in the carpet. Three more agents heard the shots and burst through the door to cover the president.

"Oh no," Cole said, surveying the damage. He sounded weak. "No. No no no no . . ."

Travis, Paige, and K rushed to his aid. "Where did he get you?" K asked, looking him up and down for an entry wound.

Cole pointed to his foot, where the 11 mm shell had traveled from Metzos's revolver and into the left toe of Damon Cole's $2,900 Tanino Crisci loafers, piercing the two-hundred-year-old reindeer leather without any consideration for the fact it had been cured in steel-cut oatmeal.

"Just relax," K said. He carefully removed the shoe. Paige looked away. There was no blood. Not even a dab. K held the loafer up to the light. The bullet had gone straight out the redwood sole without grazing a single toe.

"Now how in the world did you manage that?" K asked.

"It's a miracle," Travis said.

Cole shook his head. "No. They're three sizes too big. It was the only pair they had left."

Of all the crazy things Travis had heard in the last two weeks, this was the craziest. "You spent almost three grand on shoes that don't even fit?"

"Yes," Cole said. "They're Tanino Criscis." Apparently, Travis's question required no other explanation.

39

It was 1:23 A.M. Governor Ben Travis and President Michael Leary stood side by side in the White House Press Room, awaiting the first question. Bleary-eyed writers flipped backward through their notebooks, rereading their scribbles from the briefing and trying to decide where to begin.

The Oval Office assassination attempt? The forthcoming corruption charges against a third of the West Wing and Big Bill Lewis? The future relationship between Texas and Washington? The aerial acrobatics of Mike McKill? For now, the president was happy to answer questions all night. After all, he had looked death square in the face and had successfully hidden behind his desk.

Travis had all the leverage in the world to break away from the Union and start afresh. Yet he knew that if there remained any chance to rescue America from its own extinction, this was it. He and the president hammered out a resolution on the winding granite walkway outside the Oval Office, allowing cleaning crews to swap out furniture and pour Lysol on every flat surface while, across town, a groggy Anatole Metzos was being wheeled into surgery and begging to speak to any one of his seventeen lawyers.

"The RRA is dead," Travis said to the president. "Though I don't know how you overturn an executive order."

"I can do it with another executive order," said Leary.

"Great system," Travis said, rolling his eyes.

"We'll review it."

"Good," said Travis. "Also, I'd like you to lift most if not all federal bans on oil drilling and allow states to pursue their own resources. You're killing jobs and sending money to criminals halfway around the world when it could all stay right here and keep us more secure."

"That's up to Congress, but you'll have my full support. In exchange, I want Texas to sign a long-term agreement not to shut off their pipelines." He was still under the impression those pipelines could be shut off with the push of a button.

"Fine," said Travis. "Now let's talk taxes."

"What about taxes?" asked Leary. He felt he was already being generous.

"My senior adviser, Professor Cole, has an idea that I kinda like. I call it the No Taxes for a Year for Anyone Plan."

"So no income tax? What about capital gains?"

"Not for a year."

"Well, still, still the payroll tax . . ."

"It's called No Taxes for a Year for Anyone. There's not much gray area in it."

The notion of it scared the president. On the other hand, if it failed to spark economic growth, it would destroy a tent pole of conservative ideology. "I'll consider it," he said.

"Fair enough. And since you're going to be needing a new attorney general, might you also consider Professor Cole for the position?"

"Don't push it. I'm down but not out."

"Fine. Fine. Also . . ."

"*Also?* Come on, Governor, let's not spoil the mood."

Travis steamed ahead. "Adam Wexler. The whiz kid who acquired the Lincoln document."

"You mean *stole.*"

"Yes. Right. As I understand it, he's currently being held somewhere around here. I think in light of everything that's happened, offering him a full and immediate pardon would be the appropriate thing to do."

"Can I assume he is also the one who hacked into all those news sites and posted that video of you?"

"Yes."

"I'll pardon him—but only if he agrees to show the FBI how he did it."

"You got it," said Travis.

"You done?" asked Leary. Travis read the tone as *You better be.*

"Yep. That's it."

"What do you say we go inside and get this written up before we old farts forget what we said," Leary said.

"Not necessary," Travis said. He put out his hand for Leary to shake.

Leary stared at it, suspicious. "What are you doing?"

"This is how Texans operate. We look each other in the eye and shake on it."

"What if I back out?"

"If you give me your word, I know you won't."

"But theoretically . . ." Leary wanted all the specifics Travis was willing to give.

"Fine," Travis said. "I'm gonna give you six months. That will take you up through the election. If you make a sincere effort to do all those things we talked about, you won't have any problems from me. If you don't, then I'm going to dig up the Texas annexation agreement with the U.S. from 1845."

"What does that say?"

"Adam Wexler told me about it one night. It says Texas has the right to split into as many as five states if it wants to."

Leary looked at him sideways. "No, it doesn't." He feared that this was one last trick of Travis's.

"Don't take my word for it," Travis said. "Look it up."

President Leary didn't want to look it up. In his mind, the only thing worse than one state of Texas was *five* of them. The president offered his hand instead and said, "How about we just shake?" Travis smiled. It was what he wanted, and they sealed the deal the old-fashioned way.

Back in the Press Room, the president pointed at the first hand he saw. "Go ahead, Ed," he said.

"Thank you, Mr. President. Governor Travis, you neglected to mention what you will do to stop tomorrow morning's vote in Texas. By my watch, the polls there are scheduled to open in about seven and a half hours."

"I'm not going to stop it," Travis said. Leary looked uneasy. He assumed his agreement with the governor included an implicit mandate to call off the vote. "I *can't* stop it. Don't even have the authority, which is how it should be. But despite what y'all may think, the people of Texas are reasonable. I'll give another speech tomorrow morning, run through the details of my agreement with the president, and urge Texans to vote no on the measure. I have every confidence they will."

More hands shot up this time. Forgetting he was sharing the stage with the president, Travis pointed to a reporter. "You." Leary pretended not to notice.

"Governor Travis, two questions. First, we heard in detail about the president's actions during the assassination attempt"—in Leary's version, his baseball bat had made solid contact with Metzos's gun, saving his own life—"but I'm wondering what you were doing while the president was being fired upon."

"To be honest," said Travis, "the gun was so tiny none of us on the couch saw it. Wait until you see this thing. By Texas standards, it was basically a squirt gun."

Leary fumed as he watched his tale of heroism get reduced to child's play.

"Second question, Governor. I've got to bring up Mike McKill. I'm curious how in the world you convinced him to fly you to Washington, not to mention land on the National Mall."

"I just asked him," Travis said. The Press Room laughed. "More than anything, I think Mike just wanted to put to bed all the talk about him not doing his own stunts." They laughed again.

Leary didn't want to be shown up a second time and pointed to a hand. He was so quick to do so that he accidentally called on a Fox News correspondent. "Yes . . . Carl."

The reporter nodded at the president, then looked to his right. *"Governor Travis."* Leary had gone from a commander in chief to a mere moderator. "You certainly talked a good game the last week or so, but how prepared were you, *really*, to wage a war against the United States?"

"Great question, Carl," said Travis. He leaned against the podium, feeling more comfortable by the second. "This is off the record, right?" The press corps laughed in delight. "To be completely honest, we were in deep doo-doo. Don't get me wrong. We had plenty of troops, plenty of citizen support, but the lack of communication with any of them was a killer. Next time we secede, we'll have those kinks worked out."

Travis turned and smiled at Leary, earning another laugh from the crowd. "Last question," the president said. He scanned the crowd carefully, looking for a sympathetic scribe. Politico? No. *New York Times?* Maybe. Huffington Post! "Yes, Melanie."

"Thank you, Mr. President. I know you've been giving all your attention to the Texas issue of late—"

"I have, yes," Leary said. *Good girl,* he thought. *Now for the softball . . .*

"—but with this crisis being put to bed, and the Republican National Convention a few months out, I'm curious how you would feel about the possibility of facing Governor Travis in a presidential election."

Leary ground his teeth together. *You ungrateful little—*

"Now, there's an idea," said Travis, interrupting before Leary could muster a friendly response. The state primaries were mostly finished, but that couldn't stop delegates from changing their mind on the convention floor.

Melanie shifted her attention to the governor. "So can I quote you as saying you're open to the nomination?"

Travis said it as a joke, but now that it was being asked with total sincerity, he was hit with the weight of his answer. He decided to take the George Washington approach. "Let's just say this. I'm not going to seek the office. I'm not going to campaign for it. But if I get it, you can be sure that I'll be obedient to the call."

Walt Thompson had arranged for Travis and his crew to fly back to Texas on his Gulfstream IV from Reagan National. Adam Wexler was waiting for them at the bottom of the stairs, having been delivered to the tarmac by Agent Dermis himself. Inside the jet was a one-line note from its owner: *Please land this at an actual airport.* The onboard fridge was lined with Dom Perignon. Travis popped the first cork and sent it ricocheting around the cabin.

They were exhausted, but no one could sleep. Mike McKill told Paige all about their midair adventures, adding his own studio-quality sound effects. Paige recounted her lunch at Metzos's house, leaving out her involvement in the swim party. Wexler relived his date with Paige, leaving out the last five hours of it. Cole described what it's like to be shot in the foot. "You mean in the *shoe*," McKill corrected. Travis sat back and enjoyed every second. Before they knew it, they were on their third bottle and an hour from Austin.

The celebration was interrupted by the ring of Travis's cell phone. Despite all the drama of the last two weeks, there were still only a few people who had the number.

"I'm supposed to turn this off when I fly, aren't I?" he said to the mystery caller.

"I'm sorry to bother you, Governor." It was Hunter Reese, his former chief of staff. Travis hadn't heard from him since the day the Lege voted to secede.

"Hunter! Boy, you are missing one hell of a party up here."

"I'm sorry to hear that," Hunter said.

Travis sensed from his tone that he wasn't calling to congratulate them. "Somethin' wrong?"

"It's Gabe Coggins. Cleaning crew found him in your office."

Travis chuckled. "Whoops. Totally forgot about him. Not a problem. He was just keeping watch while I was gone. He didn't get arrested, did he?"

"No. He's dead. The police called Fran. She didn't know what to do and called me."

Travis moved away from the noise toward the rear of the plane. "What are you talking about, Hunter?"

"EMTs tried to save him, but it was too late. Said he had some diabetic episode and didn't have his insulin with him."

Travis's first impulse was anger. "Well, why the hell didn't he—" He stopped. He knew why Gabe hadn't sought help. It would have revealed the fact that Travis was gone.

"You still there, Governor?"

"Yeah, Hunter. Still here."

"Do you need my help with this at all?"

"Yes." Travis's brain fought to form a coherent thought. "Make sure the cops keep this to themselves for a few hours, will ya?"

"You got it," Hunter said.

Travis hung up and dropped the phone into his pocket.

Paige came by with an open bottle to top off Travis's champagne. "You okay?"

"Tell the pilot we're going to Houston."

40

It was 4:30 A.M. when they landed. Despite K's predictable resistance, Travis rented a car like any other Texan and drove with just Paige to Sugar Land, a half hour outside Houston. He'd never been to Gabe Coggins's house. He'd thought about driving by plenty of times when he was in town, just out of morbid curiosity. He'd wanted to see if Kate had traded up or down. The fact Gabe lived on the north side of Sugar Land answered that question. The houses were big, surrounded by big oak trees, big yards, and lots of BMWs. Kate had made a good choice when she married Gabe Coggins, and not because of his money. Travis knew that he should never have assumed anything less.

"There it is," Paige said. It was a two-story colonial-style house, yellow with a warm green door and matching green shutters on every window. Kate loved yellow. She'd asked Travis more than once to paint the ranch house that same shade, and he'd refused, saying that he didn't want the place to look like an oversized Easter chick.

Travis pulled the car around the circular driveway and parked. He hadn't thought about what he was going to say or how he was going to say it. For the first time, a lack of the right words gave him pause. He sat in the car for a minute without moving. He didn't even take his hand off the gearshift.

"You can do this," Paige said.

Travis nodded. He fumbled for the foreign handle in the pre-morning dark and stepped onto the cobblestones, still wet from the late-night sprinklers. He could smell the St. Augustine grass, freshly cut. Paige met him on the other side of the car, and they walked side by side toward the darkened house.

He found the doorbell and gave it a single short ring.

They waited in silence. After a few seconds, Paige put out her hand. He took it.

"You sure she's home?" Travis asked.

"She's home," Paige said.

They waited another few minutes. The porch light flickered on. Paige squeezed her father's hand. It was softer than she remembered.

Acknowledgments

Thank you first and foremost to Jim Hays. He planted a seed in the fall of 2009 with a phone call from Prosper, Texas, where, as usual, he cut to the chase. "I got a book idea for you," he said. Unlike most ideas generated by a writer's family and friends, his was a good one. A partnership was born, and throughout the process Jim changed hats by the hour, acting as a researcher, story guru, sounding board, on-call Texan, pep talker, and whip cracker. Quite simply, this book wouldn't exist without him. Not even a little.

It also wouldn't exist without the support of Rick Gordon, Hayden Fleming, Bob Tway, and Rob Hays, who—along with Jim—enabled me to put other projects on hold for this one. Thank you.

I'm grateful to Thomas Dunne for laying aside his self-admitted socialist tendencies to see the potential in a newbie conservative novelist. Also to my wonderful editor Margaret Smith, a New York City Texan whose notes were so good they left little room for rebuttal. India Cooper copy edited the manuscript with jaw-dropping excellence.

I'm indebted to Rebecca Oliver at William Morris Endeavor for loving this story at first read and, no less important, convincing a publisher to love it, too.

My parents left plenty of red ink on early drafts, and this book is better because of it.

Doug McConnell and Adam England answered my four hundred aviation questions.

Jennifer Chambers graciously provided a tour of the Texas capitol. Mary and Dan Pennington provided the perfect writing space. Matt McConnell provided his old Con Law textbooks. My wife provided unwavering enthusiasm for a subject about which she confesses to care little.

Finally, thank you to my children, whose demand for bedtime stories sharpens my storytelling skills every night.